FINN

finn

A NOVEL

JON CLINCH

RANDOM HOUSE
New York

Copyright © 2007 by Jon Clinch

Published in the United States by Random House, an imprint of The Random House Publishing Group, a division of Random House, Inc., New York.

RANDOM HOUSE and colophon are registered trademarks of Random House, Inc.

ISBN-13: 978-0-7394-8459-3

Printed in the United States of America

Book design by Simon M. Sullivan

For Wendy and Emily,

without whom, nothing.

HE WENT and bent down and looked, and says:

"It's a dead man. Yes, indeedy; naked, too. He's ben shot in de back. I reck'n he's ben dead two er three days. Come in, Huck, but doan' look at his face—it's too gashly."

I didn't look at him at all. Jim threw some old rags over him, but he needn't done it; I didn't want to see him. There was heaps of old greasy cards scattered around over the floor, and old whiskey bottles, and a couple of masks made out of black cloth; and all over the walls was the ignorantest kind of words and pictures, made with charcoal. There was two old dirty calico dresses, and a sun-bonnet, and some women's underclothes, hanging against the wall, and some men's clothing, too. We put the lot into the canoe; it might come good. There was a boy's old speckled straw hat on the floor; I took that too. And there was a bottle that had had milk in it; and it had a rag stopper for a baby to suck. We would a took the bottle, but it was broke. There was a seedy old chest, and an old hair trunk with the hinges broke.

———

MARK TWAIN
Adventures of Huckleberry Finn

FINN

Under a low sun, pursued by fish and mounted by crows and veiled in a loud languid swarm of bluebottle flies, the body comes down the river like a deadfall stripped clean.

It proceeds as do all things moving down the Mississippi in the late summer of the year, at a stately pace, as if its blind eyes were busy taking in the blue sky piled dreamily deep with cloud. There will be thunder by suppertime and rain to last the whole night long but just now the early day is brilliant and entirely without flaw. How long the body has been floating would be a mystery if any individual had yet taken note of its passage and mused so upon it, but thus far, under that sky of blue and white and upon this gentle muddy bed aswarm with a school of sunfish and one or two smallmouth bass darting warily as thieves, it has passed only empty fields and stands of willow and thick brushy embankments uninhabited.

A crow screams and flaps off, bearing an eye as brown and deep as the Mississippi herself.

Sunday morning, early, and the river is without traffic.

An alligator gar, eight feet if it's an inch, rises deathlike from the bottom and fastens its long jaw upon a hipbone, which snaps like rotten wood and comes away. The body entire goes under a time or two, bobbing and turning, the eggs of blowflies scattering into the water like thrown rice. The urgent sunfish eddy. The bluebottles hover, endlessly patient, and when the body has recovered its equilibrium and resumed its downward course they settle once more.

Boys note its passage first, boys from the village taking the long way to Sunday school, and their witness is as much nature's way as is the slow dissolution of the floating body into the stratified media of air and water. The corpse is not too very far from shore and clearly neither dog nor deer nor anything but man.

"I'll bet it's old Finn," says one of them, Joe or Tom or Bill or perhaps some other. On this Sunday morning down by the riverbank they are as alike as polished stones. "My pap says they'll fish him from the river one day for sure."

"Go on," says another.

"Yes sir. A worthless old drunk like that."

"Go on," says the other again. He picks up a flat stone and tests it in his hand, eyeing the crow, which has returned and sunken its beak into a pocket of flesh. "Shows how much you know. That ain't even a man."

"I reckon you think it's a mule."

"It's a woman, no question."

The lot of them go jostling together and squinting into the sunrise and blinking against the glare on the water as if the only thing superior to the floating corpse of a man would be the floating corpse of a woman, as if seeking in unison for a lesson in anatomy and never mind the cost.

Finally, from one of them or another but in the end from the childish heart in each save the learned one, this confession: "How can you tell?"

"Men float facedown. Anybody knows that." Skipping the stone across the water to flush the crow, ruining his good trousers with the offhand brush of muddy fingers.

They draw straws, and as the unlucky boy lights out toward the village to enlist an adult the rest of them locate a skiff and cast off and make for the body. They hook her with a willow switch, these boys inured to dead things, and they drag her like bait to shore. One of them has been keeping a dead cat on a string for a week now, a kitten really, just a poor stiff dried husk won exactly this way, string and all, in a game of mumblety-peg.

The corpse floats low in the water, bottoming out in the mud that sucks at heel and buttock and drooping wrist. During its journey down the river it has failed to swell in the common way of corpses left in the sun. It lacks for skin, all of it, from scalp to sole. Nothing remains but sinew and bone and scraps of succulent yellow fat that the crows have not yet torn free.

One boy panics and loses his balance and falls into the water, his clothes spoiled for Sunday.

———

THE BOOTLEGGER STIRS his fire, oblivious to the sparks that circle upward into the night sky. He hears everything, every whisper in the dry grass of the pathway that leads from behind his shack, every snapping twig in the surrounding woods, every wingbeat of sparrow or jay or owl. "You can't steal whiskey from old Bliss," he likes to say, as if anyone would stoop so low as to steal whiskey from a blind man.

He repeats this reassurance now to Finn, who has proven him wrong before. "That's so," says Finn.

Pleased with himself, Bliss cackles until he coughs. Then he spits between his crooked teeth into the fire, where the sputum lands with a satisfying sizzle. "You got a jug?"

" 'Course I got a jug." Finn is as regular around these premises as the weather, even more regular than Bliss knows. But tonight his first purpose is neither to buy whiskey nor to steal it but to dispose of something in Bliss's perpetual fire. He has a tow sack between his feet, filthy even in the firelight and slowly leaking something into the dust. He bumps the blind man's knee with his jug, a signal.

"Go on get it yourself," says Bliss. "Can't you see I'm occupied?"

"I'll tend. You pour. Give me that stick."

Bliss won't let it go. "Leave an old man be. I reckon you know where I keep it."

"I reckon I do, if I could find it in the dark."

He has a point, so Bliss hands over the stick and limps off into the woods muttering to himself like an old priest.

Finn unties the tow sack and lays out its contents, long strips dark and dimly glistening, pieces of flayed flesh identically sliced save one. Their regularity in width and length and thickness speaks of a huntsman's easy skill and a plotter's furtive patience and something else too. He chooses one and throws it upon the fire, where it sizzles and smokes and curls in upon itself as sinuously as a lie.

"Hope you brought some for me," says Bliss from the depths of the woods.

"There's plenty." Throwing another piece into the fire to blacken. "Bring a couple of them jars when you come back. We'll have ourselves a time."

Bliss, weighed down with Finn's crockery jug of forty-rod, adjusts his course and shuffles down the path toward the cabin. Halfway along he uses his head at last, plants the jug midpath like a tombstone, and makes for home unencumbered, counting off the paces so as not to stub his unshod foot during the journey back.

By firelight Finn locates the piece he's set aside for his host. He clears hot ash from a rock and places it there in the manner of an offering.

"I ain't had nothing but beans all week," says Bliss as he squats on his log. He swirls whiskey to cleanse a pair of canning jars. One of them is cracked about the rim and fit to tear someone's lip, and this one Bliss chooses for himself as long as Finn is paying. He minds the crack with his thumb. Bliss is a poor drinker and he knows it. Not mean like Finn, but morose and persistent and beyond satisfying. "A little of your fatback would've gone good with them beans."

"You'll like it well enough plain," says Finn.

Bliss sniffs the air with satisfaction and mutters something unintelligible, pours himself another whiskey.

"You be sparing with that." But Finn doesn't mean it and he knows that Bliss will pay him no mind anyhow. Once you get Bliss started there's no slowing him down until the jug is empty. "Besides, I ain't paid for it yet."

"Don't worry none. I'll put it on your account." Tapping the side of his head with a finger.

They sit in silence while the meat cooks.

"I've broken it off with that woman," says Finn.

"You've made such a claim before."

"This time I mean it."

"We'll see."

"I reckon we will."

Bliss points his nose toward the spot where the meat sizzles on the fire just as surely as if he had two good eyes to guide it. "When'll that be ready, you suppose? I don't want it burnt."

"Soon." Tossing in another strip or two.

"Ain't no good to me burnt."

"Hold your water."

"I'm just saying. Yours must be about black by now. The one you put up while I was in them woods."

"I ain't having any. She's all yours, on account of how good you've always been to me."

"Aww. Tain't nothing."

"A token of my gratitude."

Bliss smiles in the odd unself-conscious way of one who has never looked into a mirror and learned thus to confine his expressions to the social norm. "So how long was you with her, Finn?"

"Ten, twelve years maybe. Fifteen, off and on."

"Offer and onner, like they say." He puts down his empty jar and rubs his hands together in a fit of glee, his whole brain a lovely jumble of women and fatback bacon. "What'll the Judge think?"

"Can't say." Stabbing the flesh with a sharp stick and flipping it over.

"You've steered him wrong before."

"I know it."

"Me, I don't believe you'll ever make a dent in that Judge. He knows what he knows."

Finn grunts.

"Your daddy's one judge that's got his mind made up."

"He's been that way all my life."

"He was that way before you was born, Finn. It ain't none of your doing." He hawks and spits into the fire, and Finn throws in some more pieces. "Sure it ain't done yet?"

"Just about. Have some more whiskey."

"Don't mind if I do."

After a while Finn stabs the meat and places it upon a flat stone that he bumps against the bootlegger's knee a time or two. "Can you set down that whiskey long enough to eat?"

"I'll do my best," says Bliss. Which he manages, just barely. And until half past midnight, while the silence in the woods deepens and the white moon looms and recedes and the owls grow weary at last of pursuing their prey through black air, the fire consumes Finn's secret. Come noon Bliss will awaken on the hard ground, and in his mind Finn's presence will have taken on the quality of a ghostly visitation.

———

HE IS BETWEEN WORLDS, this boy. Between the river and the town, between the hogshead and the house, between the taint of his mother and the stain of his pap. He knows some things that he can never say, not even to himself.

He has trained his companions well—these boys forbidden to associate with him on account of his mother's suspected stigma and his father's famed trouble with whiskey, these boys who associate with him nonetheless and perhaps all the more intently for being forbidden his company although they do not generally encounter him at school or at church or at any of the other places ordinarily deemed suitable for boys of the village. They find his dark history as dizzying as a leap from some great bluff into a Mississippi pool and his scrapes with his violent pap as thrilling as a narrow escape from Injun Joe's cave and his deep broad knowledge of woodsman's lore and slave's superstition as enchanting as a spell of protection against nightwalking spirits or werewolves, these boys forbidden to play with him yet drawn into his wake like needles to a lodestone, these boys whom he has trained well enough that at least one of them knows what he'll say before he says it and indeed has said it already, that the body is not a man's at all on account of it floats faceup.

When he can extricate himself from the widow's he sleeps in a great barrel nearly as tall as a man and twice as big around, a sugar hogshead washed up among the rushes at the edge of the village. The barrel lies upon its side and he lies upon his side within it. Sometimes he locates a place between the staves where the rain and the riverwater and the barrel's former purpose have conspired to leave behind a concealed crusty ridge of old sugar solidified, and with his clasp-knife he pries it loose for the pleasure of sucking upon it while he drifts off to sleep.

———

IN THE END it falls to the undertaker to load the corpse upon a wagon and remove it from the indignity of public display. Except perhaps for O'Toole, the giant who owns the slaughterhouse in the next county, there is none other who might possess the stomach for it. So here he is, rolling the sticky fly-blown thing into a square of old canvas and wrangling it up onto the bed of his wagon as if it were the featureless corpse of a slug and he an ant, strong beyond his size. His name is Swope, he is rail-thin and dressed in rusty black, and he has been a fixture in the village of St. Petersburg for longer than anyone can remember. From long association he has acquired both the air of death and some of its permanence, and his pale hair bursts from under the brim of his slouch hat like a pile of sunbleached straw.

The corpse for its part is well mannered, patient, and perfectly amenable. Leached clean of all fluids, it barely stains the canvas tarpaulin.

Swope mutters to himself as he works, complaining about the hour and the uncharacteristic heat and the unfairness of the world. He has long made a habit of talking to himself, since no one else will do it. The children believe that he speaks to Death, which hovers invisibly over one of his shoulders or the other, although their parents believe instead that he addresses his harmless old horse, Alma.

"As if I weren't busy enough without goddamn half-pay charity cases come floating downstream. Won't barely cover my expenses, may God damn the goodness of my goddamn bleeding heart, but who in hell else is going to do it? And at this time of the morning, as if the old gal couldn't have kept till noon. A feller gets himself the idea to go skin somebody like a goddamn rabbit at least he ought to have the decency to set something by for the proper obsequies, mail it anonymous to the paper or the marshal or some such. A goddamn crime is what it is. The feller what done it deserves to be tried as much for one as for the other. Pitiful goddamn half-pay charity case."

The corpse has a high rotten smell that sifts through the canvas and rises into the morning air like supplication. Swope rumbles down the main street of the village cursing his luck and bemoaning his fate while in his dim little office the marshal scratches his head and his chin and his belly and lays plans to consult with the authorities upstream, from whom he is certain to learn nothing.

———

HE SLOPS PAINT onto the wall as if he has it to spare, which he does not. The money that he discovered in the woman's apron pocket, a dollar and change which he reassures himself he must have given to her at some time or another for he is no murdering thief—he may be many things but he is at the very least no murdering thief—the money that he found in her apron pocket bought the better part of a three-gallon pail of whitewash, although at the rate he's going it will be barely enough to cover the four walls and he'll still have the floor to do after that, along with the ceiling if it holds out. The furniture, what there is of it, is huddled midroom. Two sagging wicker chairs, a chest, a wooden frame bed of simple country carpentry. Perhaps he'll paint these as well, provided he has the opportunity and the materials. Laid out upon the chair are the woman's clothes, just where she took them off.

Two gabled windows front the river, looking west toward the Missouri side. The rising sun lights the tops of fir trees with pale gold and the river steams like slow soup in the cool morning air but Finn pays it no mind. The world is a distraction. With his thick brush he paints over the windows when he comes to them, glass and mullions and frames and all, as if to establish a seamless barrier between himself and the world outside. The whitewash, thin as the water that sulks by directly below this overhung house of his, seeps into every crack and cranny, cementing the windows shut and promising a long airless season ahead.

He is not entirely certain that he will sleep up here anymore. There's a horsehair couch downstairs, on the long west porch with the river running underneath, and he thinks that perhaps he will take up sleeping there from this day forward as a visible sign of the invisible change that he has wrought within himself. This bedroom he will leave naked and plain as a mausoleum, with the bed and the chairs and the off-angled broken-hinged chest positioned talismanic and the walls stripped bare and every single surface painted white.

As the morning advances he realizes that he ought to pace himself lest he grow weary before the job is done, even though the urge that drives him is more spiritual than otherwise and not to be denied from mere physical weakness. Sweat drips off the tip of his nose. Dirt and grease have caked his long black hair into ropes that hang thick before his face and he ties the filthy mess of them back with a strip of fabric torn from the hem of her dress, bedecking himself half like a pirate of the Spanish Main and half like something odder and less knowable. Aside from the knotted strip of fabric he is naked, splashed with paint, white on white. His overalls, washed in the river this very morning before the sun was up, hang dripping from a cane pole slung out over the river from the porch downstairs like an empty gibbet, the faintest faded ghost of a warning to all traffic upstream or down.

He slackens his pace and still has three walls finished by noon with half the paint left at least. Upon hard bare feet he goes downstairs out of the eyewatering smell of solvent to help himself to a dipper of water from an old sugar hogshead he keeps as a rainbarrel in one corner of the porch where the collapsed roof lets the runoff sluice down into it. Naked he stands behind the boards that rim the porch in the way of ramparts, watching the river traffic.

"You Finn."

"What is it." He swivels his head with the urgency and precision of a crow, following the voice. Water runs down his chest.

"Reckon it's laundry day." The marshal, up from St. Petersburg on the Missouri side.

"I reckon."

"Mind you don't get your pecker sunburnt."

"That happens, you're the first I'll show."

"Don't do me no favors."

"I don't mean to."

"I expect that woman of yours ain't to home, you running around like that."

"No she ain't."

"Unless I caught you in the middle of something."

"Not likely." Finn dips more water. Half of his work is done, a breeze has arisen from across the river, and he is feeling expansive. He has always been a big man, broad of shoulder and well muscled as befits one who draws his living from the river. "So what brings you to the big town," he says to the marshal, "other'n that steamboat?"

Lasseter, Illinois, is the county seat and a more prosperous place than St. Petersburg, from whence this Missouri lawman has come. His journey upriver has taken him well out of his proper jurisdiction, but not beyond the limits of his curiosity.

"Official business," says the marshal. "A little legwork."

Finn sips his water wishing it were something else.

"You see anything unusual float by last night, yesterday?"

"Calf come by last week. Monday, Tuesday maybe."

The marshal, gone bald before his time and thick around the middle, sags a little and puckers his lips as he turns away and scans the water. "That all?"

"Yes sir."

"How do you suppose your daddy's holding up?"

"Same's always."

"That a fact."

"I reckon."

The marshal chews his lip. "Same as always." He spits into the brown water, hikes up his trousers, and bids Finn goodbye with the back of his hand.

"Like I said," says Finn to the water in his rusty dipper. He scratches his crotch, studying the places along the river where his trotlines are fastened into the muddy bank with long iron stakes and rusty chains fit for a dungeon. Every hook must have found its catch by now. Two days have passed since he last ran the lines, one day given over to the work and one more given over to Bliss's forty-rod, of which he brought home a full jug. He ought to get out there on the river if he means to have any money for food or liquor, take up once again the old reliable routine about which he has hung the tattered rags of his life ever since he fell out of favor with the Judge, but instead he rehangs the dipper on a nail by its twisted handle and returns to the upstairs bedroom as if pursued. Certain stains have bled through the whitewash during his conversation with the marshal, tinting portions of the wall a pink as ruddy as flesh and necessitating there a second and more careful coat.

By nightfall he has finished the job and the room gleams ghostly by the light of his candle. He returns the bed and the chairs and the broken-backed chest to their rightful places, and he hangs the woman's clothes on their usual peg alongside the window where they may serve him as a reminder. Downstairs he finds a little whiskey left in the jug and a little bit more left in the bottom of another cracked one on the porch. The battered old jug's contents are mostly crumbled clay and rotten cork but he passes the slurry through a square of cloth and chokes it down all the same, followed by the dregs of Bliss's more recent handiwork. In the end, even after he's taken the cloth into his mouth and suckled it like a woman's breast, it is only enough to fuel his need for more.

He dons his overalls and frees the skiff and poles upstream past his trotlines to a place where other skiffs on the order of his and worse are tied up like a stringer full of fish gone belly up, and he attaches his own to the last of these then walks ashore across the unsteady lot of them. The steps to the riverside tavern grow out of the hillside where nature and convenience have placed them: flat rocks, dead limbs, curved roots cradling dried mud. Finn plods upward and makes one last futile search of his pockets before stepping inside, into a room where the day's heat lingers undiminished and the dark of night is not dispelled by so much as a single candle. Men play cards on the jutting porch beyond but he greets them not.

"You Finn," says Dixon, the proprietor.

"Hey Dix. How happy are you to see me?"

"No happier'n usual." Wiping down the wooden countertop with a filthy rag.

"I take that for a good sign."

"I take that to mean you've got empty pockets in them overalls."

Judged strictly by the regularity of his appearances and the quantity of his consumption, Finn is Dixon's best customer. The circumstance is not without its drawbacks. Their transactions are mainly in the way of barter, and Dixon's wife has lately decided that she would rather not serve her customers catfish with Finn's scent upon them, nor any other kind of fish that he's touched for that matter.

"If you won't stand me to a few then I reckon I'll find somebody who will," says Finn. His eyes have adjusted to the darkness and he scans the room from under brows knitted tight with urgency and desire. Only one figure resolves from the smoke and the gloom, a black man nearly as large as he and surely half again as strong. For all the world like a carved monument or a heathen totem, his burnished face glows and fades in the pulsing light cast by his corncob pipe. Finn looks through him or past him and throws up his hands in frustration. "Come on now, Dix. I'm good for it."

The black man, a gray-headed veteran whom everyone knows as George, rises from the table with his empty glass in hand. He moves with the grace and purpose of a storm cloud from his table to the bar behind which stands Dixon rubbing at an invisible spot with his filthy rag and contemplating Finn's sad destiny. "I'll have another'n," he says. "And this feller here'll have the same, long as you're pouring." Coins spill across the bar.

"I ain't that thirsty." Glowering at Dixon.

"Come on, Finn."

"That's all right."

Dixon pours one. "I ain't never seen you turn down a drink."

"There's a heap of things you ain't never seen."

"I know it."

"You ain't never seen the day I'll take his charity, for one." To Dixon, for Finn will not so much as cast his eyes upon the man who would be his benefactor.

George permits his teeth to gleam briefly in the dark.

"I didn't hear the man mention no charity," says Dixon. "You mention anything about charity, Mr. George?"

"No suh."

"Hear that, Finn?"

"I ain't never in my life been beholding to no nigger," says Finn, "and I ain't about to start now."

Dixon grows thoughtful behind the bar, and moves his hand in ever smaller circles.

"You going to stand me to that drink?"

George stacks his change into two separate piles, one for each drink he has in mind, and he gives them the faintest suggestion of a push across the bar. "Just being neighborly," he says in a voice like gravel and velvet. "Ain't a loan, ain't charity, ain't nothing but a drink."

"Tell him to drink it himself," says Finn, contrary to his own most imperative instincts but in keeping with his higher principles. "Tell him he ought to learn how to keep his money in his pocket."

Finn leaves the bar by the other way and stalks out onto the porch among the cardplayers. For the most part they look up, one at a time or in small groups like nesting owls, reflexively but without any excess of interest. Insects swarm their candles and collect in their glasses and get swallowed up one by one in the manner of Jonah but perhaps a bit more content for the anesthetic specifics of their dying. One of the men raises a glass to Finn, a trifle ironically and at some personal risk, but Finn pays him no mind and stamps off down the path toward the river from which he has come.

The evening has gone cool, and a sharpness in the air suggests to him that by and by his waterbarrel will resume crusting itself over with the thinnest frangible film of overnight ice. Everything changes, he thinks. The woman is gone and the world turns. Free niggers try to buy a man a drink for no reason. He troops down the steps with his head aching for whiskey and his boot-heel, the one into which he's driven a cross of nails to keep away the devil, leaving its own highly particularized trail in the dirt. He frees the skiff and it finds its own way into the current, reliable and wise as a bloodhound. Many's the time it's taken him well past home on a night like this. Perhaps the skiff knew best after all, perhaps he should have lingered down where it willed him, permitted himself to drift deeper and deeper into the slave states. Everything might have gone differently.

This evening though he's wide awake and fully alert, perhaps more so than is entirely healthy for a man of his habits and inclinations. He sniffs the air, listens to the lapping of water and the creaking of oars from downstream and the clinking together of glasses from up on Dixon's porch and other sounds too from various other locations along the river—sounds of argument and talk and singing and work, always work, for it seems to him that someone is forever chopping wood or wielding a saw or dragging some heavy object somewhere along the amplifying reach of the water, even at the deepest hour of the night. He comes abreast of his most upstream trotline and pictures its swarming struggling catch; tomorrow he'll run them all and gut the slick fish clean and cache them one after another in a bed of wet reeds like Moses in the bulrushes, and then he'll bring them up into the village to sell. Thus tomorrow night will not be like this night in the least, for he will be flush and able to do as he pleases. A flicker of light in the woods catches his eye and he considers pulling ashore for a while, following a certain path well known to him and hitting up old Bliss for a drink or two on account, an idea that sparks up in his mind and distracts his attention just long enough that as he's considering the tortuous walk into the deep woods to where the old man keeps his works his drifting boat bumps against another, this one not moving with the current but rather holding steady against it.

"Hey. Watch where you're going." The voice of a boy, no older than Finn's own son, which gives him an instant's pause.

"You boys." A powerful scent of fish above the omnipresent smells of the river and the night helps Finn realize just where he is and why the boys' doubtlessly purloined skiff is hanging steady in the water here of all places and exactly what the young miscreants are up to under this blanket of darkness. "Them's my trotlines," he says in a level voice.

"Shitfire," says one of the boys, and he goes plunging overboard rather than confront Finn's well-known wrath.

Everything is wet: fish arching in the bottom of the stolen skiff, the air erupting as two more boys dive to evade capture, Finn himself as he catches hold of a watersoaked and half-rotted paintless gunwale and makes fast. Only one boy remains, the youngest of the four and the most innocent and the least equipped to be out on the river in this kind of a fix, a black child barely visible in the stern until the moon breaks through overhead cloud and reveals him there. He has a tear in his glistening eye and a hook in his palm that he's been trying to nurse out with no success.

"You boy."

"It warn't my idea, suh." Fussing with the hook as if it possesses mystical qualities.

"Is that a fact?"

"Yes suh."

"Whyn't you go over with them others?"

"It warn't my idea."

Anyone could see that this one has been a good boy all his short life, and that the act of throwing himself on the mercy of adult authority comes as naturally to him as breathing. Upon this one occasion, however, the truth serves him exactly as well as it has served ten thousand men who have come before Finn's father in his time, which is to say poorly. He offers up that palm with the hook in it, a bead of blood gleaming there by moonlight, as if this explains everything, as if he has already endured all of the punishment that he deserves.

"Aww," says Finn, and without a second look he grabs the line that leads from it to draw the child within striking range. He has acquired a natural caution about such things from his years on the river, an instinctual feel for the tension of the line and the power of the hook and the secret breaking point of the tender pad of flesh within which the barbed iron has buried itself. The boy rises like a perch, fighting his natural inclination to resist capture, judging furiously the relative risks and advantages of the two paths open to him. And before he can make up his mind to come along or jump Finn is upon him with the back of his brutal right hand. A spattering of the boy's teeth precedes him into the river and the hook flies free, nearly but not quite catching Finn in the cheek. There's a spot of blood on the gunwale where the boy's head hit after the blow and whether or not there's any thrashing to be heard from the river is no concern of Finn's, certainly not as regards a thieving nigger boy and a sissy at that, blubbering away about a hook in his goddamn hand. He kneels and bends to take up the gasping fish, tenderly as a shepherd.

2

THE WINTER COMES ON and Finn wears every article of clothing he owns and works the trotlines every day but they are less productive. When he does catch something it's usually carp, which nobody has much interest in buying except perhaps a certain oil-black trader in darktown with whom he'd rather not do business. He fuels his stove with fallen branches and on one occasion finds a wooden door floating down the river from the north, frame and all, which he considers burning but in the end decides to use for its intended purpose. He mounts it at the foot of the bedroom stairs where it serves as insulation against intrusions and loss both thermal and psychic. The downstairs room is warmer now and he's brought the horsehair couch in from the long porch and often as not he spends the better part of the day napping on it with his back to the world. The house creaks in the wind and shudders when something in the water strikes one of the pilings on which it stands and at such moments Finn awakens with a start, picturing an insistent floating corpse long gone downstream.

The sky is pressing low over the river when he decides to walk into the village. He dons his broken slouch hat and wraps a blanket around himself, more for effect than for warmth. Lasseter is empty, abandoned to the wind, and he passes before its shuttered windows like a wraith. In the diffuse gray light he casts upon its walls not so much as a shadow.

WM. FINN, ESQ. says the shingle that sways creaking in the manner of a ghost ship over the boardwalk along which he treads. The paint upon the shingle is fresh, white and black as judgment, and at the sight of it Finn stops to consider. Then he mounts the porch and admits himself at the door.

"Look what the wind blew in," says his brother, Will. His cheeks are apples and his hair, as black as Finn's own, is thick and neatly parted in the middle.

"Will."

"Pull up a bench by the stove." Rising he is his brother's purified image, although where Finn's bulk has long been the product of exercise and whiskey Will has derived his from sedentary habits and a fondness for good food in plentiful quantities. They are nonetheless clearly two branches of the same tree, each bent by circumstance in his own way.

"This ain't no social call," says Finn, drifting mothlike toward the fire all the same.

Will encourages his brother with a soft hand set upon his shoulder. "Warm yourself anyhow."

"No harm in it."

The two sit for a moment, wordless, listening to the fire. The wind tries the latch and passes on.

Finn nods toward the door and the trail of footprints that followed him in, bits of white snow and black mud mingled. "Forgive my manners."

"These old planks have seen worse." If they have, it does not show. Even in the pale meager wash of light that sifts through the curtains on this grim day they gleam as if lit from within, as if all of the sunlight that has ever fallen upon the trees that gave them birth has somehow taken residence within their depths. The residue of Finn's passage melts over their waxed surfaces like butter on a hot griddle. It cannot penetrate, and thus it will not long endure to mark his presence here. Will looks his brother in the eye. "Hard winter."

"Hard," says Finn.

"How's the fishing been?"

"Poor."

"So I'd imagine. And Mary?"

"I give that one up a while back." All nonchalance.

"Is that so?"

"Broke it off."

"I know you."

"This time I mean it," says Finn. "No going back."

"You want me to tell the Judge."

"I reckon he'll find out on his own, this way or that." Finn crosses his legs, fingers the nails in his boot-heel. "Folks talk."

"That they do."

"I ain't the one brought it up just now."

"I know."

"You make a note of that."

"I will. You're correct." Will is the younger of the two, and he learned long ago the importance of letting his brother assert his claims.

Finn coughs into his fist.

"So I guess that's not what you came to see me about."

"No. Not the woman."

"No."

Finn examines the stove, admiring its flue, which glows red as a cherry.

"What then?"

"I need a little money." Staring at the floor.

"I give you a little money. First of every month, although I'm not supposed to."

"I need a little more." Finn raises up his head and his eyes flare with something that may be anger but is more likely plain unembroidered helplessness, helplessness that rages against its own unmistakable self. "I could use a little more, is all."

"I don't know how I could manage it."

The muscles in Finn's jaw bunch.

"He knows where everything goes. Every nickel."

"Not every."

Will angles his head a few degrees from level and looks steadily at his brother. "So just because I lie about one thing, I'm supposed to lie about another."

"I didn't say nothing."

"That house of yours. That house of yours is different. The paper-work says it's in Pike County, for one thing, on a riverbank that flooded back in '32. Strictly uninhabitable. A total loss."

"I know it."

"And do you know what it cost me to set that up?"

"How much?" As if dreaming that he could recapture it and spend it on food and drink.

"It cost me more pride than you'll ever possess." He steams where he sits. "At a risk far greater than any you'll ever know."

"I wouldn't be so certain as all that," says Finn, with the air of a man who possesses a secret idea of his own superiority.

"Have an apple before you go," says Will with a gesture that includes both a bowl on the desk and the door itself.

"Don't mind if I do," says Finn. "I see you've got plenty to spare."

———

A LITTLE BLACK BOY WHISTLES through missing teeth as Finn approaches down the far side of the snowy street and his mother draws him to her hip instinctively, muffling his music with her long strong fingers. Nothing about the boy commands Finn's attention, including the possibility that he may be the child whom he struck for purloining his fish so many months back. Not even this living potential for absolution draws his attention to the boy, for he has lost not so much as a moment's sleep worrying about the child and his fate. But the boy's mother seems to know everything, even things she cannot possibly know, and she pulls him close to her flank as Finn approaches on the other side of the street, harmless or at least too distant for trouble.

Finn has eyes only for her. She is tall, elegant of movement, haughty of aspect. The only parts of her skin that he can see are her face and her ankles and that one strong hand with which she has restrained the boy, but even that much is sufficient to set his imagination afire. He pauses on the boardwalk and squares himself perpendicular to the frozen-over street, reaching the apple to his mouth. In spite of his rags and his blanket and his broken slouch hat he studies her slow passage with the proud indifference of a proprietor, giving his apple one great cracking bite that unleashes juice to trickle down his chin and nearly freeze there. She pauses not nor looks up. Only the boy, whether or not he recognizes the man who might or might not have been his assailant those months ago if assailed he was at all, turns his head beneath his speckled straw hat in acknowledgment of Finn's presence.

———

DESPITE THE BITTER COLD in the house Finn drops his overalls and sits on the horsehair couch with its view of the river and thinks of the woman, not his Mary but the woman in the street with the boy he'd barely noticed, and even though he can conjure up all of the usual details in a mind sufficiently fevered to warm the premises with a kind of sickly heat he can find no pleasure in them. He sighs and throws his head back and tries again, baring himself to the cold with his mind aboil, beneath his bony ass his ragged blanket spread and by his haunch a stack of castoff newspapers that he collects for sanitation and kindling although for the most part their words are to him the most impenetrable of mysteries. After a while he succeeds and cleans himself with newspaper and sleeps.

Guilt and cold and darkness awaken him. He shakes the grate and starts the stove with the newspaper he has lately used, which flares damply and dies but catches the kindling nonetheless. Drawn back from the ash his hand bears a stain that catches his interest likewise. Down his bare chest beneath the blanket he draws one finger, marking a line from sternum to navel, halving himself thus, and thus cloven he proceeds to mark his leftward portion with signs and signifiers in charcoal drawn from out of the ash. Crosses to keep away the devil and charms to ward temptation. Strange native markings geometric and spiral. They overlap and merge and bleed into one another with a dark procreative fury until only he might know where one ends and the next begins and he is halfway all over dusty dusky black. By firelight he makes a raging discovery and returns again to the couch for another go with that blackened right hand, watching as he does certain lights make their slow passage along the river at his feet until he finishes and grows restless and desires whiskey. The great jug is nearly full, two gallons from old Bliss, corn transubstantiated by heat and cold. Finn dresses and puts flame to his one lamp there upon the table and sits by it with a glass, the jug within reach. He vows to drink just so much and no more, but when the warmth of the whiskey finds its way down his throat and into his belly and out into his arms and legs, some of those extremities still residual white and the others blackened beneath his clothes—when the warmth penetrates his body as first it penetrated Bliss's cool complex works in the alchemy of transmuting raw corn into raw whiskey— he yields as he always does. Motes swim in his vision as the night progresses, black spots the inverse analogues of the lamps that drift by upon the river below. They persist for a moment, dart from one corner of his vision to another, and vanish in the furtive manner of spiders. From time to time he slaps at one of them, suddenly certain that the phantom thing is an arachnid indeed for the house is after all inhabited by hundreds of their worldbound brethren. His movements grow wilder the longer the night goes on, and before he corks the jug and thumbs out the lamp and crawls to the horsehair couch he has begun seeing snakes.

3

THIS PLACE HAS BEEN HERE from the beginning and it will be here in the end: Adams County, hacked from the wilderness by naming's brutal baptism long before Illinois was a state or a territory or even so much as a dream. This single overwhelming certainty has belonged to the Judge for as long as he can remember, accompanying him in his youth and uplifting him in his adulthood and sustaining him in his old age. From his vantage point in the great white clapboard mansion alongside the grand white limestone courthouse on the finest block of the highest street in Lasseter, the most cosmopolitan village in the county and by nature its seat, the place has become the Judge and he has become the place in return.

He was born here, born James Manchester Finn on a straw pallet in a one-room shack in the Year of Our Lord 1762. His own father, adrift in an unnamed wilderness where every turning in every trail concealed a rattlesnake or a grizzly bear or a bloodthirsty Indian of unappeasable appetites, his own father before him had been a drunk just like his son. The one he hated for it and the other he pities but not enough. Drink he understands, the Judge tells himself, because it is a thing of vast and nearly indomitable power—like the law, like the wilderness, like history itself. Like them it makes certain promises and keeps others, warping the world according to its own mysterious will.

—

HIS WIFE HAS ALWAYS BEEN one to keep her own counsel, and she has profited greatly thereby. See her in the early years of their marriage, seated upon the porch or working in the garden or idly poking the keys of the piano while her mind returns unbidden to the Philadelphia of her youth, its streets crowded with life and its air still redolent of revolution. The Judge knows how she misses it. He can see it in her downcast eyes and in her pale cheeks and in the listless way she pumps water or works her needle. In truth he detects this drear longing more often than she feels it and by this subtle indirect means she conveys over time the entire burden of her past to her husband and in so doing frees herself of its weight but not its import. He read law in Philadelphia, between the sea-bound Delaware and the winding Schuylkill, and when at last he knew all there was to know he sought again the broad Mississippi of his youth. "*I'd learned enough to know where I belonged,*" he says to anyone who will listen, theatrically perhaps but with so much practiced earnestness that his overwhelmed listeners decide that he could not but mean it. They smile and nod at his late-gained wisdom and bask in the bright glow that it casts upon their own, for they have never been so foolish as to leave at all. He is the only man in the county with clean hands in these early days, the only one to earn his living by means of paper and pen, and all on account of his implacable aim of re-creating for his wife a brilliant cosmopolis in these dark woods of his youth regardless of how widely he might need to travel in order to accomplish it. Adams County lacks a sufficient number of property disputes and bankruptcies for his liking and so he sets out southward into Pike County and eastward into Brown and Schuyler and even northward into Hancock until he is well known everywhere and well accustomed to the life on horseback that will be his even after he rises to the judiciary. It serves to elevate him over other men, and thus elevated he rules that his house unlike any other in the village shall employ not ordinary black servants but a white hired man, an extravagance that doubles the demands upon his finances and his time. "*I'd rather be gone four days of five and know that my wife and boys are in proper society,*" he likes to say, "*than stay at home and have us all live among common niggers.*"

———

THE SILENCES OF THE JUDGE have as many shades of significance as uttered speech in the way of assent, of doubt, of negation. He speaks not a word nor makes the slightest sign when his wife reports how the younger boy, her fine obedient Will, has been in bed all week long with a fever, and only by evaluating his silence and his fixity of expression can she gauge his possible opinions regarding the boy's health and faithfulness and fate, opinions that may lie almost anywhere upon a multifarious web strung from extremes of mistrust and sympathy, pity and apprehension. Soon, having arrived home weary from his weeklong horseback pursuit of the usual round of trouble and woe across counties far and wide, he will climb the stairs and see about the boy for himself. But not now. He is in no hurry.

The older boy is healthy as a goat and twice as energetic and nearly as flexible in matters of conduct and digestion. These nights, listening to Will's rasping breath and his sad weary cough and his repeated cries for the ministrations of their mother, he has lain awake upon his adjacent bed in a perpetual state of stoic puzzlement. The doctor has come and gone and come and gone again and despite the august old man's best efforts Will has steadfastly refused to improve, which seems to his brother a failure of strength and imagination. The boy must desire nothing more than this, he thinks; his own younger brother must want nothing more in all the world than to toss in his bed and cry into his pillow and be fussed over by his mother and clucked at by the ancient white-haired doctor with his shuffling walk and his tobacco-stained fingers and his goiter the size of a cannonball. Twice the boy brings Will's assignments home from school, but when his brother cannot find strength to complete them he gives off and does not bother returning to the schoolhouse himself for the rest of the week since it is springtime and he yearns like some fenced animal for the restoration of his utter and unproscribed freedom.

Long after dark the Judge comes up the stairs as if still bearing upon his shoulders the weight of every issue set before him for counsel, and he lights the candle on the bedside table and sits upon the quilt and draws a single small breath as he lays his square hand upon the boy's hot forehead. The older boy can read concern in the set of his shoulders but the younger, poor burning Will, can detect nothing in his implacable face of stone.

"Buck up, young man."

The Judge rises and steps out to the head of the stairs, where he calls down for his wife to prepare the boy a good hot bath in keeping with his understanding of certain homeopathic principles. She disputes with him for a moment or two, arguing that the doctor has been here twice already and has on neither occasion ordered such treatment, but the Judge prevails in this as in all things—for after all the boy is not yet well, and thus the doctor's recommendations are of suspect value at best.

The older brother, the brother for whom a bath under any circumstance is a painful indignity, records in the book of his life yet another reason to congratulate himself upon his fine health and strong will. The younger brother, the enervated brother, who possesses no choice in the matter of this treatment or any, endures the bath and is returned to his bed in a gasping agony of debilitation like some fish half boiled alive. In the morning he will be some improved, and the Judge will take credit, but another week will pass before the doctor pronounces him fit to return to school.

The child will in fact prove susceptible all his life long, prey to influenza and catarrh and neurasthenia and the vapors. He will require attention. His brother, the elder Finn, will learn to do without.

4

D IXON'S WIFE, from the back room, pitching her voice above the noontime sizzle of catfish in oil: "You tell him we've got all we need today. I won't be encouraging that one."

Finn cannot help but hear, for whatever his other faults and failures he is not deaf, and Dixon lifts his shoulders in apology but takes the best of the man's reed-wrapped bounty all the same, making a note of where this transaction has left the complex calculus of their financial entanglements.

"I done read about that boy of your'n."

Finn decides he's misheard, nods toward the whiskey jug, and ignores the man's words for all his recent generosity and demonstrated, if subrosa, willingness to defy the instructions of his wife, a harridan as famous for her temper as for her fried catfish.

"Quite a fortune he's landed himself in."

Which gets Finn's attention at once and allows Dixon's earlier sentence to coalesce in his mind all over again, properly this time and with undeniable weight. "Where you been reading about Huck?"

Dixon draws the weekly newspaper from underneath the bar and places it square before Finn, where it would serve better as a placemat. With a stubby finger he points to a black funnel of headline and subheadline and boldfaced text the gist of which Finn can make out despite his youthful avoidance of the schoolhouse and his willful lifelong neglect of such book-learned skills as he could not help but have acquired: *Boys, Gold, Fortune, Caves, Indian, Murder.*

"I ain't heard."

Dixon places his whiskey on the bar. "Guess he's fixed, that Huck."

"I guess." Finn sips at the whiskey.

"Him and that other boy, that Sawyer."

"So they say."

"Found a regular fortune in gold, they did."

"How much?" He draws the index finger of his left hand down the page as though he could locate the figure even if he hunted for it all night, as though his finger were a divining rod tuned to dowse the facts from this dry desert of language.

"Six thousand."

"Go on."

"Right there, boss." Pointing to the number. "Twelve altogether between him and the other'n. That makes six each."

"Good God."

"I know it."

"Whereabouts?"

"Them old caves, south of St. Pete."

"I seen them." Finn drinks the whiskey in silence, shakes his head, and studies the paper. After a while he speaks. "Funny."

"What?"

"Looks like I'll be getting my inheritance after all, don't it? Only it come upstream instead of down."

"Looks like."

Finn tilts his head back and closes his eyes and pours the whiskey down his throat like the veriest medicine. Then he sits up straight, deposits the glass on the bar, and indicates a bottle on the backshelf. "I believe I'll be drinking the good stuff from this day forward." He touches the glass with a finger or two, urging it toward Dixon. His eyes are watery.

"I'll stand you one, Finn."

"By way of celebration."

"By way of celebration."

Dixon pours.

"Leave that bottle."

"Now Finn."

"Just leave it."

"I oughtn't."

Finn looks past Dixon toward the back room. "Suit yourself," he says, with a cracked smile that lasts too long and then vanishes too suddenly. He turns his attention to the whiskey and works on it for a while, methodically as a banker. He labors over it without any special appreciation, but as if he means to burn its impression into his palate for use under circumstances when such drink as he can get is of far lesser quality. "That boy," he says after a while.

"That boy."

"God love him, Dix."

"I know it."

"He's lucky I didn't sell him a long time ago."

"Reckon you both are."

"That's a fact," says Finn.

———

SOME OF THE LUMBER that drifts downstream has squarecut nails still in it and as the wood burns the iron falls out and settles down through the ash like panned gold and gets caught in the grate. Over the years Finn has made a collection of the best and straightest and least rusted of these siftings. Some of them he employed to mount the doorframe at the foot of the bedroom stairs and now another handful he hammers out as straight as he can on a flat rock one by one, his breath blowing smoke. When he is satisfied he puts them in the pocket of his overalls and returns to the house.

On the floor he has laid out everything that he will require. Hooks and lines. A jug. A shotgun he stole from somewhere, more useful in the summer and the fall than at this time of year but still. The last of a carton of shells in a tow sack with dried beans and salt pork and some bread. A blanket and a tarpaulin. He kneels among these, touching each element in turn like an alchemist of old, and then he rises and opens the door and goes upstairs to the room he has painted white. The pale sunlight on the painted-over windows glows like moonbeams on milkglass and merges the details of the room and its furniture into a single soft undifferentiated blur against which Finn, his own skin gone fishwhite with the winter and his hat and coat as black as sin, comes and goes like an illusion. He drifts around the perimeter, trailing his fingers along the whitewashed plaster from wall to wall to wall, humming to himself in a low guttural singsong. Twice around he goes as if casting a spell upon the place. He stops just once, at the peg where hang the woman's calico dress and her secret underthings and her old sun-bonnet, and he stands rapt for a moment to bury his face in them and breathe in what remains of her scent. Then he goes 'round one more time, slowly and thought-fully and with an altogether dreamlike air, before descending at last to the room below.

He takes up his hammer and fits the nails into his mouth like jagged teeth and working swiftly seals the door against intruders. His errand downstream may take days or weeks or the remainder of his life if he is lucky, and should good fortune or bad prevent his return to this place he desires that no man should desecrate it. The fire is dead by the time he finishes and he steps outside into the greater cold to run his trotlines one last time and bundle the gutted fish in wet icy reeds for the trip downstream where they will serve him as either meat or trade. The skiff finds the current, a river within the greater river. On either side the trees stand bare and the brush juts raw from the mudbanks. The sun is at its peak, a faint glow through high overcast luring the skiff downriver. Finn follows it with no will of his own. How long since he has seen Huck? A year and more, at the very least, and under circumstances that he cannot recall.

He stops at a waterside trading post just north of St. Petersburg to exchange catfish for beans and sugar and a bottle of better whiskey than is his usual. Black letters on the bleached piling spell the name Smith but Smith is not here. The man behind the counter has one withered arm and he lists to the right when he walks and he eyes Finn as if he's found himself trapped in a cave with a bear. "Where you bound?" Hoping it's some distance from this lonesome spot.

"Where's Smith?"

"Died last week."

Finn grunts. "St. Pete."

"Nice town."

"I reckon."

"Business or pleasure?" He ventures a tentative smile and then puts it away.

"Business. Might take me a little pleasure in it all the same, though." His eyes are unreadable. "Depends."

"You suit yourself, then."

"I will."

"And good luck with it."

"It'll come out just fine," says Finn.

———

HE TIES UP just below town in a little copse of willow and conceals the skiff as best he can behind dry brush. He recalls a cabin not distant, an abandoned pile of wood and stone far past human habitation, built by some woodsman or hermit or lunatic long gone. He tramps the woods until he finds it again and then he moves the skiff to a place nearer by and hauls his poor goods inside, wishing that the boy were here to do the work but satisfied that he will be along soon enough, satisfied moreover that with the boy's newfound wealth his own circumstances are even now upon the threshold of reversal.

In the afternoon he collects firewood and sets out some lines in the river and sits on the bank drinking whiskey from the bottle. Fish bite and he catches some and cleans them, throwing the loose ropes of their guts spiraling back into the river and wiping his hands on the snow that clings to shady spots here and there beneath the evergreens. He buries the fish in the snow, not caring if they're found by dog or wolf or fox or some other, for the river remains crowded with their shining brethren and his son possesses six thousand dollars and he is himself drunk on whiskey.

By dark he decides that he ought not wait until morning to question the boy. Better to surprise him by night, there in whatever room he inhabits in the Douglas house where the widow has imprisoned him out of the goodness of her heart, than to abide alone here in the woods and permit more time to pass without commencing negotiations over that six thousand. By night he'll have the advantage of surprise in addition to strength and pure mean fury and whatever vestige of paternal respect he can cause to flourish in the boy's heart either by argument or by force. He corks the bottle and takes up his blanket and strikes off through the woods toward St. Petersburg in his black coat and his broken hat as a thin dusting of snow begins to drift through the arms of the evergreens and the leafless maples like flour from a sifter.

He skirts the cottages at the margin of the village, edging past them remote as a wolf from the haunts of man. Behind the village rises Cardiff Hill, its summit commanded by the Douglas house, its green sward lightly blanketed, its near slope from this southerly direction cratered with diggings. The quarry has been here forever but Finn has forgotten about it. Not until he stumbles across the whitened mounds of its tailings does he remember and take note of it, and then he lifts his hat to give his head a scratch and sits down upon a pile of rock to uncork the bottle. The whiskey passes down his throat with a welcome heat and settles in his stomach like home comfort long remembered. He pants some for the walk has been long and lately steep, settles the blanket upon his shoulders, and looks uphill where the lights of the Douglas house have either been extinguished for the night or merely vanished behind an outcropping. The longer he sits the wearier he grows and the less sense it makes to be carrying this bottle all the way up the hill and down again, so he finishes it directly and throws it over the edge into the quarry where it lands with a distant suggestion of breakage and the snowflakes turn to spiders lowering themselves on threads of moonlight and he sleeps.

———

COME MORNING he awakens beneath a blanket crusted over with snow and he shakes off a loose flurry of it in his struggle to rise. His breath comes slow and makes a cloud that drifts toward the precipice as he labors erect, cold air passing in through his mouth and downstream through his lungs to gather warmth and then out again steaming with the conveyed heat of his body, for Finn has become as any man will an unstoppable engine of change and transformation. He leans back upon his elbows for a while and then lies prone again, this time with his forehead in a little patch of snow that cools his brain and warms by contrast the remainder of him.

A thin patch of trees stands behind the widow's house and he materializes from the post-dawn dimness of them with a great show of stealth, crooked so far over that he needs to take one hand from his pocket to keep his hat from falling off, studying the blank windows from beneath lowered brows. A fence stands before him and a gate, and he lingers there with one hand freezing in his pocket and the other hand freezing on his hat brim and the cross in his boot-heel warning away any devil save himself. He takes a few tentative steps in either direction, craning his neck for any sign of which bedroom window might belong to the boy, and when he spies one with the markings of unclean hands on the mullions and a littering of thrown gravel on the windblown shed roof below it he knows that he has found his mark. The boy will be off to school or elsewhere soon if he is not gone already. The woman for her part will be busy in the kitchen or in the parlor or somewhere else, roaming around the house with a rag in her hand and a song in her heart and her ears wide open.

Understanding that he has arrived too late to take up that six thousand with the boy, he curses the whiskey and the long walk and the sudden stoneworks that interrupted his purpose. Then he gives the fencepost a kick for good measure, knocking loose a soft sheet of snow from a crossbeam, before turning his back on the blind house and retreating to the woods from which he came.

He returns at suppertime to conceal himself in the trees behind the house, where the shadows are their longest. The boy leaves on some errand after supper and the man loses him in the woods and curses his luck but climbs upward on the drainpipe to take his place, over the shed roof and in through the window without a sound. With his hat on his knee he sits in the chair behind the door and waits patient as stone for his son's return. Night comes on and the house goes quiet save the opening and closing of the front door and some murmuring between the boy and the widow. Listening to their voices Finn neither tenses nor worries himself, but crosses one leg over the other and rocks back on the chair in his pitchdark corner, fully at ease. He is relaxing thus when Huck enters with his candle and his carelessness, and not until the boy shuts the door does he stir. Huck, despite his city airs, has retained enough of his father's woodland stealth to freeze at his sudden threatening presence.

"How much you miss your old pap?" Holding out his hand not for a greeting or God forbid for an embrace but for that other, of which he knows the boy has plenty.

The boy leans on his rearward foot and backs away edgewise. He once crept beneath a tent to see a lion tamer in a traveling show and to look at him now in this dark room with his candle clutched in one grubby hand he may have copied this slow sly movement direct from that slender man in his brilliant clothes, with his gun and his whistle hung gleaming about him like charms against mortality.

"Come on, boy. Give. High time you was good for something."

"I've only got a dollar." True, because this very day he has assigned his fortune to Judge Thatcher for safekeeping and received only that much in consideration.

"I didn't bring you up a liar."

"I ain't one."

"They teach you that in school?"

"*I ain't no liar.* I told you."

"You drop that school now, hear?" For he has reminded himself of one of his favorite subjects of conversation, more beloved even than money or whiskey for about these last two there is little to say.

"The widow makes me go."

"Ain't nobody can make you put on airs over your own flesh and blood. Not unless you want to."

"I."

"Your own mother couldn't read nor write before she died," Finn interrupts.

"I know it."

"So you leave off."

"I will." For he has had this conversation before.

"Now give." Holding out his palm.

The boy burrows in his pocket to produce a fishhook and a bone and the dollar, which the man snatches away.

"But I wanted it for."

"I'm thirsty, boy." As if he needs to construct an argument. Still he is the boy's father and there may be some useful sentiment to be mined there. Moreover the urge for whiskey has worked its weakness upon him and at this moment he is feeling for the stuff a kind of paternal tenderness that anyone could perceive, even this child. "Now where's the rest?"

"I give it to the judge," says the boy, and Finn's blood turns cold.

"You didn't."

"I did."

"No. He wouldn't have it."

"I swear."

He unsheathes his belt, drawing it forth snakelike from under his coat and sending his stove-in hat tumbling to the floor as he does. "He wouldn't have it nor nothing else. Not from you." Rising to his feet in the dark corner of the dark room, his shadow cast large behind him by the light of the boy's receding candle.

From out of his other pocket the boy produces a thick sheet of vellum, densely lettered and sealed and signed, and in his high ringing voice he reads it off to his father like a lesson.

"Judge Thatcher," says the man when he has finished, understanding this much at least. A different judge entire.

"I told you," says the boy.

"I'll see about him," says Finn, and out the window he goes with the dollar clutched tight in his fist.

———

DOWN THE FROZEN CENTER of the street he marches like some mud-formed golem drawn by revenge or moonlight until the lamps of a tavern catch his fierce eye and he turns at once, lighter on his feet than any observer might guess, and mounts the steps to the door and enters into the place accompanied by snow and black wind.

"You Finn," says a voice from the darkness. "You old dog, you."

And welcomed thus, without so much as responding or even looking to respond, he steps to the bar and presents the dollar with ceremony befitting a magus and the barman brings the bottle. "There'll be plenty more," says Finn grandly. "You'll see." But as the night wears on and the whiskey dwindles he offers up no further proof of his assertion, and so having kept his apocryphal riches to himself by morning he awakens in the village jail with his head afire and his dollar used up and his black coat stained with vomit.

The marshal works a splinter of firewood between his teeth and leans backward in his chair. "You'll be seeing Judge Thatcher."

"I know it." As if he has planned it this way from the beginning.

"That boy of yours."

"What of him?"

"You know what of him. I'm surprised it took you this long to get down here, is all."

"I come as quick as I could."

"I'll bet you did."

Finn washes himself and eats a breakfast of fried eggs and flapjacks swimming in butter and syrup brought over from the Liberty Hotel and he wonders for the briefest moment if it might be worth giving up whiskey to luxuriate in a fancy start like this every day of the week for about the same money. Then he remembers the six thousand and comforts himself that he will no doubt be enjoying the twain of these luxuries before long, both the whiskey and the cooked breakfast too and God knows what all else besides. But the eggs go straight to his gut and the marshal has to escort him out back to the frozen-over jakes before they head out to see Judge Thatcher, who isn't holding court today but is instead sitting peacefully in his study at home surrounded by lawbooks.

"We haven't seen this one around for a while," says the marshal by way of introduction. He is still working the splinter in his teeth, only now he's grinning around it as if he and the judge are playing a lovely joke upon their guest.

"Time served for the drunkenness," says the judge, who needs no more evidence in the case than Finn's wasted appearance and high acrid smell. "And open that window a crack if you insist on bringing foul creatures like this into my presence." Pointing imperiously.

The marshal leaps to do his bidding. A girl skips past the study door on her way to school, oblivious to the men within. She has two long braided pigtails the color of caramel, and Finn takes subtle note of her from the corner of his eye.

"You," says the judge, marking Finn's wandering attention, one finger aimed straight between his eyes like doom.

"Your Honor." Finn's attention regathers itself into a fine point and he blinks away the last tatters of his headache. He can't remember if he needs to call him Your Honor here in the house but he figures it can't hurt.

"I'll thank you to keep your mind where it belongs."

"Sir."

Thatcher tamps tobacco into his pipe and puts flame to it. "I don't know where that son of yours got his intelligence."

"His mother, Your Honor." Sycophantish, though the judge seems not to notice.

The marshal laughs through his teeth, a single wheeze like a dying concertina, the gasping end of merriment in spite of itself. "He got that right, Judge."

Thatcher blows smoke, theatrical. "What *of* that woman, Mr. Finn? What does *she* think of your habits? Does *she* know what to do with you?"

"No sir. I reckon she don't. Not no more."

A clock ticks in a room down the hall and Thatcher sucks on his pipe, considering, letting time pass as if he owns all of it in the world, as if in fact he runs the manufactory where it originates and owns the patent for it too. He is a small man, neat and unprepossessing as a country parson, with a pale thin thatch of gray hair and sunken cheeks. Finn wonders if there is a connection between the meager proportions of some men and their grandiose desires.

"At least that boy of yours has some intelligence. More than I had imagined, if you want to know the truth."

"That's why I."

"I have not yielded you the floor, Mr. Finn."

"I know it."

"As I was saying, the boy has some intelligence. Perhaps even wisdom."

Finn bites his tongue.

"Which came as an altogether *unexpected development,* as I was saying."

Finn composes his face into a blank.

"An unexpected development with *unexpected implications.*"

No reply from the well-behaved Finn.

"By which I mean unexpected implications for *you,* Mr. Finn. Including the fact that however greatly you might desire otherwise, the documents that he and I signed yesterday make it impossible for you to lay so much as a finger upon that wise little boy's fortune."

Down below the desk, out of Thatcher's line of sight, Finn balls his fists upon his knees like a pair of nine-pound hammers. The marshal braces his feet square beneath him but nothing comes of it.

"Not so much as a finger—at least until he reaches his majority, should you be fortunate enough to live that long. And by that time I suspect that he will have matured into a figure quite beyond your grasp." Thatcher levels his gaze at Finn and draws thoughtfully on his pipestem, indicating that he is for the time being not only finished with his argument but quite satisfied with it and with himself and with the balance of the universe as well.

"It ain't right," says Finn.

"Oh, but it is."

"It ain't right that the widow takes the boy and you take the money and his own father his own goddamn flesh and blood gets left with nothing."

"I did not *take the money,* as you suggest. I have merely become, at the boy's request, its trustee."

"Same difference."

"Not at all, I assure you. I have merely taken upon myself certain *fiduciary responsibilities*—not limited strictly to the estate but also in fact to the boy himself, which the evidence of my senses"—here he sniffs—"*the evidence of my senses* tells me is more than his own flesh and blood has ever done."

A nerve in Finn's cheek commences to twitch. "I'll sue."

"A protracted lawsuit costs money."

"I can get it. I come from it."

"By my measure, Mr. Finn, you've come a *very long way* from it. A very long way indeed." To gauge by how his smile wrinkles backward into his sunken cheeks, the idea lightens Judge Thatcher's heart.

"Don't remind me," says Finn, but everything about the judge and his house and his lawbooks and the row of tintypes arranged like mathematical theorems on his great walnut desk reminds him. These reminders, these and the presence at his elbow of the marshal with his gun, are powers that keep Finn bound to his chair as none else could.

"It does a man good to remember his beginnings," says Judge Thatcher. "Even Satan remembers his beginnings. And therein lies the root of his eternal torment."

———

FINN SITS against a fencepost in the sun and studies St. Petersburg with a kind of magisterial detachment, distant as a wild beast or some grim god beyond petitioning. Even more than his brain desires the six thousand, his heart burns with shame over a single remark made to Thatcher—over how, at the commencement of their interview, he'd said that the boy's intelligence derives exclusively from his mother—for this is precisely the kind of self-effacing lie that any fawning nigger might produce so as to deflect blame and curry favor. Beast or god, he desires little at this moment beyond eradicating this remark now cemented into his history by time's passage, for as he has said it to the least of them he may as well have said it to the greatest.

Beyond this and perhaps as manifestation of it he desires to return home rather than linger penniless and disgraced in St. Petersburg or even in the woods at the squatter's shack. He pictures his riverside house and the open ladderwork of stairs leading up to it and the nailed-up doorway to the bedroom. Behind the nailed-up door he sees the stairway and above that—above the first floor just as the mind is above the body and as the spirit is above the flesh—above that he sees the painted-over and rectified room.

He sees it now not as he has left it but as it once was: her clothing strewn over the chair and his bottle standing empty upon the windowsill and starlight from the river casting a recondite message upon the far wall, and the woman asleep alongside the depression he'd made over the years in that sagging straw tick laid hard upon its homebuilt frame (for her, he'd hammered that frame together for her, as if she required or deserved better than the mere plank-thrown pallet that would have suited him well enough). He sees her sleeping there as content and enduring as a stain upon bedlinen or history or heart and he kneels beside her as if meaning to utter some confessional prayer and instead reaches out to cradle her neck and press his thumbs against the softness of her throat and thus put an end to it.

The starlight fades and the sun comes up and he has all day. He takes himself downstairs and brews coffee and fries salt pork for breakfast and then he goes outside down the open ladder of steps to the ground where late summer has dampened the hardpacked earth with dew. At river's edge he unbuttons and fishes himself out and sends a long tense stream arcing into the moving water, not the last time today that he will return to the river some of that which it has given him. His trotlines prove strung with catfish great and small, and by noon he is done harvesting them and back home with money in his pocket. He lays out a tarpaulin on the bedroom floor and step by lumbering step walks an old empty barrel up the stairs to stand centered upon it, and then he throws a rope over a high beam and with the rope he binds her feet and from the apparatus thus arranged he swings her ceilingward over the waiting barrel. His knife stinks of fishguts but he keeps it honed sharp as the Judge's vengeance, and as her red blood drains into the barrel and fills the hot room with the smell of iron he steps to the open window and coaxes the last drop or two of whiskey from the bottom of the bottle and out onto his parched tongue. Then he raises the other window and hauls the body down and lays it on the tarpaulin. Like a supplicant he kneels and applies the knife in a straight line unwavering from clavicle to crotch, and thinking of fox and beaver and deer and other beasts whose pelts he has learned to separate from their edible or worthless meat he extrapolates the details of this new chore with some atavistic portion of his brain. Thus with brutal thrust and tender prod does he remove all trace of skin, arranging it in strips and sheets beside him on the tarp for disposal in Bliss's fire. Fastidious in his methods, he arranges each portion upside down or inside out, its inner surface made outer to show red and slick and fibrous but never allowed to reveal the dark curse of its hidden face. He arranges the pieces thus to speak of death and death only without particulars, as if by such transformation he can alter all that has gone before and begin anew, clean and pure and washed in the indiscriminate blood. By nightfall he is finished and he walks the barrel down the stairs and tips it into the dark river. He returns to the upper room and wraps the woman in the tarpaulin and stows the leavings in a tow sack and carries her down the stairs likewise and likewise tips her into the river with a silent ominous unfurling as of one great bloody wing.

5

Out of pure meanness the boy takes down some underthings from the neighbor's washline and douses them in the shallows and hangs them up again muddy to dry, and when the question comes he blames the mischief on his brother, Will. Which everyone, including the boy himself, knows is so far beyond possible as to qualify as a confession.

The neighbor, a narrow-jawed halfwit named Tyrell, stands in the parlor door with his wife's brown drawers bunched in one fist. Muddy water runs down his arm to his elbow where it gathers like blood and drips down onto the freshly polished floor. The track that it leaves down his forearm is by some small measure cleaner than the remainder of his skin, for Tyrell has been digging potatoes and bringing in hay since before sunup, but this irony is entirely lost upon him.

"My hired man seen him do it," he says. Fixing his eyes upon the boy but speaking to his mother.

"Your Lester. *Your Lester* saw him."

"Yes'm. So don't you pay that boy no mind when he denies it."

"Your Lester's word against that of my son." She does not doubt for a moment that the boy is guilty, but the specifics of this means of indictment are to her so abhorrent as to require refutation. *"Your black Lester's word."*

"Yes'm. A man sees what he sees. Color don't make no difference."

The boy stands in the corner barefoot, willing himself to merge into the shadows gathered there.

"Go get your shoes, boy." Squeezing the damp drawers as if to wring out a confession. "We'll see from their bottoms where you been."

"That will *not* be necessary." She speaks like some old Divine Right royalty, and from across the room she fastens the boy to the wall with the thrust of an imperious finger. "The Judge will decide this matter when he returns at the end of the week."

"I reckon he will," says the halfwit, for by his lights this is surely the best resolution imaginable.

In the family Finn, justice delayed is justice magnified. Two days of stony looks and silent recriminations from his mother are two days more than the boy is prepared to endure, although as he grows into manhood he will learn to suffer such treatment by the yearful. With equal intensity he yearns for and dreads the moment when his father will return, and he desperately seeks out the words to tell his mother so.

"You'll get such punishment as you get when you get it." She repeats this formula any time he lifts up his fears before her, either these self-same words or others equally well calculated to suggest the unknowable and ineluctable qualities of his fate. From time to time she adds, "There's no use in borrowing trouble," for she knows that there is indeed plenty of use in borrowing trouble, so long as she is not the one doing the borrowing.

In a shameful hidden chamber of her heart she desires that the Judge will wreak upon the boy some kind of rough frontier justice. At home in Philadelphia the decorous Quaker boys of her youth told stories of men staked out by Indians to suffer and die in the hot sun of places far deeper into the wilderness than Adams County, places populated by rattlesnakes and venomous insects and mountain lions and worse. In marrying the Judge she tied her fate to a land where such barbarity, whether the accidental work of animals or the calculated work of man, is not only possible but inevitable, and she believes that the day will surely come when through no knowable fault of her own the Judge will turn brute despite the veneer of his Philadelphia education and set about establishing an ancient and uncompromising justice in this fierce Eden to which he has delivered her. Everything decays. In this move westward with the dying sun she has taken within her breast the universal principle of dissolution, whether as cause or by effect she cannot say and does not wonder, although she does know that here beneath her feet she detects both the dawn of primordial rule and the ultimate destruction of everything and to her they look quite the same.

The boy begins to ask. "Will he."

"I can't say what he'll do, and I can't say what he won't."

"But."

"It's not your place to know the mind of the Judge, nor is it mine."

"I'm just."

"Everything happens for a reason." Which to her is an article of doomed faith and to him is an explanation of the webwork of causality in which he finds himself trapped.

———

RETURN THE JUDGE DOES, in due time and burdened down with his own ideas and understandings. He drags a divisive trail of misery behind him as a mule drags a plow, and by its passage the landscape in his wake is altered day by day. The Judge's reputation, a reputation long and fairly earned, is that none save himself shall be satisfied by his rulings. Some say that even he despairs with each grim final blow of his gavel, for the harsh justice that he measures out can neither sufficiently punish the guilty nor fully restore the wronged. Some say this, gathered muttering in damp prison cells or sipping tea in the parlors of great houses, but they cannot know for certain and the truth is more likely that they are manufacturing ordinary human emotions to overlay upon his transient and inscrutable self and make him thus both knowable and known.

The boy returns from a rare and contrite day at school to find the Judge's black bowler hat already brushed clean and hung upon its hook in the entryway like some inky aperture in the white wall, and his dizzy dreamlike urge is to escape by squeezing through it and out the other side into a place where men are neither parted nor linked by such fierce impassive implements as the Judge shuttles day by day across the virgin hills of Illinois.

His mother is in the kitchen and with the blank thin expanse of her back she instructs him to linger not but instead to go direct to his father's study, which he does, and when the door opens to expel him later like the whale casting out Jonah he is neither in the mood for sympathy nor likely to receive it. He is to do the neighbor's laundry for a month, and moreover he is to do this penance and everything else in purposely muddied drawers of his own, donned damp and sticky and permitted to dry into a harsh scratchy encrustation upon his legs and his ass and his privates. The halfwit Tyrell finds this punishment amusing to no end, a circumstance that might refute the Judge's alleged belief that justice, though necessary, is never fully possible, and he lingers about the laundry room when he should be at his chores, eyeing the boy's leaking shorts.

"You shit yourself again today, boy?" With an inquisitive sniffing that makes his narrow face look even more like a rabbit than usual.

"No sir."

"Then what you got up there?"

"Nothing." Bent over the washboard.

"You hiding a nigger up in there somewheres?" His head cocked.

"I don't reckon I could."

"You don't know much."

"I know enough."

"Next time, you have that nigger take a bath a'fore he climbs in."

The boy rakes Tyrell's things across the washboard as if to abrade them down to nothing but scraps and buttons and loose wet fibers of homespun. Some residual urge causes him to wish that the Judge were present to defend him against Tyrell's weirdly troubling innuendo, but in his heart he knows that this is precisely the punishment or some variant thereof that the Judge has had in mind from the beginning. And so he steels himself. "I don't have no truck with niggers," he says. "Filthy or clean."

"They's only one kind." Tyrell laughs with a kind of fierce hiccup, the halfwit proudly superior to the boy. "They's only one kind of nigger. That's the first thing you got to know."

"I know it," says the boy.

6

FINN LINGERS at his fencepost and permits the heat of the sun to draw him back from his reverie of that upstream house sloping riverward under its burden of remembrance. Two men stroll past his resting place, one black and one white, each of them paler and more bookish than the other. Head to grizzled gray head they converse like a pair of old philosophers. The black man is by a slight degree the more fastidious, dressed like a diplomat in a gleaming white shirt and a woolen suit the color of a chestnut, balancing upon his head an elegant brown bowler and bearing in his right hand a silver-headed cane that he uses only sparingly, as if he is loath to soil its chalk-white tip upon the ground of St. Petersburg. He walks with his shoulders thrown back and his narrow chest cutting the Missouri air like the prow of a ship, his slender hands are gloved in a pale off-white only shades lighter than his yellow skin, and from time to time he opens his mouth wide and laughs a deep round laugh from between bright white teeth as if everyone within earshot were appreciative of his refined sense of humor. Finn squints at him as he would squint at a bright light or the arrival of apocalypse.

The two men pause a little distance away to greet another gentleman, this one known to the white but not to the black. Once their introductions are complete and their gloves have been removed as needed to permit the shaking of hands and then donned all over again, the third gentleman tips his hat and proceeds on his way with an appreciative nodding of his head—while the other two continue toward Finn.

"New in town?" says Finn from his seat by the fencepost. "Your friend I mean." Looking straight at the white man and the white man only, with an intensity that makes a show of excluding the other.

The white man has been so long so far beyond contact with an individual like Finn that he accepts his question without reservation and stops as eagerly as if he has been invited to dance. "Why, yes," he says, and again: "Why, yes indeed."

"Thought so."

The white man folds his hands at his sternum and begins to declaim. "Professor Morris is visiting from Ohio, where he teaches at Kenyon College. He'll be speaking tonight at the Reform Church."

"You fixing to sell him?"

"I beg your pardon?"

"Not that he's likely to fetch much." Here he permits his gaze to wander over the black man's regally slim figure. "Not by the look of him."

"Sir."

"Ain't nothing worth any less than a puny nigger. Other'n a puny nigger in a ten-dollar suit, putting on airs."

"Come along, Professor," says the white man to the black. "We're late for your introductions at the church." He takes his associate by the elbow but finds him immovable, for the professor has been turned to stone by Finn's effrontery. He spreads wide his legs and cocks his head to one side and leans forward upon his cane, transfixed by their interlocutor as he would be by a Siberian tiger in a circus parade.

"You mind your master," says Finn with a dismissive wave of his hand. "Git along now, boy."

"No man is my master," intones the black man, with the theatrical air of an individual winding up to deliver a lecture or a sermon.

"Is that so?" Addressing the white man, parting his knees to scratch at his crotch.

"If you please, sir," interrupts the black man with a schoolroom kind of sarcasm, "you may direct your questions to me. Dr. Bale here is my colleague, not my translator. And above all he is most assuredly not my keeper."

"I told you," the white man puts in, "he's a college professor. From Ohio."

"I got ears."

"He's a scholar."

"I heard."

"He comes from an extremely progressive state—a state where a man like Professor Morris is not only free, but free to vote."

"Bullshit," says Finn.

"Not at all."

Finn grunts.

"You have a lot to learn," says the professor.

"I might."

"Change is afoot."

Finn cogitates for a minute. "If a nigger can vote," he says, "then I don't reckon I'll ever vote again."

"Suit yourself."

"I don't care what state."

"Time and events will overtake you."

"Maybe they will."

"Perhaps they already have."

As the gentlemen go on their way Finn has an idea. He returns to the jail where he finds the marshal on his knees in the one cell, bent over a bucket and bearing a rag, cleaning up after Finn's own mess of the night prior.

"You tell me something?"

"What is it?"

"What's the rule for claiming a loose nigger in this state?"

"Depends."

"What on?"

"Where he's from. Certain conditions."

"From Ohio, let's say."

"You be talking about a free man?"

"So far."

The marshal drops the rag into the water and sits back upon his heels. "Anybody particular in mind?"

"I won't lie to you. That professor."

"The one over to the church tonight."

"That's the one."

"Finn, you're either the smartest man in this town or the stupidest."

"I need money. You heard that judge same as me."

"I did."

"Lawsuits cost."

"I wonder how much you'd need before you couldn't spend every bit of it on whiskey."

"I aim to find out."

"You never will."

"We'll see. So what's the rule on that professor?"

"You won't like it." He goes back to daubing the floor with his rag. "Six months to claim."

"He ain't here six months."

"I know it."

"I claim him, I'd even sell him back to that Ohio college they like him so much. He don't look like a worker to me."

"You can't do it, Finn."

"You sure about the six months?"

"I am."

"That long?"

"That long."

"A man could starve."

"Or work."

"I've run up against the law before."

"I know it."

"I don't mean this." Indicating with a flick of his eyes the cell, the crust of vomit still visible upon the bedframe, the recent past. "I mean the Judge."

"I know."

"Him and my own rightful inheritance, which it looks like I'll never get as long as I live."

"Stealing a nigger ain't the way to fix your problem."

"I reckon."

But Finn is not without alternatives. When evening comes he takes up a position in the doorway of the Reform Church, where Professor Morris will be speaking, and assumes the pose of a mendicant, hat in hand and cheeks hollow and eyes brimming with woe. To the forward-looking faithful he is the veriest picture of need, unbesmirched by such associations as his figure may possess for those acquainted with the taverns and the marshal's office and the courts, and they do unto him as they would have others do unto themselves.

He is gone before the professor climbs the steps to the pulpit, and on his tramp back to the cabin he stops at the riverside redoubt of a bootlegger for a gallon of whiskey that will hold him until he has an opportunity to use the rest of his newfound riches to lay in proper supplies.

———

JUDGE THATCHER PERMITS the boy three dollars and before he can make use of it Finn has claimed it for his own. He awakens in the marshal's office to discover that Thatcher is riding the circuit and he'll be seeing a new man instead.

"This one a kindly sort?"

"Don't know. Mostly he's on the circuit."

Finn looks as if he's just been cheated at poker. "Time served's always enough for Thatcher."

"I know."

"A person gets in the habit."

"I know it."

"Ain't there a law on that subject?"

"Not that I know."

"How one of them has to do like the other'n already done?"

"You mean following precedent."

"Think I'd be smart to mention that?"

"I wouldn't. No."

Stone is the new judge's name and he has a house in the village where he lives with his wife and his son and his daughter, a fine Christian gentleman presiding over a fine Christian family, and for Finn he has nothing in his heart but forgiveness. "I believe that a fellow such as yourself can be improved," he says, careful not to say "saved" although "saved" is what he means.

"I do too. I believe it."

Stone looks childlike to Finn, cherubic as a soprano in a boys' choir. Tall and thin and pale, his high forehead crowned by a frill of swept-back hair the color of rust, he eyes Finn with the look a gardener would use upon a hedgerow that he means to prune.

"I have made a promise to myself, Mr. Finn. A promise that I shall never permit myself to give up on so much as a single soul. And I have kept that promise, regardless of how much evil and criminality I have witnessed."

"You ain't been a judge long."

"No."

"You giving me time served or some other?"

"Time served," says Judge Stone, "with the admonition that rather than visiting a tavern tonight you spend the evening dining with my family and myself."

In order to make Finn presentable to his wife and children the judge takes him to a dry-goods store and has him fitted with a new suit of clothes and a sturdy overcoat and a felt hat and a pair of boots, all at his own expense. Finn observes out loud that he will need to bedeck the left boot-heel with a cross of nails in order to keep away the devil, an idea that Stone receives as if it were the quaintest superstition from out of some impenetrable African jungle. "Don't you worry about the devil," he says. "He's not permitted across the threshold of my house."

Finn knows better but he will not say.

The food at Judge Stone's table is not elegant but it is rich and varied and there is plenty of it. Mrs. Stone has even baked a pie, not because they have a guest for supper but because she bakes a pie most every day of the week. For Finn, whose diet changes month by month as the year unwinds, the preserved huckleberries speak of a season long gone and hitherto irrecoverable. As he chews, methodical as some old ruminant, these baked-black berries beneath the latticework of their pale and tender crust speak also of innocence undisturbed, of childhoods spent around tables like this and around others less elevated and bountiful, of secrets buried beneath time and earth and flowing water; and even in the forced absence of whiskey a vision passes before his eyes unbidden not of snakes or of spiders but of the turgid Mississippi beneath his window on the Illinois side crossed and recrossed with a cumulative ghostly weavework of fishing boats' accidental paths and steamboats' cautious trajectories achurn with white foam beneath which and supporting all lies dark water and darker history.

Only the children fear him. The boy is perhaps seven or eight, his sister older than that by a year, and they are formally dressed in a way that distinguishes them from the ordinary run of children, a condition that has made them disdained on one hand and elevated on the other but has nonetheless left neither unbaptized by the river of rumor that laves all of St. Petersburg's children, a river heavy with detail about the hideous habits of Pap Finn. All the same their father is present, and their visitor is well enough dressed and better behaved, and they are safe by their own homefire, so by the time Finn has loaded up his plate with his third piece of pie and drunk his second cup of coffee the boy works up sufficient nerve to ask him a question.

"That dead body that came down the river awhile back: Did you know some folks thought it was you?"

Finn holds his fork in his fist like a club, and he freezes with it poised over a dessert plate clotted with syrup. For some seconds he does not move, not so much as an eyelash, and his presence at the table takes on by its very stoniness a kind of fearsome potency, like a mountain lion coiled to leap or a hunter waiting behind some leafy blind for the inevitable moment when his prey will step into full and vulnerable view. He is pure potential, dead silent and for all human purposes outside time, and as he hangs there during those few interminable seconds the boy realizes that he has made a dreadful mistake—until with a visible effort the dinner guest slides his lips back over blue teeth as tipsy as tombstones and gives the boy a ferocious smile and moves his head toward him just perhaps a quarter of an inch or even less, a cobra lining up his strike, and returns question with question: "What body?"

"There was a woman," says Stone with a certain disinterest.

"Well," snorts Finn. "I sure ain't no woman. And I reckon I ain't dead."

"Where on earth did you ever hear such talk?"

But the boy apprehends neither his mother's question nor Finn's grim reassurance regarding the obvious. His ears pound with urgent blood and he grips his chairseat with both hands to keep himself from toppling off or running.

Finn decides to pursue a course of nonchalance, so he pensively addresses himself again to his pie and watches from underneath his shaggy brows to see what sort of punishment is about to unfold before him. His own boy he has horsewhipped for daring to enter a school spelling bee, and he is certain that in this house of judgment the child's stoic refusal to answer his mother's direct question will unloose consequences most immediate and dire. But Stone reaches not for his belt, and after a moment the woman answers her own question on behalf of the tongue-tied boy, saying to her husband something that by the sound of it she has repeated a thousand times prior: "Those children at school are a poor influence on him."

"Amen," says Judge Stone, which remark leaves the boy reprieved and the dinner guest both dissatisfied and stunned, as if he has been expecting a mouthful of honey and received a bee sting instead.

After supper the adults arrange themselves around the fire in the parlor, where Judge Stone speaks of temperance and charity and the overwhelming redemptive power of Christ Jesus. He folds his hands in his lap and squeezes them together until his knuckles go white as bones and Finn cannot decide whether his impulse is to pray or to prevent himself from snatching up his guest by the collar and baptizing him in the washtub. The room grows warm and Finn grows comfortably drowsy, until after a while it seems to him that Stone with his inverse-named Christ Jesus has turned the world upside down and back to front, making it over from the hard place he has understood since childhood into a place altogether different, a place where forgiveness is not merely possible but indeed the expected order of the day. Warm and full of supper and his head aswim with sleep he sees his own hands in his lap as unclean things yet things not fully beyond redemption, and he elevates them in the firelight as if they desire on their own to perform an act of invocation or some other arcane magic.

"Those hands once belonged to a beast," says Judge Stone.

"I know it."

"But they can be washed clean."

"Is that a fact?"

"Rest assured."

"Then so be it."

The judge rises and takes Finn's right hand and shakes it without reservation. "Will you do us the honor of staying the night? It's a good long way back to your cabin."

"I will." All that he desires is sleep.

Around midnight he awakens faceup on the sofa with the fire banked and his new boots on the floor and his new coat draped neck to knee like a blanket. His mouth is dry and his stomach is sour and one arm lurches out from beneath the coat to arrest his dead weight as he falls and falls and falls in the last remnant of a dream until his knuckles crack against the hardwood floor and the shock draws him full awake. He lies still for a time listening to his own ragged breathing and his own pan-icky heartbeat and the stealthy slow rearrangement of coals in the fire, trusting that he will sleep again soon, but sleep will not come no matter how hard he tries. The coat collar tucked beneath his chin smells pow-erfully of lanolin and he envisions sheep which he attempts to count but to no avail, for his numeric skills are as limited as his wakefulness is vast. Finally, temperance and redemption notwithstanding, he decides that in order to get a proper night's sleep he is going to require a drink.

He laces up his boots and dons his coat and hat and lets himself out through the front door and onto the porch, where a light dusting of snow has covered everything over. His tracks, tracks that by dint of his newly unmarked heel the devil himself might follow, go straight down the hill to the nearest tavern in the village, one about to close up for the night until Finn presents himself at the bar.

"Throw another log on, Willis," says the barman to a huge figure bent low over a table by the near-dead fire. "Look who's come in."

"Whiskey," says Finn.

"Turn out your pocket."

Finn fishes therein with an apologetic look, as if he has somehow neglected to transfer his wealth. "New drawers."

"Should have saved your money for the finer things." With a nod toward the back bar.

"I know it."

"You've run out your credit."

"But my boy."

"Bring him in and bring his six thousand too and then we'll talk."

"How about the coat?" He shucks it.

"Got no use for a coat."

"It don't resemble your usual," says the giant Willis from his place near the fire.

"It ain't. Brand new." Showing it off adangle from one finger, like some odd and desperate haberdasher.

Willis rises like a breaching whale. The coat will no more fit him than it will fit his horse. "Give you a dollar for it."

"Paid three and a half just today."

"Not likely."

"Shows what you know."

Still the coat is clearly worth something. "I'll give you two. Take it or leave it."

Finn calculates not the true value of the coat but the duration of the walk back to Judge Stone's as measured against such a quantity of whiskey as he can acquire as fortification, and upon reflection he decides that two dollars is not only a fair price but the highest bid that he is likely to get anywhere at this time of night. He folds the coat as meticulously as it stands to be folded ever again and lays it over the back of the chair opposite Willis and holds out his hand.

"Put the two on his tab," says the giant to the barman, simplifying the transaction for all concerned.

"I ain't open all night," says the barman.

"I know it," says Finn.

"Whiskey, I reckon."

"Just bring the bottle and leave it."

"I can't leave it for long."

"I should have gone somewheres else."

"Willis ain't somewheres else, and then you'd be out of luck."

"I know it," says Finn, and he commences to drink.

When he has used up two dollars' worth and the barman has restored the cork and Willis has thrust his arms into the arms of his new coat like paired sausages and gone happily home, Finn trudges back up the hill to Judge Stone's. The powdering of snow has become an inch and he moves as rapidly as drink and footing will allow, stumbling to his knees once or twice and recovering with a curse. The cold amplifies his purpose and assists his concentration but at journey's end the slick fresh-painted boards of Judge Stone's porch conspire with the fresh snow to trip him up and so down he goes, ass over teakettle, arms aflail and hat taking wing, to land hard on the flagstone walk. He is there still when Stone comes upon him in the morning, dead asleep or else merely dead, covered over with snow, his left arm oddly bent and buckled beneath his fallen weight.

The doctor, an ill-tempered hogshead of a man awakened far too early for his liking, has nothing in the way of sympathy. "This should teach you to handle your own anesthesia," he says to Finn with a glance toward the judge. Neither one of them is amused.

For a while he squeezes and pokes the broken arm like a joint of meat, and when he's satisfied he commences twisting it this way and that like a pump handle, and once Finn has finally had enough the doctor instructs him to take a seat in a straight-backed chair and plant his feet squarely upon the floor. He removes his belt and ties it around the patient and the chair both, and he orders Stone to kneel behind the chair with his arms around Finn's chest. At last he takes Finn's wrist in both his hands, and with a curse and a grunt he throws all of his considerable and compacted weight in the opposite direction.

Finn deflates like a balloon and his shoulder nearly separates and the pain in his arm screams louder than any whiskey could possibly mitigate, much less whiskey drunk six or eight hours previous, but the arm goes straight or nearly so. The doctor mops his forehead with his sleeve and ties Finn's arm to a splint, and in the aftermath he presents his bill.

"If this is yours, Judge, I'll forgive it. If it's his, I reckon you'll have to lock him up before I get so much as a nickel."

"Now, now, that's not fair to you." Reaching for the paper.

But just as death outpaces justice the doctor is faster than the judge, and he snatches up the bill and tears it to bits.

Judge Stone: "Do you see that, Mr. Finn? Do you recognize basic human kindness when you see it?"

"I see it," says Finn, testing his arm. "I'm obliged."

"Damn right you're obliged," says the doctor, "not that I'll ever see any good from it."

"Where's your coat?" The judge.

"Drunk it."

"So this is where my kindness leads." Indicating the arm.

"I reckon."

"Pray that I never see you in my courtroom again."

"I will." With a little dip of his shaggy head. Then he turns to the doctor. "Obliged." And he shambles out, holding his arm across his chest like a baby child.

"You gave him a coat?"

"I did. And a suit of clothes and a pair of boots and a hot supper and more. Never again."

"He has limitations, that one."

"I see."

"The earlier you learn that, the better."

"I've learned it now."

"The only way you'll ever improve him," says the doctor, "is with a pistol." A locution which the judge finds so very amusing and insightful that he repeats it at every opportunity, until at length it enters the common lectionary of the village and becomes thereby Finn's calling card and his sentence and his fate.

———

FINN WORKS SOME NAILS out of a piece of lumber that's come floating down the river and caught on a snag upstream of the cabin and he straightens the nails upon a rock and then with another rock he drives them into the heel of his new left boot to keep away the devil. Thus girded he scrubs out his breakfast dishes in the river and sets them upon the bank to dry and climbs aboard his skiff with a two-gallon jug and a couple of empty sacks and a mess of fish gutted and wrapped in reeds. With his one good arm he poles upstream to St. Petersburg and ties up at someone's dock just as bold as if he owns it and half of the others strung along the waterfront too. With the jug adangle from his forefinger and the reed-wrapped fish bound up neatly in a sack he makes for the white double front door of the Liberty Hotel but thinks better of it at the last second, his cross-heeled boot barely on the threshold. So down the boardwalk he goes toward the river again and then up a narrow alleyway to a weed-grown yard aswarm with feral cats and mined with fishbones and dotted with the inverted skeletons of ruined rowboats. Beyond the jakes and the overgrown garden he finds the kitchen, and he kicks open the door with the toe of his marked left boot and heaves the sack of fish up onto a counter within. "Where's Cooper?" He addresses a black woman of middle age, her name unknown to him despite years of nodding acquaintance.

"It's Monday."

"I know it."

"Mr. Cooper ain't in on Monday."

"Since when?"

"Since ever' Monday I can recall."

"Well these fish won't wait."

"I don't reckon they will." She dusts the counter with flour that sifts down like snow or scattered seed and she rolls out a great lump of dough upon it and scatters some more flour and then bows to her kneading, oblivious.

"A dozen good-size cats there and a couple of bluegills. What'll you give?"

"I ain't authorized."

"Not money. I ain't talking about money."

"I ain't neither." Locating the wooden rolling pin in the depths of a drawer and setting to work. In a mere moment, precise as Noah with his cubits, she has fashioned this lump of pure white dough into a flat slab as round as a dinner plate and three eighths of an inch deep and no deeper from edge to edge and back again.

"Come on now." He takes a single step toward her, turning as he does one shoulder away from the bundled fish as from a child either defended or left to its fate.

"I ain't authorized. I tole you."

"Who'd know?"

"I just ain't."

"Those fish there are worth three pounds of salt pork anyhow plus a fill-up." Bringing the jug down on the countertop hard enough to raise a cloud of flour from the entire surface, bare wood and flattened dough dusted alike and alike disturbed.

"I don't know where he keeps it."

"You do."

"No sir." She picks up the biscuit cutter and touches it to piled flour to dust its edges. The palms of her hands are as pale as frog bellies and the backs as black as oil, covered all over with a thin film of flour that serves only to intensify their soft inky sheen.

"Don't lie." Another step and he takes her forearm just below the elbow.

"I won't." And then, since he is touching her with more tenderness than she had reason to expect from him though no less urgency, this: "He keeps it locked up." She is tentative with her confession but not entirely begrudging.

"Whereabouts?"

She has given off with the biscuit-making for now and stands alongside Finn with her haunch against his and her arm cradled in his strong fingers. Delicately she advances her forearm just the slightest to point toward a padlocked pantry door, drawing his hand along rather than pulling loose of it.

"I seen bigger locks."

"It's no use."

"A man should get what's coming to him."

"I ain't authorized."

Taking her arm more tightly and leaning in: "You always do as you're told?" His breath is excoriating but not without precedent.

After a moment: "I'll get whipped."

"Damn right you will." Which sounds like a promise.

She leans into the counter, easing off the pressure between the pair of them, and she finds the cutter again with her other hand. "You go see Mr. James behind the bar. See can he help you."

"Barkeep's got no use for fish." Throwing her arm down into the flour like a gutted channel cat.

"I could maybe slip you a biscuit later."

"I've got as much use for a biscuit as a barkeep does for a catfish."

"Suit yourself." Stamping out rounds as if the cutter were a dagger and the dough were flesh.

"I ain't looking for charity."

"You looking for *something*," she says.

In the end Finn poles upriver to Smith's old trading post, whose current crippled proprietor is more amenable to persuasion. He stows salt pork and some beans and flour and sugar aboard the skiff along with the whiskey and continues north to Lasseter where he ties up to one of his own rotted pilings. The river has seen some ice lately especially in the shallows and he imagines a great glacial wall of it pressing downstream from the north to scour away every unclean thing in its path, his precarious house included.

He leaves everything in the skiff and toils up the street to his brother's office. The door is locked but he finds the spare key right where an individual of Will's trusting nature would have secreted it, and he lets himself in and helps himself to an apple from the bowl and sits by the fire as contented as he believes he has ever been. By and by he falls asleep with his chin on his chest. Neither the needless rattling of the key in the lock nor the cold blast of air from the open door awakens him when Will enters, and rather than arouse his sleeping brother the lawyer takes up his seat at his desk and goes about his largely silent business. The room grows close as he consults his lawbooks and scratches meticulous notes across wide sheets of foolscap, and slowly his brother's proximity to the stove yields up the dense and furtive funk of the barroom, the river, and the slaughterhouse. Will puts down his pen and opens the window behind him a crack. He sits with his chin in his hand and his elbow on his desk and contemplates the figure collapsed upon the bench as if studying some primitive artifact that he has never seen before and will never see again, as if comparing this strange sad monster to a kinsman he was once quite certain he knew.

In time this gaze brings Finn warily awake. The apple core falls from his grip and tumbles beneath the bench, where it will stay until his brother bends down later to retrieve it. Finn starts, drawing breath as if it pains him, and pulls himself erect. "Will."

"To what do I owe this pleasure?"

"The last favor I'll ever ask."

The brother laughs out loud. "You're full of surprises. I'll grant you that."

"Honest." He removes his hat and holds it in his two hands, circling the brim around and around between dirty fingers as if he desires to wear the shine off of it or to take up praying some kind of newfound rosary. "Honest," he repeats, "the very last favor."

"How much do you need?" As if he intends to consider it.

"Can't say."

Will very nearly barks out another laugh but something in his brother's expression stops him. "What do you plan to do with it?"

"Get back what's mine."

"Good luck." Thinking of the Judge and such obstacles as have come to lie between Finn and his discarded birthright.

"I'll need luck. I'll need luck and patience too, if I'm to get back my son and my fortune."

"I'll tell you right now, you can leave the boy out of it."

"I can't."

"The Judge has no time for that boy and you know it." Will closes his lawbook and runs his finger along its spine. "Whatever you've got in mind you ought to leave the boy where he is, if you want my advice on the matter. Don't so much as mention his name."

"I got nothing without the boy."

"It's not like you to be sentimental."

"I ain't."

"Suit yourself."

"It's the boy's money."

Which removes the blinders of time and custom and habituated preoccupation from Will's eyes and brings him hurtling not merely into the present but beyond it and forward into the future as his elder brother imagines the future might be, a place informed by that newspaper article from the week prior or maybe the week before that about how Huck and that other boy had come upon twelve thousand dollars in gold.

Leave it to the illiterate Finn to obtain such information through mysterious sources of his own when everyone in the world would have been better off had he not.

"The twelve thousand. You're talking about the twelve thousand dollars."

"Six is all."

"Six or twelve, it's his."

"So you'd think." And with that much infuriating introduction he commences his tale of how Judge Thatcher has stolen away the boy's fortune and permitted the innocent child to be raised up by a widow woman of uncertain intent. "He's a slave in that house he is. A slave to that widow and her Bible and what all else I can't say."

"So you're going to sue."

"I am."

"You'll go bust in the process."

"Justice will be done."

"Where on earth did you get an idea like that?" Wondering how the two of them could have come of age in the same household.

Finn is nonetheless implacable. "You're the lawyer. How much you reckon it'll cost?"

"Everything and then some."

"Answer me."

"You'll die before it's over."

"I won't be scared off."

"There isn't a lawyer in Missouri who'll take the case."

"You don't know every one."

"I know Thatcher."

"I know him too."

"It's a fool's errand, and you'll not waste my money on it."

"You never meant to give me none." Standing up and screwing his brand-new hat down over his ears.

———

HE IS IN THE BOY'S ROOM again that night, having climbed up to the shed roof with his one good arm and nearly lost his footing on the scattering of pebbles thrown against the window by one mischievous child or another and made his silent way inside nonetheless without waking the widow only to find the boy gone as usual. Soon Huck enters that same way, his shadow on the pane a black repetition of his father's, and he is unsurprised to discover that he has company.

"I'm broke, Pap."

"Is that all you think of?"

"I know you."

"You don't." Eyeing the boy and his new school clothes from his hiding place back in the deepest shadows, wondering what bad habits the widow and her refined ways have sown in his mind.

"Suit yourself." The man doesn't seem to have been drinking, and the boy doesn't seem to know if he should be emboldened or alarmed thereby.

"Find your own clothes and put them on."

"These are my own."

"I ain't leaving here with no dandy."

"Leaving?"

"You can come along the way they brung you or you can come along stark naked. It's no affair of mine."

"Where we going?"

"To a proper home." He casts his eyes around the dark room as if the place is a museum or a prison cell. There is a lace doily under the candlestick and he eyes it suspiciously. "This ain't no suitable place for a boy."

"I won't have to go to school, will I?"

"Try it and I'll whip you good."

This cheers the boy, for he is the kind who always finds his shoes too tight and his obligations too confining. "Not to church neither?"

The man brightens for a moment, remembering that Huck is a child after his own heart. "Not to church neither. Now strip and find them clothes."

"But these."

Abrupt as a rattlesnake from its rockbound fastness he strikes, fluid despite the darkness and the nighttime need for stealth and his crippled left arm, and he brings the boy down without so much as drawing breath. He lies upon the child's pinned body on the bedroom planking and there is in his overwhelming presence something oddly maternal or at the very least possessive, something suggestive of a force that would swallow up the child rather than let him go.

"In the bottom drawer," says the boy. And even these poor rough-used things, ragged overalls three sizes too large and a shirt of butternut homespun worn through in more places than not, even these the widow has scrubbed into submission and mended like precious relics and pressed so stiff and square that the boy looks by moonlight as if he has just emerged from a packing crate.

"They'll have to do," says Finn.

"Truth is, there's more comfort in them."

"You ain't just saying that for my benefit."

"No sir." The boy fills his familiar pockets with odds and ends transferred from his newer pants and makes a beeline for the window but his father arrests him midstep and tilts his head toward the bedroom door.

"We'll leave like decent folk."

Something passes across the boy's eyes indicating either that he fears to wake the widow or that he regrets the loss of this one final opportunity for passage down her iron drainpipe, but in either case he resigns himself to his father's fierce intransigent will.

Finn lifts the latch and presses the door open and steps out into the hall upon boots that squeak with newness and grind with their one modified heel a staccato trail of signifiers into the plank floor. The boy follows on silent feet.

"Huckleberry?" The widow, her voice muffled by bedclothes and the intervening door, surprised because to the best of her knowledge the boy is never up roaming. Like others of her age she has largely given up on sleep, and she retires to her bed each night mainly from habit and propriety and futile hope. "Are you well, Huckleberry?"

The father spins on his heel, his face drawn down into a threatening mask, and clamps a hand over the boy's uncertain mouth.

"Huckleberry?" With a rustling of bedclothes. The slats of the bed creak as she stirs herself. "You boy?"

The father whispers in the boy's ear and eases his hand from around his mouth.

"Just on my way to the privy, ma'am."

"Did that pie disagree with you?"

"No, ma'am."

Her feet strike the floor and something else does, too, making a third harsh clacking step in counterpoint to the two soft ones, for the widow has lately acquired a cane. Finn vanishes into the disused bedroom across the hallway and conceals himself in the darkness, steady and watchful as a cat. Before his eyes the light of a candle blooms from the crack under the widow's door. He hisses at the boy to gain his attention and there in the darkness upon a little oval scrap rug he commences dancing a kind of nervous jig, looking for all the world like a pagan priest stamping out his heathen dance by firelight to invoke some savage god, and with his eyes he indicates that the boy should do likewise.

Just in time Huck catches his father's meaning, and he takes over the dance just as the widow's bedroom door opens. "Beg your pardon, ma'am." The boy is all urgency from head to toe, big-eyed and nervous as a tadpole.

"Oh, my, my, my," clucks the widow, leaning on her cane and craning her neck to one side so that she can examine him by the light of the candle on its stand by the door. The flame must glint in two places from off the wet orbs of Finn's eyes, but she has left her glasses on the nightstand and requires them if she is to see that far. Besides, her concentration is all upon Huck. "Are you certain you're well, boy?"

"Yes ma'am. Quite certain." With an abject and beseeching look.

Finn considers the candlelight and narrows his eyes to cunning slits, an adjustment that causes him to vanish as completely as if he has turned into pure malevolent spirit. He is careful to narrow them no further, else the scene before him vanish likewise.

"May I go, ma'am?"

"By all means." Shooing him with her free hand.

He turns and slips down the stairs.

"If you're not feeling better in the morning, we'll go see the doctor."

The boy calls some hasty bit of reassurance up the stairwell and then he dashes in the dark through the parlor and out the back door, leaving it open behind him to ease his father's passage.

Come morning the widow will recollect that the boy was dressed, and not even in his ordinary clothes but in his old retired things, and she will find his bed empty and the floor clawed and the pantry ransacked and she will alert the marshal and complain to Judge Thatcher but it will do no one, neither her nor the boy, the slightest bit of good.

———

THE SPRINGTIME IS COMING ON now and the river is running faster, and they set out trotlines and run them and shoot squirrels and rabbits with the gun, or at least the father does. He keeps the weapon either locked up in a trunk or close by his side, and he keeps the shells buried somewhere around in the woods for safekeeping. The lock on the trunk is not the only one he possesses, for there is another on the cabin door and no window fit to crawl out through. He vanishes for days at a time, leaving the boy sealed in. He says that he is prosecuting a case to have the money released and he reassures him that once they get their hands on it they will prove to the world that the two of them know how to make better use of it than any judge ever yet born, just wait. Yet the more he ruminates over the injustice of it all and his secret inability to restore his own rights the angrier he gets, not with himself but with Judge Thatcher and with The Other Judge and with his own cowardly brother and with the boy who brought on this sorry situation in the first place. He finds himself netted in by enemies and incompetents, and the only thing for it is to travel to St. Petersburg or Lasseter or Smith's or some other village or town or trading post and swap such dead things he has been able to draw forth from the river and the woods for the various simple staffs of his particular life: ammunition, flour, salt pork, cornmeal, whiskey. He keeps a low profile in St. Petersburg, sticking mainly to back alleys and the narrow passageways between buildings and never venturing far from the most riverbound of the village's precincts. When he returns the boy is generally famished and ready to eat whatever poor makings his father has brought back without expressing much in the way of gratitude or even appreciation.

"I suppose you've gotten used to finer things than your old pap can provide," says Finn one evening when he's had enough.

"No sir. This suits me just fine." Not looking up. "The widow never cooked no better."

"All right."

"I do get hungry, though."

"Fatback bacon don't grow on trees."

"I know it." Busy with his spoon.

"It's hard enough feeding just the one."

The boy stops for a moment to offer a suggestion: "I'm right handy with a fishpole."

"I know you are."

"I sure do hate wasting my time in this here cabin."

"It's for your own good. The law is man's work."

"That don't mean I can't take the air now and then."

Finn reaches for the jug and uncorks it. "I'll be the judge of when you can take the air and when you can't."

"I wish you'd let me pull my own weight."

"You done pulled it already with that six thousand if you hadn't give it away. Let me do my duty and get it back, and then we'll see who takes the air."

He believes that as long as he has the boy he has the advantage over the others. "Possession is nine tenths of the law," he remembers hearing someone say from his youth although surely not his father for the Judge would never have stooped to so reductive a formula, but he takes a kind of comfort in the familiar saying still, as if he could wring the boy out and get six thousand dollars in gold if only he knew exactly how.

There is a sweetness to the spring days that the two of them spend together, mending lines upon the cabin porch in dappled sunlight; waiting on the banks for salable junk to come floating down the river; gutting rabbits over a basin behind the cabin, the man showing the boy precisely how to make their loose flayed skin come away from their long muscular bodies like wrapping. The father doesn't mind if the boy smokes a corncob pipe or two even though he has never acquired the habit himself, and from time to time he brings home a little tobacco as a gift, a pleasant reminder that he has not been too busy to think of him while in town pursuing their legal options.

While Finn is busy strategizing and cursing his evil luck and seeking out markets for their catch, Huck passes the days of his confinement with the rusted scrap end of a woodsaw that he's found discarded in the rafters. There is an old horseblanket nailed to the wall opposite the cabin door by way of insulation and windbreak and he addresses himself methodically to the lowest and largest of the logs behind it, aiming one day to remove a segment large enough to enable his escape to freedoms far greater than this. The sawdust he disposes of in the fire.

———

THE BOY IS ASLEEP in the cabin one night when his father arrives and labors for much longer than usual at the business of opening the lock. His efforts are so futile and frantic that the boy, roused only halfway from his sleep, takes him for a raccoon until the cursing begins.

"Pap!" from a spot directly behind the door. Considering his father's condition he knows that he would be better advised to play possum as he has done so many times previous, but he has been alone for the better part of three days now and this sudden commotion at the door has about it some of the qualities of the resurrection.

"Boy."

"You got a light out there?"

"Come on give your old pap a hand."

"I can't. You got a light?"

"Bestir yourself." Hammering on the door, the lock jumping in counterpoint to his blows.

"You locked me in."

"Don't blame me."

"A light would help."

The father gives the door one last frustrated pathetic blow and leans his head against it.

"There's some matchsticks," says the boy, and he is referring not to their generalized presence in the cabin but to the four in particular that he has pushed through the gap beneath the door. "Right there on the floor," he says. "By your foot."

Finn drops to his knees as if seeking mercy from some force infinitely greater than he, and with blunt urgent fingers he locates the matches. The first of them he loses unlit down a gap between the floorboards. The next he strikes while still on his knees only to watch it burn out before he can recover his footing. The third he conserves until he is erect. Its flame lasts long enough for him to extract the key from the pocket where he has absently put it, but it sizzles out between his thumb and forefinger before he can bring the key to the lock. By the light of the very last of them, upon which he concentrates a rapt and almost holy attention as if this were the last matchstick on earth and mankind's final illumination, he springs the lock and admits himself to the squatter's shack.

"There's groceries in the skiff." For even in his present condition he knows that the boy will want them.

Want them he does, so much so that in his hunger he forgets himself and instead of merely vanishing into the woods while his father is conveniently half blind and incoherent he transfers sacks and boxes from the skiff to the cabin one after another and then commences to eat everything in sight.

"Go easy."

"I will."

"That's got to last."

"I know it."

While the boy eats, Finn returns to the skiff to fetch the gun he has forgotten there. Then he comes back and locks the door behind him and helps himself to a dipper of water and a square of cornbread and a piece of jerked beef over which he ruminates alternately each of them in turn until by and by he seems refreshed and ready for more whiskey. He grows stern and loquacious as he drinks, earnest as a judge and yet oddly confidential too, as if he has had a premonition that his opportunities to settle accounts with the boy are limited and has decided therefore that he must during this one night pass on everything he has learned in close to fifty years. The whiskey helps.

"You beware," he says, curling his hand around a glass fiercely enough to break it and pointing with his index finger at a spot between the boy's eyes. The whiskey in the glass quivers until it very nearly jumps out. "You beware where this world is headed."

"I will."

"Good. You do that and you'll be all right." He drains the glass and claps it down upon the table with an apparent measure of relief.

"I hope so."

"You will." There is nonetheless a light in his eyes that suggests he might remain unconvinced.

"I'll do my best. Don't you worry none."

He holds the bottle with one hand, and with the other he distractedly combs the damp greasy ropes of his hair, his fingers leaving psoriatic trails of cornmeal and filth where they pass. "I seen a nigger not long back," he says, "right here in St. Pete, a free nigger from Ohio. A mulatto he was, near as white as a white man. And he was wearing the whitest shirt you ever seen and the shiniest hat too."

"What'd he do?"

"It ain't what he did."

The boy waits while the man pours more whiskey.

"That goddamn free nigger was the awfulest old gray-headed nabob you ever seen. Walked with a silver-headed cane. Said he was a college professor."

The boy fusses with some crumbs on the table.

"I tried to claim him for a runaway, but it weren't no use."

"He put up a fight?" Suddenly interested.

"I wish he had. I'd have broke his back and skinned him alive."

"I know it."

"Marshal said it weren't legal, claiming him that way. So I give it up."

"It weren't legal?"

"Said I had to wait six months."

"I've heard."

The man pours himself another and favors the boy with a conspiratorial leer. "Seemed to me even a nigger college professor would be smart enough not to stay any six months, considering."

The boy laughs over his father's wisdom, and awash in the happy shower of approval and companionship thus unleashed Finn downs the whiskey as if it were the foulest medicine but necessary all the same for what ails him. Then he turns on the boy like a snake, his thoughts gone rushing back to the professor.

"Goddamn nigger can *vote* in Ohio. I reckon any nigger can. Any goddamn nigger. And after he gets done with that he can come down here six months at a time and look at me over them gold-rimmed glasses any way he likes and there ain't a goddamn thing I can do about it." He looks daggers at the boy, either imitating the black or else imagining him.

Bit by bit he descends to the level of drunkenness that he had attained previous to arriving home and then he proceeds beyond it, venturing into territory that the boy has seen before only on occasions when the fish have been especially plentiful and the harvest of whiskey has thus been particularly bounteous. For a man who enjoys his drink he permits it to make him miserable. He rages against the blacks and the government and the law, all of which he insists have conspired to bring him to ruin. Something about his drunkenness gives him the idea that he must stand up in order to orate properly, and every time he attempts to do so he loses his balance and falls, spilling his drink and catching himself with his sore left arm. This only fuels his wrath and his urgent sense that remaining successfully upon his feet is essential to his thwarted purpose and so he rages against the table and against the chair and against the tub of salt pork over which he takes a tumble for they too just like the blacks and the government and the law have been laying for him since the day he was born.

At length he collapses beaten onto the bed and the boy sits alert in the chair waiting for sleep to overtake him. The sawn log behind the horseblanket is not yet freed but the key to the lock is in the man's shirt pocket and he figures that he will make use of it once his father gives up tossing and turning and commences to snore, but sleep is no more kind to the man than the chair and the table and the law have been. He thrashes and groans without letup, hollering at the walls and at the universe and most furiously at the boy himself telling him that he'll put out that candle like a decent white boy and quit studying on him like some prowling thieving infernal white-shirted free nigger if he knows what's good for him.

The boy unwittingly sleeps first but is soon awakened by a scream that signals the appearance in his father's bed of an invading army of snakes and spiders. They are crawling up his legs, he says, and squirming in his tattered underwear and biting him on the buttocks and the chest and the face and any other place where they can sink a mandible or a fang. He leaps from the bed and throws himself upon the floor as if he has woken up entirely afire, screaming and tearing at his hair and kicking his feet like a mule possessed.

"Take him off!" His snarl is desperate and guttural and whether he is referring to a snake or a spider or the devil himself is beyond the boy's knowing. At once he is on his feet again racing in circles this time around and around the cabin stirring up a whirlwind of fishing tackle and tin pots and kindling until the boy fears that he will accidentally take down the horseblanket and leave his work with the handsaw exposed come morning and what then. "Take him off!" he cries again and again and the boy does not oblige but in a few moments the man is nonetheless either satisfied or sufficiently exhausted to surrender and so he lies back down to rest. His face presses into the ticking as if he aims to leave his likeness there for posterity. One eye gleams in the darkness like a bloody gemstone and with terrible effort he focuses it upon the boy. Lying there transfixed and panting he strains his ears and listens to something, perhaps the terrifying mysterious surge of his own blood, perhaps the calling of wolves and owls in the encroaching forest. The boy is listening too, frozen in his chair as still as some hunted creature, and while he concentrates his attention upon his father as if to subdue him by pure will or hypnosis or some other childlike strength the man digs in his pocket for his clasp-knife.

"Tramp, tramp, tramp," he intones with a grim doomlike rhythm. "Tramp, tramp, tramp. Them's the dead come to claim me. But I won't go."

The boy opens his mouth as if to reason with him and then claps it shut again.

"Their hands are cold. Take them off. Make them leave a poor devil alone." Fiddling blindly with the knife, his fingers numb as sticks.

The boy sits without hope or alternative and waits for sleep to overwhelm the man at last, but it does not for he is altogether too furious to be overtaken. His mind has gone aboil and he cannot rest for its constant seething.

"You." Narrowing his one panicky red eye.

The boy waits.

"You." Again. Softly and a bit more coolly this time, as if he is leveling not a word but a shotgun.

The boy tenses.

"You're the Angel of Death, ain't you," says the man, and with that assessment he pries open the clasp-knife and springs from the bed, hurling himself at the boy like a cannonball. "You can't have me. Not yet." Flailing madly with the knife.

The boy steps neatly to one side and the man hurtles past him but miraculously recovers.

"I reckon you can't take me if I take you first." Righting himself on his two bandy legs. "I'll show you."

He leaps upon the boy with all of his considerable unbalanced weight, nearly crushing the air out of him as he falls, and then rising up again upon his elbows to exhale a sour and choking miasma composed of cheap corn whiskey and persistent indigestion and rotten teeth.

"Pap." With such breath as is left to him.

But the man is blinded by drink and darkness and either he scoffs at this doomed demon's futile attempt at self-defense or he does not hear it to begin with. He has cut his own forefinger on the knife and the running blood makes him lose his grip for a moment but only for a moment. He fumbles with the slick handle, regains his grip by means of some automatic animal instinct, and presses the filthy point of the rusty blade against the tender underside of the boy's pale chin. The boy quivers and squirms and cranes his neck up gasping and the man presses the knife upward taking pleasure in the fierce delicacy of it in assessing the soft precise pressure at the tip of this blade that at his touch has slit throats and bellies uncountable times previous as reliable as an old friend and perhaps his only. The boy scrabbles for purchase against the hard dirt floor feeling the pinpoint of the blade against his throat like a needy thing desirous of entry and possession and then risking whatever unforeseen results any such sudden movement might bring he holds his breath and drives one bony knee into the man's crotch. Now it is the man gasping as the boy regains his feet. The man rises slow and ineluctable, but this time the boy takes the initiative and throws himself toward him before he can attack again, which initiates a brief scramble during which the man grabs for his shirt and the boy slips out of the tattered thing as if performing magic. The man slashes what remains of the garment in twain and believes that he has accomplished his goal of executing the Angel of Death and keeps right on believing it until he falls on his face and the knife clatters off under the bed and he sleeps at last. The boy gives up all hope of extracting the key from his father's pocket and takes up the gun from the corner instead, trading the promise of escape for a small measure of security. He trains it upon the man's still and shaggy head from over the back of a chair until he too nods off and abandons the remainder of the nighttime hours to the lonesome needy calls of owl and wolf.

"Boy."

No answer.

"Get up, boy."

No answer.

"What were you doing with that gun?"

At which the boy comes yawning awake at last in the warm soft glow of daylight from the cabin door. The river is just beyond and he can see its dancing reflections aswarm upon the walls and hear its urgent movement within its banks and detect the buoyant morning rise of birdsong. "Somebody was trying to get in here last night," he says. "I was laying for him."

"Next time, you roust me out." The man looks sick and sore. "You roust me out and I'll see to him, you hear?"

"I will."

The boy cooks a breakfast of flapjacks and bacon while the man sits blinking on the porch nursing a dipper of water and studying the river and attempting to recover his lost equilibrium. He remains pensive all the day long, suspicious of some connection that he senses but cannot quite puzzle out among the prowler and the misery in his head and the boy that he is bent on keeping safe from harm. The current is strong and the river is thickly laden with debris and it takes all of his strength to navigate the skiff along the trotlines when the time comes. He blames it on his age and he wonders what sad fate the future will hold for him if he cannot obtain the boy's six thousand dollars as a bulwark against sure decline.

"Your grandpap is as rich as a king, I ever tell you that?"

"I know. How'd he get that way?"

"By never giving me a nickel," which as far as he is concerned might as well be true.

"Is that so?"

"That man was so by-God stingy he wouldn't give me a whipping."

Huck laughs as only a boy can, illuminating the river valley with an arc of sound that bends across the water like a handful of thrown coins.

"I mean it. He wouldn't so much as lay a hand on me. What kind of father is that?"

The boy must confess that he does not know.

"When I done wrong he'd cook up some other sort of punishment he reckoned would suit the crime."

"Like?"

"Like extra chores maybe. I don't know."

"You don't remember?"

"Not no more. Not too good." Scratching his aching head and marveling at how much of his experience has vanished into nothing.

"Too bad."

"I suppose."

They take note of a broken-up raft just drifting into sight in the shallows around the upstream bend and light out after it in the skiff.

"Might be eight or ten good logs to that one by the look of it."

"I reckon."

"Be worth catching."

They pole to it and make fast while it's still well upstream and then they proceed cautiously back using the current to their advantage as best they can but nonetheless struggling against the stubborn willful weight of the thing.

"My pap used to tell me I had it good."

"Did you?"

"It don't seem so."

"You weren't hungry," says the boy.

The man flashes him a boiling look and heaves on his pole as if he is driving the boy himself into the soft muddy bottom. "Are *you* hungry, boy?"

"No sir."

"All right." The pole sticks and he strains to haul it loose and loses ground in the freeing of it. "Be grateful for what you've got."

"I am."

"My pap said I had it good on account of we didn't have to live among no niggers."

"Who helped out?"

"We had a man."

"A white man?"

"A white man, Petersen. His wife too."

"Slaves?" The boy has never heard of such a thing.

"They was hired." They draw near the shore and the man jumps out into water hip-deep. "More'n once when I misbehaved Pap said he'd just as soon let the neighbor's nigger have a go at me." Straining with skiff and raft against the current. "Just so I knew how good I had it."

The boy jumps out now himself and ties the skiff fast to a tree.

"Said I'd get more than a whipping. Said I could count on being buggered up the ass if it come to that. Buggered up the ass by a filthy good-for-nothing nigger."

The boy has a pained look.

"You know what I mean by that, boy?"

"Yes sir. I know it."

"My pap told me that damn one-eyed nigger would bugger me up the ass if I didn't watch out." Tramping up into the mud, wringing out his trousers. "You think he was just talking?"

"No sir."

"Damn right." He makes to enter the cabin for an early glass of whiskey, since the ten clean logs of this raft are sure to make for a handsome windfall. "Damn right," he says again, leveling his eyes at the boy. "That's how good I had it."

———

RATHER THAN WAIT for fish or game or some other added bounty that he might bring upstream and sell in St. Petersburg he unfastens the broken raft from the skiff and poles off on it alone, making certain to lock the boy in before he goes. He reflects on how this valuable cache of lumber has passed this very way unnoticed once before, and when he reaches the St. Petersburg landing and strikes a bargain to shed himself of it he congratulates himself that merely by the exercise of his sharp riverman's eye and his main strength he has captured it and brought it back and sold it for enough money to purchase a gallon of forty-rod with change left over if he's careful. Thus does the wise and wary man turn all things to his advantage, as the river turns all things to her will. He rises up from the riverside and moves toward the village proper like some slow revenant, his feet dragging but his heart light with the idea of pleasures to come. Up an alley he goes past the rear of the Liberty Hotel wishing he had a catfish or two that he could trade with Cooper who's generous with his whiskey as long as it's not Monday which he does not believe it is.

"You that James?" To the man behind the bar.

"I am."

He spills coin onto the hardwood and brings the jug down beside it. "Whiskey."

"This is a decent place."

"I don't mind."

"We sell by the drink or we don't sell at all."

"Cooper gives me a fair trade for provisions."

"What Cooper does is Cooper's business." Turning away to adjust a bottle in a grand array behind the bar. From beneath his eyebrows he keeps an eye on Finn's reflection in the mirror.

"He's always been fair with me."

"Then go see him." His hands are busy with the bottles for no reason.

"You saying my money's no good?"

"It's plenty good by the drink." He turns to assess the jug and then raises his eyes to the man's face. "But you don't look to me like a by-the-drink kind of individual."

"Not here I ain't," says Finn, taking the jug in the crook of his arm and scooping up the coins. "There's friendlier places in this town."

"Suit yourself."

Finn can tell when he's been bested and he knows when to leave off beating a dead horse and he has no time or patience to spare for any individual who would thwart his desires, so he puts the lobby of the Liberty Hotel behind him, walking through the double doors and out onto the broad sunny front porch all set about with white-painted rocking chairs. In one of these, her back to him and her expectant face to the street, sits the widow Douglas waiting on some lunchtime companion for this is the third Sunday of the month and such is her usual routine. She ceases rocking at the scent of him and turns. "What have you done with that boy?" Without any preliminary, as if he neither requires such nor deserves it.

"Took him where he belongs." He tongues a tooth and gives her only a portion of the attention that she surely believes is her due, for he is busy scanning the street and deciding where he might most profitably continue upon his errand.

"I must warn you, Mr. Finn."

"Is that so?" He fixes her with his gaze and speaks the words by way of returning threat unto threat, for now she has his attention in full.

"I must warn you," she goes on oblivious, for as a dignified and refined lady of the old school she is unaccustomed to the need for fear or even for cautious restraint in her dealings, "I must warn you that Judge Thatcher and I are taking steps to recover him."

"Is that so?" he says, more slowly this time but the same, for what else is there.

"Legal steps."

He commences to tap tap tapping the empty jug against his haunch with a slow tolling rhythm as insistent and long-suffering as any heartbeat. "Now what am I supposed to think about that."

"Think whatever you like." For rectitude and certainty and recent proximity to the judge have contrived to make her bold.

"The boy belongs to me."

"He deserves better."

"Don't we all."

He turns his back upon her and steps down off the porch into the street where his boots raise dust and leave a cross-marked trail.

"I'll have him," calls the widow from the safety of her chair on the porch of the Liberty Hotel.

"We'll see," says Finn as he goes, mainly to himself.

Later, penniless again as usual and armed with a jug full of whiskey and fortified with as much beyond that as was possible given the quantity of his coin, he goes down to the riverside and stands on the bank eyeing the tied-up skiffs and wondering where his has gone. In the gathering dark he paces from one to another rejecting each in turn while a spark catches somewhere in his brain fueled and nursed by the whiskey without intervention or even awareness on his part. He begins to suspect that his skiff is missing not by accident or as a matter of some other individual's convenience—for he has helped himself to many a handy boat when exigencies have demanded it, not excluding perhaps the very skiff that he has been using these days, although of this he cannot be entirely certain—but missing as part of a plot to separate him from the boy and thus from his rightful treasure. What, he wonders almost aloud, what will happen if he cannot return to the boy with all possible dispatch? Have the widow and the judge already sent some emissaries into the woods to track him down and steal him away? Was that cunning old widow counting upon the empty whiskey jug of his—for surely she took note of it—was she counting upon it to occupy his time and cloud his judgment and provide the ideal cover under which she and the judge could accomplish their plan? For a moment he nearly strikes out for her house or the judge's to wait and see but he cannot decide between the two, so in the end he cuts loose a likely boat and poles home to the cabin where he discovers his old skiff tied up safe and sound. He sets his recent one adrift rather than tie it up for he likes it less than the original and has no use for a second, and then he enters the cabin and finds the boy asleep and sleeps himself.

—

THE FATHER STANDS looking at the river for a minute and then turns his broad back to it. "How about some breakfast?" Indicating by the direction of his look that the boy should have undertaken its preparation long ago.

"You sell that raft?" Huck, from over the eggs.

"You bet."

"How much?"

"Enough. Some of them logs was rotten." As if he needs to make an excuse for how little he got or how much of it he spent on drink.

"Looked good enough to me."

"You don't know."

After a while the boy scrapes eggs and bacon onto the two tin plates and serves them up with hot coffee boiled black as tar. They sit eating side by side on the edge of the cabin porch with their legs adangle. "You're back early."

"I did my business."

"You happen to fetch any tobacco?"

"You didn't ask."

"You left in a hurry."

"I know it."

The man finishes his breakfast and drains his coffee cup and licks his plate clean and then the boy does likewise in turn.

"I don't like that town much."

"St. Pete?"

"I don't like it."

"I reckon it's all right."

"You'll get over it."

He lets that notion or threat or promise or whatever it is hang in the air while the boy considers.

"I've been giving thought to pulling up stakes. There's a different cabin I know where nobody'd never find us."

The boy understands his meaning perfectly.

"Downriver a few miles."

"Why?"

"Change of scenery."

"I like it here."

"I know it. But sometimes a body gets too comfortable."

The boy chooses not to press but hopes that he will have just one more opportunity to address his work with the handsaw before his father takes him away downriver to some secluded place from which he may not return alive if at all. Another two or three inches on the one side and he'll be free to do as he pleases forever and ever, unburdened by this man and his desires and unburdened even by his own infernal accidental fortune of six thousand dollars, which he has already done his best to wash his hands of to no apparent avail.

"It ain't like me to run," says the man later in the boat, offhand and out of the blue, fundamentally to himself but in the boy's presence and as if, having considered some course of action all the day long, he is now about finished persuading himself to pursue it. The boy takes this for a good sign but vows to redouble his efforts with the handsaw the instant he gets an opportunity.

While they watch, the corpse of a mule comes sagging down the river on the current, miraculously holding to the channel where the water is deep and fast and it can travel without hanging up on rocks or snags or mudflats. High upon its haunch presides a funereal black buzzard, silent and evilly intent, its wings half spread and its shoulders hunched and its talons hooked into flesh like some great grim angel of death. "I'm going upriver," says the man, and the boy does not ask why for he is relieved by the direction and eager to be locked safely inside the cabin just this one last time.

———

"I TOLD YOU I'd waste no money of mine on your pipedream." Will, not in the least hesitant about making himself clear to his brother.

"You'll pay."

"I won't. I told you." Looking out the window.

"Before I'm through you will."

The brother returns his attention to his immediate problem. "And what on earth might you mean by that?"

"You know what."

"Are you threatening me?"

"A body could say so."

Will rises to his feet and slams shut his desk drawer. "I see you're continuing to get smarter by the day."

His brother, slumped in the chair opposite as if he has grown there like some man-shaped fungus, moves not at all.

"What do you have to gain by threatening me?"

"I'd say it's more in the line of a bargain."

"You'd say that."

"I would."

"Then it's a poor bargain and I'll have none of it."

"You ain't even heard it."

"Where does that leave you?"

"You ain't even heard it."

"I've heard enough."

"No." Eyeing his brother. There is a good deal of sincerity in his look and no belligerence whatsoever, a combination that may as well be calculated to take Will off guard. "I don't mean you no harm."

"How practical of you."

"I don't."

"How foresighted."

"Honest. I been thinking about telling the Judge where his money's been going is all."

"I see," says Will. "You've been *thinking*." He sits again, incredulous.

"Where's the harm in telling? Ain't honesty the best policy?"

"So they say."

"I don't reckon the Judge'll be as happy with you as you've been with yourself."

"Or as happy as *you've* been with me," says Will.

"I ain't ungrateful."

"No. You're not ungrateful. You're just stupid and self-destructive."

"He'll cut you off once he knows. I know that."

"And where do you suppose that will leave you?"

"Same place I always been."

"Only worse."

"Maybe so."

"You'll have nothing."

"I can tolerate it. How about you?"

Will does not flinch. "The Judge isn't my sole support. Far from it."

"Is that a fact?"

"Absolutely. Most of what I get from him I steal by cunning."

Finn stirs in his chair.

"And every cent of that I give to you."

"Pshaw. You could take more anytime you want."

"There's only so much leeway."

"There's plenty, I bet."

"I'm only so smart."

"You're smart enough."

"Believe what you like. Do as you see fit. And at the end of the day, any hours I'd have spent managing his affairs I'll spend on some other paying client. No harm done."

Finn takes a deep breath and holds it in for a moment, cogitating. "You'll be disowned." As if he's drawn slow aim and fired. "Just like me."

"Which I've risked from the beginning."

"I reckon you have."

"On your behalf."

"I appreciate it."

"All he needs to do is take a close look at the ledgers."

"He won't."

"He could."

"He don't."

"He might. And I guess if I could take that chance all these years on your behalf, I can take one more on my own. Whatever you care to offer up."

Finn cannot tell if his brother is working on his loyalty or his self-interest, but he sees that the time has come to alter the terms of his argument. "They'll steal him. The boy." Sad-eyed and abject as a mourner.

"Unless you intervene."

"First chance they get."

"Tell me," raising one hand and speaking to him not like his brother but like his attorney, for this is the relation between them most likely to produce an agreeable outcome. "So they take him. Exactly where is the harm in that?"

"He belongs to me."

"You've been something less than assiduous about exercising your parental rights."

"That don't matter."

"It will in a court of law."

"All the same." With dirty fingers he picks at something on the knee of his trousers. "He's mine."

"Here's an idea. If Thatcher and the widow feel so strongly, why not be generous and let them enjoy the use of him for a while?"

"He's all I've got."

"Maybe so. But if you force their hand they'll pursue that lawsuit just as vigorously as they can and take him away for good. No doubt about it. And then you'll have nothing."

"Nothing but you."

"Free legal advice and a roof over your head. You could do worse."

"I have done worse."

"I know it."

"You know and you don't know."

Will cocks an eyebrow.

"It don't matter either way. I'm back on the straight and narrow."

"I can see that."

"That's why I want the boy. Bring him up right."

"You'll get your chance."

"I know it."

"It'll happen."

"By and by."

"Give it time."

"I will."

———

WHEN FINN RETURNS to the squatter's shack he finds the place transformed by violence. The door is ruined, battered in and splintered all over with ax strokes, hanging listless as laundry from one bent hinge. Before entering he turns by reflex and scans the area close by, the tree-line and the riverbank and the patch of grass outspread before the cabin door. Though he finds sign there of neither boat nor intruder, the part of his brain capable of detecting a single fish aslumber in dark water discerns a strangeness in the lay of the dooryard grass and he bends upon one knee to judge for certain. Sure enough there is a trail flattened between the door and the riverbank, as of some heavy thing dragged. He leaves it unexplored for now, this shining path of green within darker green, and pokes his head into the cabin to find the dirt floor soaked with blood.

"You Huck."

No answer comes from within or without, and the single room lies empty not just of his son but of his own every earthly possession. Food and fishlines and matches, skillet and coffeepot and jug. All of them gone. Only the ax remains, bloodied all over and with a bit of hair stuck to the back of it as if from a blow to the boy's head, and from this significantly ostentatious detail he deduces not Huck's actual plan for counterfeiting his own murder and stealing away under cover of it, but a different and more cunning plan altogether—this one contrived by Judge Thatcher and the widow Douglas.

"They think they can steal him that easy," he says to himself as he rubs the axhead clean with the heel of his hand. "They think I'll give him up for dead like a goddamn beast." He plucks away the tuft of hair and brushes it off on his pantleg.

He walks the path to the riverbank and discerns there in waist-deep water all he needs for confirmation: a sack, a perfectly good and useful sack, filled with rocks by that wasteful Thatcher or some other in his employ and drawn across the grass to the water as if Huck's body itself had been there dragged. He vows to deny Judge Thatcher the satisfaction of misusing his property, and wades in to recover it less its burden of rocks. Sitting to wring it out upon the bank he catches sight of further sign, footprints in the dirt and a drop or two of blood, and he scouts down along the waterside until he comes upon marks where someone looks to have nearly lost his balance throwing some other thing into the water, some other thing that proves to be a half-grown pig with its throat cut, nearly bled-out and still foggily abloom and staining the Mississippi a vague dark red. The source of that floorstaining blood. He wallows it out and skins it and cleans it with his clasp-knife, and he pledges that none shall have a bite of it save himself. Surely not that son of his, who probably went off without a fight and is now living high on some other hog at either the judge's table or the widow's.

Loading up the skiff he considers reporting the boy's apparently tragic end to Thatcher or even the marshal, who might have been the one to have counterfeited the scene of the crime, but in the end he decides against it. Avoiding St. Petersburg altogether will be the best policy from this moment forward, lest he and the boy cross paths. When the time comes and he has established either a reliable source of income or some other more cunning means to obtain his due he will swoop in to recover the boy and his fortune, but meanwhile he will return to his place by the riverside in Lasseter and bide his time.

7

UPSTREAM IN A CLOUD of fog and memory steams the *Santo Domingo*, a sternwheeler bound for Rock Island from Vicksburg. Just how many years ago this is Finn could not say, although it is surely from a time before the boy Huck was so much as a dream. Yet at this very moment, poling northbound alone on the dark river, he can see the boat in his mind's eye with so much alarming detail that she may as well be hurtling down upon him again just as she did on that night when everything changed.

———

THE *Santo Domingo* is huge and powerful and she churns upriver with the reckless outsize belligerence of an African elephant enraged. The cloud thrown up by her wheel obliterates the stars and looms upward as if she is intent upon vaporizing the river behind her and thereby emptying it as she goes, her transient purpose served and an end made to it, yet her silent steam engines let Finn's ears ring with music played upon the main deck by a pair of black men who have made up a band with a fiddle and a banjo. They sit side by side on a fat bale of cotton, and the tune they play is a number so well known to him as to be as unremarkable as breathing.

Finn has been drinking, and now he is lazily adrift from Dixon's place to the public wharf where he customarily ties up. The skiff finds the channel and he sets down his pole and permits himself to take a seat and then in his weariness and disorientation he lies down flat upon his back to watch the stars wheel overhead. He has done this before and drifted for hours downriver like a dead thing only to awaken in the morning aground on some midstream island or hung up on a log, his head afire and the full sun upon his face like a brand. As he lies and blinks and breathes he lets the music wash over him as if in a dream, as if he is making it up himself or at least imagining it, as if some secret door to the shared consciousness and tradition and history of the river and its men white and black and mingled has opened itself to him and this is what has emerged.

The music might be coming from some house downstream. But rather than rising up and reaching its peak and then diminishing again as he floats past, it swells in volume and increases in clarity and keeps on swelling and keeps on increasing long past the point that would suggest that he has come abreast of some riverbank musicale and is about to drift on past—until finally, at its loudest and most crystalline, it is shattered all at once by the noise of his skiff colliding with the prow of the *Santo Domingo*. He plummets through planking torn asunder and into deep black water where he finds nothing that he might cling to save the steamboat's charging hull, which has established a powerful countercurrent of its own and now seems intent upon drawing him under and back toward the cruel blades of the paddlewheel.

"You there!" A voice godlike from above.

He gasps and sucks in breath and pushes off from the hull using both his legs, but try as he might he cannot force himself free of the churning water for the boat is moving too fast and the current is too strong. He threatens to become mere debris.

"You there!" The face hanging over the rail above him is closer than he imagined, and rather than gazing remotely down from some heroic elevation it is studying him fairly closely and with a certain grave amusement, as if his peril is merely a game for small stakes. "How about I get you a rope?"

"Your hand," says Finn. "Reach." For there is no time to spare and he has little faith that the man, should he vanish upon an errand, will return again at all.

His rescuer, his face a black vacancy against the stars, falls dutifully to his knees and reaches beneath the rail to take the hand that Finn offers up. If the crash has caused any alarm aboard the steamboat it has been but short-lived and minor, for when Finn climbs over the rail and leans gasping against it he observes that the fiddle and banjo music is still under way down here on the heavily laden main deck where there are but a few individuals loafing about, blacks exclusively, whispering among themselves in corners and promenading arm in arm around the stacked cargo and penned livestock as if they were guests upon the grandest ship of the line. Floating down from the dining room on the deck above comes the delicate chiming of silver and glassware, cushioned upon the low hum of dignified conversation.

"Why ain't you tied up somewheres?"

"Running late, suh."

With a nod of his head he acknowledges the river whose grip he has so narrowly escaped. "I'm obliged."

"T'warn't nothing."

"Still." Flatly and with a look that is almost a warning, for he is not one to give thanks lightly to a black man even for an act such as this one and he cannot abide the idea that his courtesy might be rebuffed.

"Happy to help, suh."

"I know it." And then adrip like a river spirit made flesh and risen up to pursue some antique unfathomable errand of its own choosing, he turns and makes for the stairway. Up he climbs to the second deck, where candles and the reflections of candles glimmer like fireflies in the dining room and the smell of food is nearly overwhelming in its variety and power. He feels completely himself, recovered from his adventure and fully sobered by it, and it does not occur to him to wonder what these fine white ladies and gentlemen must think of this wet shambling creature passing by so close to their tables. He takes note of the bar with its gleaming bottles rank upon rank and thinks that he will demand from the captain the run of it as part of his restitution. The stairway to the upper deck is narrow and has a turning midway along and gives directly onto the texas and he climbs it as if he has done so a thousand times before. He opens the door to the pilothouse without so much as rapping upon it and admits himself into a small high room with a panoramic view of the river, dominated by a great oaken wheel and a compass housed in a brass binnacle and occupied by two dignified gentlemen and a single black girl of perhaps sixteen who looks as if she would prefer to vanish into the deep shadows if only she could.

"Ahoy there," says the younger and more sociable of the two men, as if he is greeting a paying customer. He is as tall as Finn and more heavily padded, dressed in a brilliant white uniform that he has recently had custom-made to his measurements. The other is taller still, rail-thin and narrow-beaked, with an intense riverbound gaze that neither sees Finn nor cares to, and the thoughtless way that he wears his threadbare uniform indicates his disdain for anything about the *Santo Domingo* other than her absolute safety. "Captain Parkinson," says the first man, thrusting out a meaty hand.

"Name's Finn." Taking it.

"Good God, man." Stricken by his visitant's damp handshake he takes the man's elbow with his left hand, which he works up along the dripping shirtsleeve to his shoulder. "Where have you been?"

"Minding my own business." His eye falls upon the girl.

"You didn't go overboard."

"Not until your boat rammed me, I didn't."

"No," says the captain, his look incredulous.

"Yes sir. I'm lucky to be alive."

"I should say."

"Lost my skiff."

"You have my word we'll."

"I know it. That and more."

"You have my word we'll make you whole, however much it requires." Whether the captain is clarifying his offer or expanding it or merely finishing his thought for the love of hearing himself speak is unknowable. "Thank God you're no worse for wear."

"Thank Him and the nigger that pulled me out, too."

"He works in mysterious ways."

"Suit yourself," says Finn with a sly look. "I come up here to see how a blind man pilots a steamboat."

The pilot slides a glance toward Finn and then returns his steady gaze to the moonlit river.

"Mr. Franklin here is the best man on the line."

"Is he now."

"Without a doubt."

"Too bad about his license."

Even this does not perturb the implacable pilot Franklin, for he has either heard worse before or placed his entire trust in Captain Parkinson or given up on the world of men for some other reason altogether.

"Accidents happen."

"I mention my pap's the judge in Adams County?"

"Did I mention that we operate under maritime law?"

"Still."

"Justice will be done, Mr. Finn. Have no fear."

"I won't."

"Were I at liberty to do so, I would write you a check at this very moment."

"I'd be obliged." He looks at the girl for a minute and wonders exactly how impressed she is by his handling of the situation. "Too bad you ain't at liberty."

"Not tonight I'm not. No."

"I reckon we can make it up somehow."

"I'll need your particulars."

"I know it." The river drifts past in the dark. Finn wonders how long the steamboat line will take to correct its error and considers just how long he might be able to wait and figures that the two time frames are not much alike.

"Offhand, what do you guess your skiff was worth?"

"Can't say."

Parkinson studies the man closely, for he guesses that fate has served him up not some unsophisticated bully but a cunning negotiator unwilling to show his hand.

"Can't say," Finn continues, "on account of I stole it."

"Is that so?"

"Hell yes. When you're about ready to steal me another'n to replace it, you let me know."

The pilot Franklin slides a look toward Finn once more but this time with the faintest of smiles atwitch at the corner of his mouth.

"Mr. Finn, what do you say we visit the medicine chest and resolve our differences like gentlemen?"

"Whyn't you send the girl down."

"That won't be possible."

"I like it up here."

"It's against regulations."

Which gives Finn an idea. "Franklin ought to have a little something, too. Send the girl down and she can get enough for everybody."

Parkinson lowers his voice. "Let's just the three of us go. You and me and the girl."

"I go wherever the captain goes." Her voice is surprisingly deep and soft and round, not unpleasant to Finn's ears or anyone's.

"*Wherever* he goes?" His mind leaps.

"Yes sir."

"All right. Come watch him buy a man some whiskey."

———

To FINN'S SURPRISE, Parkinson is not much of a drinking man. The captain sits clutching his glass as if it contains the purest poison, or as if he has learned that the universe radiates out from it and he intends by this action to remain pegged in one spot rather than risk spinning off into eternity.

"How about the girl?" Finn hazards after a while. She stands behind the captain like his shadow, unmoving even in the tidal rise and fall of the dining room crowd. Her arms are soft and gray-black as ash and they hang before her as if she is a mere marionette, her hands belly up like fish deep in the single pocket of her apron. Her eyes are sleepy but she starts when Finn mentions her, picking out his words over the conversation like some kind of strange angular music or a coded message. Were he looking her way he would witness the automatic adjustment of her every molecule so as to focus her attention on that sonic space where his words live.

"She's something," says the captain.

"How much?"

"Not for sale." Gripping his glass. "Not for sale, I'm afraid."

"How about a loan?"

"That's out of the question."

"Between friends." Raising his glass.

Rather than answering, Parkinson waves for the bottle and pours, taking some for himself to replenish what little he's had.

"You owe me."

From the kitchen door past the end of the bar comes a compact and whiteclad black man in a languid sort of hurry, a towel hung over one arm and a laden tray balanced on his upturned palm. His suit looks made for someone else and he looks made for other work entirely and he makes eye contact with the girl as he goes. Finn notices and turns his inquiring eye toward Parkinson.

"The father."

"Ain't that nice."

The captain drinks. "He has aspirations."

"I do love a nigger with ideas." Tapping his glass for more whiskey, thinking on the father and the daughter. "No wonder you won't part with her."

"I can't do it."

"There was a pretty little nigger girl just the match of this one used to walk past my house when I was her age."

The girl pricks up her ears and Finn can see her do it.

"This would have been in Adams County," says the captain, filling space with remembered detail.

"That's right. My pap said they was all just filthy beasts and we had to keep our distance or we'd be in for disease and eternal damnation and what all, but like I said she was a pretty one and I couldn't see no harm in it."

"I'll bet."

"I reckon we done it eight or ten times before we was through, and I'll never forget it. A man don't, no matter what they say."

"No matter what."

"And the only harm come of it was my pap made me sleep with the hogs for a month."

"That can't have been pleasant."

"You'd be surprised. I've done it since, the weather gets cold enough and you're out in it."

"What became of the girl?"

"She passed on."

"I see." He pulls down the corners of his mouth, taps the rim of his glass with one finger. "And you? No eternal damnation?"

"Not yet."

"Let that be a lesson."

"Amen," says Finn, raising his glass.

———

FINN GOES TO SLEEP in a secluded place on the main deck trusting that someone will wake him at the next scheduled stop, the farther upriver the better because the less chance there will be of anyone's ever identifying the skiff that he will most certainly steal and bring home to replace his ruined one. His clothes are dry now and he is warm and deeply contented and thanks to the high quality of the *Santo Domingo*'s expensive whiskey he is free of the most severe and colorful consequences of his habit: He has neither vomited nor seen beasts that are visible only to him, and he folds his hands upon his chest like a dead man and closes his eyes with an easy and luxurious grace.

"I tell you, we can go no farther than Fort Granger." The captain's voice, hushed. "We require provisions. We require coal."

"We've got sufficient." A voice unknown to Finn, deep and resonant and with a touch of gravel.

"You're mistaken."

"Make it stretch."

"Impossible. Besides, when the sun comes up and the passengers learn that we've passed Lasseter."

"Explain it."

"How do you propose I do that?"

"You'll think of something."

Unwillingly surfacing through a miasma of alcohol and sleep Finn hears these voices in the dark as if the speakers had taken up positions at his very elbow, and when he slits his eyes open just the least bit he discovers that they have. Rather than lie still and listen to their curious talk and risk being discovered he kicks out one leg with a spasmodic twitch and coughs theatrically and heaves over on his stomach with his cheek mashed into the deck. The speakers start and move away but not far. He sees as they go that there are three of them, the captain and the black man from the dining room and his daughter.

"I mean to get to Iowa," says the man, drawing forth from the breast of his formal white jacket a bowie knife of considerable scale.

The captain must have seen this object previously, for he is unmoved by its sudden appearance. "Illinois is just as good."

"Not by me."

"We've been steaming past it all night long." He thrusts out an indicative hand, which startles the man and the girl both but they recover their composure and maintain their positions without incident.

"I don't want Illinois."

"Trust me."

"I do." Studying the starry gleam of the knifeblade in the darkness.

"I've made no attempt."

"I know."

"I've told no one."

"I know it. Myself, I've told half the coloreds on your goddamn boat." Whether or not he should be parting with this information is a strategic question unanswerable, but it seems to do him no immediate harm.

"Are they armed too?"

"Some." For he is not dishonest.

"Iowa, I see, is in for quite a celebration."

"Yes it is."

"And your mistress is in for quite a surprise."

"She never should have taken this boat. I told her it wasn't safe."

"How on earth will she ever get by without you?" Parkinson clucks and asks the question as mildly as if he were merely musing to himself here alone on the deck, and to judge by his lack of answer the black man with the bowie knife seems to consider the question beneath notice.

Finn, who has no interest in riding this steamboat as far as Iowa, yawns and stretches and rises wearily to his feet. To the rail he steps with an exaggerated little stumble and from there he leans out over the water putting a finger to each nostril in turn and blowing out like a steam engine. He is wiping his hand on the leg of his trousers when he takes obvious note of the three standing nearby or at least of the captain.

"Parkinson!" he says with a kind of mingled astonishment and delight. "You're up late."

"Mr. Finn."

"These two giving you trouble?" With a wink at the girl which includes her father also and in the process subdues them both.

"Trouble? I should say not."

"That's one beautiful child you got there."

"Thank you, sir. I've been told." He has hidden away the knife behind his back and he permits his gaze to swivel toward Parkinson as he wonders what secrets other than this the captain has been sharing abroad.

"Mr. Finn is a guest of the *Santo Domingo*," says Parkinson. "In our northward haste, we ran afoul of his boat and had to bring him aboard."

The father looks at Finn as if there could be no creature in all the world more to be pitied than the victim of a shipwreck.

"That's right," says Finn, his attention shifting back to the captain. "When you reckon we'll hit Fort Granger, us running behind and all."

"That would be hard to say."

"Can't be long now."

"I wouldn't think so."

"*You wouldn't think so.*" He hawks and spits into the dark water. "Tell me who's running this boat." With a smile indicating that he knows the captain would be wise not to give an accurate answer.

"It's a complicated world, Mr. Finn."

"I know it."

"Some things are beyond our control. Rivers like this one, for example. They're full of surprises."

"Wake me up at Fort Granger then," Finn concedes, and with two arms he shoves off from the rail. "Much obliged." He puts out a hand as if to shake but instead of taking Parkinson's hand he slides past the startled captain and reaches into the deep single front pocket of the girl's apron where her hands have been conspicuously hiding since he first set eyes upon her. There he finds the pistol and by the combined powers of brute force and startlement he makes it his own. He does not remove it from its hiding place but turns it instead and holds its barrel square against her belly. In his fury he nearly lifts her up against the rail. She gasps and casts a helpless eye upon her helpless father.

Finn's voice is tight with rage and effort. "Drop that pigsticker of yours, boy."

The black man lets his knife clatter to the deck.

"Now ain't you just the cleverest son of a bitch. Kick it over before I blow this pretty little girl a brand-new hole." Prodding at her belly with the urgent barrel.

The man does as he has been told, and the knife slices into the water without a sound.

"Now bend over."

He keeps the man on his knees until Parkinson can return with some rope.

"There are others," says the captain.

"There won't be," says Finn.

They strip the man of the white suit that is not his and they tie him naked to a stanchion where his crime and his disgrace will be public come daylight.

"How can we repay you?" says the captain.

"I might have an idea," says Finn.

———

"YOU SHALL GET a whipping when we return to Vicksburg," says an elegant old white-haired woman no bigger than a child but as ferocious as some avenging angel, approaching the bound black man with baleful speed.

"Don't count on it," Finn puts in from a nearby deck chair, where he reclines with the pistol jammed ostentatiously into his pants. The girl is on a stool alongside him.

"You child," cries the woman, wringing her hands and hurrying toward her on tiny tapping feet, ignoring Finn as if any individual of his wretched appearance must surely be beneath her notice.

"That boy ain't seeing Vicksburg again, whipping or no."

The woman assesses him quickly and dismisses him for an ignoramus and a bloodthirsty one at that and turns again to the girl.

"I reckon you might bring him home in a box if you've got a mind to, but myself I never took much pleasure in whipping a dead nigger."

Captain Parkinson arrives and declares himself at the old woman's service and explains to her that Mr. Finn here is correct, that her man can look forward to enduring some extremely sharp punishment for his barely averted attempt to commandeer this rivergoing vessel and kidnap its many innocent passengers. A whipping would be insufficient punishment for such a crime were the perpetrator white or black, slave or free, and most likely the man will be hanged by the neck until dead after a rapid and businesslike trial in the federal courts at which the captain himself will be honored to testify. If she has any words to say on the man's behalf she might consider them directly and plan to make an appearance in court, although the captain does not imagine that anything she might possibly have to say will do this criminal the least good or prolong his life by any more time than it will take for her to make her futile statement.

As the dining room fills for breakfast a wary assortment of blacks both free and slave files past the stanchion, each one indicating by the angle of his head and the set of his jaw precisely where he stands in the delicate shading of responses to the roped man's predicament. Finn is correct that whatever uprising may have been under way has been quelled, and he celebrates by ordering one of the porters to bring him a rasher of bacon and a stack of pancakes and a bottle of good whiskey to wash it all down. The girl volunteers to go on his behalf but he does not permit her.

"You stay put now."

"Yes sir." Eyeing the pistol.

"Your father made a mistake."

"I know."

"I could have shot the both of you and nobody would have given a good goddamn."

"It's our lot."

"You have me to thank."

The girl will not cast her eye upon Finn and she cannot cast her eye upon her father and so she looks instead at the river and the steadily unreeling promised land of northern Illinois which in the end is not Iowa but still.

"I hope you appreciate my generosity."

"I do."

Which Finn knows is untrue or at best premature, and yet because he is of a hopeful nature in such matters he raises his whiskey glass to her with a wink and takes her compliant duplicity for a good sign.

In the end the captain writes a check on the steamboat line for the price of the girl because Finn is going to take her one way or another and the elegant old woman deserves fair value. The mismatched pair of them disembark at Fort Granger with the girl's baggage, which is grand enough and sufficiently well stocked to have been the entire equipage of the old woman herself.

"This is a nice town," says the girl, for it is and she is not merely making conversation and moreover she needs something else to think about.

"Don't go getting used to it."

"Where's the house?"

"Mine?"

The girl does not answer, not because she is recalcitrant or ignorant but because she is too busy taking in the river traffic and the movement of laden carts along the dockways and the jumble of people and horses thinning off uphill toward the higher reaches of the town.

"Mine ain't here. It's in Lasseter, a day south."

He chooses a skiff from out of many unattended and they load it with her bags and untie.

"Don't you have something that needs doing?" she asks as he looses the last rope.

"I need to get us home."

"In this town I mean. In Fort Granger. Didn't you."

"No. I never meant to come up this far."

The girl considers his appearance and his lack of baggage and his cavalier ways with a boat that apparently does not belong to him, and she decides to inquire no further.

In a compartment he locates a fine net on a wire frame which he drops over the side according to certain signs and indicators that are invisible to the girl. "Quick," he says when a moment has passed and he has become occupied with the pole. "Pull it up." And she pulls it up, and the spread net emerges all ashimmer with silvery minnows so small that their gasping is beneath notice and so brilliantly alike that they dance upon the net and upon one another less like imperiled creatures than like slick stones come magically to life. He fills a bucket with riverwater and saves half of the minnows and lets the rest go. Then he baits lines with the first unlucky few and drops them over the stern and waits.

"We were going to live in Iowa," says the girl.

"I know it."

"Mrs. Fisk has people in Rock Island but we were going to go and live in Iowa, my father and me and some others we happened on."

"It was your father's idea."

"Mrs. Fisk wasn't going to take him at first."

"To Illinois."

"Not to begin with. But I persuaded her."

Finn tests a line.

"It wasn't until sundown yesterday he gave me the gun and set me on the captain."

"Where'd he get it."

"Somebody back home."

They sit for a moment.

"I reckon you're brave enough."

"I didn't know any other way." She has fixed her eyes downstream as if thinking that she could ride all the way to Vicksburg and return thereby to a past that has been ruined long since by circumstance and desire and bold inexpugnable action.

Finn pulls in a little channel cat and puts it on a stringer and drops it back into the water to continue swimming as if it were yet as free as it is alive. He intends when he has caught enough of them to seek out a trading post on the river somewhere and clean the fish all at once and sell them as a lot, for he has with him no means of making fire and thus cannot prepare a meal for the girl and himself. Failing that he can always hail a passing boat and part with his catch for money or something else in trade, salt beef or biscuits or beans or what have you. Thus is he ever the link between the way of the river and the way of man, believing without reservation that he does daily service to each.

"Mrs. Fisk schooled me herself."

"Did she now."

"She was always kind to me."

"Not kind enough to let you go, I reckon."

"No."

He can tell that she desires to argue her point, to explain Mrs. Fisk's decency by means of a dialectical process that in itself would demonstrate the tolerance and generosity of spirit that the old woman always showed her, but in the end she lets it pass as they both know she must. There will be time for this later if there is time for anything.

"I never had no patience for schooling."

"Is that so?"

"If I had a child, I don't believe I'd let him go. My pap made me, but often as not I went somewheres else instead."

"My father couldn't decide what to think."

Finn looks out across the water for a moment. "I reckon he didn't figure it'd do you no good. Less'n you made Iowa."

"I suppose."

"Which weren't likely."

"I know."

"Anybody could have told him that."

"People do desperate things."

"I reckon."

The girl pulls up a line with another catfish and treats it as she has seen him do, and then she baits the hook with another minnow from the bucket and drops the line back into the water. "Will they hang him?"

"They'd hang a white man for what he done."

"He did it on my account."

"That don't matter. Be glad you're shut of it."

"I had the gun."

"That don't matter. You're shut of it."

"I suppose I ought to be grateful to you."

Finn considers this for a moment as a purely intellectual proposition, and then bends in earnest to his poling.

———

BEHIND THE JUDGE'S HOUSE is the barn. Behind the barn and concealed by it is the cabin where Finn retreated when he came of age and took on the work done for pay in his youth by the hired man Petersen and his wife both dead these many years. Such is his inheritance and such is now the patrimony to which he introduces the girl on a night as dark as she and moonless.

"You ain't allowed in the main house."

"Who cooks?"

"The old woman. Her and a girl from town comes in to help. We'll eat back here just us."

Bringing her bags up from the river through the dark and empty streets of the village makes him desire a wagon or at least a horse which in some other place and under some other circumstance he would have borrowed but not here and not now and not with the girl.

"This place could use some tidying up." By the light of a single candle she can tell.

"You'll do it in the morning."

"I know."

"I'll be obliged." Which is as tender an expression as he permits himself.

Come morning he fetches eggs from the barn and provisions from the kitchen at the back of the house before anyone is up. His mother and the Judge when he is not on the circuit have grown accustomed to his irregular habits and they expect little from him in the way of conversation or even presence. In his entry into the life of this new community he has forged in the hired man's cabin they will see only further withdrawal, if they take note of it at all.

8

WITH THE BOY DISAPPEARED or stolen or otherwise run up against some temporary fate, Finn returns home from the squatter's shack below St. Petersburg as from a long voyage. The world to which he recovers himself is unchanged by his absence, for the particulars of his surroundings—the rotted beams that keep the house from falling into the river, the filthy horsehair couch upon the porch, the trotlines mended so often that they have been made new a thousand times over and look none the better for it—the particulars of his surroundings have about them a quality of long disuse and advancing decay. He nets minnows and sets out his lines and assesses his need for supplies, all the while wondering if perhaps he would be better served by behaving as if that nailed-shut door to the bedroom stairs did not exist at all. He avoids it thus for three days. Then with his own clawhammer and a rusty pry bar borrowed under cover of darkness from the shed behind another man's cabin he addresses himself to it in a slow reversal of a burial itself reversed. When he is done he feels not a burden removed from his shoulders and not an easing of his load but a strange sagging sense of disappointment, as if by unsealing this chamber he has deflated something whose power might have raised him up.

He sets down his tools and climbs the stairs from full darkness into darkness diminished. Before him in the air hangs a dim light, the pale and dissipated glow of the moon through milky painted windows, and he feels himself drawn in its direction equally fearful and expectant. The bedroom when he sets foot upon its white planking has about it a purity that nearly repels him. In order to move forward he reminds himself that he is in a place of his own creation, this room transmuted by blood and cleansed by whitewash and kept safe from the eyes of men by the found lumber and nails with which the river—the river that in its infinite wisdom and patience carries all things—by these elements with which the river has blessed and absolved him.

He enters into the upper room and stands in its center by the white bed and the white trunk and the white chairs all luminously set about. There is no sound save his breathing. In the damp dim light certain artifacts and instances stand out in relief upon the walls, white-painted each identical to its surroundings but each made distinct by dint of its individual edging of shadow. A windowsill. A hinge. A picture frame painted over. Her sun-bonnet. The nail upon which his own clothing once hung. He proceeds to this last and reaches out with one finger to touch its head and to touch its square shank and then inquisitively at first but by and by with more urgency to merge the relative darkness of his pale skin with its cast shadow. Tracing that dark line upon the wall with his unclean finger he discovers that he is able to manipulate its extent and add to it by means of the dirt that he has introduced to this place upon his hand. One finger after another he rubs against the white wall as if he has become some artist of reversion. He decides without thinking to trace as best he can the shadow outlines of each visible thing, an act that fixes them into permanent and grotesque signifiers of this moment. His fingers are soon clean enough to be of no further use to him and he goes downstairs and brings back up a fistful of burned charcoal and continues with redoubled fury to create upon the walls these markings which signify his return and his reclaiming.

———

"AMONG ALL OF THE POWERS and principalities, there is none on earth so mighty as a man's unsatisfied desire."

The orator gives the appearance of possessing little firsthand experience with the subject at hand, for he is enormously fat and dissipated-looking at the same time. His stomach rolls abundantly out over his trousers despite a half-pair of home-knit galluses, and his threadbare crotch strains as he sits. He is bald as a lizard and his skin is the color of a fish belly, so white as to be nearly blue and spotted all over with moles and tiny scabbed lesions. He has done his beard the disservice of attempting to shave it with a found blade or some other scrap of metal within the past week, riverwater his only lubricant and no mirror in sight, and the result is that his flaccid cheeks resemble bottomland poorly tended and gone to brush.

Finn has no time for him. "You let just anybody drink these days?" he says to Dixon.

"Anybody who pays," says Dixon, devoting an abundance of attention to the motion of his rag upon the bar.

"I'll have money tomorrow," says Finn, which may or may not be the case and Dixon knows it.

"Note," the baldheaded man goes on, "note that I said '*unsatisfied* desire.'"

"Don't he look poorly for a preacher?" To Dixon.

"Be civil."

Finn could not say which part of the question Dixon thinks his strange pale new customer might find offensive, the idea that he looks poorly or the suggestion that he might be a preacher, and so he minds his tongue.

"I might've done a little preaching," says the man.

"Try it somewheres else."

"Now Finn."

"Aww," answers the stranger, "I don't mind him none." And then directly to Finn, with a paternal look almost kindly: "I like you, boy. I do."

Finn drinks.

"You've got backbone."

"Enough of it." He drinks again and sets the empty glass on the bar.

"Let me stand you to one of those."

"I'll need more than one."

The fat man takes his purse from his pocket and spills out money across the bar.

"I reckon you must be some preacher," says Finn.

"So people say," says the fat man. "Although I also fill in with some phrenology if need be. And a little mesmerism and a bit of the old *laying on of hands*." At this last he raises both of his eyebrows together, wrinkling back his pale forehead. "Not to mention Shakespeare, if you like that sort of thing."

"I do not."

"Some do."

"I reckon." Which is the last he says until the preacher has poured half of his savings onto the bar and down Finn's throat transubstantiated into whiskey and thence again transubstantiated into Finn himself.

"What's a fellow do around here for a good time?"

"This," says Finn.

The preacher rises up kingly and surveys the room. "Any *women* in these parts?"

"Not here," says Dixon from a stool at the back end of the bar, near the door to the kitchen past which his wife snores on her pallet. "Not that sort. I run a clean place."

"I can see that," says the preacher, "however much the observation pains me." He has a bag at his feet, a thing of greasy carpet with a hinged top, bulging and lumpen and disreputable as himself. "A traveling man has certain *needs*," he says, giving the bag a halfhearted kick by way of indicating his trade or at least the apparent trappings of it. "Remember what I said about the power of a man's unsatisfied desire."

"You'll have to satisfy it somewheres else," says Dixon.

"I am but a stranger here and friendless."

"You've made the one." Indicating Finn, nearly facedown.

"I should hate to impose upon his gratitude."

"Don't you fret. He'll be a long time showing it."

"Sir," to Finn, placing upon the riverman's shoulder a paw as meaty as a cured ham. "Might you assist me?"

Finn gathers himself up.

"I require companionship."

Which Finn takes the wrong way.

"A woman."

Finn has never before assumed the role of procurer but why not. The preacher hoists his bag and the two of them exit down the steps worn into the hillside to the black river silently moving.

"We'll take yours," says the preacher when they reach the landing where a dwindling handful of boats are tied up. And so they climb aboard Finn's skiff and head downstream. Finn poles absently and the preacher plants himself amidships upon his carpetbag like royalty.

"I believe I'd like to sample something of a darker shade."

"I can't help you."

"There must be places."

"They don't mingle."

"Places that *specialize*." This last word comes off his tongue with a long lazy hiss.

"I wouldn't know."

"Surely you know where they *live*."

"Niggers."

"Amen."

"I know where they are well enough."

"Then lead on."

Finn urges the skiff downstream past the skeletal pilings of his tee-tering house and past the brush and the mudflats and the weeping willows that intervene and past the quiet piers of Lasseter proper toward the less-lit depths of darktown, where he ties up to a post at the end of a dock with more boards missing than intact. "Mind your step." Although considering his condition he ought better to be minding his.

The preacher bestirs himself sufficiently to bend double over his bag and withdraw from it certain articles that Finn cannot make out in the dark. He conceals them in a long denim coat that he throws over his shoulder in a theatrical manner and then, panting like a locomotive, he rights himself and follows his guide toward the packed dirt landing.

"What you got."

"What we'll need."

"I won't be needing anything."

"We shall see," says the preacher.

They move in the secretive manner of grim spirits from the waterside to the single narrow street that runs through darktown like a vein. "Here she is," says Finn. "You're on your own, I guess."

"Come." The preacher takes his elbow in the crook of his arm and by dint of his greater bulk commences a gay promenade down the center of the street. He has Finn's interest now and leads him without difficulty,

for there is something about the certainty with which he commences
upon this adventure that draws Finn to it.

"How do you know where you're headed?"

"Experience," says the preacher. "Experience, and a practiced eye."

Every shack here looks the same to Finn, and at this hour of the
night they are silent and dark as ranked tombs. "Don't look like a busy
night for nigger whores."

"Ahh. You have to know what to look for."

"I don't."

The preacher raises one stubby finger as if to point out something to
Finn or else to silence him, and together they stumble to a halt. On one
side is an alleyway leading back down to the water. The air smells of
gutted fish and spilled shit and the river, but the preacher breathes it in
as if it were a zephyr wafted from Arabia just for him. Down the alley,
silhouetted against the sky, is a clothesline bearing a pair of drawers, a
woman's underthings, and a boy child's overalls.

"This'll do," says the preacher. From his pocket he withdraws a pistol
which he hands to his companion.

"What's this."

"You know what it is."

Finn jams the barrel into his belt reckoning that either the man is
needlessly cautious or else he has a history of encountering tight spots
in places like this.

"Put this on." The preacher has drawn from his pocket a pair of black
cloth masks of the sort that common bandits might wear. He ties one
tight around the great humped mass of his white head, making his
ghastly and misshapen visage into something more loathsome yet.

"You look like a stoat with a sore tooth."

"Put yours on."

Finn obliges.

"And you keep that gun handy."

"I don't see why." Drawing it nonetheless.

Thus reassured and without further explanation the preacher holds
his breath and hurls himself against the shack's half-rotted door and
plunges within as a leviathan plunges into water.

The shack consists of one room, and moving like a thunderbolt he makes for the child's bed in the far corner just as if he can see it in the near-perfect darkness or as if it is here in this particular place that his prey is always doomed to lie. A man and a woman are asleep on a pallet of corn husks in the near corner and they rise up hollering and upon the preacher's command Finn lifts the pistol and fires one lucky shot square into the man's throat. By the flare he sees the man's eyes grow wide in anticipation and shock and takes note that his woman is the very woman he has seen in the street with this very child. She catches his eye once again as before. He cannot help it or help himself and he moves to put the gun away or at least drop it to his side as the preacher snatches up the boy and his blanket and his speckled straw hat and fairly knocks his stunned accomplice on his ass in making his exit.

———

THEY ARE ON THE SKIFF the three of them, and Finn is poling upstream.

"You'll stay put if you know what's good for you." But where would the child go. The preacher takes the gun from Finn and removes his mask and drops it unceremoniously to the planking, where it lies pelt-like. Finn does the same. In the darkness he can make out the great bulk of the preacher as he bends over the child only if he squints and studies upon it, and he would prefer not to. He prefers instead to reflect upon the boy child's mother with however much intensity alcohol and excitement permit his befogged brain, and so he attends as best he can to her memory and to his poling as the stars wink from behind the bankbound willows and his head gradually clears. The preacher addresses the child in tones alternately guttural and tender and there is a furtive scrambling in the center of the boat as of a small beast attempting to free itself from a trap. After a while the child cries out and gasps and lies still, and the skiff rocks unevenly upon the face of the black water until the preacher unleashes from his throat a great roaring animal bellow.

"What do you mean to do with him now."

"Throw him back," says the preacher. "I believe he's too damn small to keep." He lies against his carpetbag like a potentate reclining or some beached seagoing monster. When he recovers himself he takes up the twitching child and lifts him over the gunwale and holds him down beneath the waters with both arms extended until he stops struggling. Then he lets go of him and rises to his feet to dress. "How about we get us another drink."

"Dixon's closed up."

"You got any at home?"

"I don't," says Finn, for he will require all of it himself.

"I know you better than that."

"No you don't."

"I know everything." The preacher elevates his voice to a kind of insinuating whine.

"This is where you get out." They have come abreast of Dixon's.

The preacher is uninterested and merely grunts.

"I thank you kindly for the drink. Now git."

The preacher bends to lift his carpetbag and rises up again with the pistol in his hand. He lets it hang at his side, glinting in starlight. "You still owe me."

"Not after that." Indicating with a snap of his chin the place where the child went into the water or at least the fact thereof.

"I surely could make use of a boat like this one."

"Steal your own."

"Very well." Raising the gun.

Finn lifts the pole to push again but waits. "Goddamn nigger-loving sodomite."

"I despise flattery." Although to judge from the glint of his teeth he is charmed without limit.

For lack of any other weapon and with no opportunity to make fuller use of the one he has, Finn angles the pole out of the water and in a single smooth motion he thrusts the dry end of it ramlike into the center of the preacher's chest. The man is too massive to be caught off balance and too broad to fall easily, but he does drop the gun to the deck where it clatters away. Whether thinking or merely acting he takes hold of the pole with both of his massive hands and props it hard against his belly and strains as if to raise his attacker up into the air fishlike, and he very nearly succeeds until Finn lets go his end and the fat man staggers backward into the bow where his feet grow tangled in a mess of lines. Finn charges him and takes him over the side into the water with his hands stretched around his neck and his thumbs probing for an Adam's apple buried somewhere unreachable beneath pale flesh, and between the water and Finn's furious grip the preacher can breathe neither in nor out and he flails and lashes out at his attacker with a fierce but steadily diminishing fury until Finn lets up and makes for the skiff, leaving the preacher to drift downstream and succumb or not.

He brings to the white room the gun which he drops into the chest and the masks which he kicks beneath the bed and the speckled straw hat which he hangs upon a nail. Then he goes downstairs and falls asleep unclothed upon the porch, his overalls slung over the rail to dry.

Come morning he awakens from a sweet dream of the boy child and his mother and he fetches himself a bit of charcoal from the stove. Up in the bedroom he chooses a wall and he moves the chest over to it so that he can reach the top, all the way up near the ceiling where a single spider has begun making herself at home, and there he commences to mark down the story of what he has and has not done. His penmanship is poor and his spelling is worse and his grammar is the worst of all but these things matter not, because not long after he begins he gives off writing almost entirely and commences to draw in a manner befitting some primitive cave painter working by torchlight to document and dispel demons both real and imagined. Here is the black man sitting up in bed, a hole torn in his throat. There opposite is his wife, unharmed and beauteous as the artist's shaking hand will allow. And in the center is the boy himself, nearly obscured by the grotesque bent oversize form of the preacher. Each mouth is open save the woman's, and from each open mouth streams a river of wordless incomprehensible language in Finn's furious scrawl. The inscrutable outpourings bend and intermix, each one a tributary unto the others, until the whole expands ineluctably into a spiraling morass that drowns the mouths from which it has come and subsumes the space almost entirely in black. Only the woman remains silent, the woman and the riverman drawn remote from her and slightly askew in a far corner with a gun in his hand and his face concealed behind a mask.

9

SHE SAYS that Mary is her name, although Finn has not asked. His practice for these first days in the hired man's cabin behind the Judge's barn has been to call her by no name at all, not even the impersonal *girl* or *woman* or some other oblique reference to their relation.

"Mary," he says. "So be it."

As the days go by he watches her in the manner of a naturalist making observations, as if fearing that at any moment she could molt and reveal some alternate self beneath her skin, some raw beast damp and ready for transformation into a different sort of creature altogether. Everything she touches she touches in a manner different from the ways of his mother and the ways of dead Petersen's dead wife. There is about her a grace and an ineffable sadness that conspire to retard her movements and make them thereby into something almost musical, transforming every act into a kind of prayer or languorous meditation. She seems always to be *preparing*—not merely his supper or a bucket of washwater or some other common thing, but herself, for that part of her life which is yet to come.

She is a fair cook and a poor housekeeper, but Finn does not notice these failings because her abilities in both matters are far superior to his. After a week his clothing is cleaner than it has been in all of his adult life despite the cabin's lack of a proper laundry room or even a washboard. These chores do not by any measure come naturally to her. She has spent her life luxuriously enslaved by Mrs. Fisk, whose opinions regarding black people are the opposite of those espoused by the Judge. Not only is the old woman happy to enjoy their company, but she believes it her duty to improve each one of them who crosses her path so as to ready their race for the day when they shall be set free.

Mary achieves such success as she does in matters of housework by concentrating her attention and focusing her will. In the absence of any other outlet, whether books or needlework or dreams of such life as might lie beyond the door that Finn padlocks behind him when he heads to the river, she can attend only to the instant in which she finds herself. "This is for your own good," he says when he takes the lock down and fishes the key from wherever he keeps it secreted about himself. She cannot imagine that he is telling her anything like the truth.

"I need to get some air," she says one evening when he comes back from the river bearing his catch. The day has been hot and the cabin is an oven.

"There's air out back." Tilting his head toward the fenced yard behind the cabin where he keeps the chopping block and a flat board for cleaning fish and various sprung and rusted implements more useful as curiosities than tools. He raises the fish to her as if they are the veriest prize, some reward for which she has labored without ceasing, the golden fleece itself. She takes them with a gracious nod and exits to the yard.

A river breeze stirs the clothes that she hung on the line before he left this morning and she threads her way between them careful with the fish.

From the tiny window comes his voice: "Mind them clothes." As if she needs telling.

She can feel his eyes upon her as she guts the fish and scales them and as she rinses her hands in the rainbarrel and dries them on a stiff rag long bloodied. By the sound of it he is occupied with starting the fire in the big iron stove but she knows that he is watching nonetheless even though she keeps her back to him to such degree as she can. Then with the fish on a platter and their guts and glistening scales rinsed from the board with a dipper of water she starts back through the thin maze of hung laundry.

"Don't forget them clothes."

"One thing at a time," she says without thinking and without implication.

"You watch your tongue."

"I didn't mean."

"I know it."

She pauses and visibly considers how she might carry two armfuls of clean laundry in addition to the platter of fish.

"Go back for that," he says. He neither reaches to take the platter from her nor moves to assist her in any other way but instead turns his back and attends to some trivial thing in the cabin. He has done enough by letting her go.

She brings in the laundry and folds it and begins to prepare the fish. She slides a spoonful of lard into the pan and puts it over the heat and while the lard melts she dredges the fillets in flour and then in milk with a beaten egg and then again in cornmeal, and then she arranges them in the pan and steps away while they sizzle. The heat in the cabin is stifling, but she knows better than to ask directly why they cannot build a fire in the yard and cook out there when it gets this way. The less she is outdoors the better as far as he is concerned, and smoke would only increase the risk.

"Your father," she hazards as they sit before their plates.

"The Judge."

"Why does he." Pausing to compose her thoughts.

"It's his way."

"But."

"Nobody knows."

"What would he do if he knew about me?"

"Don't ask."

This night he tells her to come to his bed rather than sleep on the pallet she has made up in the corner. Why he has waited this long she cannot say although she has begun to think that he might have a good heart. She obeys without hesitation for she lacks alternative. Before bedding down he swung wide the door for ventilation and propped open the shutters, so now a small breeze moves through the cabin bearing upon it the sound of crickets and the smell of the barnyard and bearing away the scent of fried catfish and the ticking of the woodstove as it cools.

When they finish he groans and rolls upon his back and places a proprietorial hand upon her thigh. In the shifting fragrant dark he keeps it there, a burning token constant while the moments pass and the air around them faintly cools and their bodies cool likewise.

She considers, lying there beneath that brand, what use she might make of the door that he has left open. A hundred schemes run through her mind, each one possible and each one faulty and each one rejected in the end. She requires her things, which would mean gathering them up from where they have gone scattered in this short time and restoring them in utter silence to her bag. He might rouse up during this operation, an eventuality that she might overcome by means of the chamber pot, but still. Obviously she must leave with only the barest of essentials. But where would she go? All she knows of Illinois is Rock Island and of Rock Island she knows only that Mrs. Fisk has people there whose names she either did not hear or does not recall. She has no means of transport beyond her own two legs. She does not even know which way the river lies, for she came to this place in darkness and has been kept in darkness ever since.

Ultimately he removes his hand and turns his shoulder away, leaving her to concentrate upon remaining alert until he should fall asleep. The night goes fully still and the breeze dies away, and she settles her own breathing to its most shallow. Some small creature, mouse or rat or other, scuttles past the doorway and as she hears its furtive steps muffled by grass and dust and then considers such noises as Finn himself might detect even from the depths of his sleep, such small courage as she has managed to collect in her heart diminishes and dims and dies. She nonetheless takes in air and reaches with her toe for the floor as gingerly as she can just to see, and it takes no more than that to bestir the man, who rises up cursing himself for a fool and stalks over to close the door and secures it with the lock.

————

FINN TOOK TO DRINK early in spite of his father's counsel. "You can rely upon whiskey to destroy a man," the Judge would say to no one in particular, waiting at the head of the table for Petersen's wife to serve him his supper. The Judge's own father before him had possessed a boundless appetite for drink, and as a result the Judge was by inclination more sympathetic to the lowest sneak thief than to any drunkard who happened before his bench. "Make no mistake," he would say then and he still does, "I am always unstintingly fair to the tippler. I can be counted upon to be perfectly just in hearing his plea and gauging his punishment. But I must confess that such judiciousness brings me no pleasure."

Thus Finn now takes a certain habituated thrill in sitting upon the porch of the cabin that he secretly shares with the girl and enjoying there in public his jar or two of whiskey. It comes from a bottle and is therefore of known quality and fair repute. His parsimonious father pays him little enough to maintain the place but between his simple needs and his patience with a trotline he gets by and routinely has more than enough extra to spend on such an extravagance as this. "That's the Judge's dollar right there," he will say to Dixon as he completes his transaction, and surely enough it is, for he is fastidious in his accounting and careful to use his father's funds for such purchases as this, which would break any such heart as the elder Finn may yet possess.

"Whyn't you plant a kitchen garden back there come spring?" he asks of the woman who sits in darkness behind the door as if the cabin is her confessional. No remark could be calculated to produce in her heart more hope, or more dread for that matter, for in it she detects both a promise of some small eventual relief and a far more dire promise of a lifetime spent imprisoned nonetheless. At least until the Judge passes on and she can emerge from her cocoon.

She asks: "Would it be safe?"

"We'll see."

"It would surely ease your burden." For she knows his habits and has read his mind.

"Put it over toward the barn, close to the fence as we can."

"Where I'd be out of sight."

"Mostly."

"Mostly."

This night she dreams herself trapped within the fenced yard by a terrifying personage who can be none other than the Judge himself or else plain Justice personified. He appears to her alternately as an enormous white man pale as death and as some ordinary inconsequential thing become animate, laundry or line or ax, and in whatever form he chooses to be made flesh he seeks to corner her and overwhelm her in some manner that her dream does not dare make specific. She awakens in the dark, pounding her fists upon Finn's chest and clinging to him at the same time, and crying out into the empty stillness of the cabin and the farm and all of Adams County surrounding that place where once there was none such as her and now there is but one and it is she and she alone.

———

WEEKS PASS and they fall into habits these two like an old husband and wife. During the days she misses him, and not only because his mere presence in the cabin means a door swung wide if not to provide freedom then at least to suggest it. He arrives at day's end like a liberating army, reed-wrapped fish in his arms and a bottle of whiskey in the crook of his elbow and the key between his teeth, and as he stands in the dusty dooryard she looks out through the tiny square of window and wishes that she were free to come outside and help him as he stands there juggling. When he finally springs the lock and gets the door open she greets him like a genie let loose from a bottle.

It must be during one of these moments that their peculiar joy is witnessed by the halfwit Tyrell. Other such moments there are, but with none to be their witness. In the dim candlelit evening, when she reads to him from a book of poetry he has found in the dry depths of a floating steamer trunk, she seems to him in her fluency a creature from some other place and time or an instrument shaped by the Almighty so that a long-dead cavalier poet might whisper his incomprehensible arcana into the mind of a benighted illiterate riverman. At night on the hard bed, as he explores her brown body with his fingers and with his tongue and with that other, she seems an astonishment and a mystery and a strange miracle, forbidden to him by his father the Judge but infinitely more precious for that.

These things Tyrell cannot see and cannot guess and would not treasure if he did. "I reckon the Judge changed his tune," he says offhand to Finn when they meet on the mudflats by the river.

"I can't say," says Finn, for he does not care what the halfwit thinks about anything and if pressed would say that he most likely thinks nothing at all, certainly nothing orderly enough to merit acknowledgment.

"Changed his tune about that girl, I mean. She's a pretty one all right." Grinning, showing his teeth. Tyrell has grown feeble with the passage of the years and his head bobs upon his neck like a lascivious sunflower.

"What girl."

"Yours."

Finn scans the river and waits.

"Your *nigger* girl." As if Finn himself is the halfwit.

Finn turns to his interlocutor and blinks once, slowly as a cat, in either assent or disbelief.

Satisfied, Tyrell presses on. "I reckon even your pap can see the worth of a sweet thing like that." He goes all moony and licks his lips as if the girl were Christmas dinner, and like a slug his tongue leaves behind a glistening trail.

Finn does not think before answering. "The Judge ain't had no piece of that girl."

Tyrell looks offended.

"He don't know nothing about her." Pointing a finger at Tyrell's chest.

"I was only."

"That girl ain't none but mine." Pushing at the halfwit with that finger hard enough to make him stagger backward a little upon his thin and bowed-out legs.

"I reckon," says Tyrell.

"She ain't no property of the Judge."

"I know it."

Had Finn denied the presence of the girl and offered the halfwit a glass of whiskey at Dixon's or some other place he might have persuaded him that she was instead some vision or mere figment. Later he will blame this lapse upon his urge to defend her reputation against the repellent notion of her having lain with the Judge, although some might suggest that the opposite is more likely the case and he was defending instead the Judge's inscrutable constancy. Regardless Tyrell shambles down the bank to his skiff, knowing what he knows and disputing within his mind what use he might make of it.

———

THE JUDGE TRIES THE CABIN DOOR and finds it locked from within, which he takes as confirmation. Neither knocking nor making any other signal he slips around to the back and pries loose the ax from the chopping block and returns to the front door, where he applies the weighty implement with a sudden fury. The raw lumber has weathered poorly and the door is instantly burst from its hinges and the Judge enters to find the two of them together in bed not even covered by a proper sheet, roused up naked and wide-eyed like a pair of nesting animals startled awake. He is even more appalled than he has prepared himself to be.

"I can trust that idiot Tyrell," he says, "but I cannot trust my own blood."

Finn eyes the ax and holds up both hands like a man accosted by a bandit. "Put that down."

"You boy." The Judge can think of nothing else to say and so has gone atavistic, reverting to the discarded locutions of his childhood. He has no further use for the ax but having been told to let go of it he hangs on.

"I'll drop her."

The woman listens and believes, and the Judge listens but does not.

"I swear I'll drop her." Negotiating either for his life or for his patrimony.

"You will."

"I will."

"But you won't come back here." He lets the ax hang down alongside his leg. "Neither in this life nor in any other."

"However you see fit."

"It isn't my decision." The Judge points briefly doorward with the ax and then stands watching in a kind of dull and horrified astonishment while his son and the girl dress and gather themselves up to depart. Adam and Eve would more likely steal apples from the garden than these two would dare take anything more than the clothing they wear and one or two necessities that come easily to hand: a hat, a clasp-knife, matches. Finn resolves to creep back later for the frying pan and the ax and a few things more.

Disheveled and displaced they proceed downward to the river's edge where he knows of a raft hung up against a snag in the shallows and long unclaimed. Some of the logs are rotten and some others are broken in two but it will make shelter enough as long as the weather holds, so working side by side they haul it from the water and into the woods where they prop it against a tree and give thought to making themselves comfortable.

"You said you'd drop me."

"Go on leave anytime you want. I can't stop you."

"Where would I go?"

"I meant to do you a favor." Thinking of the *Santo Domingo.*

"I know it."

She gathers up some pine boughs and finds a straight stick and then with line salvaged from the raft she binds them all together into a passable broom. With it she sweeps out a smooth place and she makes up in the center of it a pallet of more boughs while he runs his lines more urgently than usual and wonders where he might acquire some tomatoes or beans to go with the bluegills now that the garden behind the white mansion is surely off limits.

"You hungry." Arriving with fish wrapped in reeds.

"How am I to cook that?"

He turns his back and walks off through the woods to the river again and poles his skiff up to Dixon's place where he trades the fish for whiskey, and then he returns to the lean-to and lies down to sleep the afternoon away. In the early evening he runs his lines again and puts the fish into a sling made of rope and hangs them from a limb out of reach of such wildlife as may pass this way. "We'll need a fry pan," he says to her and she follows him up the hill into their own retreating shadows while the sun finishes setting.

They gather what they can from the cabin and bundle it up into a blanket, certain that the Judge will never discover their thievery and not caring if he does. When they finish they slip down the pathway between the Judge's property and Tyrell's until Finn takes note of the halfwit himself silhouetted in his parlor window smoking a corncob pipe as contented as a sultan.

"Wait," he says. Lowering the bound-up blanket to the grass in a single smooth movement and slipping away catlike.

The house is ramshackle and swaybacked and he enters through the back door as if he owns the premises and is free to dispose of it in any way he sees fit.

"You Tyrell."

The halfwit takes the pipestem from his mouth and surveys his visitor with the offhand grace of bemused royalty. "Now what brings you here?" As if Finn's appearance upon these premises is a common thing but one that never ceases to bring him delight.

"You know."

"Need somewheres to bed down?"

"I don't."

Tyrell luxuriates with his pipe for a moment.

The visitor asks his question. "Why'd you tell him?"

"Why not?" For there is no other reason or at least none better.

Finn strides to the old man and takes the vegetal stalk of his neck in one hand and presses upon it. With the other he knocks the pipe to the floor and covers the old man's mouth lest he cry out. Through the window he sees Mary waiting and he presses harder taking no pleasure in it but hanging on to the old man as he would to a rattlesnake got likewise by the throat or some other dangerous beast desirous of doing him harm. When he is finished and Tyrell lies limp he locates a jug of coal oil and empties it upon the halfwit and his threadbare couch and scatters red embers from the corncob pipe thereon rather than waste matches.

Under full dark they crouch in the woods along the margin of the property and together they watch as Tyrell's house burns to the ground. They have barely gotten themselves settled when the halfwit's wife hobbles shrieking from the front door in her nightgown bereft of home and husband and flings herself full upon some sympathetic neighbor. Finn has forgotten about her entirely and he is taken aback to witness her standing there big as life and solid as denunciation, describing no doubt the atrocity she discovered upon the parlor couch when she came down to call the old man to bed.

Mary cherishes the inch or two of space between their crouched bodies and she brushes away a tear with the back of her hand. But for their shining eyes the lurking two of them are invisible in the dark woods, she in particular, despite the light cast roundabout by flames.

At the height of the blaze Finn bumps against her and takes her forearm in his hand and speaks without turning away from this bright thing he has created. His voice comes to her amid the crackle of fire and the crash of falling beams and the roar of wind through flame as if from the throat of some reassuring demon. "I done this for you."

She sits wordless but does not dare pull away.

"You remember that."

———

THEY PASS THE REMAINS of the summer without difficulty and the autumn too, but soon enough winter comes on. He has kept himself alert for such floating timber as he may salvage from the river and added it piece by piece to the raft until their poor habitation has grown from a mere lean-to into a certain kind of disreputable-looking shed. The one original side supports some brushy overgrowth and has begun to tolerate the dense-furred encroachment of moss, with the result that the place has begun to look not so much lived-in as like an abandoned relic of some ancient civilization lost and long forgotten by the sons of man. Only the firepit provides a clue as to its inhabitance.

One deep snowfall after another pushes conditions toward the untenable. The woolen blanket that she hung upon found nails for a door no longer suffices to keep out the wind and needs reinforcement by pine boughs and a deadfall better used for firewood. They huddle outdoors around the firepit when they can and long for its warmth and light when they cannot. He experiments with building a fire inside for cooking, but as they lack proper material to construct a chimney of any sort or even tools to cut a venthole in the roof the trial ends without success. The shallows freeze over and Finn chops his skiff away from its moorings with the ax each day to run his impoverished lines.

When his brother finds them they are not so near death as he has feared but sorely afflicted nonetheless.

"Will." In an astonished voice from beneath a pile of clothing and stolen blankets and pine boughs.

The brother's instinct is to stamp off his feet before coming indoors but the margin between inside and out is so thin as to be past notice. He has come through the woods with an oil lantern for light and he places it on the frozen mud of the floor, where it sits at an angle and radiates a welcome incidental heat. "I can't bear this," he says.

"You can't?"

"No. I can't."

"You ain't inviting me home."

"No."

"What then."

"The Judge'd never have you."

"Nor I him."

"I'm taking a place of my own, and I thought you might do the same."

"I already done it." Indicating the frigid room and its fire-blackened walls by means of a hand thrust out into the cold.

"This. Honestly. I can help."

"I don't require it."

"He'd let you die."

"I won't die."

"I know it. Still."

"I'm obliged for your concern."

Will jams a hand into his breast pocket and draws forth an envelope folded over many times and wrinkled into illegibility. He shows it to his brother as if in itself it has meaning. "I've arranged a place for you."

"What."

"That's right.

"With you."

"No."

"Where then."

"A house. On the river. Maybe a half-mile from here." Will is beginning to shiver in the cold shack.

"Have a blanket," says his brother, and he throws him one, diminishing the pile strewn upon himself and the girl. She has been witnessing all this in silence, wearing a look of studied uninterest.

Useless though it is, Will throws his brother's ragged castoff over his shoulders. He returns the deed to his pocket and prepares to go on.

"What house?" asks Finn.

"The Anderson place."

"That old fool."

"He's dead."

"When'd it happen?"

"Maybe a month ago."

"It's no loss."

"Still."

"I know it."

"He was a squatter, it turns out. After he passed on one thing led to another, and certain opportunities presented themselves."

"I reckon money changed hands."

"It did."

"Where'd it come from?"

"I'd rather not say."

"I hope my own brother didn't do nothing unethical."

"As I said, the Judge would let you die."

"I know it."

"He's through with you. Absolutely. But I'm not."

"I reckon I'm obliged."

"I can't help myself."

"I know it." For what individual can.

Will lowers himself to a crouch so as to look his brother dead in the eye. "One thing. You can never tell a soul how this came about."

"I don't rightly know myself."

"Good. And it had nothing to do with me."

"I'll remember that."

"You will." With which he removes the blanket from his shoulders and picks up his lantern and excuses himself from the shed for the walk home. Come morning Finn and the girl will awaken shivering in a thin cloud of their own exhaling, and wonder for a moment each of them if Will's appearance before them was dream or vision.

———

ANDERSON'S OLD PLACE IS FIT only for dying in, as lately he has had the misfortune to demonstrate. One room downstairs with a riverfront porch and an iron stove, one smaller claustrophobic one upstairs with a pair of gabled windows looking out upon the river. It rises from the water on rotten pilings, to one of which is yet tied the painter of Anderson's sunken icebound rowboat. In the rising wind this habitation creaks like a sailing vessel on the high seas, and snow swirls up from between the downstairs floorboards. Rats have infested the place, lured by food scraps and other leavings, and on account of their plenteous excrement and occasional corpses the squalid rooms smell worse than does the outhouse at the edge of the woods for being less thoroughly ventilated. Yet there is a pile of kindling by the stove and a stack of split logs beneath the house where the snow eddies in the wind and is less deep, and Finn and Mary make themselves at home without hesitation.

"Your brother is a very kind person," she hazards once the fire gets going. She is on her hands and knees, packing straw from an old tick into the worst of the gaps between the floorboards.

"He has his good points."

"I don't doubt it."

"We ain't never had much in common."

She salvages what she can from the kitchen and puts the blankets on the pallet in the upstairs room, while he complains that he ought by rights to move his trotlines down this way even though the fishing may not be as good here as it has always been in his usual spot. Anderson left some rusty iron stakes driven into the ground with chains attached and then ropes and then his old poorly mended lines, the lot of which Finn reckons he can now make his own just as he has made his own the house, although his usual things are no doubt superior to these and it will mean a good bit of work and a day's lost fishing to bring them down here when he gets around to it.

In the early evening a steamboat goes upstream, not the *Santo Domingo* but its equal for all earthly purposes, its tall stacks steaming doubly in the cold.

"Don't you get any ideas," says Finn as he chews at a piece of corn-bread she has made up from meal sifted clean of rat droppings.

"What kind of ideas?"

"You know what kind."

She does, but she cannot confess them even to herself.

He passes his arm across the river scene before them, magnanimous. "Not after all I done for you."

She can tell that in his way he means it. And because he cannot help himself, as the months and years go by he is faithful to her as to nothing else in this world.

10

Finn has torn a rusted hasp from a barn door floating downriver and fashioned a nail into a loop that serves well enough, and with these and his venerable lock—relic of his months in the hired man's cabin with the woman, relic of his subsequent days in the squatter's shack with the boy—he secures the door to the bedroom stairs before going out to steal whiskey from old blind Bliss.

"Ain't seen you around, Finn." Bliss pricks up his ears and speaks these words without irony the instant his visitor emerges from the treeline.

"I been busy." Crestfallen at having been discovered, but making the best of it.

The bootlegger, teetering on a broken rocking chair, laughs until his shoulders jump. "I know my customers, don't I?"

"You do."

"How much you be needing?"

"Some."

"Help yourself." Throwing his head back and to one side, toward the trail that leads to his cache. "I guess I know you're good for it. What with that boy of yours and all."

"I reckon."

Bliss's sharp hearing is not limited to the crackling of twigs and the barking of foxes, and in Finn's voice he detects uncertainty. "Something happen to the money?"

"No."

"You can tell me."

"It's tied up."

"How so?"

"Legal business."

Finn sounds so in need of comfort that the bootlegger's charitable instincts get the better of his business sense. "Help yourself anyhow," he says, uncertain of how dearly his generosity may cost him for he cannot assess the capacity of Finn's empty jug. "Help yourself, you poor benighted bastard."

"Poor benighted bastards ain't all saddled with the Judge."

"Amen to that," says Bliss.

When Finn returns Bliss has fetched a pair of canning jars so that he might share in his own largesse. "Speaking of your daddy," he begins.

"Don't."

"You still free of that woman?"

"I am."

"How's that suit him?"

"I can't say."

Bliss rests his drink on the arm of his chair and leans toward Finn as if his customer's hearing has gone bad, as if Finn is an imbecile who does not fully understand the English language. "What'd he say when you told him?"

"I didn't."

Bliss sticks a finger in his ear and runs it around, probing for something, incredulous.

"I ain't worried. He'll find out one way or the other."

"What's wrong with you, Finn?"

"Folks talk."

"You can't trust folks."

"I know it."

They drink for a while, the two of them, on that falling-down porch in the woods.

"I ain't been back long," Finn says after a while. "Ain't seen Will yet."

"So maybe the old man knows."

"Could be." The woods are filled with birdsong and he attends to it while he drinks. "For a while I didn't think I cared no more, what with the boy and all."

"The six thousand."

"The six thousand."

"That kind of money'd go a long way."

"It would."

"It ain't bugdust to the Judge," says Bliss, shaking his head like a woeful old horse.

"I know it."

"Still. It'd go a long way."

Finn refills his jar. "With six thousand in my pocket," he says, "I believe I might never give that Judge another thought."

"Could be." Bliss creaks forward and back in his rocking chair, pushing his lips together and ruminating upon Finn's fate. "If you don't mind my saying, enough whiskey'll give you that same advantage."

"I know it," says Finn.

After Finn leaves, old Bliss troops back to his cache and despairs over the damage. This is the last time, he says, the last time that he will ever take pity upon that individual. And although he knows that he is lying to himself he takes some comfort in the idea all the same.

———

FINN SITS DRINKING on his old horsehair couch above the river with his hair drawn back in a tangle and his beard brushing his bare chest, wondering if perhaps old blind Bliss is correct and he ought to brave the Judge in his lair after all. How much time has gone by since he told Will that he'd finished with her he cannot say, but with a brain full of forty-rod he reasons that it must be weeks at the very least or even months. Long enough for him to have gone downriver and rescued the boy and run into trouble with Judge Thatcher and that other judge, the new one with his ideas of improvement. Long enough for him and the boy to have passed a certain number of days together in that squatter's shack where the river ran slow and time seemed as if it would go on forever. Long enough to have alarmed the widow Douglas and set her and Judge Thatcher upon the task of not only taking from him his rightful fortune but taking from him his child.

He resolves that come morning he will walk up the hill to the white clapboard mansion alongside the limestone courthouse on the finest block of the highest street in town and find therein his father. The Judge is old now, nearly as old as judgment itself, and as the years have passed he has come to see his son only obliquely if at all. How an impoverished riverman such as he might maintain that house upon the water he cannot tell and does not ask, for he knows without doubt that the answer would require certain adjustments. The cabin behind his barn stands uninhabited, lair of snakes and spiders, and the current hired man resides in his own tidy house in town, living high upon the extravagant wages that the Judge pays rather than let any other set foot in that accursed place again.

Finn lies down upon the horsehair couch and struggles toward sleep but sleep will not come on account of the whiskey. His head spins and he lies awake turning now faceup and now facedown over and over until the spinning in his head gives way to a pain like a railroad spike thrust through behind his eyes, and he falls in and out of sleep dreaming of the Judge, who upon less than half of the present evidence would condemn him for a drunk like his grandfather before him, both worthless and beneath contempt. A steamboat passes by lit up unearthly and it blasts its whistle at some other boat in the channel, and Finn holds his ears as if upon his willing it the world might vanish or at least accommodate itself to his desires.

A chill awakens him. The evening warmth is gone and the heat of the whiskey has dissipated itself likewise through his liver and limbs and out into the greedy atmosphere, leaving him cold where he lies there uncovered and alone on the couch. The sun has yet to rise but will.

He fortifies himself with an outsize breakfast. Coffee, eggs, and salt pork as usual, but also on this occasion a plate of biscuits made the way she used to. He is thinking not of the old paradisiacal days in his cabin behind the barn, a time when she had not yet learned the making of them or much else, but of the years that followed, after they had retreated to this place on the river. The biscuits in their dusting of flour sit white upon his blackened tin plate and he devours them.

Beyond his porch the river steams.

He licks crumbs from the plate and reflects upon the uselessness of her education with Mrs. Fisk, those brief irresponsible years that had left her with hardly the skills to fry a catfish, and he congratulates himself over having required her to come into her own after all. Whether she learned in the general store in Lasseter or in some other woman's kitchen in darktown or perhaps elsewhere was no business of his as long as she had supper on the table.

He puts the plate away and checks the lock on the bedroom stairs and heads out. Up the sloping street he climbs into the sunrise with his long shadow astretch behind him all the way to the river's edge as if it would cling there still and thereby ground him, and near the top of the hill he passes his brother's shuttered law office before which the shingle, WM. FINN, ESQ., hangs without motion. A spider has fixed an egg case to one of the hinges and Finn considers its precariousness and walks on.

The house when he reaches it would seem to be asleep. Like an itinerant he knocks upon the door, tentatively and as if he does not exactly belong here, and the hired man's wife comes to crack it open just the slightest and study him through the gap.

"Morning." With a tip of his slouch hat, which would pass for comical were not his expression so fierce.

Behind the door her one visible eye narrows. Something about him is familiar but not sufficiently so or perhaps not in the proper way. These premises have been haunted previously by men of his type and better who have believed themselves wronged by the Judge and sought compensation at least or revenge at worst.

"The Judge in?"

"No." She looks instantly as if she has made a dire mistake, as if in the absence of the Judge this man will surely have his way with her and with anyone else whose unlucky presence he detects on this besieged property.

He takes the latch in his hand and she flinches as if stung.

"Reckon I'll have to see *her* then," says Finn. "Seeing's how I come all this way."

"Your mother," says the hired man's wife, realizing.

"There any other about?" Stepping inside and trooping off down the long central hall toward the kitchen while she slumps against the plaster wall in the wake of fate forestalled. His mother is not in the kitchen of course but the coffeepot is, and he returns the cup to the sink before climbing the great circular staircase to her bedroom. There is a parlor adjacent and here she passes her days.

She speaks his Christian name as he enters but she stirs not from her chair. Save a small furtive gleam in the old woman's eye, which she dares not expose to her son's view, a person watching would suppose that he presents himself in her parlor daily. Time has diminished her, and when the undertaker comes to carry her out she will weigh no more than a wish ungranted.

"Where's the Judge?"

"Sit."

He stands his ground instead, wringing his hat in his hands. "He out on the circuit?"

"You know better than that." Patting a vacant place on the settee. "It's been two years since he rode the circuit."

"I forgot."

"No one even asks his opinion anymore. All of that learning gone to waste. All of that wisdom."

"He had his run."

"He'd be surprised to see you here."

"I reckon."

"It must be a special occasion." The look that she gives him is sly and knowing and coquettish all at once.

"I guess he ought to know I've broken if off with that woman."

The mother dares to speak her name, as if there could be any other.

"That's the one."

"After all this time."

"I know it."

"Your father knew you'd come around."

"Did he."

"He had faith in you."

Finn gives off with his hat and turns to unlatch the shutter and look out. The view from this elevated spot is the finest in Lasseter and it extends all the way down to the river, although thanks to the deep summer greenery of the trees and the comfortable clustering together of neat clapboarded houses one against the next he cannot make out his own place.

"He did," she says, as if to make herself believe it.

"You think so."

"I do."

"Then you tell him." Squinting at a boat upon the river and past that at a plume of smoke rising into the air from somewhere over on the Missouri side.

"No."

"Tell him I was here and tell him what I done."

"I will not."

He stands chewing his lip for a moment and then turns to face her. There upon her settee she has drawn herself up to her largest and most imposing aspect and although she doubtless intends to demonstrate her resolve thereby she looks to Finn like a foolish and willful child.

"I'll not run your errands," she says.

"You never would."

"Come back."

"I will."

Finn leaves his mother in the parlor and proceeds back down the long hill toward that house upon the river which now stands empty of all life save his own. His lines need running and he will get to them by and by, but no sooner has he passed his brother's office than he finds himself waylaid by the open door of a tavern. The proprietor is mopping up from the night previous and he shows him his back along with as much uninterest as he dares.

"How about a whiskey on account."

"I ain't open."

"Your door is."

"That's no matter."

"It is to me."

"I can't help you." Swabbing intently at a place he's already done.

"I'll take my custom elsewhere."

"Be my guest."

"I will." Looking away out the door he came in. He abandons the pursuit of whiskey not because the proprietor has successfully dissuaded him but because he sees across the street, just about to turn down the alley that leads alongside the Adams Hotel, a certain tall and lovely black woman with a bundle of laundry balanced upon her head. Bedsheets or towels, he reckons, done at home and brought back. He can imagine the misery and duress of her life well enough, for he knows without looking twice that she is managing somehow to get on without the boy whom the preacher drowned in the river after buggering and without the husband whom he himself shot clean in the throat mainly by a stroke of good fortune. He can see in his mind's eye the line upon which those towels or bedsheets have dried, for it is the selfsame line upon which the preacher spied the boy's overalls silhouetted. He desires to speak to her but denies himself the pleasure, not because he fears that she would recognize him without the mask—for her attention at that fateful moment in darktown was no doubt occupied by the preacher's assault on her boy's pallet and by the harsh report of the pistol that slew her husband—but because of the conversation that he has just had with his mother and the promise that he has made both to her and to himself regarding his reformation. Yet something inexorable within him stirs. And after she has vanished down the alley he returns home as if drawn by some power, and he climbs the stairs to the bedroom, and there upon the wall in anguished word and picture he describes the story of his urge and of his longing and of his despair over the fate of his poor doomed immortal soul.

———

HIS HAND IS BLACKENED and his face is blackened from the damp dirty recurring touch of it. The long ropes of his hair are drawn back and bound in a scrap torn from her dress, a scrap fingered likewise dark and thoroughly soaked as well for he has been hard at work in the airless bedroom documenting his dissolution. On the porch he drinks a dipper of water and then another after it without pausing. Sated and wet of hand he goes to the kitchen and fills a glass with whiskey and drops it and it shatters upon the planking, and before the whiskey can

soak in he has flung himself prone and lapped up such of it as his desperate tongue can locate. He pays no mind to the slivers of wood and
the rusty ill-driven nails that get in his way, although now and then a
shard of glass does serve to impede his progress. He reckons that the
more he presses forward the less he will have reason to mind, and in this
he is after a fashion correct.

When he has recovered all that he can he rises upon knees now
bloody inside his pantlegs and searches for the other glass in the jum-
bled depths of the cabinet. Slick with blood and whiskey his hand falls
upon it at last, and he hoists it tenderly out into the last dying rays of the
riverward sunset only to be disappointed, for he has unearthed not the
glass at all but a baby bottle, a baby bottle gone cloudy with dust and
cobwebs and perhaps a lingering sentimental scum of milk. Packed into
its open end is a rag stopper half gone to dust. He considers for a moment whether or not such a bottle will do for whiskey, but in the end he
decides that he would prefer something more capacious. Still he keeps
it in the pocket of his overalls even after he has found the other glass
and begun making use of it.

The air on the porch is cooler and the traffic on the darkening river
provides distraction or at least a pleasant counterpoint to the whiskey.
He leans against the rail and hollers once or twice across the water to
passing rafts, with no intent beyond livening up the evening. Upon the
ears of whatever raftsmen or wanderers or runaways are aboard these
silent craft his voice from the elevated porch must fall like that of a lunatic or an idiot or an idle god, speaking from on high in a language unknown to ordinary men. His tongue bleeds in his mouth and from time
to time he nurses it by causing it to lie still in an anesthetic puddle of
whiskey until he can wait no longer and must swallow, and from this act
so elegantly combining self-medication with restraint he derives a certain unmistakable satisfaction.

Black with coal dust and blood he lies upon the horsehair couch and
drinks straight from the jug, for his glass is on the railing and he is too
encumbered by drink to reach it. The baby bottle is still in his pocket
and it pokes into his hip by way of reminding him of itself until he reckons that he knows exactly the place where it belongs and resolves to

climb the stairs and place it with such care as he can manage into the broken-backed chest along with the gun belonging to that preacher. Up there in that hallowed place must go these things for which he dares hazard no further use, these things that ought by rights to go straight over the porch rail and into the slow hungry mouth of the river if only he were strong enough in spirit but he is not. And so he gathers himself and climbs the steps one by one to his limbo and his purgatory, where contrary to his best intentions he falls asleep on the hard frame bed and the bottle slips out of his pocket and drops to the floor without making sufficient sound even to awaken him.

11

Iₙ ᴛɪᴍᴇ Mᴀʀʏ ᴄᴏɴᴄᴇɪᴠᴇꜱ and they are to have a child. During the months prior he imagines the burgeoning creature aswim in her belly, needful and blind and oddly imperious, as enigmatic as some new constellation hung in the darkness over the face of the Mississippi. He knows within certain limits what manner of fish his lines will bring up each day and how many, but the nature of this new thing is inscrutable and troublous.

"It's mine, ain't it?" he says to her as they lie side by side in the frame bed one morning, light coming in through the gabled windows. The lean flat surface of her belly has begun to distend and he is fascinated by it.

"Who else's would it be?"

"I don't know."

"You think too much."

"I know it."

She is unwell these mornings and she visits the outhouse in a desperate hurry and then returns to the upstairs room not entirely better but at least some relieved.

He takes up his thread again, for he has been considering something in her absence. "Boy or girl, you suppose?"

"I don't care." Lying back down with her face to the ceiling and her hands folded upon her stomach.

"I hope a boy."

"I'm sick enough for it."

"What's that mean?" For he knows nothing of such matters.

"They say you're sicker with a boy is all."

"Do they?"

"They do."

He lies contemplating. A steamboat passes on the river and in its wake he asks, "White or nigger?"

"They both say it the same. Everybody knows it."

"I mean the child."

She turns her head to look at him.

"White or nigger?"

She understands now. "The child could look either way, I suppose."

His gaze flicks down to her belly and back.

"You suppose."

"There's no telling."

"It could be someplace in between."

"Bound to be someplace in between. Just where in between is the question."

"I know it." He lies thinking. "I just thought maybe."

"Just maybe on account of how much experience I have with this kind of thing?"

"Just maybe you had a feeling."

"This doesn't come with any kind of a feeling."

"I don't reckon so."

"If I had any kind of a feeling I'd surely tell you."

"I know it." For he trusts that she would and he understands that there are some mysteries in the world that must wait until the lines are run.

Later he ties up at Dixon's place and climbs the rutted steps for whiskey. He has been ruminating about his prospects and considering the shape of his future in light of both his shameful devotion to the woman and his own wondrous and overweening potency, and as he sits he concludes that someone other than the two of them ought to know about the child and that it may as well be Dixon as any.

"I reckon I ought to make a better father than the Judge," is how he introduces the subject, hardly above a whisper.

"You mean that?" says Dixon. There are others in the place, six or eight boisterous men gathered around a table playing cards and a handful more on the porch, but Finn prefers to sit by himself and nurse whiskey from a jug without distraction.

"I do. I mean it."

"With that one?"

"There ain't been none other."

Dixon cogitates for a moment. Whether he is pleased for Finn or embarrassed is beyond saying, but either way it is none of his business. "You old dog."

"I reckon."

"This calls for a little something." Reaching for a bottle.

"Long as it's on you." He has not had a taste of the bottled merchandise since the Judge threw him out and ruined his financial prospects.

"It is," says Dixon. "It's on me for sure."

"Just a small one then." Knowing that a small one is all he will get as long as Dixon's eagle-eyed wife is in the kitchen. "You having some?"

"Not while I'm working."

"Then let me have yours too."

"I can't."

"I know it." But it was worth a try.

Dixon sets down the bottle and goes to the kitchen. One of the card-players, McGill by name, passes by on his way to the jakes and observes Finn with a bottle at his elbow instead of the customary jug. "What's the occasion?" His clothing has a scoured-clean look to it and his hair is greased back with a pomade that Finn can smell from where he sits.

"Ain't no occasion." He does not know whether to ignore the bottle or to help himself as if nothing has changed, so he does neither.

"You certain." The dandy cocks his head.

"I am."

"I was thinking maybe you come into some money."

"I wish I did."

Indicating the card game. "We could use another."

"I'd spend it on whiskey before I'd throw it away."

"Just being neighborly," says McGill, looking a little crestfallen over how the indicator of this riverman's improved finances has misled him.

Dixon returns to the bar to find the two conversing like old conspirators and he asks if McGill has heard the news.

"Way I hear it there ain't none."

"You heard wrong." Without thinking and surely without seeing the look by which Finn means to silence him. "Finn here's going to be a pappy."

"Well now," says McGill, who knows the same truths as everyone. "Under those circumstances I believe I'd get drunk too."

Finn removes one foot from the barstool and braces it upon the floor. "You be careful."

"I'm just saying."

"I know what you're saying."

"Just saying what I'd do."

"You mean the woman."

"I prefer the free and easy life."

"You mean the woman."

"She's no concern of mine."

"I know she ain't." Considering that McGill seems to have withdrawn his objection or perhaps not even to have stated it specifically in the first place, Finn returns to his less coiled position on the barstool and helps himself to an additional dose of the bottled whiskey with no threat of interference from Dixon.

"There's alternatives," says the dandy as he turns to continue on his way to the jakes. "There's always alternatives."

"I reckon you'd know." Finn rises and reaches out to take McGill by the collar. The man is two thirds his size and he arrests him without effort. "You and your free and easy ways."

Dixon restores the whiskey bottle to its place behind the bar and advises the pair of them to head outside if they have differences in need of settling. "Go on now, you two."

"I like it fine right here," says Finn.

"I'll not have it."

"You brung it on."

Which Dixon does not dispute.

"I didn't mean nothing," says McGill.

"So you say."

"Honest."

"Next time you don't mean nothing, maybe you oughtn't say nothing."

"I won't."

Before he lets him go Finn gives him a shake hard enough to rattle his teeth, like a lioness toying one last time with some ravaged carcass. McGill goes off leaving his cards and his money on the table and he will not come back for them this night.

"I'm proud of you, Finn." Dixon, mopping the bar.

"I figure I ought to get in the habit." Which is easy enough to say while the child is still mere potential.

"You ought."

Finn nurses his jug whiskey and looks over at the card game, which shows no sign of breaking up. He puts down his glass and goes in three steps to McGill's empty seat and pockets the coins left stacked before it upon the table. Then with a drunkard's rough disdain he pushes the man's abandoned cards back toward the dealer. "Go on shuffle these back in if you've a mind to. I believe he's finished."

———

THE BOY EMERGES squalling from his mother's womb as do all children regardless of parentage: dark with contorted rage and the bare willful containment of his own pulsing lively fluids, adrip with blood like some wrathful demon plucked from hell. His mother gives him his name, perhaps in anticipation of a dusky quality of skin that to his good fortune never quite returns after the first fading bluish-purple blush of his entry into this world.

Huckleberry.

It is a poor name for a boy but then she is poor in judgment, hardly past childhood herself, and the father is more interested in celebrating the boy's pale skin than in helping her choose. It is a name doomed to suggest not only the boy's curse but the raw pure accident of his creation and the unstraightened path down which he must tread. It is a name that bespeaks the simplest and most natural of freedoms, given at birth to a boy whose accursed birthright may prove to admit none.

His father pays the midwife with a bundle of fish and they resume their life as if nothing has changed. In a few days Will sends a note that his brother cannot read but Mary can. Its contents are not entirely congratulatory but more in the line of acknowledgment and advice.

"I reckon word gets around."

"Be glad he thought."

"People got no right to talk."

"Now Finn."

"They don't."

"You can't stop them."

"I'd like to."

"You can't stop them all." Taking the child to her breast.

"I know it."

In the back of his mind is the individual to whom no one speaks other than the variously accused and the constitution of the State of Illinois and under certain circumstances Almighty God Himself. No doubt the Judge will have heard of the child nonetheless. Possibly he has foreseen his coming for months. Finn looks at the boy and his mother nestled together content upon the horsehair couch and he half wishes that the Judge could see his circumstances now if only to condemn his behavior even more stridently than has previously been his habit. The woman and the child are a strange and cumbrous burden but they are a burden his alone, and he believes them thus deserving of acknowledgment.

———

WILL REMAINS CHILDLESS and unwed, and so Finn is the only one of the pair to have engaged in the continuation of any sort of family life however attenuated or odd. It is as if Will has decided that the Judge's lineage shall descend this far and no farther, or as if by agreeing to handle his father's financial affairs he has given himself over to the preservation of a dynasty long dead and thus finds himself with no spirit remaining for the pursuit of any living future.

"And how are you today, Mr. Finn?" asks the waitress at the Adams Hotel, a tall slender woman of middle age whose name Will has never made a point of catching.

"Quite well, thank you." He waits for her to finish filling his water glass and then waits another moment or two before reaching out for it and lifting it to his lips so as not to seem overeager. He dines alone as usual. Others in his line of work have never dared associate with him, some because they fear seeming to cultivate his friendship so as to influence the Judge, and others—those who know the Judge better—because they know that they would gain no benefit from bothering and might even come to suffer for it. And so he has become a highly esteemed pariah.

The waitress observes no such boundaries. On the contrary, over the years his solitariness has persuaded her that he must be more in need of human contact than her other patrons. Although it pains Will to accept her unbidden daily attentions he nonetheless persists in lunching here, for the Adams is directly across the street from his office and the food is both familiar and plentiful.

"That brother of yours," she says with a rueful shake of her head. He is seated at his usual table in the corner near the dead fireplace and far from the other customers, and she adopts for the occasion of their interchange a hushed kind of exasperated cluck.

Will looks helplessly at her over the menu.

"I suppose it's not my place."

"No." Yet he maintains a thoroughly professional smile that she mistakes for something else.

"But you'd think."

"You would." He orders the fried chicken, which he settles upon every day after a thoughtful examination of the entire menu.

"I suppose it happens in even the best of families." She tips her head just a hair's breadth toward the busman, a sepulchral octoroon known only as Lovett, whose grandfather was rumored to have been not only a wealthy Virginia planter but a hero of the Revolution.

"Even the best." Unfolding his napkin. "Which I am not suggesting mine has ever been."

"Oh come."

"Please."

She has no trouble detecting his embarrassment but blames it upon her forthrightness with respect to his lineage.

"If you don't mind," he goes on, aligning the silver upon each side of his plate, "I'm not entirely comfortable."

"Of course." Very nearly reaching out to touch his shoulder as she would any other individual this familiar to her and managing at the last instant to stop herself. "Forgive me."

"I do."

"These things."

"Yes."

Weeks pass before the Judge makes mention of the child to Will and then only in a fiduciary context. They are sitting together in his dim study surrounded by lawbooks and dust, the Judge himself with his black frock coat hung upon a peg but Will still dressed as formally as if he were trying some case before him. The room is close and sultry and dust motes dance in the light that slices in through the drawn shutters. The Judge holds his great noble head such that two stripes of blinding light cut across it from left to right, one upon his broad wrinkled forehead and one across his upper lip, where it illuminates a neat mustache long gone gray. They have finished reviewing his bank accounts and his investments in various stock exchanges and his positions vis-à-vis certain farmers and miners whose fortunes have lately suffered. He closes the ledger and squares it upon the desk before him and gives his son no word of thanks.

"Have you given any thought," he says, "to addressing our complication?"

Will grasps the subject immediately, and for just an instant he mistakes the question for a sign of his father's awkward and long-delayed entry into some kind of good-heartedness. He wonders if perhaps the Judge actually intends to make provision for his brother's bastard child, if only to keep him at arm's length. So much time has passed since Will has heard his father consider engaging anyone in this way—it has been his entire lifetime really, and then some—that he wonders if perhaps the man has somehow managed to soften without his noticing. He blames himself. Yet he makes only the most cautious and noncommittal answer. "How so?"

"The will. You've checked it."

"No."

"It's in your files."

"I know."

"We had not prepared for this."

"For the *child*."

The Judge wrinkles his brow in irritation but he does not dignify the creature by granting him a naming even this impersonal, not even within his own mind. "Yes."

"He'll get nothing."

"Who."

"My brother. And through him the boy." Still testing the waters.

"You're certain."

"Yes."

"You've checked."

"I know it."

The Judge ruminates. "Then alter the papers. He shall receive one dollar. One dollar exactly."

"Which?"

"*Your brother.*" His eyes flare behind his reading glasses. "I'd not name that other creature in any writing of mine."

"Of course not."

The Judge goes on. "See to it that your brother receives one dollar, so that he'll have no cause for complaint. I'll not have him claiming that I forgot him altogether. I'll not have him accusing me of an oversight. I'll not have him dragging down my good name in the interest of whiskey and his nigger whore and that infernal offspring of theirs."

"Thy will be done," says Will, for this is a formula that never fails to provide the Judge a certain measure of delight—even though he is forever at pains to conceal it.

12

THE BOY GROWS STURDY and takes after his father from the start. Anyone can see it. And although Finn never intends to enjoy such moments as they spend together he catches himself taking pleasure in them nonetheless, for even in the cradle his son is so full of mischief that looking at him is like looking into a mirror capable of reflecting the past. When the child is yet in diapers he wants to take him aboard the skiff to have his company while he runs the lines. Mary tries to dissuade him, not because she mistrusts his ability to keep the child safe from harm but because she knows too well his lackadaisical habits of sanitation. Nonetheless he prevails and does as he wishes, making a show of striding down the back stairs with one arm full of linens and the other full of boy, although once he has gone out of her sight beneath the house where the skiff is tied up to a piling he follows his own inclination and leaves the linens on a rock and climbs aboard with the boy flung over his shoulder like a floursack. And when inevitably he shits he rinses him off in the river, a proceeding that brings unstopped joy to father and son alike.

Such is the child's baptism, and by such means does his father claim him for his own. He places no demand upon the boy as he grows save that he pull his own weight, and so the river and the tavern and the trading post become his classrooms. From his mother the boy learns different lessons entirely: songs inherited from her father and her father's father before him all the way back to Africa, poetry memorized under the pathetically hopeful tutelage of Mrs. Fisk, mysterious folk wisdom passed down from the circle of women who have woven from their tangled skeins of belief and superstition her particular history.

From her, Huck learns how to divine the future from the hairballs of cats and oxen and how to circumvent curses by means of stump water and moonlight. He listens wide-eyed and his father listens too, although he feigns some other occupation all the while, either repairing lines or drinking whiskey, thinking as he listens that from this mingled trove of the primitive and the poetic he might likewise acquire some knowledge worth possessing.

The child, perhaps five or six years old now, sits with him in Dixon's place drinking a glass of milk and watching the other men play cards, and although he longs to ask if he may join in he does not. In this way, in a world populated by none such as himself, he learns his place.

"That your boy," a cardplayer known to Finn either asks or states.

"It is."

The cardplayer has approached the bar to refresh the ale he's been drinking and has put down upon the damp wood an oversize portion of his winnings. He is in a generous mood and so he offers to stand Finn to his next round. "Assuming there'll be one."

"There will be."

He nods to Dixon who nods back, refilling his glass. "And how about something for the boy."

"He's got his."

Huck sits with his milkglass clutched in both dirty hands and looks up at the cardplayer as if nothing in all the world, neither wealth nor plaything nor talisman, could make him any happier than he is at this moment.

"Time comes to put away childish things." Taking up his drink.

"Time ain't come yet."

"Let him try."

"I ain't ungrateful, but."

"Not even a black and tan? Dix, help the boy to a black and tan." The cardplayer hoists his glass and winks at Huck. "May as well get used to it, son."

Finn coils. "He ain't your son."

"I'd not have him. But that don't mean I can't be gentlemanly to his kind."

Finn rises like weather and steps around Huck with one hand graz-
ing his small shoulder in an instant's offhand tenderness, and with his
greater bulk he moves to pin the cardplayer against the bar. The other
falls backward and drops his glass which shatters spilling ale upon hardwood and piled coin alike. Amid the wreckage the thick bottom of the
glass remains intact with its remnant jagged rim and Finn's hand falls
upon it in a black rage. "I'll teach you to talk."

Behind the bar Dixon dares neither arrest Finn nor speak up in defense of the cardplayer or even of basic civility so he comes around and
takes the boy and puts his milk on the bar, and removes him to the
kitchen while his father attends to the defense of either his boy or himself or some other.

The cardplayers at the table turn as one and for a moment they believe that the activity under way at the bar is merely the usual. Which of
their number first spies the glint of that bit of glass cannot be said and
will become a point of prideful contention in the years to come, but
glint it does in the light of the lamps behind the bar and the candles on
the tables, and as they watch transfixed Finn raises its sharp jagged circular end to their fellow's blasphemous mouth. He twists it and blood
bubbles up black from around its perimeter and although the man dares
not scream or even breathe the other cardplayers fall upon his assailant
and drag him to the plank floor. One of them will remember bringing
his boot-heel down upon Finn's wrist and thereby knocking free his
makeshift weapon. Another will recall kicking the ugly gleaming
bloodstained thing off into the darkness beneath a table, where a third
will remember trying to find it for use on Finn himself but to no avail.
In the end they subdue him with their fists and the task requires all of
them even in his state or perhaps because of it.

Two of them help the cut man down the steps and up the hill to
where the doctor lies dreaming of a place where incidents such as this
do not happen. Finn sleeps off his injuries and alcohol on the floor and
his boy gets a pallet in the corner of the room behind Dixon's kitchen.
Come morning they head home to find Mary frantic with worry, but
after one look at Finn she knows better than to complain or demand
reason. He will tell her when he is ready, later on in the day once the boy

has gone off somewhere, and when he does she will not know whether to respond with satisfaction or with alarm.

———

HE IS ASLEEP in the skiff when the marshal comes to arrest him. The marshal, a boneyard of a man in loose gabardines whose deputy sits by his side brandishing a pistol, looks no more equipped to wrestle Finn into compliance with the tenets of civilization than to outswim an alligator gar, but the deputy with the weapon provides all the authority he requires. They bump Finn's boat with the bow of theirs and rouse him up.

"How I hear it," the marshal says, lazily leaning against his pole, "that feller may not talk again."

"He'd be smarter not to."

"Now Finn."

He has not seen the interior of the jailhouse previously and so he knows not what to expect. The marshal leads him down a gray hallway and locks him behind iron bars and advises him that he may smoke if he likes provided he has makings. His lawyer will be along presently.

Will.

"You look like hell," he says when he arrives.

"I feel it," says Finn.

The marshal has given Will the key on a great iron ring and he admits himself to his brother's cell and takes a seat on the hard bed. "You know what you've done."

"I reckon."

"He may never talk again."

"That would suit me."

"You ought to keep your voice down."

"If you say so."

Will clears his throat and tugs at the knees of his trousers to preserve their crease. "I hear he had some words to say about the boy."

"He did."

"You didn't like them."

"No."

"This can't go on."

"I know it."

Will sits silent for a moment and draws a deep breath to remind himself of the reason he is here with his brother in this prison cell and not merely consorting with him in some spot less full of portent. "This is going to be terribly serious."

"How serious?"

"It depends on the prosecutor."

"They all know the Judge."

"I would advise you to take no comfort in that."

He does not, but he has other ideas for his defense. "Look what they did to me." Indicating his raw face.

"That came later."

"So they say."

"The chronology is plain enough."

"They were drunk, the lot of them."

"Those men won't be on trial."

"So put them."

"I can't."

"Then go after them on the stand."

"You leave the law to me."

"I'd like to."

Three days pass before he sees the courtroom. Mary and the boy visit him twice, and upon each occasion he is so pained by the thought of their witnessing him in his caged state that he insists they leave. On the third day they come not at all, or at least not in time.

"Which judge you suppose?" Finn inquires of the marshal as he leads him out, for he knows them all at least by name and reputation.

"Can't say."

"You don't know or you can't say."

"I can't say, on account of I don't know."

The marshal plants him in a chair within a small chamber containing a high bench and several rows of empty seats and then stands behind him waiting. Neither of them speaks for the longest time until at last the door behind the bench opens and out steps the Judge.

He speaks first to the marshal. "You may go."

"I believe it's my duty."

"Not today."

"But."

"I can handle this."

"Yes sir." Leaving Finn hard up against his own father for the first time since that day when the Judge broke down the cabin door and turned him out.

"Properly speaking, I ought to have recused myself."

"I know it," says Finn, and know it he does, for he did not come of age in that white mansion belonging to his father for no reason.

"It's a matter of conscience, though. As I see it, so long as I am of the belief that I am capable of executing my duties in a fair and impartial manner, I shall proceed."

"Are you sure."

"You don't need to ask." Studying a paper before him. "You have no right to ask, come to that."

"Where's Will?"

"He'll be along."

"Where's the prosecutor?"

"He'll not be needed."

At which idea Finn's spirits rise unaccountably.

"I've already spoken with him at some length, and although we are not precisely of the same mind on all points he has seen fit to yield to my greater wisdom." He speaks to his son as to a child, flashes a brief and reflexive smile, and bows his head to his paper again.

"I understand."

"You do."

"Yes sir."

"Then you understand why you'll be spending the next twelve months in the state penitentiary at Alton." Without so much as looking up.

"Where's Will."

"He'll be along."

"I'll appeal."

"You'll get nowhere."

"This ain't right."

"I shouldn't think that you would be a trustworthy judge of right and wrong." He deigns at last to lift his eyes unto his son.

"You know it ain't right."

"I know you need to be taught a lesson."

"Where's Will."

"He'll be along."

"When."

"Be patient."

Finn sits plaintless for a moment as if compliance will do him the slightest good. His bruised face pains him still and the beaten muscles of his arms and shoulders and chest are sore but he touches them not lest he be judged even more severely than he has.

"That's better," says his father, just as sweet as pie. "You're learning already." He adjusts his reading glasses and tilts his massive head back and draws out a pen with which he signs some lengthy document to which his prisoner is not privy. While he blots up the ink Will enters and stands between the two of them wearing upon his face a look of resignation.

"This ain't been much of a trial." Finn to his attorney.

"I suppose not."

"You have no idea," says the Judge. He motions to Will, who approaches the bench and takes the pen from him and signs.

"While I'm gone," Finn hazards to his brother's back, "what's to become of."

"I'd counsel you to travel no further down that line of reasoning in my presence," says the Judge.

"They're my concern."

"They're none of mine. Should those creatures go feral and starve, then perhaps their deaths will teach you the full wages of your sin. It might be the best thing for you."

"Father," says Will.

"Your brother has always been recalcitrant. He has always been willful. He has always, dare I say it, been perverse in the extreme."

"Cruelty is no."

"Hush. I'll cite you for contempt."

Will retreats.

"He has gone his own way without regard for decency or history or God's will, or even for the merest wishes of those who gave him birth. He is by nature cross-grained and rebellious, and the longer he has lived upon this earth the more devoted to these traits he has grown. The time has come at last for him to be reformed whether he likes it or not, for I shall tolerate his ways no more." He pauses to draw breath. "If that qualifies as cruelty, then so help me God I stand abidingly unrepentant and guilty as charged."

"As you see fit," says Will.

If he is to be sent to prison Finn desires to be done with it, and he desires in any event for his father not to think that he cares. "Do I leave right off?"

"In the morning."

"That suits me fine."

"Good. And may you return a changed man."

"I can't say about that."

"God knows I have asked little enough of you."

"I know it," says Finn.

———

BECAUSE THE JUDGE has sequestered himself in his study, Will dares collect Mary and the boy to say their goodbyes. If he should fail his brother again in even this insignificant duty he is certain that he could not live with himself, so he borrows the wagon and the matched Arabians from the Judge's barn and fetches mother and child back up the hill to the jailhouse. The boy takes no end of pleasure in the ride, which cheers Will some, but the woman collapses on the box wordless and woeful.

"Neighborly of you," says Finn from his cage. His tone when he speaks has a kind of resigned gratitude, as if he has recently made a vow to savor such decency as he can witness while he yet tarries in this world.

Will opens the cell door to admit them and locks it again behind, and then absents himself to the marshal's office, where he waits.

"How much he tell you?" Rather than tell it again himself.

"That you're going to the penitentiary," she says. "For a year."

"I reckon that'd cover it."

"A year."

Finn nods.

"Seems like forever."

"It's supposed to."

"I'll wait for you."

"You don't have to. I'd not blame you if."

"But I will."

"I know it."

"And we'll come visit you."

"I don't know they allow it."

"We'll come anyhow."

"It's a ways."

"Not that far."

"You'll be busy. With the boy and all."

"I know it."

In the end she does not come at all and he does not blame her because he understands the reasons. Her heart breaks over not doing it more than his does over her failure.

—

THE PENITENTIARY AT ALTON is the state's original and Finn is among its earliest inmates. A low stone fortress asquat by the Mississippi, it houses but twenty-four prisoners and admits into their presence nearly no air and less sunlight. He has inhabited worse places than this and he surely will again. At Alton the prisoners wear uniforms with alternating stripes of black and white, and each man's head is shaven on one side lest he escape and attempt to enter society by stealth. The prison hires them out to work in the fields, and on these long summer days out of doors Finn can smell the river, which makes him long for home more than usual.

The other inmates are murderers mainly, which gives him neither comfort nor inspiration. He aspires only to return home and reunite with Mary and the boy, and to this end he keeps his nose clean and indicates the passing of the days by scratching marks into the wall alongside his bed although their array soon grows beyond his counting. The warden has imposed a vow of silence upon the inhabitants of his fiefdom, which does not bother Finn in the least. From time to time he gets a letter from Mary, which he struggles to decipher, and deep in the silence of the prison he believes that if only he could read its sentences more perfectly he would hear her very voice speaking them aloud within his mind as if by magic or miracle.

Whenever he can get out into the daylight he relishes it despite such labor as he has been assigned, and in the winter when the prisoners' work schedule is sporadic and the pale sun leaks down into their frigid stone bunker through high windows as narrow as gunslits he remembers the river and the woman and the child and he dreams of them all alike. Snow falls sometimes from that great windowed height onto the black-and-white shoulders and the half-shaven heads of the prisoners, and once during the winter Will comes by to visit but his brother denies him entry for denial is the only power he yet retains.

———

ON THE SUMMER DAY that he leaves Alton for good the barber shaves his head entire. Thus restored he steps forth from the prison door in his own clothes, ill-fitting now for Alton's food has been even poorer than that to which he has previously accustomed himself, and follows his instincts straight to the riverside. Children spy him marching hatless along and can tell that he is recently released by the two colors of his scalp, burnished brown on the one side and pale as a fish belly on the other. Beyond this visible bifurcation and a redoubled urge to take up his former life he is apparently unchanged.

At the river's edge he seeks transportation upstream to Lasseter, but opportunities are few and he finds no willing souls. The few rivermen he meets take him for a murderer most likely unreformed and they desire nothing to do with him or any other such risky cargo. Upstream he walks along the mudflats past green islands and snags and shallows, past children playing hooky and rivermen running their lines, until he comes to a spot where a few battered skiffs are tied up to a post and to one another and there above the river he spies a place not much different from Dixon's. With a dollar that Will left for his release burning a hole in his pocket he climbs the stairs.

"So what'd you do?" says the man behind the bar.

Finn has had plenty of time to reflect upon this question, but on account of the vow of silence prevailing at Alton he has had during the entire year's passage no opportunity to answer it aloud.

"I run afoul of the authorities," is what he says.

"Next time," says the barman, "don't get caught."

"Easier said than done." His voice has gone a little creaky from disuse but the barman takes pity upon him and starts him off with a decent whiskey on the house. Finn has missed the drink more than he reckoned and he fishes out his dollar and places it upon the bar.

"Got folks waiting at home?"

"I reckon so."

"And nobody come to get you. Ain't that the way it goes."

"I got a brother would have tried."

"What put him off."

"I did. He ain't no use to me."

"Any man who'll provide passage home is of use."

"I can provide my own." Pushing the glass forward for more whiskey.

When the dollar is gone he descends the stairs and helps himself to a skiff and poles upstream. Someone shouts down from the bar but too late and they know neither his name nor his destination. He keeps his head low lest there be gunfire and stays to the shallows, thrusting with the pole and feeling strong and a good bit drunk and happy to be out upon the river again.

———

WHEN THE NIGHT GROWS too dark for navigation he ties up and sleeps beneath the cover of an overarching willow. In the morning he plunges his face into the water and wishes he had not parted with his dollar so rashly, and then he leaves the skiff tied where it is and sets out upon a path leading inland to a cabin. He detects the smell of breakfast from the place long before he sees it, biscuits and fatback bacon and coffee too. A woman of his age or perhaps a little less is alone in the kitchen.

"Take what you want," she says to him when he comes to stand in supplication at the door, for she can see the hunger in his spare frame and the strangeness written upon his face.

"I'd be obliged."

"If they ask, I ain't seen you."

"They won't."

"They've asked before."

"Not about me they won't." He takes from his pocket his release papers and flattens them upon the table. Between the two of them they have sufficient reading to confirm his freedom, and she gets another plate from the cupboard and invites him to sit if he will.

"I believe I could set here just about forever," he says in a moment of candid relief and gratitude, for he realizes that under certain circumstances he just might. She does not ask him his crime nor inquire as to his destination and he admires the curve of her throat as he helps himself to her provisions.

After breakfast they adjourn to a pair of chairs upon the porch and she tells him of her husband gone these many years. The woman's voice soothes him after his months in the harsh silence of Alton and makes him wonder how far it is back upstream to where he belongs, and she tells him exactly how far it is then asks what's his hurry. For he has told her nothing about himself.

"Folks waiting."

"They know you got out?"

"I don't reckon."

"Someone would've come for you."

"It ain't that easy." He sits and studies the woods and thinks of the river, imagining its southward flowing and picturing overlaid upon it his own unfinished journey north. "Besides, they know I can look out for myself."

"They can count on you."

"I reckon."

He splits a pile of wood in exchange for her kindness and then drinks a dipper of cool water from her well, and as he prepares to go he catches her looking at him despite his shaven head and his particolored skin in a manner suggestive of certain possibilities that he has already rejected. If he were in possession of his old slouch hat he would tip it as he leaves but he goes on his way in the absence of such niceties, back to the river and the skiff and his long day's journey upstream, penniless and indelibly marked but heading for home.

———

AT THE OVERHANGING frame house he steps into his own captive skiff from out of the one he has poled all this distance, leaving the borrowed one to find its way back downstream however it might. Thus is one more displaced wanderer set free in this time of transformation.

He climbs the stairs in the dark and admits himself without knocking, whereupon she greets him with the gun as she would greet some common criminal. She very nearly fires to see him there in the doorframe with his shaven two-colored skull, imagining him some odd tattooed fugitive from the carnival recently passed through town and now returned to work mischief, but at the last second he takes the gun from her hands and speaks her name in the softest whisper so as not to awaken the boy.

"Mary," he says. "I come home."

She throws herself upon him and he drops the gun in his startlement but the clatter does not begin to rouse the boy, who sleeps out on the porch over the river as upon his own mother's breast. They take themselves to the bedroom upstairs where every particle of her body returns to his consciousness inch by inch, replacing the dull repetitive textures of Alton with the thrill of her life and her liveliness, and although when they are finished she would rather talk than sleep he is too hungry to do either for long. There are biscuits in the breadbox and she brings him a plate.

"I missed you."

"I missed you. And them biscuits."

"I'll make another batch come morning."

"Make two or three."

"I will."

"While you're at it."

"I don't mind."

He holds up the last of them into the moonlight and riverlight and studies it as if it is some fetish or source of wonder. "How'd you get by all this time?" Thinking of Will, and of whether his brother may have worked to redeem himself while he was gone.

"I wrote you how kind people have been."

"I know it."

"I mean I don't have family, but."

"Neither do I."

"But you'd swear I did."

"We'll make it up to them, every one."

She sits at the end of the bed and smiles upon him as if he is a dear child who has come to her with a notion ten times as big as he is but entirely too lovely for deflating just yet.

When morning comes he stands on the porch studying the steaming water and watching the slow early-morning traffic float past his high place like a procession in a dream, while the boy sleeps at his feet upon a pallet of corn husks. His sleeping place looks more the dwelling of a muskrat than a human child, but the boy curled there upon it smiles a smile so unconscious and beatific as to befit an angel. In repose he is the same Huck.

Finn leaves him there and goes down to see about his lines, which some samaritan has coiled up and hung on nails beneath the house to keep them safe from the weather in his absence. He locates a good deal of rot which he cuts away and mends, and some of the hooks are broken off and rusted through which he can do nothing about just yet, but in the end these raw makings yield two lines for every three original and he trusts that this will be sufficient for now. The shallows are agleam with silvery minnows just as he recalls, and he catches a netful for a place to begin again.

The skiff needs patching. He can see that the boy has been working to keep it bailed, for it is only half sunk when he sets foot in it, and he figures that he ought to find a little pitch later on when he has the chance and show him how it's done now that he's big enough. Between the bailing bucket and the lines he is busy out upon the water, so busy that he does not look back up at the house until he has drifted some distance and there upon the porch, with his straw hat askew and his hands upon the railing, stands the boy. He is even taller than his father would have imagined possible, now that he is awake and upright. They meet beneath the house, the child paying no mind to his father's strange appearance, and since there is nothing to do about the lines now but wait they join hands and return upstairs to Mary as one.

13

Finn knows the woman's shack by its location and by its stove-in door and by the line strung across the alley upon which hangs drying a batch of sheets and pillowcases from the Adams Hotel. Working silent as some bereft spirit in his own empty house above the river he has gathered together his washing—a ratty woolen blanket, two pairs of socks that he won't have use for until winter, and such else as he can make do without for a time—and he has bundled them all up and brought them here to this place as offering or bait or some other. The laundress, whom he has seen both in town and in her farthest extremity, struggles to swing the door open on hinges that she has thus far lacked the means to repair. Someone has run a bit of rawhide through the broken part of the upper and hammered the lower almost straight, but the door is still not right and looks to remain thus. Between the ragged bundle in his arms and the air of trepidation on his face she takes her visitor for an itinerant, and although she would wish it otherwise she has nothing to offer him and says so.

"No ma'am. I got laundry." Offering it up.

She considers the bundle and the figure carrying it and although she is poor beyond knowing and could make use of whatever he might desire to pay she wants nothing to do with either one. "I don't do much," she says. "Just the hotel, mainly."

"I sure could use the help."

"I know it, but."

"I'm all alone in this world."

"I understand." For she of all people does.

The look that he gives her is so laden with beseeching that her heart nearly breaks and she realizes that she cannot bear to turn such a one from her door. She takes to herself the bundle and names a price, which he calculates in forty-rod whiskey and agrees to. He asks when.

"I'll need two days at least. Maybe three."

"Don't hurry on my account."

"I won't."

"You around most times?"

"Same time as this in three days, if that suits you."

"It does."

"Fine then."

"I'll be obliged." He hates saying it to a person of her color, but he reckons it can do no harm this once.

———

FINN RETURNS to the mansion at the top of the hill and lets himself in this time without the assistance of the hired man's wife. He is in the kitchen scavenging through the cupboards like some sneak thief or stray starveling beast when she comes upon him, and although she has seen him infrequently enough until that recent prior visit one daunting glare from beneath those shaggy brows and she identifies him as the Judge's son all right and none other. She leaves him alone to do as he pleases.

Fortified with coffee and a slice of pie consumed over the sink he mops his face and beard with a sleeve and proceeds down the back hallway to the Judge's study. The door is closed as it has always been. Even with no living creature in the house other than his own cowed wife and the timid ghost of the hired man's woman, the Judge requires for himself isolation or at least confinement.

Finn knocks at the door and there is no answer.

Within, the Judge assesses the tonality of the knock and evaluates the silence that went before it and chooses to hold his ground.

"Pap." Finn, with his lips to the door.

Nothing.

"I seen your carriage in the barn."

Nothing. Nothing beyond perhaps the merest whistling breath of an old man, which the son detects as he would detect the twitch of a cornered rabbit's eyelid or the slow rhythmic underwater pulsing of a carp's fin.

"Pap."

"Don't think I'm hiding from the likes of you." Lifting his voice to be heard through the door.

"I don't."

"You're not welcome here."

"I know I ain't."

"Neither in my house nor in my study."

"I know it."

"Nor anywhere upon these premises."

"I broke it off with that woman." Daring to unlatch the door, which for all its constant closure is nonetheless unlocked.

"You'll find another." As if he knows.

"I won't." He stands back and lets light spill in from the hallway to his father's dark precincts, where it gleams muted against picture frames and polished hardwood and gold-stamped leather bindings all thick with dust.

"You probably already have." There behind his massive oaken desk the Judge is as broad as he ever was, smaller perhaps by a shade than his son remembers but no less fierce for the bow of his back and the slope of his shoulders. The light of a single oil lamp illuminates his collapsed visage from below and casts shadows that creep upward along the creases and protuberances of his face and then merge together into one great blackness above the line of his heavy brow, giving him in this small space the ghastly judgmental aspect that he possessed in even the brightest of daylight for those hundreds of poor damned miscreants who passed before his bench during his prime. "No doubt you've *already* found yourself another nigger bitch," he continues, proud of himself and of his wisdom, "if I know you."

"I ain't done it." Then a pause. "Maybe you don't know me like you think."

"I know you better than you know yourself." He uncurls two fingers from around the corner of the lawbook he's been studying and uses them to wave his son off as he would shoo a fly.

"Maybe not."

"Go," says the Judge. "You and your ridiculous claims are dismissed. Your presence here is neither required nor tolerated."

"I know it. But if I've changed."

"Even if you have, I shall be ten lifetimes forgiving you."

"But."

The Judge tilts his head back and his eyes vanish into the shadowy reaches above the lamplight. "In the meantime," he says, "you are at liberty to wait for that day in some more hospitable location."

"A man can only do so much."

"Do as you wish, but you'll get nothing for your troubles from me."

"I ain't asking for money." Thinking of his boy's six thousand.

"Good. For you'll get from me neither funds nor forgiveness nor any other sort of gratification."

"I know it," says Finn. "I know it now."

His mother has been drawn downstairs by the murmur of their two voices and she awaits him in the kitchen. She has poured him coffee and drawn him a glass of cool water from the well, not knowing which he will prefer or guessing that in the end he will want neither.

"You told him." Her mouth drawn up into a little incipient smile in spite of the evidence written large upon her son's face.

"I see why you wouldn't bother."

"It's not that."

"You knew he wouldn't change his mind."

"I thought maybe if you'd."

"You said he had faith in me."

"I had faith in the both of you." Lifting the coffee, an offering.

"Only one of us deserved it."

"I didn't mean any harm." For who truly means harm in all this world.

———

RAIN COMES EARLY on the second day and settles in, and he crouches in his skiff to run the lines and then lets the little boat find its own way downstream along the mudbanks of darktown, where under better weather he would expect to see his blanket and the rest of it drying upon her line. He thanks God that he can produce an income fair weather or foul, then waits another day before returning on foot for his things, which he can hardly recognize when she presents them.

He shakes his head in wonderment and fishes in his pocket for a coin. "This is a help."

She stands in the open door holding up the laundry, tall and slim and elegant as some Egyptian statuary. He makes such a show of searching for his money that she suspects for a moment he might be intending not to pay at all, and even as this possibility comes dawning upon her she remains impassive for she has endured worse.

At last he yields it up, presenting it to her as if he has minted it himself.

"Thank you, mister."

"Finn."

"Mister Finn."

"Finn alone'll do."

"Thank you." Perhaps acknowledging his request and perhaps ignoring it.

"Folks around here used to know me." He tests the waters for some sign of the ill fame that his presence engendered in the period after he'd come back to Mary and Huck from his imprisonment at Alton.

"I don't." Shaking her head.

"Now you do," he says with a display of teeth.

"I reckon."

"Whyn't you see can your husband fix that door."

"He can't."

He gives the hinge a look of respectful puzzlement, as if it has somehow bested a better man than he, but he inquires no further as to the reason. "I could give it a try. It won't be no trouble."

"No. Thank you. But I'm obliged."

Nonetheless he returns in a day's time with a sack of tools purloined from the shed where old Bliss keeps such things, prepared to rectify at least this one wrong and earn thereby her gratitude. At the outset she looks upon him as if he has taken it upon himself to desecrate a holy shrine, but he seems so intent that she can find within herself no strength to resist. He removes the door entire and takes the hinges off and hammers them straight upon a rock. The bit of rawhide he discards upon locating the upper pin where it fell unseen on that awful night, in a crack between the floorboards and covered over with a scrap of rug. He refits the latch and with a plane and a file and a crosscut saw for which he can imagine Bliss having no earthly use he trims the rough splintered edges away from the door before rehanging it.

"That'll keep out the weather," he says. Swabbing his brow with the back of his forearm.

"It weren't the weather broke it."

"Is that so." Inviting her to tell more or nothing, howsoever she might desire.

Although every woman, child, and man in darktown knows the story, she can see that he does not. Such is the manner in which information, like water or blood, flows only where it is admitted and fills up only those places wherein it may be confined. Permit two white men to batter in a darktown door and steal a woman's child and murder her husband by means of a bullet through the neck, and from that night forward those two masked men or their simulacra shall be forever breaking down doorways into the dreams of every last mother and child in that forlorn place—while elsewhere their fame shall go unbespoken. The white children of Lasseter may have monsters of their own, but none of them are exactly these.

The sadness that creeps into her eyes Finn either does not notice or else takes for appreciation of his kind act.

" 'Tweren't nothing."

"Thank you," she says, perhaps the slightest bit late. "I'm obliged." The hand in her apron pocket clutches tight to the coin he gave her yesterday and he can see it hiding there just as he once saw a certain girl's hands thrust into her own apron pocket for other reasons altogether. Concealed things of this order are to him like fish lurking just beneath the surface of a placid river pool, endlessly fascinating and deeply desirable and capable of being read only by one who knows how to attend to their signs.

"How about we take it out in wash," he says.

"That'd be fine."

"Though it ain't necessary."

"It is."

"Fixing that door was my idea." He is gathering up the tools taken from Bliss and returning them one by one to his sack. "You never said you required it."

"But I did all the same. I required it."

"But you never said."

"I know."

"So it was my idea."

"I know it."

He finishes with the sack and ties it off and leans it against a log that marks the edge of the street, and then he makes himself comfortable on the ground alongside it. "Might you have a dipper of water handy?" Such is the least she can do.

14

T HE MORNING FOG has just begun to burn off the river when he returns from baiting his lines. As he draws closer a man appears on the steps beneath the house, the darkness of his form wavering and unresolved within the white density of the fog that still hangs palpable along the margin of the river and up into the dense riverbound trees and even beyond the trees up the slope thinning along streets of increasing prosperity until it surely gives out altogether near the place where the village reaches its height and the white mansion and the limestone courthouse stand side by side implacable. Finn steadies himself and narrows his vision to assess movement, desiring to know if the figure is going up the stairs or down or merely standing upon them in wait for someone, perhaps himself. The boy and the woman are still in bed so far as he knows.

The figure of the man moves not as Finn approaches in his skiff, and as they draw near the two of them eye one another like phantoms arrived from differing realms.

"Morning." By his voice alone Finn can discern the man's color.

"It's that." Wondering if this interloper has come to call upon Mary and for how long this kind of behavior might have been going on among these creatures whose ways are inscrutable to him despite the years.

"Them lines hold up?"

"I suppose." Perhaps the man has come to trade for fish, although now that they have come nearer together in the fog he can see nothing about him that would suggest preparedness for trade, neither bundle nor package nor jug. Which suits him fine for he would hate for this waterside place to become a nigger trading post on account of its location and his own untoward preferences in women.

"They was in the water a good while 'fore I hung them up."

"They spend a lot of time in the water."

"When you was in prison I mean."

"I know when you mean." Tying up and gathering his things and un-bending himself, yet seeming for all of his readiness incapable of ever coming entirely ashore—as if he is not a man at all but some yearning spirit bound to this place for remembrance or repudiation.

"A year's a long time," says the black man.

"I know it."

"I guess you ought to."

"Whyn't you go on home, boy."

"Name's George."

"That's fine."

"I just come to see about them lines."

"You thought I ought to know my benefactor."

"I thought."

"What else you done around here while I'm gone?" Finn has begun to move down the length of the boat toward the big black man.

"That's all I done."

"You certain."

"I am."

"Then I suppose I ought to be grateful for that too. Like I ought to be for them lines."

"I don't reckon." Stepping down from the stair and making as if to move off.

"You want gratitude, you can get it from her."

"I won't."

"That's a good idea."

Finn goes from under the house toward the open stairs and the samaritan George backs away from his path, stepping cautiously through the rough dry tangle of late-summer weeds and keeping the distance between them constant.

Above in the house the boy is asleep and she is adding wood to the stove. "Were you talking to somebody?" When he has come in and closed the door behind him.

"I was not."

"I thought I heard."

"It weren't nothing."

"So it *was* somebody then."

"A nigger."

"I see." She purses her lips and takes down a bowl of eggs from the shelf above the dry sink. "You fetch me that bacon, just a little for the pan?"

"You can fetch your own," he says, "if it ain't too much trouble." Then he goes out to the porch to sit resting his feet upon a corner of the boy's pallet and watching the river steam past until she has finished readying his breakfast.

"I expect the man had a name," she says when she brings his eggs and biscuits and coffee to the table.

"Let it go." Sitting and digging in with a kind of urgency. "He come around here looking for something I don't have."

"Manners, I might think." Distracted by the sight of the boy stretching himself awake on his pallet out on the porch, she says it half under her breath in the way she has acquired through no fault of her own during the past solitary year, more to herself or to no one at all than to him.

"How dare you."

"I didn't mean." With the beginnings of a dismissive look.

"You apologize."

"I didn't mean a thing."

"First that presumptuous old nigger meddles in my business, then you dare judge my manners."

"Which presumptuous old nigger would that be?" Angling to distract him and get her answer all at once.

"The one fooled with my lines."

"You mean George."

"That's the one."

"He doesn't mean any harm."

"He wants to keep out of my business if he knows what's good for him."

"He did what he thought was right."

The boy stands and yawns and approaches the table, where sits his father with his face twisted into a scowl and his particolored skull bent over his plate like the lowered head of some scavenger.

"He did what *was* right," his mother goes on.

"Don't you tell me." Without looking up.

She rises and fetches some biscuits for the child. "Without help from the likes of him, I don't know what we'd have done. Isn't that right, Huck?"

"Yes ma'am."

"You didn't take no charity." Without looking up from his plate.

"Share and share alike was more the nature of it."

"I couldn't abide you taking no charity. That ain't respectful of me. Nor of my wishes."

"You was in *jail,* Pap." From a mouth clogged with biscuit.

"I know it."

"So she done."

"I know what she done." Raising his head to cut the boy short and then looking from him to the woman and back again as if drawing a line between the two and then erasing it by an exercise of his solitary will.

———

HE AND THE BOY are on their haunches beneath the porch, gutting catfish and bluegills and looping their intricate gleaming viscera back into the water like pagan offerings, when she appears on the downward path among the weeds with a bundle of white laundry piled high upon her head. She proceeds like a goddess, erect and effortless and perfectly balanced, and Finn can see from the look of placid resignation upon her face that she has gone this way and its reverse a hundred times before under like burdens.

"What are you about?"

"My work. Laundry for the hotel."

"Your work is here."

She approaches the stair and reaches up with both hands and lowers the bundle down to rest it upon the third step. "My work has been taking care of that boy."

"You can't take care of him doing other men's laundry."

"And I can't feed him if I don't."

"Now you can."

"I couldn't while you were gone."

"I ain't gone no more."

"You never know." And with that she picks up the laundry and goes on up the stairs and into the house. She crosses to the stove and adds wood to the banked fire thinking of how she has done this for a year now—this fetching of the laundry and this splitting of the wood and this boiling of the water, this scrubbing of the linens and this drying of them upon the line and this meticulous pressing of them inch by inch with a three-pound iron heated red upon that selfsame stove—thinking of how she has done all this for a year now on behalf of herself and the boy, and of how she intends not to give it up for anyone who would dare threaten to take from her such independence as she has managed through devotion and determination to earn.

He leaves the boy to finish gutting their catch, and he climbs the stairs and enters in through the door to come stealthily up behind her and take her arm and whisper his rage into her ear. *I done it for him.*

"You did it because you couldn't help yourself."

"Why should I."

"And you did it because you'd had too much to drink."

"He wronged my boy."

"So you say."

"He did."

"Some would say he spoke the truth."

"That don't matter."

"I suppose not."

Strong in the belief that he has triumphed, Finn takes up a kingly position at the head of the table and watches her work for a moment and then returns to his previous concern and instructs her that this laundry is the last she will do for anyone but her own household.

"There's no disgrace in it." Not arguing, but merely stating something that seems to her a fact.

"Maybe not for you."

She does not ask for clarification but keeps her back to him and takes up some lye soap and a peeled branch that she uses for stirring the pot.

He waxes expansive nonetheless. "I reckon it comes natural to some, but I won't have none of mine washing sheets for white men to sleep on. I won't have a string of no-good white drummers and fancy white lawyers coming through this town sleeping on sheets you washed."

"There's no harm in it."

"It ain't right."

"It's an honest trade."

"Besides, you don't need to do it no more."

"The money's good."

"We'll get by. We always did."

"It would ease your burden."

"My burden don't need easing."

"Suit yourself."

Which he will. The only difficulty is that after a week or so, when her pay from the Adams Hotel has run out and they are left one and all to subsist again on such sustenance and trade as he and now the boy can draw forth from the river, a brief dalliance with high-quality bottled whiskey at Dixon's bar comes to its natural end and he returns dejected to his customary poisonous forty-rod. She has set aside a few dollars in a tobacco sack at the bottom of the sugar barrel but he does not know it, else he would have spent that too on drink.

"I can't give you no more credit," says Dixon early one evening when Finn has barely gotten started.

"You'll have my best cats tomorrow. Them nice little fiddlers, sweet as pie. I'll save every last one just for you."

"I'd be obliged."

"Then let's proceed." Finn fingers his glass toward Dixon along the bar.

"I'm afraid not."

The cardplayers at the long table quiet down to hear what comes next but Finn disappoints them all by merely looking slowly at Dixon from under his eyebrows.

"The missus thinks you're in a little deep," says Dixon.

"The missus does."

"That's right."

"And what do *you* think."

"I reckon she's correct."

"Tell me," Finn says. "How deep's too deep, exactly? I mean according to the missus."

Dixon pulls a ledger from beneath the bar and adds up some numbers and shows the total to Finn, who possesses enough mathematics to recognize generosity and disaster when he sees them tallied together into a single figure.

"That adds up to a passel of catfish."

"It does."

"Even them precious little sweet ones."

"Amen."

"I know when I'm licked." He pushes his stool away from the bar.

"I'm obliged," says Dixon.

"I appreciate your kindliness."

"Come back tomorrow with some of them sweet little fiddler cats, and we'll start to whittle it down."

"I will."

———

MORNING FINDS HIS SKIFF overburdened and alive with thrashing fish, as if some god has smiled down upon him and arranged for the richest of his bounty to surface hook after laden hook and fairly leap into his boat. He guts them and cuts reeds and binds them up damp for safekeeping, and he takes a few of them up the steps into Dixon's place.

"The world has conspired against me." He intones the words with a forlorn look as he drops his bundle on the bar and unwraps it to reveal two or three decent bluegills and a couple of fat sunfish.

"They ain't so bad."

"I don't reckon."

"You had me fooled."

"I didn't mean to."

"Got more in the boat? I'll come on down."

"Don't bother."

"It ain't no bother."

"This here's the lot."

Dixon gives him a look both incredulous and sympathetic.

"I know."

"This ain't going to make much of a dent."

"I know it. Do what you can."

"Better luck tomorrow."

Finn sorrowfully dons his broken slouch hat and descends the steps and unties his skiff. Before he poles away he removes his long coat and flings it wide and uses it to cover up his catch, or at least as much of it as he can, in case Dixon should happen to glance over the side and spy him as he heads downriver.

South of the village on the left descending bank, just a mile or two above St. Petersburg, he comes to a trading post. He hates coming all the way down here but he reckons that since he could give everything he has to Dixon and still be in the hole he ought to take the greater part of his bounty where it can be turned to profit free and clear. The proprietor of the trading post is a choleric old swindler named Smith, a gigantic slug of a man who gasps for air when he walks and coughs up yellow phlegm into a tin cup and hates Finn all the way down to the ground, but no more than he despises the rest of mankind. On his first day in business he painted his name in black on a bleached piling and hung a sign on the door reading CLOSED. He has neither improved nor altered either one of these indicators over the intervening years.

Finn ties up the skiff and selects some of the catfish and enters through the door marked CLOSED as he has done so many times previous. He takes off his hat and jams it underneath his arm and lays the bundle of reeds and fish upon the counter.

"What'd you do to your head?" says Smith from the shadows.

Finn has not forgotten his year in the penitentiary but he has let himself forget that his skull yet bears the evidence. He runs a hand over the stubble. "They done it to me at Alton."

"What'd you do?"

"I let them. Didn't have no choice."

"I mean to get sent."

"Killed a man wouldn't buy my catfish."

Smith laughs his gasping laugh. "I won't make that mistake." But Finn can see that he does not entirely mean it.

"So how much you think?"

"Is this the lot?" Eyeing them greedily but doing his best not to let it show.

"This ain't but the beginning."

"Somebody's had a good day."

"Don't you dare ruin it."

"I hate to."

"You won't." Finn takes Smith by the sleeve and pulls him from behind the counter and sets him on his breathless path to the door. From there they look over the side of his pier to the spot where the skiff is tied up below bearing its bounty of succulent cats barely concealed and cooled by their wet wrapping of reeds.

"Why, most of them's just fiddlers."

Listening to Smith breathe. "Folks like them better small."

"I know what folks like."

"They're sweeter."

"Don't tell me my trade." He hawks and spits into the river and turns to make his way back inside. "Them little fiddlers don't hardly weigh enough to charge for."

"You'd charge a man to breathe your air." Hollering after him through the open door.

"If I could."

"Them little ones are just as much trouble to catch."

"Not for me they ain't."

Back at the counter Smith names a price by the pound and says that although it pains him to do so he'll take the whole lot of them.

"That'll make my life easy now, won't it?" says Finn.

"I reckon."

Finn makes as if to begin looking around the trading post for his necessaries. "I'll wait here while you go on fetch them up."

"You will not." The mere walk to the pier and back has left his face ablaze and his bald head running with sweat. He collapses upon his stool and begins mopping at his brow with a muddy handkerchief.

"Suit yourself," says Finn. "But I might have to charge for cartage." And he returns to his skiff and sorts through the fish, leaving out most of the small ones and wrapping up the rest and bringing them up to Smith.

"I thought you had more."

"You were mistaken."

"They's not so many young ones as I thought." Calculating his loss by the pound.

"It's your lucky day."

"I reckon." Not knowing whether he has been bested or not, yet unable to walk out on the pier again and see what quantity of fish his visitor may or may not have left in his boat for more profitable sale elsewhere.

Finn takes Smith's money and spends some of it on things that Mary has requested and puts them in the skiff. He denies himself a bottle of whiskey this once because he has plans to take some of his earnings around to the old blind bootlegger and get a jug of poorer-quality stuff as a means of sacrificing on behalf of his dependents. Then as the sun burns heavily overhead and the river sulks nearly to a stop in the shallows he boards his boat and poles northward to a place where he knows he can get full value for the remainder of his catch.

———

ON THE EDGE of darktown is a long low shack as collapsed upon itself as its proprietor's toothless visage. The building has a covered porch with a rusted tin roof that lets in the rain and a single rotted and sprung step that none of the regulars dares use anymore. Finn treads upon it and it nearly gives way beneath the weight of him and his tow sack full of catfish, and he vows to be more circumspect on the way out. Two men huddled over dominoes on the porch watch from under their bent brows and wonder exactly what business he might be here to conduct. He passes them without acknowledgment and enters the still and tomblike interior of the store.

"Mr. Finn."

"Hey."

"Don't see you much."

"I can't hardly see you neither, you keep it so goddamn dark in here."
Waiting for his eyes to adjust.

"If I could afford another window, I'd open it." The man is black as
tar, squat of build, and powerful across the shoulders as a bull, and he
approaches Finn with a gaiety and a toothless grin which together suggest that every human being on earth—even this unlikely one—is his
boon companion. "What brings you here today?"

"Got cats. Them little ones."

"My, my, my." He calls to the men on the porch that they should
come and see this if they know what's good for them, so they begrudgingly lay aside their dominoes and sulk in through the open door.

Finn backs away as if they are contagious but keeps one hand on the
sack. "Them's good eating," he says to no one in particular.

"I know it," says the proprietor.

"How much?"

"This all you got?"

"All I got left."

The proprietor names his price, which is less than Finn believes the
fish are worth but more than he would have gotten from Smith.

"Done," says Finn.

The proprietor makes a little shooing motion, just enough to let the
domino players know that he and Finn might like to speak in confi-
dence. The two black men are safely back out on the porch when he resumes, yet he whispers nonetheless: "You plan to put some of that on
the lady's account?"

Finn tilts his head as if the man has begun addressing him in a for-
eign tongue.

"You know."

But Finn does not know.

"The tab she been running. While you was down to Alton."

"Alton's my business."

"I know it." Understanding the man's shame or secretiveness or whatever else it may be, but needing all the same to navigate past it if he is to begin recovering his losses. "And if I was too generous, then that's my business. I know it. I'll have to pay the price."

"Too generous."

"I just thought."

"Generous how."

"Some folk need more credit than the rest. Generally them as can't be counted on to make it up. You know how it goes."

Finn eyes the fish aglisten on the counter in the dark room. "I should have thrown them back."

"Let's just keep this between us gentlemen. I expect she wouldn't want me asking." The proprietor nods as he speaks, in time to his own slow and sleepy rhythm. "She said she'd be keeping up best she could, with the laundry and all."

"I put a stop to that."

"I didn't know. I just thought I'd."

"Go on, then." Finn grinds his teeth and the muscles in his jaw bunch. "Go on and put it all on hers. Every bit." The words come out of him as if he is deflating all at once.

"Yes sir." The proprietor's eyes brighten. "That'll go some way."

"I'll not have her obliged."

"That's a fine policy."

"I don't require your say-so."

"I need more customers think like you."

"Good luck."

Finn leaves with the same next to nothing in his pocket that he came in with and a freshly discovered debt on top of it. As he walks with his empty sack down the lane and back to his skiff he weighs in his mind the relative merits of the two courses open to him: to never visit this place again and thus remain beholden but aloof, or to come back straightaway and pay off the debt with all of the speed and dignity that he can muster. He has not yet decided between the two when he arrives at the skiff and casts off, and he has still not decided when he realizes that thanks to her he is now shy the money he had hoped to spend on whiskey.

———

BLISS'S SHACK LIES so deep in the woods as to be nearly past locating for those with ordinary sight. He labors in the open air down a path hidden behind that disreputable falling-down ruin with none but his fire and his boiler and his ranks of empty jugs for company, and he stores what he produces God knows not where. The surrounding forest serves as his guardian, for not so much as a rabbit can move among its dense overwhelming greenery without the old blind bootlegger taking note.

Finn has heard the way to this spot described as often and as erringly as one might hear tell of the path to glory, and from these thousand fragmentary and conflicting reports he has triangulated an idea of his own. He is not too far wrong, as it happens, and so after fighting his way through a mile of tangled underbrush and recovering from a few false turnings he detects from up ahead the unmistakable mingled aromas of fire and forty-rod.

Bliss when Finn spies him is hunched close by his works in a broad clearing burnt barren as a holy place, head tilted and sniffing the air, his right hand atwitch on the ivory handlepiece of a pistol.

"You Bliss."

"Step no further."

"I won't." Raising his hands and then seeing his mistake and dropping them again.

"Now go on back the way you come."

"I can't."

"Git." Bliss swivels his head in tiny increments, and when he has satisfactorily located Finn he raises his gun and points its barrel toward the unseen man's unseen heart with a preternatural accuracy.

"I'm lost." From where he stands Finn can see the man's eyes, one of which points off in a direction that seems riverward but may be otherwise. The other one has a gray glaucous film over it, as thick and obscurant and mysteriously portentous as a caul.

"Lost, are you?" Bliss creaks out an appreciative laugh but refuses to unaim the gun. "I've heard that before."

"I ain't no liar."

" 'Course you are. No man ever found this place by accident."

"I'll grant you."

"Not even me."

"It ain't easy."

"Damn right."

"I been lost since noon."

"Bullshit."

"I have."

"I won't hold it against you."

"You mean happening on you like I done."

"I mean lying about it."

"I ain't lying."

"You are. But since you're so intent on it I just might reconsider." For there is something about Finn's conviction that he admires.

"Either way," concludes Finn. "It don't matter to me."

"How about a little taste of my corn?" Lowering the pistol. "Just to speed you on your way."

The old man's stuff is as clear as kerosene and nearly as poisonous, the kind that gives certain strains of bootleg whiskey the reputation for taking a strong man down at a distance of forty rods. Finn learns in a hurry that Bliss enjoys the taste and potency of it as much as anyone, perhaps more, and the riverman is wily enough to use such weakness to his advantage.

"So how'd you find me here?" the old man asks after he has mellowed some under the influence of his own drink.

"I got lost," Finn confesses again.

"Tell the truth."

"I got lost. But it weren't for lack of trying."

Bliss wheezes in a good-natured way. "Who told you?" He names three quarters of the barmen and trading post operators in the region, at places as low as Dixon's and Smith's and as elevated as the Liberty and Adams hotels. He names them in miraculous alphabetical order, a fact that Finn would not notice even if he could.

"Nobody told."

"You can level with me," says Bliss. "Whoever it was, I swear I'll do no more than cut his balls off. *Next time I see him.*" As if to indicate the potency of this promise he tilts his head downward and his one dead filmy eye travels straight from Finn's visage to his vulnerable crotch.

"There's lots of rumors," says Finn. "I ignored every one of them and ended up here."

"But you do like your whiskey."

"I do." Helping himself to the jug and refilling Bliss's portion too.

After a while they bank the fire and leave the clearing and walk together to micturate in the deep woods. Then they adjourn to a pair of rockers on the old man's porch, all of which gives Finn the opportunity to make a study of the premises. The sun is well down toward the horizon before he brings up his name and his predicament and his inability to pay more than a few pennies for the whiskey he's drunk.

"Judge Finn's boy. So you're the bad seed."

"I reckon."

Bliss puffs himself up and intones the father's full name as if reading it from an engraved card for introduction before royalty. "James Manchester Finn."

"You do know the sonofabitch."

"Ever since I was born, or thereabouts."

Finn gives a sly smile whose contribution to the tonality of his answer goes not unnoticed. "He never mentioned you."

"The world ain't a fair place."

"So they say."

"But I knew him. Since I was a boy."

Finn sips whiskey. "The Judge weren't never a boy."

"Neither was I."

"Maybe not."

The two sit listening to the night come on. At the margin of the woods a flurry of brown bats drops one by one from their hidden haunts to pursue one another riverward, and thus Finn recalls the way home or at least the direction.

"So you're the one took up with that nigger woman."

"I reckon I am." He asks no question but Bliss can hear his curiosity in the silence as clearly as if he had given it voice.

"People talk, is all."

"What people."

"I ain't saying."

"What do they say."

"You know."

"I reckon I do."

Bliss stops rocking and squares his odd gaze at Finn. "Me, I say what business is it of theirs."

"Amen."

Bliss lowers a fingertip into his jar to assess the level of whiskey in it, finds it satisfactory, and resumes rocking. "A person's color don't matter to me. I never gave a tinker's damn for it one way or the other."

"It matters."

"You're the one to talk, ain't you."

"You wouldn't think."

"You wouldn't. But I reckon you'd know after all."

Finn sits and rocks and speaks not.

"Now don't take me wrong," says Bliss, trusting in the defensive powers of his hospitality and his supply of forty-rod and even perhaps his long-dead connection to the Judge, come to that, "but I ain't never had no nigger gal on me."

"Your loss," says Finn.

"Is that a fact."

Finn nods in the dark.

"I had a feeling."

"You was right."

"Then it's like they say." Not wanting to go any farther along this path. Finn will be back to buy whiskey and keep him company, he can be certain of that. And there will be time then to discover each other's secrets.

"I reckon it's like they say," says Finn. "It must be, for all the trouble."

When they are both sufficiently drunk the bootlegger provides his visitor with instructions for finding his way home, instructions that can be followed reliably only in utter darkness or by a blind man fully undistracted. Finn does well enough with them because such dim light as he can make out from the sky overhead is more than offset by his inebria-

tion, and thus he can proceed methodically and slowly with his attention undiluted by sight. When he reaches the river at last he seeks out
his skiff, which he has missed by less distance than he had feared. The
things he bought for the woman at Smith's are gone, either stolen by
men or eaten by scavenging animals, but this he does not notice until he
ties up beneath the house and by then he does not care.

———

"You forgot the flour."

This is how he wakes up, this and a head that feels as if Bliss had fired
that pistol of his straight through it and then dragged him here to this
bed and left him bleeding in it to die. She is calling to him up the stairs,
calling to him as if he can do anything about her lack of flour from
where he lies in his bed of pain.

"You forgot the flour."

Silence.

"There'll be no biscuits today."

This suits him fine as long as she goes quiet for a while in the bargain, which she does.

Later he troops down the stairs and plants himself at the table and
stares across the water with a headful of poison. The coffee tastes vile
but he drinks it boiling until he begins to sweat and then he drinks some
more and when the pot is empty he goes outside to relieve himself. All
the while the woman and the boy eye him as they would watch a snake,
and maintain a safe distance.

"You go on run them lines," he says to the boy when he returns. "I
didn't get to them last night."

"All by myself?" The boy is as thrilled as he is uncertain.

"I said *you go.*"

The boy does, gladly and with some pride in the newfound role into
which he can feel himself maturing. The woman says nothing as he
leaves. She has no fear for his safety nor doubt that he will produce a
fine catch, but like any mother she desires all the same to advise caution
and invoke good luck. Yet the chill that the man has brought into the
room suggests that they will all be better served if she permits the boy

to go about his father's business without remark, and so she sits in silence. He is barely down the stairs when his father begins.

"There weren't money for flour once I begun paying your debts."

"My debts."

"Weren't money for flour nor nothing else. And we're still in the hole."

"I don't know what you mean."

"You know what I mean and you know where I been."

She picks up a dish and rises and moves toward the kitchen.

"Sit."

She sits, and she says what she knows. "You been to Mr. Connor's store."

Finn lifts an eyebrow. "That his name? Even a sly old worthless nigger like that one got to have a name, I reckon."

"He does."

"And you'd be the one to know it, you running up your tab there and all."

"I had no choice."

"You living on credit like the goddamn Queen of England while I ain't here."

"It's not what I wanted."

"A person don't do what he don't want."

She looks him in his bloodshot eye. "And I suppose you wanted nothing more than to spend our grocery money on corn whiskey."

He raises a finger, indicative of his entire ready hand. "Don't question me."

"I wouldn't dare."

"You got yourself in deeper'n you know."

"Did I."

"And white men's laundry ain't the way out. Not no more it ain't."

"He told you."

"I figured."

"I wanted to keep it quiet," she says. "I knew you'd be."

"You knew right."

He rises and strides out to the porch, where he can stand looking across the river with one hand visoring his brow. For a moment he watches the boy running the lines. All along the valley the sky is stacked high with clouds and from time to time one passes between the boy and the sun drowning him in a temporary space of moving shadow. The father draws water from the rainbarrel and stands drinking it while shadows of his own making pass across his face. "You ain't to go down there no more." Showing her only his broad back.

"Down to Connor's."

"Down to darktown I mean. You got to be broke of that, now I'm home." He lowers the dipper into the water and raises it up and drinks some more. "I aim to break you of it right quick."

"Where was I to go."

"That's no business of mine."

"You were in the penitentiary."

"I know it."

"I hope you don't mind my saying so, but white or colored, people aren't generally solicitous of a woman in my position."

He turns like machinery and neither puts down the dipper nor hesitates as he steps back inside the door to where she sits at the table with her hurt feelings and her effrontery. The dipper is an old one he found somewhere long ago, its bowl half eaten with rust and its handle twisted like a branch, and he grips it tight enough to slice a less callused hand across the palm. The momentum of his passage brings him to her straightaway and gives the backhanded swing of his right arm untold power, and accelerates the arc of that rusty implement into a stroke as fierce as a lash. Had she not flinched she might have lost an eye but as it is the jagged metal edge cuts her temple down to white bone, white bone instantly drowned in red blood and black flecks of rusty iron and a spattering of residual water that trickles down her face like the tears that she will not permit herself to shed either now or later.

"I'll teach you to tell me my business," says Finn, craving solitude and silence and perhaps a little whiskey.

15

A<small>LL ALONE IN THE WORLD</small> he passes the shacks and the sheds and the shuttered storefronts of darktown. Along past Connor's he goes, a place where he is known for having years ago paid off his woman's debts and then kept his own promise never to trouble those premises again unless burdened by a parcel of carp or some other worthless fish that no other trader in the valley would lower himself to buy. Today he has no catch and only the memory of any closed obligation, and so he directs his tread toward the door of that regal woman whose life he not only helped ruin but has since set about rebuilding according to his own lights.

He finds her tending her cauldron on the riverbank behind the house, and he admits himself into her presence uninvited. He had meant to bring an item or two of laundry but forgot in his eagerness and haste, and so he produces from the pocket of his coat an undershirt that he stripped off while still afloat on the skiff. His shirt is haphazardly tucked in and he fears for a moment that she will surely guess his deception, but if she does she gives no sign of it or at least none that he can detect.

"I figured your husband'd be home."

"He ain't these days."

"Ain't *home*." Making a grim little unobtrusive joke to himself but not to her for she cannot know that he knows.

"Ain't been for a while," she says.

"He'll be coming back, though."

"I don't reckon." Stirring with a peeled branch she edges around the pot in Finn's direction, which has the result of putting her slender back toward him. He is uncertain what to make of this shift for he cannot see the tear gathering in her eye, and he would still be uncertain what to make of it even if he could.

"He run off?"

"He got himself killed." Her voice rises barely above the inaudible, and a single crack from the fire would be sufficient to drown her out and wipe clean her slight speech from the consciousness of this world forever.

"I'm sorry," says Finn.

"Two men done it by night."

"No."

"Stole my boy and killed my husband."

"You had a boy." As if he has forgotten or never known.

"The two of them broke down that door and come in together."

"You was home?"

"We was all of us asleep. Until then."

Finn cogitates for a minute, watching the steam rise and inhaling the dizzying smell of her homebrewed lye soap. "At least they didn't touch you."

Turning to show him her face. "I'd die right this minute if I knew how." Turning it away again.

Finn considers asking whether it was white men or black who committed the crime, and then wonders for a moment whether he should ask if the murderers or kidnappers or whoever they are have yet been found, but by the set of her shoulders even he can see that the time for such curiosity or whatever else it might be is well past.

He turns to go. "I'm glad I could make that door right." Almost as if it doesn't matter.

"You didn't have no idea."

"A person notices."

"I'm obliged."

"Don't worry none. You got troubles enough."

16

SLICK AND GLISTENING with bluegill scales the boy slides onto the couch alongside his mother there on the sunshot porch, and together they watch as his father poles upstream with the morning's gutted catch. The boy is surprised to find her resting here at a moment when she is usually occupied, but not as surprised as he is to detect a kind of despair both in her posture and in the dispirited way she answers his greeting. And not half as surprised as he is to discover the bandage on her swollen and pale face when she turns to look upon him and admit him thereby into her shame and her fury.

"What happened?"

"It was an accident." Which she means to make true, because it is her intention that a thing such as this shall not be permitted to happen again.

For his part Finn sells all his catch but a handful and invests most of the proceeds in a quantity of Bliss's forty-rod. The remainder he spends begrudgingly on certain necessaries, and after he returns home and ties up and tells the boy to bring in the groceries *and you'll be careful with them jugs if you know what's good for you,* he takes the last few of the fish and bundles them freshly in wet reeds and wraps them in a clean cloth sack and starts uphill.

"I thought you could use some," he says to his brother when he finds him.

"I don't cook much."

"I know it."

"Perhaps I'll have them fry them up over at the Adams. For lunch."

"Beat the hell out of whatever's on the menu."

"I wouldn't doubt it."

"Don't know who they're buying from these days."

"Some lesser supplier, no doubt." He sighs, flicking bits of dust from the gleaming top of his desk and sniffing the unwelcome odors of fresh bluegills and his own kin.

"I didn't come here to talk about business," says Finn.

"Or fish."

"Neither one."

"What then?"

"I come here to let you know he's right."

"The Judge."

"Not all the way right, but."

"But he has a point."

"You could say."

"He's right about some things."

"I reckon."

"Nobody's wrong all the time. Not even the Judge." Will wrinkles his nose and points with one finger at the sack. "Let's take those across the street right now, shall we?"

The sun is directly overhead, high as the smell of bluegills and brother as Will locks up and the two of them step down from the porch into the street. They enter the dim cool fastness of the hotel lobby through great swinging double doors, Will first and his brother behind by only a step or perhaps two yet nonetheless visibly subordinate. The lawyer gives the impression that he was born here. The riverman on the other hand looks as if he is hunting something or perhaps being hunted himself.

Beneath the arched doorway to the dining room Will whispers in the ear of the octoroon Lovett, who takes the bundle from him as if it is infected and strides with it toward the kitchen. Will waits to be shown to his table, where he takes up his usual post and lets his brother sit where he may. He raises one hand to dissuade the waitress from leaving menus and orders tea with lemon for himself. His brother orders whiskey but then thinks better of it and in the end orders nothing, not so much as a glass of water to wash down his own catch.

"So what's the old man right about?" Leaning forward to create a space of confidentiality between them in the vast high-ceilinged room.

"My troubles."

"That covers a good bit of ground."

"The woman."

"Oh." He flutters his napkin loose and arranges it upon his lap. His brother tucks his own into his collar and smoothes it down. "I see."

"I don't believe she's worth the trouble."

"So you're giving in."

Finn goes ruddy above his white napkin. "It ain't that simple." But keeping his voice down, intimidated by the high room and the bustling staff and the lunchtime crowd just beginning to filter through the door, lifting their hands in restrained and respectful greetings to his brother one by one.

"It is to him. To the Judge it's every bit that simple."

"Still."

"I suppose you've had some revelation."

"I've had a few."

Will leans back as the waitress brings their plates, the bluegills arrayed upon them delicate and fragrant in ways that Finn has never imagined much less witnessed. They have left his presence ordinary and returned transformed, and he barely recognizes them for his own nor dares disturb them with knife and fork.

"Eat up," says his brother. He selects his cutlery with the intensity of a duelist. "So you've learned some lessons."

"I have."

"That will please the Judge to no end."

"I know it."

"Is that what you want?" His mouth full.

Finn thinks. "I reckon it may as well be."

Will gives his head a rueful shake, not as if he disagrees with his brother but as if he is reflecting upon the tragic loss of him. "Times have changed."

Before Finn can ask him to clarify his meaning a gentleman dressed all in white linen approaches from across the room, one hand outstretched. "Will, you old hound dog," he calls, although by the appearance of him and the refinement of his voice he seems unlikely to have been much in the presence of hound dogs.

Will stands to greet him and while they shake hands the stranger takes the attorney's right elbow in his own left hand as if the two of them are the dearest and most long separated of companions.

"Senator Farraday," says Will. "Good to see you again. Do you know my brother?"

The senator runs the fingers of his left hand through the gray tangle that rides high upon his head like a storm at sea. He leans theatrically back to assess Finn from his great height, a stance yielding the impression that if he were wearing galluses he would be about to snap them. "Only by reputation," he says. And then he plunges a hand toward Finn and smiles from under his mustaches as if their entire encounter is the purest of delights. "The pleasure is mine."

Finn does not even have a chance to follow his brother's lead and rise fully to his feet before the senator is through with him and gone, striding back to his table where he dampens a napkin and wipes his hands and calls for the waitress to bring 'round a replacement.

"He didn't mean anything by that," says Will.

"How do you know."

"I just know."

Finn turns his head to one side and the other, assessing his position in the room. "The way people look at me." His voice low.

"*The way you look to them*, if you don't mind my saying."

"That ain't it." Reaching a filthy hand toward a mountain of hot biscuits piled under a gleaming napkin.

"It's some of it."

"I am what I am."

"Leaving her won't change that."

"It might for the Judge."

"Don't get your hopes up."

"Look at you," says Finn, pointing with a biscuit. "You fit in. You got a place in the world."

"So do you."

"It ain't much. And half of it I owe to you. More'n half."

"That's nothing. And anyhow it's not what I'm talking about. I mean you've found your own way. You've taken your own direction. With no help from the Judge."

"Which is more'n you can say for yourself, I reckon."

"I reckon," says Will.

Finn sops up what remains on his plate with the biscuit and studies the filmy residual streaks of butter and grease as if hoping to divine some truth from them.

"Besides," says his brother, "he won't love you any better for abandoning that woman."

"He might."

"I suspect he'll hate you more."

"Why."

"He'll decide you're weak. He'll accuse you of vacillating."

"He might."

"He'll dismiss you and your best intentions altogether."

"I reckon he could."

"You know the Judge."

"I do."

Will raises his hand for the check. "No matter what you do now, he'll never forgive you for what you've already done. That's his way. All you can do by struggling is make things worse."

"I know it." Like a fish on a line.

———

NONE BUT BLISS has time or temperament for him.

He poles past Dixon's in the lowering rainy dark, looking up from the river as Dixon's wife lights the lamps and draws the threadbare curtains. Under circumstances such as these even so poor a place as this acquires an ethereal and inviting glow for those who are forbidden its delights, among which scattering of sad outcasts Finn must number himself on account of his continuing indenture to Connor for the woman's debt. He'll be damned if he'll buy whiskey from that black bastard with the few cents he permits himself and he lacks enough to so much as get started at Dixon's, and back home under his own roof confined with those two he feels as if he may as well be back at Alton. So these days he can be counted upon at nightfall to tie up to a branch and thread his way in the darkness to that secret spot in the woods where Bliss's fire is constant and his whiskey is cheap and his hospitality is reliable if not quite freely given.

"I ain't running no tavern hereabouts," says the blind man as Finn emerges from the treeline.

"I know it."

"You bring a jug?" Poking the fire.

"Damn. Left it in the skiff."

"Ain't you the great idiot." In all the world there live only two sorts of men who speak with the luxurious immunity enjoyed by this blind bootlegger: those in positions of great power, and those locked safely behind prison bars. Bliss imagines himself to possess certain qualities of both, and about this he is correct.

"I reckon I'll just have to drink it all at one go."

"I reckon."

The delight that Finn takes in Bliss's whiskey begins at a level hardly describable as such and perhaps more accurately understood as its inverse. So it is with the bootlegger's company. But over the passage of an evening's time each one of these variables—whiskey and companionship alike—improves on a steady upward curve whose course proceeds through ascending parallel strata of pleasure and brotherhood. Still they both must peak eventually, and as the moon completes its circuit and Finn's head begins to throb he usually begins to ruminate upon the course of his life and the various hurtful influences upon it and how they have conspired to bring him to such a sad destination as this. Drinking in the deep woods with a blind man who tolerates him for pay. Tomorrow night he will return, but he will like it no better.

———

THE WOMAN IS HUNGRY and the boy is hungry and Finn is hungry too, but he of them all does not care much. He has eaten a little during the day, bits and scraps acquired by bargaining and stealth along his circuitous route, and so his stomach although empty is not quite so entirely void as theirs. She lacks sufficient flour to dredge the sunfish he has begrudged them for their supper, and the tobacco sack that she once concealed in the bottom of the sugar barrel now lies exposed like a bone unearthed in a hard land. The boy has thought to ask her about it on more than one occasion, but each time the shame attached to having opened the sugar barrel without permission has overcome his curiosity.

"I'd think Connor must be paid off by now," she says with a kind of dreamy resignation, in a voice pitched to suggest neither harm nor doubt.

"You'd think."

She chews thoughtfully and slow, the muscles in her jaw sliding over and alongside one another as patient as the haunches of moving cattle. She chews as if she might by rumination extract more value from these poor scraps than they contain, the way a scholar might by study glean more from some volume than its author intended to be contained there.

"Could be you got in deeper than you knew." Desiring neither acknowledgment nor admission.

"You would have more understanding of that than I would."

"Amen."

She has been for the past year and more a prisoner in this slanting riverside house and the boy a prisoner too, although for the most part he has had the good fortune to be asleep during those black hours before dawn when his father stumbles up the stairs from his nightly rendezvous with Bliss. She sleeps then too because there is nothing else for her, but he awakens her each time with a rough hand upon her shoulder or her breast or her leg—and once, by the most evil of chances, upon that tender place high on her temple where the wound from the jagged rusty dipper was not yet healed. At first he took her at these moments, facedown or faceup or however he happened to find her, but lately while the food has dwindled and his misery has ripened and increasing sums of the money that should by rights have gone to Connor have been going to Bliss, he has found himself frustratingly unmanned and blamed it upon her and sought thus his furious satisfaction in other more brutal ways.

I'll not be starved to death in my own house, she tells herself one damp autumn morning when he has left to go about his business. *And I'll not be beaten to death, for that matter.* And so she fetches the money from the tobacco sack and calls the boy in from where he has gone digging for worms in the yard, and they gather up such belongings as they might claim for their own into a single tow sack, and together they walk south along the mudflats toward Lasseter proper.

"We going to darktown?"

"Not this time. Not ever again, if I have my way."

They stop at the landing, mother and child. Beholding the two of these ragged fugitives any observer would think them far from home and despairing of potential return, a sad pair of wasted refugees displaced from such lives as they might have ever hoped to know, rootless and lost and doomed to wander forever beyond the reach of the familiar until misery and death shall take them at last. The society and commerce of Lasseter, even here at the landing, where anything can happen, eddies around them at a decent remove as if they have been poisoned.

Traffic upon the river is light, but at this nexus it folds inward upon itself and commences to clot like blood. A flatboat laden with coal, the skiffs of fishermen whose lines and haunts are downstream of those kept by Finn, rafts piled high with grainsacks and other goods for sale both upstream and down, these mingled vessels and more interweave their complex courses in silence save for the shouts of the rivermen and the occasional blast of a steam whistle from a sidewheeler not yet visible around the long rightward bend to the north. Mary's heart rises to hear it as it always does, even as it has thus risen unfailingly during her years in the riverside house, for the distinctive high warning bellow of that instrument reminds her of her lost childhood and her daring father and their single great doomed adventure aboard the *Santo Domingo*. It stabs at her eardrums and it reverberates in her gut and it brings to her heart unbidden thoughts of freedom.

Yet she lacks sufficient funds to book passage anywhere. This much she knows without inquiring. And so it is that she begs transport upon a keelboat bound downriver to St. Petersburg, a place she does not know but that can only be superior to this. The captain is a stern and pious individual as broad as a cotton bale and just as tightly bound, but the look of her and the look of the boy conjure up within his heart a reflexive pity that he mistakes for the irresistible will of God. St. Petersburg is not far downriver but it is as far as he shall go today, and Mary and the boy hardly notice that they are stepping out upon the banks of Missouri when they leave his care.

The village is not large, although it is larger by far than her experience of the world. Her inclination is thus to remain on its periphery, and although she would like nothing better than to march up the main street and forge there some instance of the new life she has foreseen for the two of them she instead takes the boy by his hand and edges off to one side of the bustling riverfront square, where they stand as if enchanted while the society of little St. Petersburg manifests itself before them. Only when the boy loses patience with what he sees—with the men unloading barges and the men bartering over fish and the men playing mournful music upon a banjo and a fiddle under the partial shade of a whitewashed gazebo—only when his attention wanes and his gaze wanders away from the square and up the adjoining grassy slope of Cardiff Hill does the village present an alternative aspect to these two wayfaring strangers, for there in the sunlight upon the hill stands a house, a shingled house slate-roofed and foursquare in aspect, angular and clean as a block of salt, imposing as a mausoleum. It draws them as if it possesses a lodestone buried in its foundation.

They climb the hill upward and away from the bustle of the village, she with the tow sack over her shoulder and he freed of all burdens save his own young life. The hill is fringed upon the far side with a crown of evergreens and tall oak trees just now in full but fragile leaf, and they move toward the house and its rearward encirclement as toward a fortified castle. A fence rings it and a wooden mailpost stands guard at the gate where like pilgrims they arrive expecting God alone knows what.

"You girl," comes a voice from the sunblind shadows behind the open door.

"Ma'am?" For the voice clearly belongs to a woman and an old one at that. Mary touches her fingertips to the gate as she would touch the head of a child.

"Can I help you?"

A question she has heard rarely enough. "I hope to find work, ma'am."

"You and the boy too?"

"He's mine."

"You don't look much alike."

"I know it."

The shadow behind the door and the voice emerging from it conspire to incorporate themselves into a resolving outline, the crooked but potent figure of a sturdy old gray-headed woman who steps now into the sunlight of the porch as if birthed there all at once by the power of their desiring. She has about her an air at once refined and severe, suggestive of the city and the frontier both, as if from her lofty post high on Cardiff Hill she has seen the future of this land and its past and has through an act of will incorporated certain elements of each into her aspect. She lowers her jaw and squints through her glasses, taking in every element of these two wanderers as if to make them her own by mere observation.

"Runaways."

"No ma'am."

"I can always tell."

The boy gives his mother a pleading look.

"Truly," she says. "I was stolen once, I suppose you could say, but I've never run."

The woman leans against the doorframe. "You surely look it."

"I know." Studying her hand where it lies upon the gate like a bundle of knobbed sticks, studying the shoes that over the years have nearly vanished beneath her tread in spite of all her caution, studying the boy, for whom anyone with a heart or even eyes would desire better.

"Where'd you come from?"

"Upstream. Lasseter."

"That's Illinois."

"I know."

"You're in Missouri now. Did you."

"I hadn't even." Not desiring to interrupt yet already sufficiently comfortable with the old woman to engage thus.

"Things are different here." Neither comfortable nor uncomfortable but oddly oracular.

"As long as the work isn't too much harder, I suppose I'll get by." Desiring to indicate her desirability as a helpmate by exhibiting both her amenable nature and a certain inborn ironic grace.

"Why don't the two of you come on inside. Let me explain a few things."

The house upon the hilltop is open to the four winds and shot through with the high clean scents of pine needles and long grass and oak leaves. Although clearly the domain of a thrifty old woman given to rag rugs and lace doilies and protective antimacassars, it has by dint of its elevated position an open and free and shiplike aspect. To the boy and his mother it feels like a place from which a person could jump off and land almost anywhere. Even the clouds seem closer.

Her name is Douglas, and her neighbors call her by the most elevated title she has ever earned: the Widow. She has lived alone in this house since her husband met his Maker in an accident upon the water perhaps twenty years ago, and although he chose this place for its vista of the river below she can hardly bring herself to look out the windows anymore. Only into the woods behind the house, which seem to her at least close and fixed and comforting.

Unaccustomed to visitors and undeterred by the oddity of these two she responds to this vagabond mother and child as she would to any forlorn and starving creatures. Her pantry shelves hold an untapped bounty which she spreads before them as before royalty. The woman helps her, this woman at home nowhere and everywhere whose child sits at the kitchen table in rapt and ravening anticipation, and together they discover a rhythm of movement that suits them both.

"Help yourselves," says the widow at last, and help themselves they do. Under his mother's gaze the boy despite his appearance eats with the delicacy and grace of a cherub. For herself the widow consumes nothing save a cup of pale tea, but watching the two of them feast upon her accumulated riches brings to her heart a pleasure far deeper and more satisfying than they can know.

"So you're looking for work."

"Yes ma'am." Pausing just long enough to swallow and answer and smile.

"You eat," says the widow, nursing her tea. "I'll talk."

The boy grins as if this is the most agreeable disposition of things he has ever hoped to encounter.

"Things are different here from the way they are in Illinois. Missouri is a slave state, you understand. I've had slaves myself, or at least I had one until I decided the arrangement wasn't doing either of us the least bit of good." She blows air across her teacup and thinks. "If you mean to stay here for long, I can't hire you. Do you understand what I mean?"

"You mean you can claim me instead."

"I could claim the both of you."

Mary looks around the kitchen as if evaluating its potential as either home or prison.

"Depending, of course, on where you came from. On your circumstances. You mentioned you'd been stolen, for example. Now, it could be that circumstances would arise under which I would have to give you back."

"I've been living free in Illinois for as long as I can remember."

"I hope that's true."

"It is."

"So how do you know your full history, then?"

"How do I know that I was stolen?"

"Exactly."

"People talk."

"What kind of people?"

"Folks." Not meaning to be difficult.

"Your parents?" Believing she has ascertained something.

"No ma'am. In fact, I was stolen straight out of the arms of my own daddy."

"And whereabouts was he a slave?"

Mary sees in this instant just how completely she will need to be on her guard, not just around the widow Douglas but anywhere at all in this treacherous godforsaken spider's nest of a state. "I don't recall," she says, and with these three words she repudiates her own history and the abortive kindness of Mrs. Fisk in the interest of freeing Huck from the perils of a past once removed. "People say various places. Mississippi. Louisiana somewhere. I don't know."

The widow Douglas sips her tea and offers to refill the boy's glass with cool milk from the pitcher. The look of delight that beams from his face at this small kindness illuminates her kitchen and her heart as has no other thing in the years since her husband died or even before; it would be worth starving the child near to death all over again if she could witness once more so miraculous a recovery.

"But in the meantime you've been in Illinois."

"Yes ma'am."

"And although you're not a runaway, you *are* running from something."

"Please." Indicating the boy, as though the widow has for one moment looked elsewhere since their interview began.

"You don't need to say it." The widow touches her hand with her own. "I may be old, but I'm not ignorant."

Mary takes some relief in this reprieve, and she sits for a moment enjoying the plain bright cleanliness of the kitchen and the cool breeze that enters through its windows without bearing upon itself the dizzying intolerable stink of fish offal. "You've been very kind," she says.

"You looked overdue for a little kindness. Your boy too." The truth of which is beyond denying. "Permit me to make some inquiries tomorrow," she says as she commences clearing the table, "and we'll see if I can't be of a little further use."

"We have no place to." Rising along with the widow.

"Pshaw." She lowers a plate back to the table with some satisfaction. "You follow your instincts and clear these, and I'll follow mine and air out a room for the two of you."

———

No one has slept in the back bedroom for years, and although it is clean beyond question there is about it an airless quality of preserved antiquity that the boy finds immediately disconcerting. "You reckon somebody died in here?" is how he puts it, and surely enough he is correct in his guess. The widow has thrown open the one window and he leans out of it headfirst with his feet airborne, halfway eager enough to crawl onto the shed roof and down the drainpipe to the ground. The white curtains billow around his ankles as if he has already taken flight in the manner of some great fledged bird or angel, and his mother pulls them aside and takes his feet and draws him back to safety. Upon the dresser by the window is a tiny group portrait, tilted away from the sun for preservation. It shows a serious-faced young woman, presumably the widow Douglas in the period before her widowhood, an earnest young gentleman with a slouch hat and a ten-mile glower, presumably Douglas himself, and a sour-looking baby child of indeterminate gender clothed in a long dressing gown that tumbles like falling water and pools in the young woman's lap.

"I told you," says the boy when he gets a look at the portrait. "That baby's the one died in here. Right in that bed, I'll bet you anything."

Night when it descends brings with it an unearthly quiet. The river traffic to which the boy and his mother have long become accustomed, with its variegated texture of curses and shouts and creaks and whistles, is lost far below, muted and attenuated by distance to nearly nothing. A light wind whispers through the branches of the evergreens behind the house, and occasionally a bough will brush against the shingles or the slates with a weary sigh, but aside from this and the widow Douglas's antiquarian snore the house is silent. The boy and his mother lie awake wondering what they have done and what they shall do. Around midnight the widow arises and lights a candle and creeps to the outhouse. Upon her return she pauses at their door and opens it just the slightest as if to persuade herself despite the impervious darkness that the two of them are here with her still, and when she is for no ostensible reason satisfied she closes the latch with a tender furtive caution and puts herself back to bed.

———

THE RIVERSIDE HOUSE IS EMPTY when Finn returns, and when he draws near he can feel its vacancy as he would feel an intruder in his bed. There is no outer indication, no lamp lit or unlit, no signifier present or missing that would suggest as he ties up the skiff and hoists his jug of forty-rod and makes his cautious way to the foot of the open stairs that he has been left abandoned by that faithless nigger woman and her white-skinned mulatto child.

He climbs the stairs and opens the door and does not even bother inquiring upstairs as to her presence for he knows that she is gone. The whiskey jug he puts in the kitchen and the slim contents of his pocket he spills out upon the table, some string, a fishhook, a button, two or three coins. Enough to finish paying off her debt to Connor, if he chooses. Out on the porch he steps around the horsehair couch to make certain about the one thing that he has decided might matter, and surely enough the boy is gone too. His pallet lies empty and oddly yearning in the moonlight.

He returns to the dim kitchen and pours himself a tall dose of whiskey in a jar and brings it back to the porch to drink by reflected riverlight. As usual at this time of night his nerves are wildly ajangle and his body is wound tight as a watchspring and he is ready for something to happen. His breath comes rapidly and his breathing is harsh as he sits taking in the few soft lights moving on the current below. One such light, at some place upstream or down, could represent the vessel in which the two of them made their escape. There is no doubt in his mind that they left by way of the river, for what other artery is there for making serious time and distance. Unless they went to darktown, which would after all be just like that woman.

He tilts his head back and tips the jar fully upward to empty what remains therein down his throat in one impatient sluicing, careless of how much may go into his mustache and his beard and run from there on downward along the sinews of his neck to soak into his shirt collar. The empty jar he places on the railing like a sacred totem, and he sits before it like a dead man with his hands hanging between his spread knees as if it might soon begin working magic. There is in fact some conjury in the way it reflects and absorbs and refracts such bits of light as come to it. Moonlight, starshine, lamps on silent boats below, the jar captures them one and all and mingles them together with diffuse reflected riverlight and trades them one for another as if they are all equal and all equally distant. From such materials as these it creates a localized and mysterious moving galaxy within which this watcher might easily find himself lost, and upon which his own deep alcoholic alchemy overlays its own twinings and taints and endless entanglements. Spots that might be spiders, and twists that might be snakes, and other dark amorphous things lurking indiscernible and beyond differentiation. One of them he fixes his attention upon, a tar-black thing that has either lowered itself down upon a filament or emerged whole from some concealed portal. He tilts his head from one side to another and back again to make it out more clearly but cannot no matter how he tries, for it seems willfully to resist him, concealing itself in the passageways of light and dark within the jar's surface like some world-destroying entity out adrift among the stars. Once he nearly catches it, and he freezes, preparing to pounce, but it slips away again as a lamplit boat drifts by below disturbing the arrangement of light and dark. Furious and frustrated he decides to leap all the same, ill timed and ill aimed, and with the back of his hand he strikes the jar, which plunges noiselessly into the water. He is too weary to go to the kitchen and seek another jar or a glass or whatever other container he may find, perhaps even just the comforting jug itself, and so he kneels down upon the boy's empty pallet and falls upon his side there with his back to the wall and drops into a fitful sleep.

———

IN THE MORNING it is either search the river or search darktown, and even with a throbbing head he is wise enough to know which of the two will prove simpler. He makes haste downstream and ties up just below the village on the invisible margin where darktown begins. Down the single street he prowls, alert for any sign that she and the boy might have passed this way. Each glance that falls upon him and caroms off in its habituated manner looks suspicious this morning, and the posture of each individual he sees—whether a naked child at play in a hardpacked dooryard or an ancient gray-headed grandmother smoking her corncob under a willow tree—speaks to him of a secret just barely kept. He stops at Connor's, turning with an appraising look to survey the low shack with its broken backbone and its long porch jammed with useless junk both for sale and otherwise. Then he goes to the door, careful as any regular to skip the one treacherous sprung step on the way, and admits himself.

The place is as empty of life as a depot after the last stage has come through, and the unaccustomed silence both satisfies Finn and sets his nerves on edge. "You Connor," he says at half-volume, the first words he has spoken all day, and the phrase as it passes from his lungs turns into a great throat-clearing cough that he stifles on his sleeve.

No answer.

"I'd reckon a nigger bastard could show himself long enough to take a white man's money," he says to the darkness, hoping that the woman is hiding somewhere nearby so as to witness both his disdain and his faithfulness. For in both of these qualities he is demonstrably and by his God-given disposition the natural superior to any of her race.

No answer.

He proceeds toward the rear of the shack, past where Connor keeps work implements hung and certain dry foodstuffs in barrels and various second- or thirdhand treasures making their sad rounds again in a display case built from the frame of a rowboat. He proceeds toward the counter, behind which that grinning squat old orangutan Connor holds court day after day. His cashbox is present, right below the counter on the little shelf where he is known to keep it, and this fact puzzles Finn as well. He bends over the counter to touch the cashbox with one finger as he would toe some dead thing he'd found lying in the road, just to assess its condition and see if there might be any danger in approaching more closely. There is plenty of weight to it, he discovers. There also may as well be a string attached, for no sooner has he pushed at it than Connor comes careening in through the front door as if the world is on fire and Finn has sounded the alarm.

Finn turns as if he himself is the proprietor of this place. "Don't hurry on my account."

"Excuse me, Mr. Finn. I was just."

"No harm done."

"Something doing back to the house." For in recent years Connor's merchandise has so filled his little shack that it has finally crowded him out altogether and into a place down the alley.

"I'll bet."

Connor ties a white apron around his barrel of a midsection, an affectation he has lately acquired from shopkeepers in the village proper, and with an eye on the cashbox with which Finn has recently been toying he moves behind the counter. "What can I do for you?"

"The usual." Finn reaches into his pocket and draws forth from it his coins, and then one by one he lays them out upon the counter. "I reckon that about puts us square."

"You are a gentleman and a scholar, Mr. Finn." He can see from the ridge of dust on the shelf that the cashbox has been lately disturbed, and he decides that the coins upon the counter are about to go back where they came from. No harm done. He will be glad to be shut of this Finn, make no mistake about that, and if he needs to pay a few cents for the privilege then so be it. He puts away the coins and opens the ledger and makes some marks therein, ending with a broad flourish. "No catfish today?"

"No catfish no more, I reckon."

"Now, now. Just because we're square don't mean you need to be a stranger." He lays his hands on the counter and puts on the old smile, but it doesn't seem to fit.

Finn has the impression that the savvy old man desires their interview to be over even more urgently than usual. "So what's the matter back at the house?" As if he has ever extended a conversation of theirs so much as one word past its necessary length, and as if he could possibly care about the private life of this individual or any like him.

"Nothing. Sick child."

"Honest to goodness."

"Honest to goodness."

"Ain't that a damn shame."

"It is that." His smile faltering a little. Finn has never attended entirely to the humanity of this being, preferring to watch him at some remove as he would observe a caged animal or some potential prey, but on this occasion he detects in his eyes and in his stance and in his weak smile a furtive quality that he does not like in the least.

"You seen her, ain't you."

"The child. Yes. My grandbaby."

"Not her. The other."

"She woke up with a mighty high fever." Not thinking that Finn cares to know this but sensing that he wants to know something.

"*The other*, I said."

"The other." A question and a reassurance and an admission of bafflement all at once.

"That woman of mine. You've seen her."

"No." Yanked back into this moment by the scruff of his neck. "She
run off?"

"Don't lie to me, boy."

"I won't."

"I won't tolerate it."

"I ain't seen her."

"Don't you lie to me." He picks up a varnished stick that Connor uses
to fish bolts of fabric down from high places and takes a single step
backward and sights down its length toward him. "It won't do neither
one of you no good."

"Come over see my grandbaby, you don't believe me."

"You think I won't."

"No. I wouldn't put nothing beyond you."

"You're one smart nigger. You know that?"

"I don't mean to be."

"Let's go." Waving one end of the stick doorward.

Connor bends to take up the cashbox rather than leave it unguarded
here once more, and along the way he gives Finn a little sycophantish
smile of explanation: "A person might wander in, take advantage of this
useless old nigra."

Finn watches the way he moves and listens to the way he speaks and
realizes all at once. "You think I done that."

"Done what?"

"Took money from your cashbox."

"Now Mr. Finn."

"You said you wouldn't put nothing past me." He raises the stick and
pushes one end of it into the storekeeper's chest, stopping him cold.

"I said that, I did. But I didn't mean nothing by it." Holding the
cashbox to his white-aproned belly as Finn pushes harder on the stick,
hard enough to back him up against the wall. His breath comes short
and he feels a building pressure against his sternum, as if this avenger
intends to lean upon his weapon until it pierces him through.

"There best be a sick baby in your house yonder," says Finn, leaning on the rod and giving the tip of it a cruel half-turn, "or I'll gig you like a goddamn bullfrog."

———

CONNOR'S DAUGHTER IS BATHING her child in a tub of cool water when the two of them burst in, her father hung at the end of a pole like a dancing marionette and the man behind him ablaze all over with a kind of dark and furious light. "Lorena," says Connor, "show this man your baby."

She believes for a moment that in spite of the visitor's terrifying appearance he must be a doctor, perhaps the only one remaining who will do business in darktown, and she is thus prepared if only for the briefest of instants to throw herself and her child upon his mercy.

The child cries out and her mother cradles her head in her hand and the ferocious white man says to both of them, "That'll do."

"Your business here's done." Connor, feeling safe in his own house and pulling away from his tormentor and clutching his cashbox to his side.

"But you seen her. I know it."

"I done told you. I ain't."

Finn cares not for his reassurance and sets about to investigate every cranny of his back-alley shack with the lever of his long straight stick. He pries open each door and lifts each threadbare curtain and tries each loose floorboard, and when he is finished he swats at the baby's basin for good measure.

"If she ever *was* here, she ain't here no more." Peering out the back door and letting himself out into a yard stripped bare and packed down hard as rock.

"She weren't."

"So you say."

"I guess you got to try somewheres else."

"I know it."

He passes down the alley using the rod as a walking stick and occasionally rapping upon a wall or fencepost with it as his anger rises and falls within his breast like respiration. When he reaches the mudflats he turns upriver and flings the stick into the water as if it is tainted, as if it harbors poor luck, as if it has been handled too many times by that black storekeeper with his recordkeeping and his greed and his falsehearted smile. It whirligigs through the air and lands flat on the surface, refusing to enter the water, and then it gathers momentum and commences to float downstream as do all things dead and useless.

He poles upstream and runs his lines and thinks. Each cat and carp rises to him like a coin drawn up from some secret sunken hoarding, and he reflects as he works that he is surely better off without the woman and the boy to live upon his largesse and take advantage of his hard work and generosity. Without them he could accomplish much more while requiring less. He could eat at Dixon's more often, move up to a better grade of whiskey, perhaps even put a little something by now that he is out from under her and her carelessly accumulated debt. He poles to the bank and guts the fish and wraps them in wet reeds then poles up to Dixon's. The packed dirt and twisted roots and fallen limbs that rise from the river like a stairway are slick with dew and will be slow to dry in the autumn damp, but he climbs upward upon them and tries the door to find it locked. The back door leading straight into Dixon's living quarters is open a crack and from within comes the sound of argument, more precisely the sound of Dixon taking his customary abuse at the hands of his harridan wife. From his own newly elevated position as a freed man Finn takes pity upon him, but not enough to let him suffer his wife's revilement in privacy. He knocks, listens, and knocks again until Dixon comes sheepish to the door.

"Hey, Dix."

"Ain't seen you around."

"Ain't been. But that might change."

"It's early for drink."

"Not that." Finn raises his bundle. "Thought maybe I'd beat out whoever else you been using."

Dixon's wife: "You tell him to go around front if he's got business."

"I reckon you heard."

"I did."

Dixon shrugs. "The counter's up there and all."

"Ain't the kitchen back here?"

"Just go on."

Go on he does, and he waits at the door while Dixon draws on his trousers and buttons his shirt and makes his way through the place to unlock it and let him in with his bundle of fish wrapped in reeds and dripping wet.

"Got a mess of cats. Fiddlers too."

"Is that so. To what do I owe the honor."

"Lucky I reckon."

"You or me."

"Either one." Shouldering his way through the door and back toward the counter that separates the bar from the backroom where Dixon's wife remains isolate.

"I reckon we can use every last one of these," says Dixon when he has pushed back the bunched wet reeds and assessed Finn's offering. "Not just them little ones. Ain't that right, honey?"

"Suit yourself," she calls from the back, as if she is ostentatiously deigning to grant him some concession.

Finn raises his eyebrows toward the woman's voice. "Mine done run off, God bless her."

From Dixon he gets a look of mingled curiosity and compassion. "Whereabouts?"

"She ain't gone home, I can tell you that. Not home to Vicksburg."

"So where."

"Ain't sure. Ain't sure I care."

"How about the boy."

"Gone too."

Dixon gathers up the fish. "He's a good boy."

"I know it."

"You'll miss that one."

"I reckon I will. Sooner or later."

———

THERE IS A BRUSH on the dresser and after a few moments of hesitation and any number of false starts Mary takes it up and begins working her hair into a smooth and glossy braid. While she sits occupied in this slow meditative manner she watches the boy asleep angelic upon the widow's soft spare featherbed, and she thinks for once that she desires for him nothing less than exactly this, forever and ever. The house is quiet, silent in itself and isolated from the rising sounds of the waking village and alive only to the music of birds and the buzzing of insects. The widow must be a late riser, which Mary thinks odd for one her age, since Mrs. Fisk hardly slept a wink and complained about her weariness with every breath she drew.

She is playing possum, the old woman, waiting to see just how her visitors will comport themselves in the absence of her guiding presence. Still as a mummy, desperate to make use of the chamber pot but committed to seeing this experiment through to its end, she lies and waits and listens like some predator. Her heart beats and she draws breath and the inner flesh of her eyelids scrapes again and again across the sticky glass of her glaucous dried-up old woman's eyeballs, but beyond these small movements she may as well be dead.

A wall away Mary bends into the sunlight of the window and removes from the hairbrush all signs of her use as meticulously as she would sweep clean a gravestone, and then she moves across the room to return the thing silently and with infinite care to its place upon the dresser. The boy is still asleep. She permits herself one last moment of rest in the ladderback chair by the door, letting her vision fall upon the vista of the river below. The positions of the window and the chair angle her view southward, far downstream, away from Finn and his riverside habitation but toward the world of her youth to which she dares not return nor cares to. She feels herself a princess locked in a turret, the sort of figure Mrs. Fisk would read to her about in the old slave days in Vicksburg, back when being royalty confined in a high castle chamber seemed the most desirable fate in the world. As often as not those stories included a banquet that materialized mysteriously upon an intruder's entry into some ruined palace, and Mary realizes that if she waits for magic or hospitality or some other power to lay such a feast before her and the boy she will have done her years under Mrs. Fisk no honor.

She goes down and makes breakfast, at which development the widow is sufficiently satisfied to don her dressing gown and shuffle downstairs herself, acting when she sets foot in the kitchen astonished and delighted but no more astonished and delighted than she truly is and then excusing herself for an urgent and long-overdue visit to the outhouse. Soon the clatter of pans and the smell of food and the voices of the two women in the kitchen conspire to wake the boy, who flings himself from the bed and darts along the hallway and slides all the way down the railing as if he has decided all at once that he owns the place.

"What on earth?" The widow, alarmed by the crash of his two-footed landing in the front hall.

"Huck!"

"Mama!" Charging down the hall and bursting into the bright fragrant kitchen with a look of such joy upon his face that neither one of the women can bear to criticize him, at least not this morning, at least not this once.

Mary has responded to the abundance of the widow's pantry by cooking everything in sight, and the widow has not seen fit to restrain her. Eggs and bacon, flapjacks and country ham, biscuits and red-eye gravy—and not a single stinking catfish in sight. This must surely be paradise. The boy is ravenous and so is she and among the three of them they clean their plates and leave not a crumb. Huck has pocketed a biscuit or two but no one notices nor minds.

"I must say you do just fine in the kitchen," says the widow.

"You haven't seen supper."

"I could use the help. Lord knows."

"You could." On her feet, looking for an oversize pot to boil water for washing up.

"Bottom shelf." As if she has been reading her mind. "The cistern's out back."

"I've found it."

"There's no well. We're up too high."

"I hadn't thought." Out the back door she goes to fill the pot.

Through the open door: "And you do seem to have initiative."

"You noticed." Returning and daring to give the widow a playful glance, enough to indicate that she has recognized this morning's activities for the test that they have been, should the widow care to confess or even merely acknowledge.

"You're sure you're not a runaway."

"Not from slavery." With a look toward the boy.

"Whyn't you get some fresh air," says the widow to him, but before he goes he lets erupt into that bright welcoming kitchen the dark question that has plagued him ever since last night: "Did that baby of yours die in our room?"

"Now Huck," says his mother.

"Shoo, you impertinent thing," says the widow. She waggles her fingers at him like twigs, but something in her manner indicates that she does not mind his having raised so delicate a question.

"Forgive him."

"He's a child."

"I know it."

"We all were, at one time or another. Rich or poor, Negro or white. We all started out the same."

"You're very kind."

"I'm very old," says the widow. "God help me if I haven't learned something along the way."

"He'll learn too."

"I know," says the widow. "He will." She sips at her tea, not minding that it has gone a little cold. "Perhaps we can even help him along some. Find a way to get him a little schooling."

Mary's eyes brighten, but the light that rises within them dies out as rapidly as it has come. "Not Huck. Not a mulatto boy."

"Stranger things have happened."

"I know it."

"Have faith."

"I don't know."

"As for me, what I've learned is that I can use some help in this world."

"So you'll take me on."

"I need to make some inquiries first. Inquiries with the marshal. With the banker."

"I see."

"Just so we know where we stand with respect to each other."

Mary stands waiting for the water to boil.

"And of course there'll be the legal ramifications," says the widow, thinking out loud as is her custom.

"This being Missouri."

"This being Missouri," she agrees, "and not Illinois."

———

THE MARSHAL HAS FEW REPORTS of an escaped slave woman with a boy child, and no reports in particular of an escaped slave woman with a decidedly light-skinned boy child sufficiently unlike her to have been stolen from somewhere, and so he assumes that these are just two more nameless elements in the constant flow of desperate mankind that runs beneath the surface of a nation divided. The widow has no surname to report to him, for Mary truly does not recall her own and has refused to part with the identity of Mrs. Fisk. Even had she confessed that one detail, no lawman in America would have made a connection to her Vicksburg childhood, since for the last ten years the kindly Mrs. Fisk has possessed nothing more of her beloved Mary than a fond memory and a bill of sale from the owners of the steamboat *Santo Domingo*.

The banker allows that on a monthly basis the widow can afford to feed two extra mouths, plus a little besides. He desires to know how much she will be paying to take ownership of the woman and the child, but the widow prefers to keep her own counsel. He will learn soon enough, is all she will say.

Judge Thatcher tells her that she will be able to claim the woman and child after six months of unfettered residency, should they desire to stay that long. "They don't tend to linger in one place, these free Negroes, but I suppose you have a plan to keep this one handy."

"I can't say that I do," says the widow.

"That would be your decision."

"We'll just have to see."

"So we shall, so we shall."

The judge makes some tentative inquiries as to the woman's identity and origin, but the widow informs him that she has already considered all of this with the marshal and has no desire to travel that road again.

"Where has she been?"

"Up Lasseter way."

"And who'd be the boy's father?"

"I don't know. All I know is she ran off." She sits fingering her sunbonnet, watching its pale yellow ribbon move beneath her bent fingers. After a moment's pause she raises her eyes to the judge: "To tell you the truth, by the look of that pale child I wouldn't be surprised if he weren't hers at all."

Thatcher raises a hand in a peculiar little gesture of dismissal, for he can guess her intentions regarding the boy and would not dream of denying them. Even after these twenty years he misses the companionship of her dead husband nearly as much as she does, and although he knows that the empty place left behind by her lost child will never be filled by this mulatto foundling he will let her have her way nonetheless. "The father wouldn't be a character by the name of Finn, would he?"

"I've told you everything I know."

"He lives up in those parts."

"I know who he is. He has a reputation."

"Took up with a Negro woman some time back. If yours is the one, I'll never know why she took this long to come to her senses."

"I can't say."

"Do yourself a favor," says the judge, "and find out. Then you come talk to me. Because if that old boy's her man, you might want to reconsider those plans you don't have."

"Understood," says the widow, rising from her chair. "But if I discover that that child is as rootless as he appears, I'll be raising him for my own instead of claiming him."

"Sounds like a fine idea."

"And Finn be damned." Jamming on her hat.

She visits the grocery for some baking powder and ground coffee and tells the man behind the counter that until she advises him otherwise a certain Negro woman named Mary will be entitled to sign for the usuals on her account.

They are in the yard, mother and child, when she returns to the house atop the hill. "I'll tell you what," she says as she drops her sack on the porch and wipes her brow with a lace handkerchief, "the first thing you can do is get in the habit of making that trip for me."

"The first thing?"

"I'm too old to be climbing mountains every day of the week."

"Are we staying, then?"

"If it suits you."

Mary cannot bring herself to inquire as to the terms of her employment—not only because the discussion seems altogether too delicate, but because it has never occurred to her that such terms are something that people might discuss at all.

The widow comes to her rescue. "I can part with room and board for you and the boy, plus a little extra. You ought to be able to put something by." She collapses upon the porch step alongside her sack. "I won't be on this earth forever."

Huck scrambles off toward the woods and Mary stands on the lawn before the house, surrounded by green grass and an ocean of blue and all of the space in the world. She lifts her eyes unto the universe and the widow and begins to ask: "What about the."

"Oh," says the widow with a smile and a wave of her hand. "We have six months to resolve that."

"Six months," says Mary, considering. "And then what?"

"Then you can be claimed."

"Huck too."

"Huck too."

Six months. Six months is half as long as Finn spent in the penitentiary at Alton, a stretch which seemed then an eternity of composited blessing and curse. She decides that six months will have to do. It may be sufficient time to alter a life for good.

"Happily," says the widow with a grave kind of reserved maternal delight, "happily, I have made arrangements for an alternative."

Mary cocks her head.

"All that's required is that we tell the world a little story."

"A story."

"About Huck." The widow pats the step beside her, indicating in vain that Mary should sit.

———

FINN WAKES AT NOON and lies in the bed listening to the river traffic, glad that for once he is not out in it. He has not lain awake in bed like this for longer than he can remember, and the activity seems to him more luxurious than any other he might name. There are fish upon his lines, this he knows, but they will await his pleasure as the woman and the boy never could.

Finally his belly draws him downstairs, and he makes himself a pot of coffee and fries up some bacon and dines kinglike on the porch. He cannot decide whether this is breakfast or lunch and he reckons that by establishing a practice of spending additional hours in bed he can economize considerably on his foodstuffs. Two meals a day for himself, versus nine altogether with those others. At this rate a person could make some progress in life, and in honor of this liberating insight he helps himself to a celebratory whiskey which turns by and by into two or three, and then he runs his lines and sells his catch half to Dixon and half to that scoundrel Smith and returns home. At suppertime he visits the dimly gleaming precincts of the Adams Hotel dining room where he has previously ventured only with his brother, but a single glance at the menu dissuades him from his intent and he wanders instead into the bar as if he has meant to come this way all along.

"Your best whiskey," he commands the barman. "A double."

The barman keeps a particular bottle for the use of the hotel's proprietor and certain influential guests like the tousle-headed Senator Farraday, and out of habit he gives it a passing glance while he considers exactly what he might pour for this uncouth apparition posted at the dark end of the black walnut bar. He reaches for a bottle of some second-rate stuff, whiskey no doubt five times as good as anything this figure has ever drunk before and ten times better than he'd have the palate to recognize, but as his fingers touch the glass Finn cuts him off with a bark.

"Not so fast. I seen where you keep the good stuff."

The barkeep nods in acquiescence and feints as if to reach elsewhere, toward another bottle just the slightest bit more elevated.

"Don't try me."

"I won't."

"I'm good for it." Spilling coins onto the bar. "No matter what you think." He fixes the barman with a vicious look that turns midway along its passage into a disdainful and predatory smile. "Or did you reckon you'd overcharge me for the plain?"

"No, sir," says the barman, "I most certainly would not. This is a decent establishment." He reaches for the bottle with one hand and takes up a glass with the other, although it pains him to present his back so nakedly to this individual.

"I don't generally trade at decent establishments."

"Is that right." Turning, and working the cork free.

"But this," says Finn, "is a special occasion."

"How so." Making a show of inspecting the empty glass.

"I done won back my freedom."

"Really." Pouring with infinite caution.

"That's correct."

The barman puts down the bottle and leaves the glass where it sits and edges closer to his customer as he might to some chained and ravenous creature brought back from the deepest jungle. "Won back your freedom." Despite Finn's layering of beard and hair and filth he draws his conclusion: "You don't look it."

"Shitfire," says Finn, taking a certain amount of pleasure in the barman's confusion and even more in being without doubt the first man to ever make such an exclamation here in the elegant bar of the Adams Hotel. "I ain't no goddamn nigger. That what I just *freed myself of,* son. A goddamn nigger. And a woman too, all at once."

"That's quite an achievement."

"Yes sir, it is." Eyeing the distant drink. "Yes sir, you could say that."

The barman presents the glass of whiskey upon a fancy coaster of darkly tooled leather, and then with a single professional glance he evaluates the pile of change that Finn has set out. He helps himself to most of it and goes to the register.

"You making change?"

"No sir." Fearing the worst.

"Live and learn," says Finn. He smacks his lips over the double whiskey and raises it to his lips like a sacrament. "There'll be more where that come from."

The barman turns and leans on the back rail to watch as Finn struggles with his conflicting impulses. Like Jacob with the angel the riverman wrestles, torn between desire and dignity, sipping and sniffing and eyeing the glass in the lamplight as if speculating on whether it contains some liquefied gemstone or the purest poison. Little by little he downs half of it before he completes this evaluative procedure, and then he sets the glass down flat on the coaster and puckers his lips. He sits tilting his head from side to side, thoughtful and slow as a bluetick hound.

"Well?"

"Smooth enough." Toying with the glass, putting it up on one edge and setting it down again.

"So they say. Myself, I've never had the pleasure."

Finn cogitates for a minute, then he raises the glass and downs the remainder in one gulp. "Don't waste your money," he concludes as he wipes his mustache with the back of his sleeve. "You'll hardly know you drunk it, and how in hell much good is that."

"You've got a point." The barman fears that Finn may decide to part with the rest of his money on refreshment of lesser quality, but soon enough learns otherwise.

"I'm an expert in these things," he says. Gathering up his coins.

"I guess you are. And on niggers and women too."

"Amen," says Finn. "And this right here," running his finger around the interior of the glass to collect the residue and lifting that finger into the lamplight and licking it clean with satisfaction, "this right here is the one thing out of those three that I ain't giving up." He stands and thanks the barman kindly and sets a course for the door across the lobby, the tall double door which is just now opening to admit the night air and something else besides: a tall elegant stranger in a luxurious woolen overcoat and a beaver hat, who holds the door wide and makes himself nearly invisible so as to permit the entry of the Judge and his wife.

In the shadows, Finn turns back to the barman. "You know that feller?"

"The tall drink of water? I don't believe I do."

"I mean the other'n."

"I know *of* him." Finn's empty glass has already disappeared some-where. "That'd be Judge Finn. The old woman's his missus."

Finn pulls out his few coins all over again and slides them onto the bar. "Tell me what'll that buy."

The barman whistles low. "Nothing much that I've got."

"How about if I said that feller's my own pap."

"I'd say you were drunk, if I didn't know better."

"I ain't lying."

The barman rubs a fresh glass with a towel and does not even look up at the man standing eager before him. "If that's your pap, then your money's no good here." Which remark Finn takes for an insult until he realizes that it is either a wager or a guarantee, between the two of which possibilities he has no cause to make any great distinction.

"You mean it."

"I do."

"Then pick me out a fair to middling bottle—none of your fancy stuff—and leave it on the bar."

———

A SPECTER SWOOPING DOWN at him from the high chandelier could surprise the Judge no more than the sudden shambling appearance of his own son within the depths of this previously secure redoubt.

"Pap." Hiking up his trousers as he comes.

His answer comes not from his father but from his mother, who speaks aloud his Christian name.

"Didn't think I'd run into you," says Finn.

The Judge stands dumbstruck beyond a theoretical margin sprung up around his own flesh-and-blood descendant, like a man tending a brushfire that has grown suddenly hotter and less amenable than he would like.

"Who's your friend, Pap?"

The Judge looks away as if distracted, and then to the tall man in the beaver hat. "Mr. Whittier, may I present William's brother."

"Pleased to meet you," says Whittier, with a smile and an outthrust hand. He teeters just the slightest, oddly like a drunken sailor in spite of his elegance, for his right leg is missing below the knee and he has never quite accustomed himself to its wooden substitute.

"Careful," says the Judge, his smile an ironic mask.

"Why? Does this one bite too?"

Finn takes his hand and churns it. "I see you *do* know that brother of mine."

Perhaps Whittier is humoring the Judge or perhaps he is blinded by the old man's legendary stature or perhaps he is himself just more a man of the people than his elegant appearance suggests, but he gives the impression of being genuinely delighted to have made the acquaintance of this ragged and wild-eyed figure. "Will you be joining us for supper?"

"He will not."

"I reckon I already had a little something." Rolling his eyes toward the bar and the barman and the standing bottle.

"Then perhaps we ought to have a little something more." Whittier indicates the bar with his upturned palm and addresses his suggestion more to the Judge and his wife than to Finn, who he can see is always ready for anything in the way of a drink.

"I'm in."

His mother demurs and starts off toward the dining room, which leaves the Judge to choose between accompanying her and looking after the best interests of his unsuspecting guest. As much as it distresses him he follows the two of them to the bar, where they have already taken up positions on either side of the bottle.

"How long you known Pap?"

"Not long."

"I reckoned so." Confidentially: "*He ain't got much patience for drink.*"

"Now, now," says Whittier as the Judge settles onto a stool and shakes his head at the ready barman. "All things in moderation. Isn't that correct, Judge Finn?" Lifting his glass.

The Judge ignores his impudence. "Mr. Whittier is out from Philadelphia, your mother's birthplace."

"I know where she's from."

"He's an attorney, representing us in certain matters having to do with her parents' estate."

Finn gawks, incredulous. "When'd they pass on?"

"They've been in the ground for years." The Judge tips his great knowing head toward Whittier for sympathy, but Whittier offers him none for he believes that his son's ignorance is a great and bracing joke.

"You've got your own way of looking at the world," he says, a step away from clapping the younger man on the back. "Do you know that?"

"I know it. I reckon I'm what you call the black sheep."

"Me too," says Whittier. "My people are day laborers, one and all. It broke their hearts when I took up the law."

"Ain't no good never come of it."

"And very little good has come of hard labor, either. Not so far as I'm concerned." He raps with his knuckles upon his wooden shin loud enough to make Finn jump. "Taken off by an overturned hay wagon. I was just a child. It reformed me then and there, and set my course in life."

The two of them put their heads together to work on the bottle of whiskey for a few minutes and the Judge watches them as he would study a nest of insects, curious about their ways but wary of their intent.

The barman whispers to him. "The feller told me who he was, sir, but I thought he was all wet."

"Thank you," as if he has received a high compliment long overdue. "Oddly enough, he seems to possess a power for entertaining my houseguest that is well beyond my own capacity."

"Folks are different."

"I know they are."

"That's one thing I've learned."

The Judge sniffs.

Finn lifts his voice. "I've been telling Mr. Whitfield here how I'm at loose ends."

The Judge to his visitor: "My son's income has always been, how shall I say it, uncertain."

"I ain't talking about them kind of loose ends. I mean the woman."

"Please." With a freezing look that would bind and gag him if it possibly could, and manacle him to the bar for good measure.

Whittier raises his glass in a toast. "Your son tells me that he and his wife have gone their separate ways."

"Not exactly. Not exactly my wife, I mean." With an animal grin.

"That's correct, Mr. Whittier." The Judge agrees with his son for once. *"Not exactly his wife."*

"Now, I'm not bothered in the least if you folks want to do things a little differently out here."

"We do not do things differently. We live by the same precepts here as in any other civilized place."

"I don't want you thinking I'm shocked is all, just because I'm from the big town back east, if a fellow wants to take up with a little old gal."

"I wouldn't."

"I've seen a bit of the world."

"I suppose you have," says the Judge.

"As I was saying," Finn resumes, helping himself to the bottle, "I done set myself free of that woman."

"And as a result you expect me to be proud of you."

"Speaking for your son, it's nothing to be ashamed of."

"I assure you that my son knows all there is to know about shame, Mr. Whittier. He could teach both of us volumes."

Whittier eyes Finn with something approaching a new appreciation.

"I shall be forthright with you, Mr. Whittier. My son has possessed an untoward predilection for nigger women since young manhood. He has lain with one in particular for many years now, and their unnatural union has yielded unto this world a bastard mulatto child." He rises a bit, as if pronouncing a sentence. "The shame that he has rung down upon his family and his race is beyond any reckoning." He excuses himself to check on his wife, and when he returns from the dining room his misbegotten son and the Philadelphian Whittier and the half-drained bottle are all three of them gone off into the night, the barman knows not where.

—

THE TWO MEN, one broad and bullying as a grizzly and the other dangerously slim in his elegant woolen coat and beaver hat, one slightly astagger and the other reeling on his mismatched legs, make their way down the hill sharing a bottle between them. It does not last long, the bottle, and Finn underhands it riverward when they reach the pier and together they stand to watch it go circling end over end upward and upward into the moonlight and then down again knifing into the water with nary a splash.

"That's that," says Finn.

"That's that."

"You got money."

"I happen to be filthy with it."

"God bless you for a gentleman," says Finn. "Myself, I'm a little poorly just now."

"Don't you worry about a thing." Whittier puts his hands on his hips and surveys the night river. He turns to his guide and presents him with a slow smile of infinite mischief and delight. "Your grandparents' estate takes good care of its executor."

"And that would be you."

"That it would."

Finn lowers his chin and cackles into his beard with a certain unmitigated glee. "Whitman, you're a man after my own black heart."

"And who would have guessed?"

"Not the Judge."

"No. Surely not the Judge."

They choose a skiff and Finn poles it up to Dixon's place and introduces his newfound benefactor all around. Dixon has plenty of whiskey and Whittier has plenty of money and between them they strike an agreement that leaves everyone happy save perhaps Dixon's wife who hates a drunkard. An angular black man playing a banjo in the corner names a rollicking number after him and the cardplayers let him win a harmless hand or two, and by closing time his misspelled name along with the date or some date close to it have been carved into the wainscoting beneath the bar by a grateful individual gone belly up and fish-like thanks to Whittier's memorable largesse.

"Where to?" says the Philadelphian when everyone else has gone home and Dixon's wife has shown these last two the door.

"I know a feller."

"I'll bet you do."

They stumble down the steps and untie and make for the dense patch of woods on the river's edge where the trail that is not a trail to Bliss's cabin begins. Even for Finn, who knows it well, the passage seems to camouflage itself anew each time he seeks it, and as he proceeds along it now he could swear that every turning has shed its prior geometry or traded places with some other. The woods are silent save the tree-to-tree movement of these two, whose steps are not half so stealthy as they would desire or believe.

"Bliss can hear a cricket fart at a hundred yards," says Finn. "So we better start stepping light."

"Won't he be asleep?"

"You can't never tell. Not with Bliss. He don't do nothing regular."

"Why don't we just wake him up and buy the stuff?"

"Now Whit," says Finn with a look of comic derision visible by moonlight through a high canopy of leaves, "where's your sense of adventure?"

"I have money. I don't need a sense of adventure."

Because Finn cannot deny the wisdom of this sentiment he chooses to ignore it, and so rather than answering he lifts a finger to his lips. Together they plunge ahead into the depths of the woods as quietly as any two staggering drunks, one of them city-bred and afoot in the wilds of Illinois for the first time in his life and hampered by a wooden leg on top of it all, possibly could.

Bliss's shack is darker than the dark woods themselves and many times as threatening. Despite his frequent visits to the still and the secret cache of whiskey and the broad tree-shaded porch, Finn has never set foot within the cabin itself and so he does not know exactly where inside it Bliss might lie sleeping or beneath which open window his ready ear might lie cocked. The crumbling place stands in its clearing like a ruined mausoleum by moonlight, the air around it still redolent of woodsmoke and alcohol. Finn spies it first from the fringe of the woods, and he reaches back to place a hand on Whittier's chest, thereby arresting his progress.

"Are we getting close?" Whittier, hissing.

"Have *you* gone blind now too?" The outline of the house is plain enough to him as to be illuminated. He cannot imagine that Whittier is having difficulty resolving its squarish silhouette from the tangle of woods and brush that surrounds it, although by the light of day the very boards and shingles and struts of the decrepit place seem intent upon merging themselves back again into the organic earth.

"Oh," whispers Whittier, making it out plain as day now that he knows it is before him. "Excuse me."

Finn believes that Whittier means to make apology for his incompetence as a woodsman, and he is about to forgive him when from the direction of the Pennsylvanian there issues a noise as of strong rain on a flat rock. To avoid his companion's inadvertent overspray Finn steps into the clearing where his foot lands with a single sharp report upon a twig laid by chance traplike upon another just like it.

"I done heard that." Bliss's voice from within the cabin.

"It's Finn."

The bootlegger's silhouette appears dark against the inner dark of the cabin against the outer dark of the woods and Finn can see it moving within the doorframe.

"You taking a leak in my woods."

"I reckon so."

"Christ Almighty ain't you got no decency at all. First you wake a man up in the middle of the night and then you start in to pissing in his front yard. God damn you." The man has clearly been in his cups and between the fog induced thereby and a certain unsatisfactory measure of sleep prematurely interrupted he is perhaps even more irascible and off balance than is his custom.

"I need whiskey."

"I need my sleep."

At which moment Whittier completes his business and tops it off with a long grateful bellow of sighing respiration. The Philadelphia lawyer's friends and family and descendants, if he has any, will be either comforted or saddened to know that he enjoys at least this one moment of unmitigated luxury before Finn's bootlegging associate Bliss raises that ivory-handled pistol of his and fires it into the oblivious dark at the woods' edge and puts a ball straight into Whittier's unsuspecting shoulder.

"Damn," says Whittier. "You weren't lying."

"Who's your friend?" says Bliss.

"Nobody special."

"Leastways I didn't kill him. My aim must be off."

"You've had a few."

"I know it."

Out from the woods comes Whittier with his bleeding shoulder darkly agleam in the light of the moon despite the layers and absorbency of his thick woolen coat. His beaver hat is gone, knocked off in the woods or fallen from the skiff or perhaps cast off back at Dixon's, and freed from beneath it his hair is wild and clumped with leaves. Nonetheless thanks to the whiskey he has drunk he is gay of mood despite having been shot, and if pressed he would even go so far as to admit that receiving a ball in the left shoulder should not slow his drinking down even for the short term but will on the contrary serve forever in his mind as a badge of honor and a treasured memento of this wild-and-wooly occasion.

They go to the porch and Finn asks for a lamp but the bootlegger has none.

"Rags then. Clean if you got any."

They leave Whittier upright in one of Bliss's rockers with a jar of forty-rod in his good right hand while the two of them go off each on his own errand, Bliss for rags and a basin, Finn for some sticks of wood and a little fire from the banked coals beneath the still. They return and make a torch and douse it in whiskey and wring it out dry, and then Finn wedges it into a knothole in the porch floorboards and touches fire to it.

Finn's course of action is clear so he helps himself to some drink and Bliss does likewise just to keep him company. They strip off Whittier's coat, the man moaning in his chair as they peel it away from his wrecked shoulder. In the torchlight the wound is mysterious and wet and black.

"Go on pour some into that basin," says Finn.

"Goddamn if whiskey ain't the most useful thing on earth."

"I know it."

He bunches a rag and wets it and dabs roughly at the wound, which causes Whittier to flinch and forces a sizzling sound from between his clenched teeth. The ball has dug itself a deep passage down into muscle which gapes and puckers like a small mouth and leaks a slow insistent pulsing of blood.

"Will I live?" Whittier's good humor returns the instant Finn leaves off mopping at the wound, and his right hand raises the jar.

"I reckon you will."

"How bad I get him?"

"I'd like to see that ball out of there."

"It can wait," says the patient. "There's a doctor in this town, isn't there?"

"It ain't in all that deep." Pulling out his clasp-knife. "I've cut further cleaning a rabbit." Finn cleans his knife with an alcohol-soaked rag and permits himself a long pull from Whittier's jar. "Have another'n yourself," he says. "You might need it." He slides the lawyer out of his chair and gets him faceup on the porch and plants his weight astride his chest, and then he instructs Bliss to take the lawyer's left forearm between his knees lest it move when he starts cutting. Between the chairs and the torch and the basin of bloodied whiskey there is some confusion on the porch and at one point Bliss's right foot is up to its ankle in the stuff but soon enough this rough-hewn operating theater is ready and Finn bends to touch the black wound with the tip of his knife.

"Ow."

"Don't be a goddamn baby." Finn grins down at the Pennsylvanian's upturned face like some willful cannibal king who has passed his judgment and whose hand will not be stayed.

"That won't help."

"It weren't meant to." Turning his gaze to the wound pulsing doubly with its own blood and the torch's flicker.

"I'd prefer a doctor."

"I'm the doctor in these woods." He reconsiders his strategy and takes the jug and splashes whiskey upon the wound, washing it clean again and making Whittier jump beneath their two pairs of clasped knees. "Drink up," he says, as if the wound were the mouth it resembles. And then he applies the knife.

Certain buried obstacles catch the leading edge of the blade and strive mutely to deflect it from its intended path, and although each one of them may be the ball each one of them in time proves itself otherwise. Whittier lies gasping and beating his legs both natural and wooden against the floor against the railing against the chair while frustrated Finn withdraws the knife and prods deep with his own rough finger.

"There she is. I swear it."

But the lump is just a round bit of bone or gristle and prying upward upon it does no good, so he mops his drenched brow and fortifies himself and the patient and Bliss alike for good measure and delves in again with the knife clenched spoonlike in his fist.

The knife scrapes against bone and glances off to press against something soft that gives way and before he knows it Finn has an eyeful of blood and Whittier is bucking fit to catapult him off the porch. The leather straps holding the artificial leg tear loose, letting the wooden thing flail within Whittier's pantleg like some furious weapon gone self-aware until it works its way free and lands spent upon the floorboards at some remove from Whittier himself who flails on while Finn squints through blood. "Let him go," he hollers at Bliss, who is eager to comply. "More rags. Dip them."

With two fistfuls of bunched wet rags he leans his considerable weight upon the Philadelphian's pinned shoulder, not caring if he breaks every bone in it so long as he exerts pressure sufficient to stanch the bleeding. Bliss wets the man's lips with whiskey and nearly loses a finger for his kindness, and as the moments tick by and the stars wheel overhead the rags grow sodden with blood and Finn nearly falls asleep with his weight upon the man's chest and shoulder and the bleeding slows but does not stop entire.

Finn comes to his knees and pulls back the rags and examines the shoulder by torchlight. Whittier's breathing is shallow and ragged but his forehead is cool to the touch, which the riverman takes for a good sign until with a burbling and a sudden hideous stench the wounded man brings up a portion of everything he has consumed since breakfast. On his back he lies strangled, not able even to gasp, while a shock goes through his body and out his helpless leg which kicks at the railing again in a kind of hopeless automatic fury.

"Roll him over for God's sake," says Bliss, whose nose and ears have detected Whittier's condition.

"That shoulder."

"The hell with his shoulder. Roll that sonofabitch or he's a dead man."

Finn does as he has been told and gets Whittier's face over the step, where he can work on freeing the passageway of his mouth with bloody fingers. His clasp-knife has disappeared in the scuffle and once Whittier has resumed breathing in that desperate and pitiful way he has acquired he slaps him on the back and goes off to find it by torchlight. He downs a little of the bootlegger's whiskey while he's at it, just to take the edge off.

———

"DID YOU GET IT?" Whittier, buckled over on the step, hard by a pool of his own crusting vomit, his ruined coat thrown about him like a cape.

"Get what?"

"The ball." Not even lifting his head to explain.

"I reckon it's in there deeper than I thought."

"Thank you, Dr. Finn." Without a weak smile or an ironic smile or any kind of smile at all.

"We got you bandaged up fine though. It'll hold."

"I can't feel a thing."

"That's good."

The two sit for a time, Bliss asleep in the chair behind them. The night air has gone cold and Finn half wishes he had Whittier's coat.

"We'd better get on," he says by and by.

"Where."

"Get you home."

"I'm happy here."

"The Judge ain't. I don't get you back he'll have my hide."

Whittier works at the torn straps of his wooden leg with fingers equally wooden until at last he resigns himself to failure and lets his head collapse down into the cradle of his cupped right hand as if this small frustration were the worst indignity he has yet been caused to suffer and the worst he ever will. Careful to avoid the Philadelphian's mess Finn kneels before him and ties the leg in place with a rag soaked in either whiskey or blood and wipes his hands on his pantlegs and rises. He is certain there must be a shortcut uphill through the woods that will save some time and keep them off the river, and so he prizes the dead torch from its hole and throws it into the yard and then he wakes Bliss to ask.

Bliss confirms it, so the two of them let him drift back to sleep and set off into the woods. Every step pains Whittier, who clutches his coat around his neck like a shroud and winces each time he runs afoul of some stump or treelimb or thorned underbrush. "How about you go back and get that torch."

"Won't do no good," says Finn. "Funny thing about this place. You can find it better in the dark."

"How about finding your way out."

"Don't get smart." Pushing the jug toward him.

"I don't have a free hand." For his right hand is busy with his collar and his left arm is pinned tight by bandages below which the remainder of it hangs down limp as an animal gutted and bled dry.

Finn pauses long enough to raise the jug to Whittier's lips and tilt it back. "Easy now."

Whittier can hardly draw breath for the tightness of the bandages wound around his chest and shoulder, but he acknowledges the whiskey and follows Finn along the trail that is not a trail into deeper and deeper woods. They press on for time indeterminate, the riverman flailing at branches and brush and the diminished lawyer calculating one step after another and stopping now and then to lean against the welcome trunk of some tree.

"We ain't stopping here."

"I know it."

"Stir yourself."

"I'll die if we don't stop."

"You won't."

"A drink then."

"None for you till we're back."

"Please."

"I'll end up carrying you, you great drunken baby." Which he does in the end regardless, the leg coming loose for all his trouble and slipping inch by inch out of its pantleg and battering him about the ankles until he frees it entire and carries that too. By moonlight he emerges laden from the treeline into a farmer's field he does not recognize and tramps onward with his back-borne burden despite fences and walls and horse-shit until the outline of a farmhouse emerges from the dark and he knows it and can tell the way home.

To his father's porch he comes like a peddler bearing death by the sodden sackful. There is a swing at the far end and into it he lets Whittier drop, and then he slumps down against the wall and listens while its poor unused rusty chains creak a little and then go quiet.

"Are we there?"

"Yes." His heart pounding in his ears.

"Nothing hurts."

"Good for you."

Finn sits for a while studying the late-night sky and the dim starlight through the vertical balusters of the porch. Whittier's left arm droops black across the marching line of them at a haphazard angle as oblique and final as a tally mark, its line other than Finn himself the only thing off square upon the spotless white porch of the magnificent white mansion on the most elevated street in town.

———

COME MORNING a rivulet of blood has dribbled down that selfsame arm and pooled upon the painted floorboards and dried to a black crust, and Finn arises to find himself jailed behind the sunlit balusters with a dead man. He rifles Whittier's coat for whatever riches may yet remain in his purse, and then he lies back down again and sleeps some more, for he will need all of his wits to handle the Judge and there is no sense in running. The wooden leg he resolves to keep as a memento.

The hired man's wife discovers them. "There's two men dead on the porch," she says to the Judge's wife, who steadfastly refuses to go out and see for herself. She edges down the staircase from her parlor and thence along the hallway that leads to the chamber where the Judge sits inviolate, and she raps upon the door and delivers to him the news.

"Two men?" From deep within. "Two?"

"So she says."

"Then you haven't seen for yourself?"

"No."

With a creak the Judge's chair gives up his weight. "I do not require a crystal ball to foretell that only one of those two men is dead," he says when he emerges from behind the door. "If you're curious, it would be the one *not* descended from your bloodline."

"My bloodline."

But the Judge has already put his broad black back to her and gone striding down the hall toward the porch where he might take in the damage with his own two eyes. He discovers the tableau exactly as he had expected it, and with a grunt he kicks his son in the ribs to rouse him.

"Ow." Turning painfully over onto his back. There is more blood on him than there is on the dead man, as if Whittier for his last gift had bequeathed every drop of it to the individual who saw fit to carry him as far as the Judge's porch. Blood has stained his shirt and his trousers and his boots and by his walking he has left upon the porch a pattern of crosses in blood, as of a man who has waded in paint. Blood is caked in his hair and in his beard and blood is dried masklike upon his face and blood is crackling from his hands like his own dead skin.

"You've made a by-God mess."

"It weren't my fault."

"It never is."

"I brung him home. That's all." He knows that offering up too much too soon will drive the Judge's suspicion and intuition to an even higher pitch than they have surely reached already.

Fingering the bullet hole in Whittier's coat: "You didn't do this?"

"No."

"Who did."

"I don't know."

"So it *was* you."

Finn sits and leans his bloody back against the white wall. "It weren't. It was two men down to Dixon's. Stole my skiff and shot Whitman here in the bargain."

"Why him."

"He weren't smart enough to let them have the boat."

"And you were."

"Oddly enough."

The Judge surveys Whittier's long and crumpled form, pale as wax beneath his coat and covered over with a thousand stray spatters and streaks of blood. "I don't believe it."

"Suit yourself." Blinking hard to clear his head.

"I will," says the Judge.

"You always do. A man can count on that."

The Judge calls forth the hired man's wife and instructs her to go fetch the marshal, and then he bends himself nearly double to fill his son's vision with his great vengeful head and forges for the pair of them a pact. "I shall not dispute your story. Moreover I shall not by the exercise of such power as I possess have you hanged by the neck until dead, however much you deserve it. Do you understand?"

"I do."

"In return you shall mark this occasion and remember my kindness all the days of your life, for as of this moment you are irrevocably and immeasurably in my debt."

"I won't forget."

"No." Unbending himself. "You won't."

"How can I."

"Repay me? How can you repay me? Why, it may not be possible. We'll have to wait and see."

"But."

"However." He shows Finn a stern finger, smudged with a little blood from Whittier's coat. "If we cannot agree upon a way, or if you should dare deny your promise, honor shall require me to inform the marshal of exactly how you lied to me."

"I didn't lie. I didn't kill Whittington. I tried to save him."

"Perhaps you did," says the Judge. He rises and wipes that one tainted finger clean upon Whittier's pantleg. "But I can no longer bring myself to care."

———

HE LEAVES his father's house and goes down to the river to bathe. At the steamboat landing he lowers himself fully clothed into the water as a sinner plunged into fire or a penitent baptized. He does not so much as remove his hat, and when he draws a gasping breath and pushes himself under the riverwater that misshapen black thing remains floating at the place of his disappearance, signaling his vanishment just as a loaf of bread doctored with quicksilver will seek out a bottombound corpse. He scrubs himself against himself, running his fingers through his beard and his hair and scraping with a fingernail at his temples and at his cheeks and at his ears to remove such bits of Whittier's blood as he can identify by their stubborn crust. The muddy current carries it all away and he rescues his hat and hauls himself out weighted down and wet. Then he walks back to shore ignoring the bystanders who stare at him as at a sideshow act, and he trudges up the mudbank toward home, where he hangs everything save himself on the porch railing and sits in the sun while the heat of the day comes up and order by means of evaporation restores itself moment by moment.

17

"WE ALL MAKE SACRIFICES." Thus Mary begins, digging the last of the onions in the widow's garden.

"I know it," says the boy.

"You do." Not a question but a challenge.

"Yes ma'am."

She brushes hair and sweat from her forehead with the clean back of her hand, leaving behind a trail of dull velvet black against the remainder. "Reach down and get those, will you?" She stands weary with her sole on the fork, letting the boy scrabble in the place where she has dug.

"I don't mind," says the boy from the dirt.

"You don't mind what."

"Working. Whatever I got to do." He is vigorous and bursting with life and proud of each contribution he has ever made to this multifarious family of his. The boy was born content to pull his own weight and draw his own oar, and so he has remained whether the work has required running trotlines on the river or digging onions in the widow's yard. "You know."

"I do."

They labor together for a while, each of them taking his turn, and the bushel basket fills little by little.

"This doesn't have to be your fate."

"I don't mind."

"You can make something of yourself."

"I'll try."

"Trying's not half of it." She thrusts the fork into the ground as far as it will go and heaves upon it. "Sometimes a person can get only so far."

He kneels in the dirt and looks up at her as at some oracle or demigod.

"I won't have you grow up a slave."

"*You* ain't one."

"Not now." She cannot bring herself to mention those six months that the law has seen fit to grant unto the likes of them, those six months already commencing their inevitable accelerating vanishment.

"So?"

"Things could change. I can't much help it for myself, but I don't want it for you."

"I don't see how there's."

"I'd give anything." Stabbing the ground.

He fetches up the onions and puts them into the basket which he bends to lift with all his might, straightening his back and swaying a little, rehearsing for a lifetime.

"I'd give anything," she says again. "I believe I might even give *you*." As he drops the basket she reaches up with a knuckle to brush at the corner of her eye.

"Mama."

Letting go the fork and kneeling alongside him in the dirt. "You hear me. From this day forward, as far as anyone beyond this house knows, you are a poor motherless child."

"Motherless." He knows her intent as any would.

"That's right. We know better, but nobody else needs to."

He sits stunned.

"You'll go to school like any white boy."

"Mama." At least now his alarm has found a focus.

"Don't *mama* me."

"Pap hates."

"I know it. But you're going to grow up different from your pap. Different from either one of us, come to that. Better too."

"How?"

"Don't you worry. I'll be here to help." Thinking of the six months. "Just as long as I can."

"But."

She points a finger at him. "You came here to St. Pete with me, but you aren't mine. That's all anyone needs to know. And let that be an end to it."

———

NIGHT HAS DESCENDED upon the widow's house, and the boy has gone complaining off to bed as boys will. His mother sits on a hard chair opposite the widow's rocker patching a hole in his trousers while the widow reads from the family Bible. The little parlor is bright with many lamps, bright enough to be visible from the river below, bright enough that these two may pursue their separate aims at their ease despite the woman's weariness and the widow's fading vision. Mary's concentration, whether on her sewing or on her fate, is sufficiently complete that the widow discovers she can lower her book and lift her eyes and study her over her glasses without being noticed. Thus she sits for a time until her lack of movement draws Mary's attention, for prior to this moment she has been sliding the tip of her finger across the page of her Bible and fluttering her lips around the lineaments of the words she finds there.

"Ma'am?"

Raising the finger that has been tracing the Gospel, and pointing it trembling at the scar upon Mary's cheek: "Did he give you that?"

"Yes ma'am, he did."

"*A white man.*" She spits out the words as she would expel a cherry pit. "A white man did that to you."

"The white man I left."

The widow closes the Bible on her finger. "You're more intelligent than he is."

"I hope so, ma'am. And thank you for your kindness." But now that the widow has unlatched this door for so long sealed Mary feels arising within herself an upwelling of grief and grievance, a burgeoning of truths forever withheld and forever likewise unresolved. She rolls up one sleeve and displays the soft tender pale underside of her forearm, marked. "He did this. And this too." Her wrist. "And this." Her ankle. One twisted finger broken and healed that way unset. A gash concealed just under the tattered collar of her dress. Beneath the smooth dark curve of her hair, a red-rimmed and puckered cavity torn from one ear by his strange and brutal teeth. Displayed and duly witnessed here in this quiet and well-lit room with the boy asleep upstairs and the river creeping past far below and the limitless darkening sky yawning over-head, she is a palimpsest of her own degradation.

"You poor child."

"Now you see why."

"I do." The widow has an impulse to set down the book and lean for-ward in her rocker and bless the poor beaten girl with a touch, but she knows not where to begin. She opens the volume and takes one last look at the place within it where her finger lies as if she might find there some eternal truth with which to comfort Mary, and then she closes it again and rests it in her lap, where it lies impotent against incarnate per-sonal evil such as this. "Did he touch the boy?"

"Not like this."

"Does the boy know what he's done?"

"Some. Enough to have come away with me."

"Yes," says the widow, and "yes" again. "Of course he does." The Bible in her lap has become a dead weight and a heavy burden and she ab-sently fiddles with the purple satin bookmark that runs its spine as the river runs the valley. After a time a question occurs to her and she rec-ognizes that there will be no better occasion to ask it and so ask it she does: "Do you suppose he'll come looking for you?"

"Yes ma'am. I believe he will."

"Mary." Fixing her with a look that will admit no denial.

Mary puts down her work.

"The man's name is Finn, isn't it. Finn."

"Yes."

"I thought so."

"You did."

"I made inquiries."

"I know it."

———

THE BOY GOES OFF to school for the first time.

"But Pap always said."

"Never you mind what Pap always said. Pap always said a lot of things."

Thus does his luxurious idyll, atop the green sward of Cardiff Hill, freed of running lines and gutting fish, in the gentle company of two women who perhaps without even knowing it have been competing these weeks pie after pie and song after song and story after story for his love in spite of his straitened circumstances and his uncertain future, thus does his idyll come to an end: with a whine and a shrug and a vision of Finn as his absent savior.

In the classroom he proves a fast learner but inconstant. The other children are of mixed ages and although the boys his own size have much to teach him about the local geography they have nothing whatsoever to show him as regards to capitalizing upon it. They point out the church, and Huck climbs to the belfry to sermonize by moonlight in the company of bats. They talk of caves high up on the riverbank, and Huck explores them with a stolen ball of yarn unwound to mark his return. They gossip of a slave reputed to own a prophesying hairball, and Huck befriends the individual and divines his own future by means of the relic's mysterious power. He becomes in short the children's secret untouchable prince, their authority on all things mysterious and forbidden, the raiser of their antes and the taker of their dares.

Parents and pastors and teachers alike urge the children to keep a cautious distance once his ill fame has risen up to the level of their awareness. Some know of Finn and some know of his extended dalliance with a black woman and some know or have at least heard tell of how that selfsame personage has lately enslaved herself and the child as well to that poor bereft widow Douglas in her child-empty house on Cardiff Hill. Some on the other hand have heard the official story of the boy's unknowable origins, and some even believe it. This footloose and misbegotten child, with his fortunate pale skin and his experimental corncob pipe, with his intimacy with slave lore and his confounded gift for looking ragged even in clothing freshly pressed by none other than a white woman or so they say, this child can surely be no positive influence on their young, no positive influence at all. By denying him they make him irresistible, and like a sturdy weed he thrives upon their neglect.

The autumn gives way to winter and the Mississippi begins to glaze over in places. From the boy's window on certain bright mornings it glints along its margins like a woodland path strewn with gemstones, and he tells his mother that he would go down and retrieve them one and all if only he could and then make for her a necklace. She laughs and tells him that she deserves neither the necklace nor him, which he denies but takes to heart nonetheless without seeing for even a moment the depths of his ready faithlessness. By the time he heads for school the frozen patches are gone and the river has recovered its quality of ambiguous bank-to-bank sameness, which the boy knows from his father's teachings is only a façade to mislead the ignorant and starve the inexperienced.

For his part the father is upon the river every afternoon, pursuing a catch that grows more scarce as the winter deepens. He mends old lines and acquires new ones and steals still others, and with them he widens his range by appropriating the fishing grounds of lesser men unwilling to contest his claim until the Illinois side of the river is his from above Lasseter to below it, traversed by a latticework that he transits each day to fuel his meager needs and then some. He thinks rarely of the boy and less rarely of the woman, mainly when there are chores to be done or a fire to be built in the old iron stove. Mornings he endures by staying in bed and evenings when he returns home longing for a little warmth he satisfies himself with whiskey. That warm-blooded African girl with her memories of Vicksburg would have kept the stove red-hot night and day, and as he swallows and shivers and swallows again he takes pleasure in realizing that at least he is not outdoors chopping wood so that she might waste it.

A storm blows down the river late one day and catches him unsuspecting past the southernmost perimeter of his workings, below Smith's trading post by half a mile, nearly as far downriver as St. Petersburg. Icicles are adangle from his slouch hat and his beard is rimed with ice and even his eyebrows beneath that sagging hatbrim are crusted over by the time he has poled to within sight of Smith's, which looms white against the white storm and looks, as usual, abandoned. On the verge of such a night as this the vituperative Smith will be in no mood to buy fish or offer credit, so Finn settles on tying up downwind against the little pier and sleeping the night there in the protection of its lee side rather than risk the fat man's reflexive and pitiless ire. The catch will keep until morning under its bed of snow.

Unbidden she comes to him in the night, a warm tender spirit coalesced from out of the cold. Mary. Under the darkness of his eyelids under the whiteness of the accumulating snow he sees her through a fog of sleep lit piercing in the absence of his usual whiskey. Snow-damped silence and the patient slow rocking of the skiff have put him to sleep beneath his tarpaulin, the night has reached some blank unknowable nadir aspin beneath ratcheting stars and cartwheeling snowflakes, and at this point or some other she comes to him unwanted but not undesired. He shivers and yearns and warms himself against her and unwittingly draws himself out to spill his milt upon the icy heap of catfish warmed slick by his sacrificial flesh. Through it all he awakens not.

Come daylight he shakes himself off and knocks on Smith's door to find the proprietor as unreceptive to his merchandise as he would have been the night before. The storm has mostly spent itself but the riverman is half frozen and dying for warmth, a thing that Smith hoards with the same miserliness that he brings to guarding his other merchandise.

"You'll frighten away my customers."

"If they're brave enough to bargain with you, I reckon they're plenty brave enough."

Somewhere deep within his mountain of flesh Smith chuckles in spite of himself, but he neither warms to Finn nor permits him to linger. "Be on your way before you begin stinking like a wet dog."

Finn obliges and tests the wind and follows it downriver to St. Petersburg, where he can trade his catch to Cooper at the Liberty Hotel. Up the hill into the village he troops with a sackful of frozen cats and bluegills, unsteady on his feet in the snow and leaving behind him a trail of crosses. Cooper gives him whiskey and pork and cornmeal from his stores and a hot breakfast fit for a king right there in the kitchen, where he and the black woman sit and yarn and wait upon orders.

"I reckon won't be many customers on a morning like this," says Cooper. "You may as well have your fill."

"I'm obliged." His coat and hat steam on a nail by the stove and the snowmelt from his boots soaks into the hardpacked dirt floor and he can hardly believe his good fortune. "I could stay here all day."

"Don't get any ideas."

"I won't."

Full and warm and drier at least than he has been, he gathers his sack and leaves down the alley. On the street he spies a group of children off to school, one of them Huck.

"You boy."

The snow is still pelting and he stands between buildings ghostly and darkly emergent.

"You Huck."

The boy turns. Deep in scheming conversation with some mischievous towhead, he recognizes his father as if growing cognizant of a dream made real before him; he notes his appearance as if a chasm in this world has opened up and let loose the inhabitants of some other.

"Pap." Soundless, just the merest dark opening of his boy's mouth in the bright snowfall. He halts and the boy behind stumbles up against him but the rest go flowing 'round about like a stream past a rock. Some look back over their shoulders and some do not and those who do avert their eyes quickly before going on their way for they have been warned about this individual.

"Where you bound, boy."

"School."

Full as he is of flapjacks and bacon and hot coffee, and pleased as he is with his haul of goods and whiskey from that burden of fish frozen solid in the skiff, he can feel the heart in his chest collapse at the sound of the word. *School.* All is surely lost. "No you ain't."

"The widow says."

"What widow." Brutal he is and single-minded but not lacking in imagination. The word upon his son's lips suggests that perhaps the woman Mary has declared herself thus liberated in her new life. Again: "What widow."

"Widow Douglas. She took us in."

"Not out of charity."

"No."

"What then."

"Mama works for her."

"Not in Missouri. In Missouri they call that slavery."

"She ain't a slave."

"Wake up, boy."

"The widow don't treat her like one. She treats her like help." Standing in the snow as it lightens around them both.

"What do you know about help."

"Pays her every week like clockwork."

"So tell me," Finn wheedles. "You all free to leave the premises?"

"Where would we go?" With a shrug.

"Sounds a heap like slavery to me."

The man has a point that rings true to the boy but only so far. "Mama never left the house upriver neither. Except when you was in prison."

"Them was different times."

"I reckon they was."

Finn watches the other boys vanish around the corner. "You ain't going to no school."

"Where then?"

"Wherever suits you."

"You fishing?"

"Not today." Lifting his sack of groceries. "Just back home."

"Can I come?" For the boy's great gift is of accommodation.

"No. I reckon you're better off here." Thinking of his own obligations and customs. "Just don't get in the habit of going to that school."

"I won't."

"Take off when you like. Go fishing maybe. Take a swim come summertime."

"I will."

Finn stands thinking. "So where's this widow's place, anyhow?"

"Top of the hill." Pointing with a hand that emerges from the sleeve of a coat of better quality than any Finn has possessed since his own squandered childhood.

"I seen it up there." He chews his lip and squints up toward the place.

"Reckon I might go on up and say my goodbyes. Ain't never done it proper, on account of how you two run off."

"It weren't my idea."

"I know it. I don't blame you. I blame that woman calls herself your mama." For it has occurred to him in this instant on this show-white street in this no-account Missouri village that if he does not desire to possess the boy then no one shall have him, least of all a nigger woman bound for enslavement.

The normally garrulous and amenable Huck knows not the words to make answer.

"Hear me, boy. Your mama's long dead."

"No."

"Breaks my poor heart to say it."

"No."

"Don't tell me what I know. She died giving you birth."

Tears come to the boy's eyes but he fights them back and turns to wipe his nose upon the sleeve of his coat.

"Now that nigger woman, she come along later. She's a runaway I done took in to be kindly."

"But the two of you."

"One thing led to another is all. That's the way of the world, boy." He hikes up his trousers and spits down between his boots. "I always had a fondness for her color, even though your own mama was as white as this very snow."

"She was."

"She by-God was. Look at your own self."

Confronted by the evidence of his very flesh the boy casts aside all previous assumptions on the matter and discovers that he believes. "Why did you lie to me."

"She done it, not me. I never."

"But sometimes you did. You'd call her my mama. You would."

"It weren't my idea."

"But."

"That nigger's a kindly old gal for the most part. I ain't taking that from her. I reckon she wanted a little boy of her own and I just up and give her one."

Huck looks away, distracted, off down the street to where the boys have disappeared around the turning. Despite his youth he desires in the manner of all people gone bereft to absent himself entirely from the known world, to break all bonds with it rather than let the pain of any yet unsevered connection bespeak the absence of those others already gone. Today he has lost two mothers, and he desires to be neither with his father nor with Mary nor anywhere at all. "I got to get to school," he says, hoping neither for confrontation nor for approval, but perhaps to wound his weakened father just the slightest by his willfulness.

"I know it."

"I don't go regular, but I got to go now."

"Then you go on."

"I will." Turning and making tracks.

"There a path up to that widow's house?" asks his father as he goes.

———

The path circles around the base of Cardiff Hill and skirts the upper edge of the quarry, where it intersects another path coming straight up from the edge of the Mississippi. Finn looks back and wonders how any son of his coming downhill from that house could ever choose the town path over the river, particularly when he faces no contrary force save a nigger woman and a useless old widow, but in the end he resolves that there are some things in this world that simply will not yield to reason.

He tops the hill and scuffs up the walk where the snow is thinner and windblown with his cross-heeled boot pinning down some of its tatters, and Mary answers his knock.

"You." Casting eyes upon him.

"I see that old widow's got you trained up well enough. The boy too, going to school and all."

"You saw Huck."

"I did."

The woman's eyes darken and she draws one short breath. "You can't have him."

"My, my, my." Finn rocks back on his heels, grinning through his mustache. "Ain't you gotten uppity?"

"He's better off here."

"I don't doubt it." Scanning the room behind her.

"Now Finn."

"A feller could be right comfortable in such a place."

"Don't you get any ideas."

"Yes sir, right comfortable. Provided he weren't growing up a goddamn nigger slave."

From the kitchen: "Mary?"

"I reckon your mistress is calling."

The woman cuts him with a look both furious and terrified if not for herself then for her son. She has grown comfortable here these last months enjoying the widow's wherewithal and accommodating the widow's habits and doing the widow's bidding, and now she despises this gleeful harbinger of fate for reminding her that all of it must come inevitably and one way or another to an end. She shall be either exiled or enslaved, and the decision between the two shall be entirely her own.

"I said *your mistress.*"

"Mary?" Stretching out that second syllable as if calling a hog, the widow bustles toward them down the hall and then pulls up short to appraise this mendicant come begging around her door with his dusting of snow and his hat down over his eyes and his greasy old sack. Rarely do his kind seek comfort this high above the more ready pickings of the village, and she is unpracticed in the ways of rejection. "May I help you, sir?" Not recognizing him.

"No ma'am, your girl is doing just fine." A delicate stab that goes unnoticed at least by the widow, or else noticed and by lack of response acknowledged as mere truth.

"Have him go around to the kitchen door, Mary. He can have what breakfast Huck didn't eat. Then send him on his way."

"Mighty obliged, ma'am," touching his hat, "but I done had all the breakfast I can hold." By the time he delivers his surprising answer she is gone, circulating back into the depths of the house like some secretive fish and leaving Mary alone to dispose of him as she has been instructed.

"I done Huck a favor," he says, leaning toward her and offering a carnivorous smile.

So certain is she of the impossibility of it that she bothers not to ask what he has done. She scents the sharp tang of him and the sour rot of his breath and draws back a step.

"I told him he weren't yours."

"You." She stops, for she dares not so much as repeat the betrayal he has described lest by stating it again she should conjure it into truth.

"I done it so he don't suffer your same fate."

"You did it because you want him for yourself."

"I don't care to rear no child."

She scoffs with the last shred of dignity permitted her. "What chance would he have with you anyhow."

"He wouldn't be no slave."

"I'll tell him the truth."

"You do that. He'll believe his own flesh and blood."

Mary turns and considers herself in the hall mirror. "Then how am I to keep him?"

"You ain't."

From the back of the house: "Mary, shut the door."

He tells her what he has told the boy of his mother's death in child-birth and his kindness in taking in this desperate runaway for a substitute. "I never said you didn't care for him none."

"Mary!"

———

HE CAN STILL SEE HER standing in the doorway of the widow's place, surrounded by that looming hilltop house like Lazarus gone stiff at the entrance of his tomb, like Lot's wife turned to statuary by the power of her own unbelief. Like her he too dares look back over his own history, and for his punishment he is tormented to distraction by a kind of desperate unholy vigor, by the inescapable conviction that he has abandoned something that he must now restore unto himself regardless of the cost. He runs his lines and drinks his whiskey and sleeps all by himself in the hard frame bed, and he dreams of Mary of Mary only of Mary after all this time and he cannot help himself.

This would be a fine time to talk with Will or even to go straight to the Judge himself and make a clean breast of it regarding his now-terminated miscegenation. He has after all found his way through these many months without her, and if it were not for his damnable weakness he could make it through as many more again and then who knows. Perhaps his kinfolk would uphold him in his efforts. He would readily pledge to reform and swear upon a goddamn Bible if they required it. And yet to be truthful with himself he recognizes these ideas for the pipedreams that they are, since regardless of such other faults as he may have he is not entirely lacking in self-awareness. In this matter as in any other he has only himself to depend upon, and regardless of his intent he grows increasingly weak of spirit.

He takes to haunting the house on Cardiff Hill, lurking in the woods for the chance to cast his covetous eye upon her. He sleeps on the edge of the abandoned quarry when the weather is fair and in the hogpen behind a farmer's cottage when it is otherwise. The boy comes and goes and he observes his passage without interest from behind a pine tree as shaggy as his own countenance. It is the woman he wants. He sees her in the yard, he sees her through the window, he sees her making her way to the outhouse and the toolshed. He reckons that the widow must judge her worth her keep, and he bemoans the unfairness of the world.

18

ALONE IN ALL THE WORLD but for his mislaid bastard son with two mothers dead—the apocryphal white in childbirth and now the unfortunate black in bloody ceremonial repudiation of her very nature and his perverse delight in it—Finn rises from his bed and runs his lines and sells the catch as is his custom. Back to his room he returns early, thinking of nothing but the laundress. He lies upon his bed in that milkwhite room half blackened and draws himself out and dreams his insistent dreams there high above the river with the dress and the apron and the underthings of Huck's mother hanging still upon their outlined nails within his view. He thinks of her flesh, not the laundress but the mother not the mother but the laundress not either one or perhaps both together and indistinguishable, merged, transubstantiate. Visions and impressions alternate in his mind one after the other each one more lurid than the last and each one doomed and empty on its own but capable of edging him that much closer to his satisfaction. In his dream the women love him, each in her turn, regardless of what he has done and how much he may further desire. He completes his act and fetches up black charcoal from the stove downstairs and draws out upon the walls the vision he has just seen in his mind's eye, himself, the woman, the laundress, his urgent shame and his satisfaction. He cannot get it right and so he tries again and again as he has attempted the act itself again and again before achieving his release, and in his drawing his cave painting his avid repeated execution of the scene formed prior in his imagination he takes the woman and removes from her the raiments of her flesh until she is reduced to mere black bone, an armature of skeletal parts broken and bent to his ministration. By the time he is done he finds himself aroused once more, and he wipes his blackened hands one upon the other and dresses and drinks a glass of whiskey. Then he unties the skiff and poles to the mudflats of darktown.

The laundress he finds tending her cauldron. He makes no pretense of engaging her in custom this time, approaching with neither clothing to wash nor coins for payment. Because he has laved his hands in riverwater then lifted them up to pole she can see the remnants of the black residue of his work shading away into his sleeves, his white skin here and there traced and carved clean by the passage of dripping water which has traveled down his wrists and forearms veinlike.

Her face brightens at his appearance, for none there are who call upon her with half the kindness of this forlorn white. Even from her low vantage she can see that he is of such reduced caste that stooping to her assistance can have caused him no loss of dignity. He has endured some grievous pain in his life and she can see it; he has suffered a loss perhaps even greater than her own and thus sufficiently powerful to bring him lower than the very lowest of his own kind. It is at such desperate points of illimitable degradation that understanding blooms.

"Mr. Finn."

"Just Finn."

Withdrawing the peeled branch and passing the back of her hand across her brow. "What brings you here."

"I was out."

She cannot help but see upon him a look of strangeness and animal hunger, as if he has emerged from forty days' wandering in the desert beyond the precincts of civilization. He looks alarmed, astonished by his own presence within earthbound skin, returned here bursting into life by means of some dire pact with the devil.

"Can I get you something?" What she owns shall belong to him, this lone white man who has shown her unbidden kindness.

"A little water."

There is a cistern by the shack across the way, a cistern shared by these dark poor too downtrodden for declaring individual right even to this the plainest of God's mercies. She goes and dips water while he stands staring at the bubbling cauldron and the crackling fire. When she returns he takes the hand that holds the dipper forth and bends it steadily in his own that he may down the water with a greedy delicacy, and then he asks for more without so much as taking his eyes away from her.

"Are you hungry?"

"No."

But she can see his need and so she begins: "I could."

"You got none to spare."

"I do. Some."

"Then I reckon I could make a little room."

There is hard biscuit and a stew of greens whose scent carries the faintest suspicion of pork and it makes him sad and weary to eat it for it signifies to him the life from which he long ago rescued that other. "Next time I'll bring you some of them little fiddler cats," he says.

"You needn't repay me."

"I don't mean to." Just so she knows he is not beholden. "They'd go good with your greens is all."

"I reckon they would," she says, lifting her eyes.

They finish and she takes away his plate, and he sits looking at the place in the corner from which the preacher snatched the child. There lies the abandoned pallet and above it a man's overalls.

"You look like you lost something," she says over her shoulder.

"I didn't," he says, but in his broken heart and his subverted groin he can tell that he has lost along with his woman and his child the impulse to pursue such possibilities as have brought him abegging to darktown. "How about I cook you them cats next time?" Picturing her in his own lair, that scene of other crimes to which he has become by habit inured.

———

FIREWORKS THROUGH THE MILK of his whitewashed windows. A ruddy glow to suffuse walls hieroglyphed with one man's history. Finn rolls over in his lonesome bed and rises up like the dead at a great noise from without, an explosion as big as what remains of the world, and he runs down the stairs to stand upon the long front porch and watch while a crippled northbound steamboat, the *Wallace P. Greene*, erupts into flame. He has not been in bed for long, and with a befogged brain he stands to observe and marvel. The *Wallace P. Greene*'s boiler has exploded, the fault of an engineer who fell asleep at his works on account of a sleepless night prior spent arguing with a cantankerous wife who had been busy all week nursing a sick child, the resultant high-pressure blast killing a sweat-greased black tender by driving the blade of a coal shovel through his throat and severing his head clean. The shock wave from the burst boiler has rocked the furnace upon its moorings and blown off its door and opened a seam from which a torrent of fire spills lavalike onto the decking. The engineer is the second to die, trapped amid wreckage and fire, but he will not be the last.

From Finn's vantage on his riverward porch the *Wallace P. Greene* is soon become a variegated fountain of flame, not just from its tall twin stacks but from the open lower deck with its cargo of cotton and livestock and coal, and soon enough from the windows of the upper deck as well. The sternwheel seizes and shudders and begins to turn backward as the mighty vessel gives in to the river, and when at last she yields up her aim and begins to turn upon the current small figures appear one by one and two by two at the railings attired wraithlike in nightshirts and nightgowns. They hold hands and assume various theatrical postures of uncertainty and desperation and woe, strung along the rail like gemstones lit by fire. Some turn to look over their shoulders as if seeking a loved one, some dash momentarily back toward the flames only to emerge once again coalescing against the fierce redness that has repelled them. Ultimately they jump alone or in small groups into the black water and thrash against it to free themselves from the gathering power of the steamboat bound ultimately like themselves downstream.

Finn watches all of this, along with the arrival of an army of men in a fleet of smaller boats to rescue those gone overboard and corral the willful ball of flame that was once the *Wallace P. Greene*, with a kingly sort of detachment. Only when the steamboat shifts—its stern running up against a sandbar and hanging there to let the bow swing broadside to the channel and with the force of the current accelerate its turning until it breaks free and takes aim downriver as if the entire *Wallace P. Greene* were itself a great cannon with its flaming maw aimed squarely at Finn's violate and piratical presence—only then does he register that there may be some part for him to play in this maritime spectacle. Straight for his overhanging porch comes the steamboat, its twin stacks crumpling over in paired showerings of sparks and its every plank afire and its cargo of livestock bellowing like demons. As intimately as he knows the current and the channel he knows that the *Wallace P. Greene* will not veer away in time, and as much as he would prefer to escape by jumping barenaked into the river and swimming for it he calculates from the boat's speed and course that he will do better running out the back door and down the stairs and concealing himself and his nakedness in the woods behind the house. This he does, his darting passage a flicker in the night, and beyond the outhouse he crouches shivering like a wild thing with his red eyes afire and his scraggly goatlike balls adangle to watch while the boat surges slow as death on the unfurling current toward his exposed overhanging house.

Upriver and down the air vibrates with a high and many-voiced keening which he does not register. The boat itself makes only the variegated noises of its burning. He watches it drift downriver like some inexorable ghost ship acrackle with the sounds of timbers popping and containers bursting and plate glass shattering from the outward force of great contained heat; he watches it drift downriver consuming itself as it comes like some cancerous thing alive, fueled and reduced at once by its own selfsame diminishing weight. The pilothouse breaks loose of the texas and tumbles forward and then down two full stories to crash upon the main deck amid bales of cotton already blooming with high ragged flame, and by the resultant burst and subsiding glow the *Wallace P. Greene* seems even more intent upon sighting its riverside target. Her high jutting prow extends out of the water far enough to spear Finn's house before she runs aground.

He can see in his mind's eye the damage sure to be done, the prow blasting at an angle upward through the pilings and into the main house in one blow, hanging there momentarily as if at rest, and then when the irresistible power of the current and the weight of the massive flaming boat take over tearing laterally southward slicing the house in two, like a sharp knife gutting a sunfish.

"Least I'll see her go," says Finn.

But he does not.

For the men in their boats have managed to get lines around one strut of the sternwheel, the only part of the steamboat not yet fully engulfed, and the sudden yank of their ropes going taut is sufficient not to arrest the *Wallace P. Greene* but to alter its course the slightest. The prow turns as the boat shifts on its axis and rather than plunge swordlike into Finn's riverside house it only clips the southernmost of its pilings and heaves on past oblivious. The piling collapses into the water like another timber of the wrecked steamboat, like the useless pilothouse itself, leaving Finn's dwelling to sag riverward as if impatient for the hour of its own destruction.

19

SPRING.

The boy has expanded his orbit through the long cold months of winter, wordlessly making clear to his mother the untruth with which his father has rendered him both cursed and cured. He has gone pale and sad during these pale and sad days. The widow has made attempts to warm him by the fireside and to help him with his studies but he rejects both her comfort and her aid for he desires them no more than he desires the attentions of the woman who once was his mother and then was his secret and now is merely a signifier of all that he has lost without knowing it. He possesses at least the sensitivity not to confront her with his burden of truth and thereby break her heart; this much he has unwittingly inherited from this figure who now, against her will, retreats into a dark corner of that which was once his life.

"Soon we shall need to make a decision," says the widow on a fine spring morning when no person could desire a single thing more in life than to remain forever upon this high and airy hill so far above the world. The boy has gone down ostensibly to school but actually to recapitulate the best and freest and most true aspects of his father's life, out on the mudflats with a cane pole and a blackened corncob pipe. He will release what he catches and eat the lunch Mary has prepared for him and stretch out full upon a sunny rock until the time has come to return to the widow's house bearing tales of the other boys' mischief-making with tacks and chairs and inkwells and braids. Neither woman will attend in the least to these stories of his, and not merely because they have heard each word of them one hundred times before. Instead they will find themselves preoccupied by the implications of a decision that even now, even while the boy loafs under a pine tree at the margin of the river dangling his line, they are about to reach.

"Where will you go if you don't stay on?" asks the widow. She sits in the porch swing and Mary sits on the step beneath her.

"I don't know."

"The boy is certainly happy here." She makes this observation as if it settles everything, which it practically does. "If you don't mind my saying so."

"I know it."

"I've treated you two properly, haven't I?"

"Yes ma'am." Thinking of winter nights at the fire, the three of them more a family than any she has known since fate swept her away from the care of Mrs. Fisk and the high hopes of her father and left her shipwrecked and friendless in the wretched cabin behind the Judge's house with Finn for her keeper. She knows that this widow woman could be Huck's own Mrs. Fisk, faithful and kind and expecting the best despite all odds. Yet. "I can't be a slave again."

"Child," says the widow, "what on earth can you know of slavery?"

"No more than what I hear." Recalling that once upon a time she lied to the widow about having been stolen away from it at an age too early to remember.

"All folks do things differently. There are circumstances and there are circumstances."

"I know it."

"Nothing will change."

Mary purses her lips and looks out at high clouds adrift like steamboats.

"I'll keep up your pay."

"Thank you kindly," says the woman, but she shakes her head.

"What will you do? Go back to that Finn?" Thus speaking aloud the changeless and unapproachable fear that Mary herself for these past months has dared not contemplate. Yet downstream lies sure slavery, and upstream lies bleak uncertainty, and across the broad Mississippi lies some lonesome solitary life deprived not only of the boy but of all who have ever known him. Finn, the devil she knows, is barely distinguishable among the sorry alternatives.

The clouds collide and separate and drift on, changed in their aspect but immutable in their nature. "If you go to him," says the widow, "you surely can't think of taking the boy. He'll hurt that poor thing too. Sooner or later. You know it sure as I do." The widow raises to Mary a finger as frail and stern as any that she has seen since she left the hopeful care of Mrs. Fisk. "Do as you like with yourself, but think of the child."

His mother sits for a moment in the spring air and the open light, drawing inward upon herself and closing some door in her mind and opening another. Then she stands and levels her gaze at the widow: "Wherever I go, you need to understand something." Drawing one slow breath. "He's truly not mine."

The widow cocks her old head.

"I love him, but I'm not his mother."

"Is that a fact," says the widow. She would have promised not to claim him anyway, even without Mary's resorting to this dreadful lie by way of repudiating his parentage and clearing his name and title. She was prepared to promise anything, any kindness within her power, if only she could keep the boy and raise him as a simulacrum of her own lost child, and so her heart wells up with love for this woman's final act of denial. "You know who he belongs to?"

"Finn. Old Finn in Lasseter, who doesn't care in the least for him."

"And his mother?"

"Dead," says Mary.

———

FINN PLIES THE RIVER with his wooden skiff and strung lines, small on a boundless expanse, as if plundering immensity itself. He sells his catch and buys back a little of it fried up by Dixon's wife and sits drinking whiskey on Dixon's high porch as the sun sets far beyond the river in wilder territory than this.

"That's it," he says after a while to nobody except perhaps the absent Dixon, and he raps his scabby knuckles on the table and shoves off. Since no one seems to be looking, he takes the jug.

He permits the skiff to meander southward on its own, standing amidships in the dark with the jug in one hand and his unloosed self in

the other, blessing the downbound Mississippi with his own slight aug-
menting stream. As long as he has it out he considers doing a little
something further with it, but the whiskey has gotten the better of him
and in the end he decides that he ought to save himself anyhow, for who
knows what opportunities tomorrow may bring.

Downriver he goes past the steamboat landing, past the huddled
shacks of darktown, past the trading post belonging to Smith. He poles
where he can pole but mainly he drifts in deep water, making good time
on the fast high springtime current that hurtles south as if eager to bear
him to his destination. Just north of St. Petersburg he angles around the
far side of an island and makes for the Missouri shore, permitting the
skiff to slide past the ramshackle docks and the deserted levee and
drawing up instead onto a muddy bank below the quarry. He ties up in
a brushy spot overarched with willows and sleeps while the rest of the
world does likewise.

In the morning he rises and strips naked and throws himself into the
river, and then lizardlike upon a rock he dries his flesh in the sun and
drinks what remains of the whiskey, growing warm both inside and out.
He dresses after a while and ties back his hair with a bit of line and
throws the jug into the river as if to turn over some new leaf, and then
without further thought or consideration he stalks up Cardiff Hill.

The woman is already out among the washlines, and she comes upon
him behind a flapping sheet as upon a spider beneath some rock.

"Mary."

He holds up a hand in a kind of innocent greeting, and she takes a
half-step backward. He keeps the hand raised and with its fingertips he
holds back the sheet, making of it a proscenium beneath which she
might witness one version of her life's remainder enacted.

"You Finn." Looking over her shoulder for the widow, who will not
come.

"Is that any way."

"I don't know."

He smoothes back his damp hair with the flat of one palm. "I been
keeping an eye on you."

"Have you now."

"I have."

"From whereabouts?"

"From around," he says.

"The boy too?"

Huck is to him a mere impediment, but the look in her eye prevents him from saying so. He remarks instead upon the length of her absence, and how it has seemed to him an eternity.

"Is that a fact."

"It is." He lets go the sheet and steps past it, and with the other hand he takes her wrist in a grip whose pressure is calibrated as precisely as any line he has ever tugged, any blade he has ever pressed, any trigger he has ever squeezed. His touch communicates a thousand shades of yearning and insistence and possibility. "Come home," he says.

———

THEY ARE TOGETHER upon the frame bed in the high bedroom in absolute dark, the dense clouds above and the sluggish river below each likewise invisible. By his potency and the rapt hypnotic attention that he focuses upon her she judges that he has given up whiskey in her absence, and this she takes for the greatest of miracles.

"At the beginning I feared you'd come for us."

"I known where you was all along." A lie for its own imperious sake.

"But you didn't." Trailing off.

"I reckoned a person wants to make her own bed ought to sleep in it a while." Upon her belly he traces with his finger a line from navel to breastbone. "It weren't so bad being all by my lonesome. I got by."

"Did you tell the Judge?"

"Thought about it. Reckoned it weren't no business of his."

"You could have told him you put me out."

"I know it."

"Years ago you said you would. When he found us in the cabin you said you'd drop me, just like that, on his account." Never again since that day has she called him on this denial, and yet it has remained all this time upon her heart like another scar.

"I know."

"Did you mean it?" she says. "That you'd drop me?"

"I didn't." He draws breath, lifts his finger from her skin, and lies back like a man on a slab. "And I reckon he knew I didn't."

She lies breathing there beside him, her mind and heart angled at cross purposes. "The thing you told Huck," she begins after a while.

Finn grunts and scratches himself.

"I believe you did him a kindness."

"I know it," says Finn.

He was ravenous for her when he found her there among the hanging sheets and now that they are finished getting reacquainted and have rested a while he is ravenous again and hating himself for it, and thinking as he penetrates her once more of nothing other than the Judge and those pleasures in life that the Judge has forbidden him. She would rather sleep but she interprets his urgent roughness for something higher and so she acquiesces. Yet when he is finished this second time, truly and unsatisfactorily finished, and when she has stood to open the window and let in some fresh air, he rises too, unsteady on his feet and damp with her, and he dons his overalls and takes his hat from its nail and heads for Dixon's. Returning he will battle serpents on the stairs and spiders in the doorway and fall unconscious upon the horsehair couch as if she has not returned to him at all, but as the months pass he will grow accustomed to her presence once more and her good fortune will come to its natural end.

20

T WICE WILL RAPS upon the door of the tumbledown riverside wreckage that may as well be his own for all the value in Finn's squatter's right, and when twice there is no answer he springs the latch and admits himself. The floor slants alarmingly downward to his left where the *Wallace P. Greene* swept one of the pilings away, and already certain flotsam has begun to accumulate in that far corner by the entry to the porch. Bottles mainly but also clothing and trash and scraps of paper and something alive that rustles invisibly there even as he looks and listens. To his right is the door to the bedroom stairs, hanging open in a frame abristle with pulled nails that sprout like so many teeth. The naked board steps before him are spattered with white paint and bare footprints marked in the blackest coal dust, with bits of charcoal littered from edge to edge and ground into each crevice and corner. He thinks the place is worse than he had imagined it, worse even than it must have been when old Anderson died intestate here and left it ripe for the salvaging, and he is half afraid to touch anything within its confines. At the turning of the stairs he begins to see if not what his brother has done then at least the markings indicative of it. They swoop and careen across the walls in great angry torrents. They intersect and overlap and contradict one another like a band of murderers making testimony. They consist where he can make them out of dead men and spraddle-legged women and lost children, of blood and bottles and long sharp knives, of words never spoken save in derision and lust and despair. Will turns his rapt gaze entirely around as he takes the last few steps, wondering what he has done by turning this riverside place into his brother's habitation and penitentiary and sanatorium. He has not long to consider the question, for even now his brother, despite the lateness of this fine bright morning when he ought by rights to be out running his lines, even now his brother has commenced to stir upon his whitewashed bed of coals.

"Will."

"What have you done."

"I can't say." For he knows not whether Will is asking about the drawings or about the things they represent or about some other perhaps less grievous crime that he may have committed as recently as last night while under the perpetual influence.

"These walls."

"I painted them up a while back, but they was too plain."

"Is that it." He asks although he does not truly desire to know.

"I reckon."

Will puts his hand on the banister and draws it back grimed over with black. "Father wants you."

"I ain't going." He staggers out of bed and slips upon a strewn deck of greasy cards, falling hard on his bony unforgiving ass. He has lost some weight since Will saw him last, lost some weight yet gone flabby in places too. He is oddly both diminished and increased, at once an echo and a refutation of his former self.

"You *ain't going.* Isn't that just like you."

"I ain't his to command."

"He seems to think you are." Drawing from his pocket a summons and clearing his throat and reading it aloud, with particular emphasis upon a certain passage regarding a promise that Finn has apparently made to his father in return for some kindness granted. He folds the note with one hand clean and one otherwise, and restores it thus contaminated to his pocket.

Finn regains his feet. "So what's he got on his mind, you reckon." Considering such alternatives as there may be to ignoring his father's summons, including a noose around his neck at best and a lifetime in Alton at worst. Having already rid himself for good of the woman and her taint, he cannot imagine what his father might desire or what he himself might offer the Judge by way of alternative penance or even perhaps proof that he has acceded already to his highest wish.

"I wouldn't know."

"I reckon I ought to count my blessings he ain't called on me before."

"I remember times when all you wanted was to talk to him."

"Not lately."

"Perhaps not."

"Them times are gone."

"Maybe so."

Finn sits upon the bed and reaches under it to draw out a bottle. He uncorks it with his teeth and takes a long satisfying pull.

"Is this all you do anymore?" Looking from his brother to the walls and back again.

"It ain't so bad." He pounds the cork back in with the heel of his hand. "I fish a little bit. Either way, it's all I got left in the world."

"You've got the Judge."

"I know it." Pulling on his drawers and his shoes. "There's always the Judge. I believe he'll outlive me, the sonofabitch."

"The Judge," says Will, "is sure to outlive us all."

The day is hot and sunny and Finn exits into it with the fierce sudden pain of the newly awakened dead. The light burns his eyes and his head throbs and he can hardly keep pace up the hill with his own perpetually deskbound brother.

"You'll go it alone from here," says Will as they reach his office door. The white sign with its black letters gleams in tumultuous leafshot daylight, and the nest of spiders has cast forth its young to scatter themselves abroad like so many rumors of catastrophe. Finn tips his broken slouch hat to his brother and walks on wordless.

Spring seems to him more advanced the higher into the village he goes, perhaps because its bright signifiers are more readily available to and cultivated by residents of higher strata. Flowers bloom in gardens and window boxes and hanging planters, and as intimate as he is with the elements of the natural world he cannot tell one of these domesticated blossoms from the next. The Judge's mansion alone remains unbedecked. Finn keeps his pace steady as he travels the walk and strides across the porch with his cross-marked boots. Then hat in hand he knocks.

"The Judge wants me." To the hired man's wife or at least a vertical sliver of her, bright in narrow sunshine through the cracked door.

"I'll tell him." She goes off neither closing the door nor opening it farther and he remains behind. When she returns he follows her down the hall to the Judge's sealed room and knocks, and lets himself in without waiting to be admitted.

"Pap."

"You look a fright."

"I know it."

"Sit." The Judge closes a ledger book and files it and spends a moment or two stacking up papers that he has positioned around about his desk like dealt cards. He makes a study of each one as he raises it into the light of his oil lamp, and midway through he stops, reconsiders, and sorts them all over again into a different arrangement.

Finn clears his throat.

The Judge attends to his work.

"You sent for me," says Finn.

"I am aware of that. Sit." Without looking up at his son or glancing away at anything other than whatever artifice of paper he is devoted now to constructing. His reading glasses have slipped down his nose and he keeps his great hairless head tipped rearward as if he has detected upon the air some troubling scent brought by his prodigal son into this place. Finally he ties the pages off in a slim leather portfolio with a tourniquet of dark red ribbon, and aligns the packet in the dead center of his desk. He folds his hands upon it, waiting.

"Pap." Beginning again.

"For some time I have been reflecting on our agreement."

"I know it."

"Do you recall its terms?"

"I do." For he has labored beneath them since the night when through no fault of his own the poor luckless Philadelphian went to meet his maker.

"You'll be glad to make an end to it, then. I can see that."

"I will be."

"Good."

The Judge slides his elbows forward and raises his hands to place the palms and fingertips together. Then he tips his hands over slowly until they point toward his son, and he angles his head and sights along them over his reading glasses as he would sight down the barrel of a gun.

"That child of yours. That mulatto creature."

"Huck."

"How old would he be now?"

"Ten years, I reckon. Maybe eleven. Maybe more." With a shrug. "He run off."

"He did."

"Some while back."

"How long."

"A year or two."

"Your chronology is a little vague." Flattening his hands back down upon the desk.

"I don't keep no calendar."

"So I see."

"I don't have much need." This audience is proceeding better than Finn had expected, and he permits himself to sag a little in his chair. He slides one booted foot out to the side, making himself just the slightest bit at home.

The Judge for his part stiffens. "Do you know where he's gone?"

"More or less." He goes cagey.

"But you can find him. You're a man of the woods, a man of the river, the sort of highly capable individual who could track down a fugitive creature like that with his eyes closed. Isn't that correct?"

"I reckon it is." Although his father's tone is abrupt and more than a trace sarcastic, the Judge has never before spoken such respectful words to his son, and so Finn receives them now with a little self-conscious smile.

"Very well then. I shall give you the opportunity to make good—not only upon your vaunted abilities as a woodsman, but upon the promise you made to me over the body of that godforsaken Whittier."

"And then we'll be square."

"Then we'll be square."

"It's been a long time coming," says Finn. "God knows I've tried."

But the Judge makes no acknowledgment. He merely swivels his head to look toward the shuttered window as if imagining a world beyond it different from this one, and then turns back to his grown son. "I want you to clear my bloodline."

Finn gives him back a look of mixed bafflement and horror.

"The creature. The child. *The boy.*"

"I already took care of that." For he has an idea.

The Judge narrows his eyes. "You said he ran off."

"He did. I tracked him down and set him straight about that nigger woman."

"As much as it pains me to admit it, I'm having difficulty following your thread."

"I told him she weren't his mama."

The Judge shifts in his chair. "Go on."

"I told him his mama was a white gal that died giving him birth. Told him the nigger gal was just a charity case I took in. A runaway."

"My God." With an incredulous shake of his head. "You are indeed gifted at bringing things to ruin."

"Oh, he believed me all right."

"He won't keep it up for long. A mulatto child like that."

"Huck's as white as you or me. I swear it."

The Judge leans back in his chair and tugs at his lip. "So that's the way you left things with him. That his mother is a dead woman."

"A dead *white* woman," Finn clarifies. "And he'll never know no better."

"I suppose he won't."

"He won't go noising nothing around, that for sure. Once he got wind of that nigger woman's lie, he broke it off with her for good. Just like his old man done."

"That's all to my advantage, I must admit it."

"My pleasure to oblige."

"But still," says the Judge, leaning forward into the light of the oil lamp, recovering his old intent, "I cannot tolerate my blood passing through mulatto veins."

"I know it." Airy and agreeable, as if the storm has passed.

"So regardless of what the boy knows or does not know, I must insist upon purging my bloodline of all trace of your willful and wicked miscegenation. By which, lest there be any misunderstanding on your part, I mean to say that I am relying upon you to end the life of that bastard creature. And bring me evidence."

"But if he don't know, and nobody else knows."

"I still know." The Judge paces his words like drumbeats. "And my knowing is sufficient cause. Let that be a lesson." He leans back and withdraws his head from the light as if he has become some mythic oracle of few words and implacable intent.

"I can't do it."

"Consider the alternative."

"I considered it."

"You don't have to make up your mind now. Take a few days. You've disarmed the creature, after all, which I appreciate. Such action is grounds for a brief stay of execution, if nothing else." The idea seems to give him pleasure.

Finn sits thinking. He pushes a fingertip into one ear and draws it back and rubs the waxy residue into a ball between forefinger and thumb. He wonders how much wastage of hair and fingernails and sloughed skin, how large an accumulation of snot and phlegm and crusted sleep he has cast aside on his passage through this vale of tears, and he figures that if he had it all collected up in one place he could make of it a boy, a thing like a tar baby or some other lifeless husk yearning for his animating breath, instead of having only the boy Huck to show for his troubles, only the boy Huck not even sufficiently aware to understand the woes of his origin or to grasp the slow sure sealing of his doom.

Perhaps, Finn thinks, he might offer some alternative penance.

"The woman," he says. "The nigger woman."

"What of her."

"I didn't break it off."

Wearily: "You will now. Or you'll risk siring another mulatto bastard. And you have seen where that leads."

"No. I didn't *need* to break it off." Finn lowers his voice to the faintest conspiratorial hiss. "I killed her."

"Really."

"Honest," says Finn. "I done it for you."

"For me."

"There weren't no other way to get shut of her. No way that I could tell. I tried losing her but I couldn't make it stick."

"With your own two hands."

"It's what you wanted."

"I'll admit that," says the Judge. He removes his reading glasses and studies his son as if seeing him anew. There is a certain grudging and tentative respect in his look, mingled with the usual contempt and a newfound measure of something like alarm. The man before him is capable of almost anything and he sees this somehow for the first time. He sees it with all the terrible clarity of a premonition. "Very well," he says at last, folding his glasses and tucking them into the breast pocket of his coat. "Where's the body?"

"That's my business."

"It was mine from the start."

"It's safe enough all right."

"I'll need to see it." For the proof and for the pleasure and for the satisfaction of seeing his son reduced.

"I thrown it in the river."

"More's the pity," says the Judge. "If you could have shown me some evidence, I just might have given you more time to consider the boy." He dangles the idea like bait. Whether he believes that Finn has lied about the murder or lied about the disposal of the body makes no difference, for the two are signs of one and the same impulse.

"Maybe," says Finn, his mind racing, "maybe it got hung up on a snag."

"You let me know if you find it," says the Judge. "And then we'll talk about that other."

21

Now that she has returned to live with him again she can do nothing right, but in any extremity there is always the potential for betterment. She awakens in the dawn yearning for the boy now lost to her for good, and as she rises in pain from her bed and begins the rounds of her endless day she permits herself to brighten for at least a moment with the last dead despairing hope of any dream-deprived soul, that the two of them mother and child might one day be reunited in heaven.

The morning hours are hers, for as has become his habit Finn rises late and loafs in bed with a bottle he has secreted beneath the bedframe. Only when he is fully restored does he come down the stairs and eat whatever she has laid out before he goes trudging off to run his lines. In the hours before he materializes, she can imagine that the riverside house is hers and hers alone, a place that she can arrange to her liking and where she can do as she pleases. She dreams sometimes that he is dead and has thus freed her to live here by herself and take in the hotel's laundry and labor over a boiling cauldron stinking of lye like the slave that she is not in order to make ends meet, and no dream pleases her more than this. Save perhaps one in which Huck returns and claims her for his own.

Finn despises himself upon arising, both for that which he has done and for that which he has not done. Try as he might he cannot imagine why the woman would tolerate returning to one such as he, although on the obverse he cannot imagine why he ought to continue tolerating her presumptuous presence. Only the boy, the boy now set loose without chance of recovery, could have reassured him by his mere existence that the doomed lust he harbors for the woman could have in the end generated something other than rage and loathing. So day by day, in the absence of the boy and the absence of his own improvement or understanding, he finds himself pursuing her degradation as if by diminishing her he might diminish his own wrongdoing.

Even Dixon finds that the subject of Mary is forbidden.

"I hear tell that woman of yours is back," is all he says, and he says it affably enough, but Finn turns on him a reptilian look of smoldering wrath.

"I don't require your pity."

"I ain't offering it." Topping up the riverman's drink out of the goodness of his heart.

"And I don't require your advice."

"I know you don't. I was only."

"The Judge given me sufficient in that area." He shakes his head and subsides, and turns his full attention to his glass.

Thinking that Finn has changed the subject and that following his lead will be the wisest tactic: "I didn't know you saw that old man anymore."

"I don't." He cranes his neck to look up at Dixon inviting contradiction, and detects none, and addresses once more his whiskey.

When he gets home he reacquaints himself with the reasons he has admitted this strange dark creature into his house into his heart into his bed and once she has satisfied him he goes down to sit naked and alone on the horsehair couch and watch the river. There are a few lights here and there and from someplace above the long rightward bend to the north he hears the uplifted voice of a man singing unaccompanied. Some drunk. He sits and lets the night chill settle into him and tells himself that any decent man would throw a sinner such as he into the river to drown, that if he were in possession of any sense at all he would throw his own self in if only he did not know how to swim. Thus stymied he drinks more whiskey and when he is finished with it he heaves the jug over the side and down into the river in his own stead. Come morning he will regret its loss, and consider such outlay as its replacement will require, and blame it all upon the woman who has made him this way.

22

Out on the river his mind is achurn with thoughts of the woman now dead and himself left as usual with nothing to show for it. He sells his catch but for a mess of sweet little fiddler cats, which he keeps wrapped in the bundle of damp reeds and brings back home. His natural inclination is to leave them in the skiff right where they lie for he has come not to care whether he shares some of his bounty with any such scavenger as may find it, be his beneficiary fox or wolf or dog or some other, but on this day in particular he has different ideas so he bends to lift the bundle in his arms like a swaddled child and he carries it up to the kitchen where he leaves it alongside his gutting knife and goes out.

He looses his skiff and lets it glide southward on the current to bear him past the landing where a small crowd has gathered for the arrival of a steamboat. Whether the boat is coming upriver or down a person could not say without knowing the day of the week and the riverboat schedule, and Finn knows neither of these for such information matters not in the least to him. Out upon his skiff in midriver he slides past the gathered assemblage of men and women and wagons and horses like a leaf adrift on a breeze, like a comet dying in the night sky, like any inconsequential thing in its ordinary unremarkable passage. He drifts past the mudflats and along the riverward margins of darktown keeping to the edge of the channel until he comes abreast of the laundress's shack, and then he digs in with his pole and comes around. Rather than seek a place to tie up he runs the skiff aground on the mud and steps off dryshod.

"I got them little fiddler cats," he says when she replies to his knock upon her door. Just that and no more, by way of greeting and invitation.

"I'm obliged." Looking at him and wondering just whereabouts on his person he has secreted the fish. "They out on that boat of yours?"

"Back home," he says with a toss of his head.

Whereupon she remembers the promise that she never reckoned he would keep. "You still plan on doing the honors?"

"If you don't mind." All gallantry.

"You're quite the gentleman."

"I know it."

She has chores to do and the afternoon is at its peak. Alongside the half-open door she rests the dark serious oval of her face. "You'll come back for me."

"Whyn't you come on up now."

"Suppertime's a long way off."

"We'll pass the time."

She tilts her head against the door, either playful or sly or suspicious.

"I reckon we'll think of something to do," says Finn.

———

A STEAMBOAT HAS ARRIVED from the north, a sidewheeler bearing upon its broad decks both cargo and passengers to be dispersed along the river from Rock Island to New Orleans. Lasseter is but one landing among dozens and not a major one at that, so the activity at the landing is confined to the unloading of a few ropebound crates and the transfer of some sacks of grain and the disembarkation of but a handful of passengers. Poling northward Finn swings wide of the steamboat in his skiff, the woman at his side dangling one hand luxuriantly in the water and gazing up at the boat's towering double stacks as if she has never before seen such marvels. Anyone can see that the nature of things has shifted for her, that the world has gone upside down entirely and she finds herself compelled now to hang on lest she grow disoriented and plummet to some alternate unpredictable earth.

One of the passengers makes for a wagon driven by an individual well known in these parts and throughout the whole of western Illinois, a fierce and imperious figure more likely to drive the affairs of men than to drive this wagon pulled by a matched pair of Arabians stamping on the shore awaiting this steamboat this passenger this attorney from Philadelphia sent to complete the work begun by the late Whittier.

The Judge raises his hat by way of identifying himself to his visitor, and that small movement—the glint of his cufflinks, the gleam of his revealed pate in the bright afternoon sun, the flicker of his black bowler hat—that small movement calls out to Finn as his skiff clears the side-wheeler's upstream limit. For a moment or two he freezes and stares as if he has stumbled across some ferocious thing in the wild, and then he regains his senses and looks away.

23

HE SITS BY THE RIVER mending his lines. He has made do without her before and when the times comes he will make do again. The months since she has been returned from the widow's have taught him this much.

If anyone dares ask about her he will merely report that he has broken it off once more. This time for good. The Judge he will tell the same partial truth, but only if pressed. He will make no public show of his reformation, and he most surely will not confess to any soul the entire truth.

Let her vanish into the collective memory like bait thrown into moving water.

He finishes mending his lines and hangs them looped from nails the way that nigger bastard did during the time of his imprisonment and then he retreats to his skiff bobbing tied up beneath the house. He smells his cooking supper and nearly has second thoughts, so he unties and pushes off and when he has cleared the porch he hollers up to get the woman's attention. "Whatever it is you're making," he says when she has come to the porch, "I'll not be having any of it." And she knows better than to ask.

He takes himself and his pocket full of riches to the haunt of old blind Bliss, where he might drink his supper rather than eat it. He finds Bliss tending his fire, crooked double over banked coals like a shaman bent upon summoning up some spirit.

"Bring me something besides your money next time," says the bootlegger as he rises. "Maybe a little bacon to go with my beans."

"I just might," says Finn, who is in a mood to take everything in the world for a signifier.

"Do a helpless old blind man a favor."

"I will."

"I don't get out much." He limps as he heads toward the cabin.

"I know it." For who other than his customers knows that Bliss even draws breath upon this earth. Finn thinks for a moment about what sort of life this individual must have lived for all these years here in his forest hideaway, secretive and self-contained, to some men but a myth or a grail and to others such as himself who know the truth nothing more than the merest insignificant enabling fixture.

"What become of that easterner, anyhow."

"The one you killed?"

"Don't say it." Spitting good whiskey.

"It's the truth."

"I didn't."

"I reckon your bullet landed in his shoulder all by its lonesome."

"I reckon it did."

Finn drinks and stares into the lowering dark and Bliss does the same, his one cocked eye wandering over the tops of the graying trees and the other, the one sealed up behind a glaucous film, fixed as fate upon some indeterminate point.

"I ain't heard nothing about it."

"I done you a favor."

"Don't tell me no more." Bliss takes a slow sip and puckers his lips around it. "I can still picture that old boy out here. Gasping like a fish."

Finn looks downward in the falling light and sees there upon the floor the traces of Whittier's passing, writ in blood nearly scuffed clean by Bliss's transit. "I took the blame and done you a favor. Leave it at that."

"I will."

"You'll do me one sometime."

"I reckon."

———

"ONE THING I REMEMBER about that Whitfield," says Finn, arising from his chair on Bliss's porch preparing to take his leave.

"Not him again," says Bliss. "I thought."

"Hear me out. You know the last thing he said?"

"I don't."

"Last thing he said was *nothing hurts*."

"Is that a fact."

"It is."

"I'll be."

"Take a little comfort in that if it suits you."

"I will." Bliss makes an attempt to rise but collapses back into his chair where he will spend the remainder of the night. "Help yourself to a jugful on your way," he says.

"It's the least you can do."

"It is."

"I hate to take advantage."

"Don't make it a habit."

Finn steals a jug to replace that other lost in the river and fills it, then traces the path back to his skiff and unties and poles downstream as if pursued by demons. The jug is alongside him but he touches it not, because the work that remains before him shall require all of his will. He thinks as he goes of the woman asleep in his bed wrapped up in her warm traitorous skin. He thinks of that which drew him to her in the beginning, her innocent brown-eyed youth, the mysterious dusk of her flesh, the hand bravely hidden in her apron pocket to conceal and ready a white man's pistol that her father had stolen from God knows where and passed on implacably to her just as he had passed on his stain and his fate. Blame it on that overweening nigger slave then, and blame it on the Judge for his part in it. And take comfort, if any comfort is to be had, in the bled-out easterner's dying words. *Nothing hurts.* Nothing hurts save duty realized too late.

The sky above the Mississippi is clear and bright and hung all about with stars, and the moon has given up its shining, when Finn ties up in his customary spot below the house and leaves the jug and goes stealthily within upon his errand.

24

THE JUDGE CANNOT HELP but note the pair of them bound upstream on the skiff, his errant son and the woman, no doubt the very same woman his son has been miscegenating with all these years, the selfsame woman he surely lied about having slain and thrown into the river, but he acknowledges nothing for he has work to accomplish with the new eastern lawyer. He is frankly unsurprised, for he has seen enough of this world to know that treachery is commonplace and the worst possible outcome is forever to be expected. From the corner of his eye he watches his son pole upstream to his destination, then he brings the attorney to the great white mansion on the highest street in Lasseter and admits him to his chamber where they spend the afternoon in counsel.

For his part Finn ties up beneath his leaning riverside house and bends to help the laundress to her feet, the first time they have touched skin to electric skin.

"What happened?" Taking in the broken piling, the sagging porch, the bent roofline.

"Steamboat."

She hesitates on her way up the stairs for the place seems unsafe, oddly cocked, a cunning trap in danger of lurching shut at the thoughtless placement of a single errant ounce, but he offers her encouragement and finally sets chivalry aside and goes ahead himself.

"See?" Giving a little jump at the landing. The stair proves stable enough.

"I'm coming."

He stands aside to admit her first, this woman so like the other and doomed to the same fate. Her familiar silhouette against the light from the porch makes him vertiginous, and he can hardly draw breath.

"You all right?" She reaches out a hand, aware that he is older than she and thinking that he has perhaps fallen away from the man that he once was.

"Fine." Taking the hand offered, indicating the porch with a dip of his head.

"In darktown," she says as they sit, "all I get is pity."

"You won't get none from me," says Finn.

"Promise."

He makes his promise and brings out whiskey in a bottle though he hates to waste any on her. They share a glass, she merely to be polite and perhaps to reduce her trepidation.

"I never known a woman liked whiskey."

"You still don't."

"I know it." Tossing off the remainder. "I don't reckon I could support one who did."

"You sleep out here?" She toes the corn husk pallet used by Huck in those long lost years, the pallet now torn asunder in places and soaked stinking by water spilled over the lip of the slanting rainbarrel and ravaged by birds for use in building other better resting places.

"Had a boy." He leaves it at that and pours more whiskey, letting her think what she chooses about such kinds of misery as they may already share in common. After a while he says, "I sleep upstairs."

"Show me."

"It ain't much to look at."

Past the kitchen they go with the fiddler cats wrapped in reeds and the gutting knife lying beside them ready for his purpose. He reckons that he will accomplish this one as he did the last with his bare hands alone, and use the knife only for the secondary work once again although this time he will need to save some part over to show the Judge. But this fate is not all that he means the laundress to share with her prior incarnation, and so he permits himself to touch the small of her back as he guides her to the bedroom stairway.

"Goddamn kids," he says when she takes note of the thorny crown of bent and halfpulled nails surrounding the door. "Made themselves a mess upstairs too."

She wonders if perhaps they deemed the place abandoned, but she chooses not to ask.

"It's home," he says. "Home all the same."

"I know."

"Just close your eyes if you don't like what they done."

And close her eyes she does, for there is too much of it and it is too uncouth for enduring. The drawings and the words and the half-breed constructs that are neither drawings nor words but partake perhaps of both cover even the whitewashed windows through which slanting sunlight comes now as through spiderwebs or the rigging of an abandoned ship. The bed is inviting nonetheless, and the woman's dress hanging upon its nail reminds her of the overalls of her own dead husband, which she has not yet had the strength to move, not since the night he died, and so between the boy's forlorn mattress and the woman's empty clothes she believes that she understands just how Finn has come to be this way.

He calls her Mary when he takes her and she corrects him not, for she pities him and would grant him this one kindness at least.

The whiskey he has drunk makes him sleep despite his intent, but the woman soon stirs and opens her eyes in the last dying light. There upon the wall she spies that speckled straw hat once belonging to her son, and for a moment she believes that she is either dreaming or dead or else fallen into someone else's dream of death, and she stifles a gasp by exercise of will. Out from beneath Finn's fallen bulk she slides without disturbing his slumber of weariness and whiskey, to pad naked over to the protruding nail and take down the charcoal-outlined hat with her own two shaking hands. There can be no mistaking it. And now that she has eyes to see there can be no mistaking certain of the mad scrawlings upon the walls either, least of all those depicting her wronged child and her throat-shot husband and her own beauteous profile untainted, certainly not those recalling the vulgar bare-rumped preacher having his hideous way and the familiar masked figure standing to one side with a pistol in his hand.

Like a cat she prowls the room in silence for some tool or weapon or other device appropriate to her aim. She recalls a gutting knife in the kitchen below but cannot muster the courage to leave this murderous monster alone here for long enough to retrieve it lest she meet him on the stairs returning or worse and more shameful still risk losing her nerve and running from the house entirely with him still asleep and at large and her still owing the two of her most beloved more in the way of faithfulness than that. In the room's lowest downstream corner, in the spot slumped most precipitously riverward by the house's meeting with the *Wallace P. Greene,* stands the sprung chest with its broken hinges. By and by she dares approach it and thus discovers in its depths not only a baby's broken bottle with its dry rag stopper but a pistol, gift to her from some vengeful god in whom she has had no prior right to believe.

———

WHEN HE HAS SHED himself of the easterner and driven his matched pair down to the river, the Judge hardly dares to climb the crooked steps of that treacherous overhanging house. But climb them he does, for he is old and has nothing to lose save such tatters of civility and self-respect as his son has seen fit to leave him. The house is dark and he creeps upward without a light without a sound without remorse over the sentence that he shall soon impose upon the son and the woman and to hell for the moment with the boy for there will be time and opportunity to find him later all the time and opportunity in the world but first things first. He has discovered the two of them in bed before, and this time he will not merely cast them out of this earthly Eden or any other. He bears in his right hand a pearl-handled pistol for enforcing his judgment.

The downstairs is empty save a bundle of fish stinking on the table, and the overhanging porch is likewise empty but for a jug and one empty glass. He turns back around and in the darkness sees the nail-toothed hole to the stairway gaping and he crosses to it and enters into its mystery as cautious as a man on ice. Black underfoot are the stairs themselves and black are the walls alongside him but a dim halo of pale riverlight hangs above his head and toward this he strives pistol in hand. Finding his son facedown in his own bed, one bullet square through his back and the sheets running red and the blood filtering down through the straw tick to pool upon the floor, is to him an anticlimax—and he desires to fire again, to slay him all over, but resolves instead to conserve the ammunition. The walls are mingled white and black with something that he reads as cobwebs and no more.

The house with its broken spine and its ruined pilings proves no match for a single strong rope and his impatient paired Arabians. Into the river it crashes in a slow shattering avalanche, sunk in water up to its roofline and bobbing faintly beneath the moon, ultimately unrecognizable to any who might happen upon it downstream with its gaping roof and its broken gable windows and its secret burden of betrayal. When the boy Huck discovers it afloat and ties up seeking adventure of his own he will know it not, nor will he desire to see or understand or much less judge the heart-shot corpse upon its slanted floor. He will take what he requires and light out.

AUTHOR'S NOTE

THIS IS FINN'S BOOK.

And although I have approached its source material with the reverence that is its due, Finn himself has always insisted upon having the last word. Which is another way of saying that in order to learn the facts about Huckleberry Finn, you'll need to seek out an older and better novel than mine.

It's not that I have discounted or denied the details of Huck's story as Mark Twain set them down. Quite the contrary. In matters of location and timing and continuity, the events retold in this novel are fitted meticulously into and around Pap Finn's appearances, both alive and dead, in *Adventures of Huckleberry Finn*. The elements of his character—his drunkenness, his cruelty, his virulent and overwhelming hatred of blacks—are all drawn whole from Twain's novel and followed here to their likely ends.

A hundred other details link Twain's novel and mine, including the contents and condition of the room where, in Chapter 9 of *Huckleberry Finn*, Jim discovers Pap Finn's dead body. My own interpretation of these particulars—the words and pictures on the walls, the men's and women's clothing, the whiskey bottles and the black cloth masks—served as a road map for charting many aspects of this book. I've made use of some of Twain's minor characters, too (Judge Thatcher, the widow Douglas), and permitted at least one other (the King, a shapeshifter if there ever was one) to appear reimagined. A few of Twain's scenes, filtered through a different sensibility, appear more or less whole in this novel. And in that "*more or less*" lies the spot where, in the company of passing time and changing critical sensibilities, and in the service of a narrative that requires its own shape and its own energy and must by its own working acquire its own meaning, this story parts company with Twain's book—and travels down its own treacherous channel.

I have assumed, for example, that the Huck of *Huckleberry Finn* may not be an entirely reliable narrator. What boy is? What boy, aiming to describe his relationship with a father as appalling as Finn, possibly could be? Thus certain encounters with his father take on different nuances here than they possessed in Twain's novel.

Throughout, I have followed such narrative threads as the elder Finn and his particular brands of selfishness and bigotry have suggested to me, dealing with the facts of *Huckleberry Finn* at least as fairly as Twain himself treated his own sources. For after all, as Ron Powers noted in *Mark Twain: A Life,* the author "took a democrat's view of fact and fiction; he privileged neither above the other and let them mingle in his work without prejudice."

———

THE NOTION OF HUCK as a mulatto is certainly the most daring aspect of this novel, and the one sure to cause the most consternation among some readers. It most definitely takes Shelley Fisher Fishkin's monograph *Was Huck Black?*—which traced Huck's voice to distinct black sources from Twain's youth—to another level altogether. But is a mulatto Huck really that unlikely an extrapolation of Twain's intent? Perhaps not.

Fishkin links Twain's satirical impulse to his experiences with the black tradition of "signifying" speech, that complex rhetorical doubling documented by Henry Louis Gates, Jr., in *The Signifying Monkey.* Fishkin traces Twain's appreciation for the rich signifying tradition to the young Sam Clemens's contact with particular black speakers— among them a youth known to history only as Jerry, whom the author memorializes in "Corn-Pone Opinions": "I had a friend whose society was very dear to me because I was forbidden by my mother to partake of it. He was a gay and impudent and satirical and delightful young black man—a slave—who daily preached sermons from the top of his master's woodpile, with me for the sole audience."

If a key part of that description—"a friend whose society was very dear to me because I was forbidden by my mother to partake of it"— does not have a familiar ring, then you haven't read *The Adventures of Tom Sawyer* recently enough. Here is Twain in that book, introducing Huck to his audience for the very first time: "Huckleberry was cordially hated and dreaded by all the mothers of the town . . . all their children admired him so, and delighted in his forbidden society, and wished they dared to be like him." Although I make no claim that Twain meant to suggest anything but a Caucasian Huck, he most certainly and consciously built his boy hero out of materials whose blackness goes far deeper than mere dialect.

In later years Twain would give us Tom Driscoll, the secret mulatto at the heart of *Pudd'nhead Wilson*. Driscoll reflected Twain's lifelong fascination with double identities, and demonstrated his growing sense of the complexity of race relations. To the reader who would suggest that my mulatto Huck subverts a cherished motif of *Huckleberry Finn*— the relationship between a free white boy and an adult black slave— I point out the similar (though reversed) revelation that comes near the close of this novel: When the elder Finn strips Huck of all traces of his true black mother, substituting in her place a dead white woman, he sets his son free to pursue whatever fate Mark Twain has in store for him. Huck's identity is thus doubled without his even knowing it, a device of which I believe his creator might have approved.

—JON CLINCH
 Plymouth, Vermont
 February 2007

ACKNOWLEDGMENTS

As MUCH AS A BOOK like this seems to spring from nowhere—even to its amazed author—I owe enormous debts of gratitude all around.

To Mark Twain, who created the world within which this interloper has dared to meddle.

To my mother and father, Joyce and Warren Clinch, who freed me early on to do as I liked. Including this sort of thing.

To a small handful of early readers and encouragement-mongers— among whom I name in my heart old pals Bob Hill and Steve Kendra, newer friends Karen Dionne and Chris Graham of Bksp.org, and faithful cohorts Zarina Docken, Kristy Kiernan, Sachin Waikar, Tasha Alexander, Elizabeth Letts, and Rachel Cole—each of whom has seen to it that I've kept going, even when the going has seemed pointless.

To my tireless agent, Jeff Kleinman. To my irreplaceable editor, Will Murphy. To the rest of the extraordinary team at Random House: Daniel Menaker, Tom Perry, Sanyu Dillon, Sally Marvin, Jynne Martin, Lea Beresford, Megan Fishmann, Gabrielle Bordwin, Gene Mydlowski, Vincent La Scala, Amy Edelman, and Matt Kellogg.

To my astonishing daughter, Emily, who would have been enough.

And above all to my dear wife, Wendy, without whom I would surely perish.

ABOUT THE AUTHOR

A native of upstate New York and a graduate of Syracuse
University, JON CLINCH has taught American literature, has been
creative director for a Philadelphia ad agency, and has run his own
agency in the Philadelphia suburbs. His stories have appeared
in John Gardner's *MSS.* magazine. He and his wife
have one daughter.

ABOUT THE TYPE

This book was set in Caslon, a typeface first designed in 1722 by
William Caslon. Its widespread use by most English printers in
the early eighteenth century soon supplanted the Dutch typefaces
that had formerly prevailed. The roman is considered a
"workhorse" typeface due to its pleasant, open appearance,
while the italic is exceedingly decorative.